THE CHRONICLES OF THE FEW

A SAGA FORGED IN STARLIGHT

By
DAWN CLARK

ISBN: Number

Printed in the United States of America

Published by Book Marketeers.com

TABLE OF CONTENTS

1   The Silent Echo 1

2   Into The Heart Of Chaos 20

3   A Path To Rediscovery 37

4   Rebirth Amidst The Stars 50

5   Shadow Of Terentia 65

6   Shimmering Bonds 106

7   The Midnight Lotus 123

8   Turmoil Awaits 140

9   A Desperate Gamble 153

10   Embrace Of Shadows 167

11	The Hidden Arbor	179
12	Dark Star Whispers	185
13	Web Of Deceit	198
14	Justice's Echo	214
15	Island Sanctuary	259
16	Cosmic Kinship	274
17	Defiance Among The Stars	299
18	Tensions And War Begins	334
19	The Push For Freedom	361
20	Echoes Of Eternity	380

1

THE SILENT ECHO

The metallic tang of blood mingled with the ozone kiss of sparking wires. Gresham gripped the hilt of his FEW blade, the worn leather slick with sweat beneath his trembling fingers. The faint lavender scent hung in the air—a cruel reminder of a bygone era. It clung to Mara's hair, a memory forever etched in his senses with unrelenting clarity.

A kaleidoscope of violet eyes, the lavender scent of her hair, the metallic tang of fear—Mara's scream echoed in his mind, a specter from a past life. For the FEW, memories were not fleeting shadows but vivid, unending specters. A curse, he often muttered to himself, to recall every detail with the precision of a crystal shard.

The Requiem, a formidable Galactic Alliance ship, hummed around him, its corridors blending advanced technology and sterile efficiency. The metallic scent of the ship's interior mingled with the faint aroma of lubricants and ozone. The steady hum of the engines reverberated through the walls, a constant reminder of the vessel's immense power.

The Council chamber, a marvel of gleaming chrome and holographic displays, fell silent as the doors hissed open. Lady Mara and Lord Gresham, bathed in an ethereal glow emanating from their activated FEW blades, strode into the room. Their crimson and black capes billowed dramatically behind them, imbued with an energy that mirrored the intensity of their gazes.

A collective gasp erupted from the assembled Councilors. Pale with awe, some faces craned their necks for a better look at the legendary warriors. Councilor Vex, a stocky man with a usually blustering demeanor, now had a nervous twitch and stammered a greeting. "W-welcome, Lady Mara and Lord Gresham. We did not expect two of the FEW to take interest in our proceedings."

Councilor Anya, a slender woman with silver hair and sharp green eyes, gripped the armrests of her seat so tightly that her knuckles turned white. "This is... unprecedented," she whispered, her voice trembling.

Even the stoic Councilor Kalen, a seasoned military leader with a scar running down his cheek, couldn't help but gape at the spectacle before him. "Legends come to life," he muttered, his deep voice tinged with awe.

Lady Mara, her blonde hair cascading over the unrelenting black of her FEW uniform, walked with athletic grace. Lord Gresham's pace was crisp beside her. His muscular form was also clad in featureless black, the glowing FEW emblem prominent on his shoulder. The emblem pulsed with a soft, otherworldly light, a beacon in the dark fabric.

Their capes, crimson and alive, swirled and snapped with their emotions. Mara's violet eyes darkened to deep purple, mirroring the intensity of the moment, while Gresham's ocean-colored eyes threatened to turn black. Their swords glowed with deep red and blue hues, ancient runes shimmering along the blades.

As they approached the central table, Councilor Kalen was transfixed by their youthful faces—so at odds with all he had heard about the FEW's long lifespans.

The attendant's tray clattered to the floor, shattering the hushed whispers of the Council chamber. Startled, he stumbled back, his eyes widening in terror as they fell upon Lord Gresham's hand resting on the hilt of a magnificent blade.

The blade, an ethereal gradient of black and crimson, pulsed with an otherworldly energy that sent shivers down the attendant's spine. Strange alien symbols danced across its length, hinting at forgotten powers. Lord Gresham, his expression unreadable, exuded an aura of authority that belied his youthful appearance.

Gresham's thoughts drifted to a past encounter with Ximon, the phantom warlord. He recalled the desolate battlefield, the smell of burning metal, and the screams of the fallen. Ximon had stood amidst the chaos, a towering figure of menace, and his eyes gleaming with malevolent intent. The memory was a stark reminder of the danger they faced.

"Yes, well... we were just discussing the uprising in the Cygnus colonies," Vex said, his voice cracking under pressure.

Gresham stepped forward, his voice low but commanding. "Ximon. He's allied with the rebels."

A murmur of shock and disbelief spread through the Council chamber as Gresham's words landed like a dark omen. Councilor Kalen's face blanched as he gripped the arms of his seat, his knuckles turning white. Ximon. The notorious warlord, a phantom who had haunted the galaxy for years, was now allied with the rebels.

"Preposterous!" Vex sputtered, his voice cracking like a twig under pressure. His gaze darted nervously between Mara and Gresham, betraying the fear his bluster couldn't mask. "We have no reports of..."

He trailed off, his words dying in his throat under Mara's steady gaze. Kalen felt the cold sweat of dread trickle down his spine, the implications of Ximon's alliance overwhelming his senses. "Merciful stars," Kalen murmured, his usually composed features now etched with dread and desperation. "If this is true, Lady Mara, we are woefully unprepared."

Mara's voice was firm yet gentle. She closed her eyes for a brief moment, and a wash of calm radiated from her, an invisible wave that settled the nerves of everyone in the room. "Councilors, I understand your concerns. This information may shock you, but we are here to help you navigate this threat. Our sources are highly reliable, and we have evidence of Ximon's movements."

Councilor Anya leaned forward, her voice trembling but steadied by the calm aura. "But how can we possibly stand against Ximon and his forces? Our defenses are inadequate."

Gresham interjected with a hint of humor. "Well, that's why you have us. We're not just here for decoration, you know."

A faint smile tugged at Mara's lips. "Indeed. We are more than capable of handling Ximon. Our priority is to protect your colonies and ensure the safety of your people."

Kalen's grip on his chair relaxed slightly. "What do you suggest we do?"

Mara unfurled a holographic map, her finger tracing a path across the shimmering constellations. "Ximon's fleet," she began, calm but authoritative, "is a well-oiled machine consisting of various warships and support vessels. We need to cut off his supply lines and isolate his forces."

Gresham nodded. "We'll coordinate with your fleet and deploy our units strategically. We can outmaneuver and neutralize Ximon's forces with our combined strength."

Councilor Vex, his earlier defiance waning, asked, "And what about the rebels on Cygnus-9? Can we trust them to join our cause?"

Mara's eyes softened. "The people of Cygnus-9 have suffered greatly under Ximon's tyranny. They will stand with us if we offer them hope and a chance for liberation."

Kalen found himself nodding, a glimmer of hope igniting in his chest. "Very well. We will follow your lead."

Mara and Gresham exchanged a look of mutual respect before she addressed the Councilors. "We appreciate your trust. Together, we will face this threat and emerge victorious."

As the meeting continued, the Council members began to debate the logistics of the plan. Councilor Vex, regaining some of his composure, questioned the feasibility of the proposed maneuvers. "How can we be sure this will work? Ximon is not easily defeated."

Gresham leaned forward, his eyes locking onto Vex's. "We have faced him before. We know his tactics and his weaknesses. This plan is our best chance."

Councilor Anya added, "And what about our own forces? Are they ready for such a confrontation?"

Mara nodded. "We will personally oversee the training and preparation. Our presence will bolster their resolve."

The debate grew heated, with Councilors expressing both support and skepticism. Kalen, his deep voice cutting through the chatter, said, "We must trust in the FEW. Their presence here is a sign that we can succeed."

Finally, the Council reached a consensus. Vex, with a resigned sigh, said, "Very well. We will proceed with your plan."

With a final nod, Mara and Gresham turned and left the chamber, their figures vanishing into the shadows of the corridor. As they walked down the corridor, Mara reached out, her fingers brushing against Gresham's hand. He turned, his stern expression softening at her touch. They stopped, and she gently intertwined her fingers with his, drawing him closer.

"Mara," Gresham whispered, his voice filled with tenderness. He lifted her hand to his lips, gently kissing her knuckles. The warmth of his breath sent a shiver through her. Their capes, the crimson of his contrasting with the stark black of hers, swirled around them like a shared secret.

Mara's violet eyes softened as she looked up at him. "Together," she said, her voice a promise and a plea. "We face this together."

Gresham nodded, his forehead resting against hers. Their proximity, shared warmth, and mingling of breaths were a sanctuary in chaos. His hand cupped her cheek, his thumb gently caressing her skin. "Always," he murmured, his eyes searching hers for strength and reassurance.

Their capes wrapped around them, creating a cocoon of intimacy and shielding them from the outside world. Their embrace lingered, a moment of stolen peace before the storm. Mara's fingers traced the lines of his jaw, memorizing the feel of him and grounding herself in the reality of his presence. "I need you," she whispered, her voice barely audible. "More than ever."

Gresham's grip tightened around her waist, pulling her closer. "I'm here," he vowed. "And I won't let you face this alone." He cupped her cheek and pulled her into a warm kiss. Lavender washed over him as they stood close, their capes wrapping around them like a protective shield.

As they stood there, lost in each other's presence, a human officer pacing the corridor halted abruptly. His eyes widened, taking in the tender scene. He felt a pang of something he couldn't quite name—respect, awe, perhaps even envy. The sight of the legendary FEW, so powerful yet deeply in love, was a rare glimpse of vulnerability that left him speechless.

With a final, lingering touch, they stepped back, their connection unwavering despite the physical distance. The mission ahead loomed large, but their bond provided an unbreakable foundation.

"Let's go," Mara said, her voice steady with resolve. They continued down the corridor, side by side, their hearts beating in unison.

Suddenly, Gresham was alone. The corridor's echoes faded, replaced by the sterile hum of the Requiem's machinery. The air felt colder, carrying the faint metallic scent of the ship. He found himself seated in his quarters, the dim lighting casting long shadows on the walls. The warmth of Mara's touch, the softness of her voice, and the vivid colors of their capes—all dissipated into the stark reality of his solitude.

He sank into his chair, the worn leather creaking beneath him. Silence greeted him, accompanied only by the sterile tang of stone and dust. Gresham closed his eyes, clinging to the memory of her fiery violet gaze and the glint of her silver necklace. The weight of their burden pressed heavily upon him, each breath a reminder of the mission they had undertaken and the love that gave him strength.

In the solitude of his quarters, surrounded by the muted sounds of the ship, Gresham allowed himself a moment of vulnerability. The ghostly warmth of Mara's touch lingered against his skin as he steeled himself for the challenges ahead, knowing their bond remained unbroken despite the vast expanse of space between them.

The admirals' voices had buzzed like a hive of agitated insects, a cacophony of strategic hubris in Gresham's ears. They had extolled the virtues of the ship's latest armaments, their animated gestures at odds with his stoic posture. Black hole artillery and neutron warheads, he thought with a sardonic smirk. Let them have their shiny new toys. Nothing could mend the gaping hole Mara's absence had left in his soul.

A muscle in his jaw twitched, then released with a tremor. He balled his hands into fists, the worn leather of his gloves straining against his grip. With Mara at his side, such a display of raw emotion would have been unthinkable. Her quiet wisdom had countered his blunt force, her calm logic disarming adversaries where his temper might have inflamed them.

He sank into the cold stone command chair, the chill seeping through his uniform. The air was stagnant, devoid of the faint lavender scent that had once been a constant, comforting presence. Silence pressed in on him, broken only by the ragged rasp of his breath. He squeezed his eyes shut, the memory crystallizing in his mind, sharp and vivid. Her fiery violet gaze contrasted starkly with the bleak reality of the sterile chamber. He saw her blonde hair cascading over her shoulders, the way it framed her face with a halo of golden light, and her serene smile that always managed to calm his storm.

The siege of Altair-7 had been a maelstrom of chaos and destruction. Gresham and Mara led the charge, their blades cutting through the enemy ranks with deadly precision. The air was thick with smoke and the acrid stench of burning metal. Amidst the cacophony, Mara's voice had been a beacon of calm.

"We need to flank them from the east," she had said, her tone steady despite the chaos. "Their defenses are weakest there."

Gresham nodded, trusting her instincts implicitly. Together, they turned the tide of the battle, their combined strength and strategy a force to be reckoned with. The memory of Mara's serene determination in the face of danger was a stark contrast to the turmoil he felt now.

The admirals' enthusiastic chatter continued, a grating discord against the leaden weight in Gresham's gut. Let them prattle on about their new tools of destruction. He thought, a bitterness surprising even himself. No arsenal could fill the void that echoed within him.

His fists clenched again, the leather groaning in protest. Beside him, where Mara would have sat, the empty space ached with her absence. Her calming voice, usually a soothing balm to his volatile nature, was a fading echo in his memory. In its place, a simmering rage bubbled beneath the surface, threatening to erupt like a star on the verge of a supernova.

He rose from the chair, his crimson cape swirling around him like a vortex of turmoil. Each step he took in the sterile corridor resonated with a hollow thud, the sound echoing through the metallic shell of the ship, a solitary drumbeat against the deafening silence within him.

The ship's interior was a labyrinth of cold steel and harsh lighting, a stark contrast to the organic warmth he remembered from days spent with Mara. The air was tinged with the scent of machinery and ozone, an ever-present reminder of the battles fought and those yet to come.

He traced his finger along the holographic map in the command center, the jagged lines mirroring the maelstrom of grief and rage within him. Once, navigating this chaotic world had been a shared endeavor, Mara's serene wisdom calming the tempestuous tides within him. Now, the silence in his mind roared, the absence of her calming presence a gaping maw where warmth and understanding had once resided.

The flickering holographic map pulsed with a network of tunnels, a seemingly endless labyrinth that mirrored his sense of being lost and adrift. The cramped confines of the command deck pressed in, intensifying his claustrophobia and amplifying the suffocating echo of his loneliness.

"Thirty minutes," he growled, his voice tense as the tremors threatened the caverns. Enclosed spaces were Gresham's anathema, his claustrophobia clawing at the edges of his control.

Colonel Graves' salute was as crisp as the click of a rifle bolt. A flicker of unwavering loyalty burned in his eyes, but a tremor in his usually booming voice betrayed the strain. Even the seasoned soldier couldn't entirely mask the weight of their dwindling oxygen supply.

"All systems are a go, my Lord," Graves reported, his voice steady despite the fear lurking in his eyes. "We'll be ready to deploy on your command."

Gresham nodded, his mind briefly flashing back to the siege of Altair-7. Graves had been a young lieutenant then, full of fire and bravado. They had faced insurmountable odds together, and now, years later, that same fire still burned in the Colonel's eyes, tempered by experience and the scars of countless battles.

The memory of their final confrontation with Ximon was seared into Gresham's mind. The battle had raged for hours, the relentless assault from Ximon's forces pushing them to their limits. Gresham had fought side by side with Mara, their blades moving in perfect synchronization.

Ximon stood before them, a towering figure of menace, his eyes gleaming with malevolent intent. "You cannot stop me," he snarled, his voice dripping with contempt. "I will rule this galaxy, and you will be nothing but a footnote in my conquest."

Mara stepped forward, her blade glowing with fierce blue light. "Your reign of terror ends here, Ximon," she declared, her voice steady and resolute.

The ensuing battle was brutal. Ximon fought with reckless abandon, his attacks fueled by a desperate need for dominance. But Mara and Gresham's combined strength and strategy eventually overpowered him. In a final, desperate act, Ximon unleashed a devastating attack, sacrificing his own forces in a bid to take them down with him. They narrowly escaped, but the cost was high.

Gresham's fists clenched at the memory. Ximon's words and actions had left a lasting scar on the galaxy and on him personally. The absence of Mara, the person who had been his anchor, made the weight of their mission even heavier.

As the command center prepared for their next move, Gresham's thoughts returned to the present. The admirals' voices buzzed around him, but he tuned them out, focusing instead on the mission ahead. His resolve hardened, fueled by the memories of their past battles and the determination to honor Mara's legacy.

The Descent into the Unknown

The Galactic Alliance, a coalition of diverse star systems, prided itself on bringing peace and stability to the universe. However, their path often involved heavy-handed policies and ruthless enforcement, sparking dissent, most notably in the mining colony of Cygnus-9.

As the team embarked on their descent into the abandoned facility, the hum of their ship and the echo of their boots were the only sounds breaking the silence. The air grew colder, and flickering emergency lights cast long shadows, creating an atmosphere thick with unspoken promises and threats. The secrets of Cygnus-9 awaited them, offering the potential for answers, redemption, and perhaps darkness deeper than they could imagine.

Hours later, Gresham and Levi stood shoulder-to-shoulder, united by grim determination. The holographic map before them revealed the depths of Cygnus-9's underground labyrinth. The rebellion, swallowed by the earth, seemed to echo from the depths, beckoning them closer with promises and perils.

"What drove these miners to rise against the Galactic Alliance?" Levi mused aloud, his voice echoing in the silence. "What secrets did they take with them into the abyss?"

Gresham's gaze hardened. "The Alliance's push for increased production quotas and the exploitation of Cygnus-9's resources pushed the miners to their breaking point. They were treated as expendable, their lives valued less than the minerals they extracted."

Gresham remembered the day the rebellion began. The miners, their faces gaunt and eyes hollow, had stormed the administration building. Explosions rocked the colony, and the air was thick with the acrid smell of burning machinery. Mara had been by his side, her blade glowing blue as they fought to protect the civilians caught in the crossfire.

"We can't let them win," she had said, her voice steady despite the chaos. "We need to protect these people."

They had fought valiantly, but the miners, driven by desperation and fury, had overwhelmed them. The memory of that day, the screams, and the blood haunted Gresham still.

The descent into the heart of this forgotten rebellion would test their strength, loyalty, and perhaps even their very identity. As they descended, the echoes of the past grew louder. Whispers of betrayal, pleas for justice, and the chilling screams of the fallen painted a stark picture of the rebellion's tragic end. Would they unearth answers or awaken slumbering ghosts?

Gresham and Levi exchanged a glance, their eyes reflecting the weight of their mission. This was the threshold, the line beyond which their lives would be forever changed. But would they emerge as heroes, uncovering the truth about the rebellion and bringing closure to its lost souls? Or would they become another tragic chapter in the facility's dark history, lost to the shadows they dared to explore?

The holographic map flickered as they reached the final descent point, revealing a hidden chamber deep within the labyrinth. It pulsed with an ominous energy, hinting at the power and danger that waited. With a deep breath and a shared nod, Gresham and Levi activated their energy shields, stepping into the unknown, the echoes of the rebellion their only guide.

Levi traced a finger along the holographic map of Cygnus-9, its labyrinthine network of tunnels glowing an ominous red. The abandoned mining facility, once a symbol of prosperity, now loomed as a skeletal scar across the moon's icy surface. "A frontal assault would be foolish," he muttered, his green eyes narrowed in thought. "We need to be surgical, precise."

Gresham nodded curtly, his weathered cloak rippling in the sterile air of the command center. The memory of Mara, their strategist lost in a daring raid years ago, flickered in his eyes. "Divide and conquer," he ordered, his voice echoing the countless battles they had fought together. "But remember, Levi, the shadows in those tunnels hold more than just echoes of the past."

His words sent a shiver down Levi's spine. Rumors of spectral guardians and automated defenses haunted the facility's history. But the unspoken part of Gresham's warning truly unsettled him. Did the shadows conceal hidden agendas, remnants of the rebellion with their motives, or something even more sinister?

Levi outlined his plan, a calculated dance of infiltration and distraction. He would lead a small, elite team through a forgotten access point, while Gresham, with a more significant force, created a diversion at the main entrance. It was a risky maneuver, but their best chance of neutralizing the enemy and uncovering the secrets buried within.

As they finalized the plan, Levi felt a pang of guilt. The memory of Mara, ever present in their strategies, felt heavier than usual. He missed her calm presence, her ability to anticipate every move, and the unspoken comfort of her shared burdens. He vowed to honor her memory by completing this mission, by bringing whatever lurked in the shadows to light.

With a determined glint in his eyes, Levi turned to Gresham. "We'll be ready in two hours," he said, his voice firm. "May the shadows guide us, and may Mara's memory illuminate our path."

Gresham met his gaze, a flicker of gratitude passing through his stoic expression. "She would be proud of you, Levi," he said, his voice gruff but sincere. "Now go and claim what is rightfully ours."

The team gathered their gear and prepared for the mission ahead. The cold metal of their weapons and the hum of their energy shields were a stark reminder of the dangers they faced. As they moved through the ship's corridors, the tension was palpable, a silent testament to the gravity of their task.

Gresham's voice cut through the stillness as they approached the yawning entrance to the tunnels. "Stay sharp. Stick to the plan.

Remember, we're fighting for those who came before us and those who will come after."

The team nodded, a collective breath held as they descended into the depths of Cygnus-9. The darkness swallowed them, each step a defiant echo against the oppressive silence. The walls seemed to press in, cold and unyielding, as if the very planet sought to crush their resolve.

The flickering holographic map cast an eerie glow, guiding them through the labyrinthine tunnels. The air was thick with the scent of damp earth and the metallic tang of old machinery. As they moved deeper, the ground trembled, sending showers of dust and debris from the ceiling.

Gresham glanced at his team, seeing the determination etched on their faces. Levi, his second-in-command, moved with a quiet intensity, his eyes constantly scanning for threats. Beside him, Zara, their tech specialist, adjusted her equipment, her fingers trembling slightly. She had lost her brother in the rebellion, and this mission was personal for her.

Suddenly, a faint noise broke the silence, a distant murmur of movement. Weapons at the ready, the team halted. Gresham signaled for quiet, his eyes scanning the shadows. The tension was electric, a tangible force pressing against their nerves.

Levi leaned in, his voice barely a whisper. "We've got movement at ten o'clock."

Gresham nodded, his grip tightening on his blade. "Stay close. We move together."

The noise grew louder and closer. They had ventured into the heart of the rebellion, where the past's ghosts and present's whispers intertwined. Rounding a corner, they confronted a group of spectral guardians—remnants of the rebellion's automated defenses. Glowing eyes fixed on the intruders, the guardians' presence was both ethereal and menacing.

Gresham's blade ignited with a fierce red glow. "We come in peace," he declared, his voice steady. "We seek the truth of what happened here."

For a heartbeat, the guardians hesitated, their eyes flickering. Then, as if understanding their purpose, they stepped aside. The team moved forward, the guardians' spectral forms dissolving into the shadows.

The team reached a heavily fortified door, its surface bristling with sensors and automated turrets. Zara stepped forward, her fingers dancing over a holographic interface. "Give me a moment," she said, her voice tense.

Gresham scanned the surroundings, his nerves taut. "Hurry, Zara. We don't have much time."

The interface beeped, and the door slid open with a hiss. "We're in," Zara announced, her voice filled with relief.

The passageway ahead was a maze of crumbling rock and twisted metal. The air grew thick with the scent of decay and the metallic tang of old machinery. As they moved deeper, the ground trembled, sending showers of dust and debris from the ceiling.

"Watch your step," Levi warned, steadying Zara as she stumbled. "This place could come down on us at any moment."

A sudden rumble echoed through the tunnel, and Gresham's heart leaped. "Move, now!" he shouted, leading the team in a sprint towards the next checkpoint.

They reached a cavernous chamber filled with ancient, dormant technology. The central console pulsed with a faint blue light, its surface covered in a layer of dust.

Levi approached the console, his fingers deftly tapping commands. "I'll need a few minutes to get through their firewalls."

Gresham kept watch, his blade ready. "Make it quick. We don't know who else might be down here."

The console beeped, and a holographic display flickered to life. "We're in," Levi said, a triumphant smile on his face.

A series of coordinates appeared on the display, leading them to a hidden alcove. Inside, they found a cache of data crystals and a small group of survivors, their faces gaunt and eyes filled with hope.

"We're here to help," Gresham assured them, guiding the survivors to safety. "Stay close, and we'll get you out of here."

As they made their way back, a rival team of government agents emerged from the shadows, weapons drawn. "Hand over the evidence and the prisoners," their leader demanded, his voice cold.

Gresham's eyes narrowed. "Not a chance."

A fierce firefight erupted, energy beams lighting up the darkness. Gresham and his team fought with a desperate fury, protecting the survivors and the precious evidence. Zara took a hit, collapsing to the ground. Commander Levi rushed to her side, his face a mask of determination and fear.

"We can't lose her!" Levi shouted, his voice breaking.

Gresham's heart ached, but he couldn't afford to waver. "Cover us! We need to get her out of here!"

Just as the last of the agents fell, a violent tremor shook the ground. "The whole place is going to collapse!" Zara shouted, her voice filled with panic.

"Everyone, move!" Gresham ordered, leading the charge towards the surface. The tunnels seemed to close in around them, debris raining down as the planet itself seemed to protest their escape.

They burst into the open air, the ground heaving beneath their feet. Gresham turned to Levi, a rare smile breaking his stoic demeanor. "We did it," he said, his voice filled with pride.

Levi's eyes shone with determination. "And we will ensure their sacrifice was not in vain. We will honor their memory and continue the fight for freedom."

Their steps echoed through the tunnels, the oppressive shadows retreating as if acknowledging their victory. Emerging into the light, they felt a renewed sense of purpose. The survivors they had rescued clung to them, their gratitude evident in their weary eyes.

Gresham looked at Zara, who was being tended to by the medic. Her face was pale, but she managed a weak smile. "We made it," she whispered.

Gresham nodded, his heart heavy with the cost of their success. "Yes, but at what price?"

As they regrouped, the reality of their mission settled over them. They had uncovered the truth, but their actions had drawn the attention of powerful enemies. The fight for justice was far from over, and the road ahead would be fraught with danger and sacrifice.

But for now, they had each other and the memory of those who had fallen to guide them. They had descended into darkness and emerged victorious, their mission complete, but their fight for justice was only just beginning.

The journey back to the ship was filled with a sense of accomplishment and hope. They had faced the darkness and uncovered the truth, and now they would return to the Galactic Alliance with their findings. The future was uncertain, but they were ready to face whatever came next, united by their shared mission and the memory of those they had lost.

2

INTO THE HEART OF CHAOS

Alarms blared, red lights pulsing like malevolent eyes. Reports spat from consoles, a torrent of data threatening to drown the bridge in chaos. Yet, Commander Levi moved with the focused grace of a dancer amidst swirling skirts. His brow furrowed, not in panic, but in calculation, his hazel eyes scanning the chaos, absorbing information like a sponge.

"Helm, steady course. Weapons target their main engines. Shields at maximum!" His voice, calm amidst the turmoil, carried an undercurrent of steel, unwavering even as a wry smile briefly flickered across his lips. It wasn't a joke, exactly, more a shared acknowledgment of the absurd reality they faced. He caught the flicker of fear in a young Ensign's eyes, stopping to place a hand on his shoulder.

"First time under fire, kid? Remember, fear and panic are just advisors, not commanders. Listen to their warnings, but don't let them take the wheel."

The words, simple yet charged with experience, sparked a flicker of confidence in the newcomer's eyes. This was Levi—a commander who strategized and empathized, his leadership woven from steel and understanding.

Beneath the calm surface, a storm churned. He knew the stakes, the potential cost of even a minor miscalculation. The weight of responsibility pressed down, a familiar burden he bore silently. A bead of sweat traced down his temple, the only betrayal of the tension simmering beneath the surface. Yet, he wouldn't let it show. Not now. Not when his crew needed him most. At that moment, he was the lighthouse in the chaos; his every breath, every command, a testament to the unwavering spirit that resided within. This spirit would guide them through the turmoil and, hopefully, toward the dawn.

Levi wasn't just a commander but a conductor, orchestrating the diverse talents aboard his ship into a harmonious whole. He knew birthdays by heart, surprising crewmates with a cake baked from salvaged ingredients. He celebrated promotions with boisterous laughter, his voice echoing through the mess hall. And he truly listened to their hopes and dreams, fueling a loyalty that ran deeper than mere duty.

He understood Gresham, the enigmatic warrior shrouded in power and mystery. Gresham needed a bridge, someone to connect him to the crew, to temper his isolation with warmth. Levi filled that role perfectly with his easy smile and genuine empathy. He was the oil that smoothed the gears between Gresham's brooding intensity and the crew's camaraderie.

The crew viewed Levi's optimism as a beacon of hope and reassurance. They trusted him implicitly, knowing that his leadership came from a place of genuine care and dedication. His friendly and outgoing nature made him approachable, and his willingness to listen to their concerns fostered a strong sense of loyalty. In contrast, Gresham's stoicism inspired awe and a hint of fear. His presence commanded respect, and while the crew appreciated his skill and decisiveness, they often felt a sense of unease around him. His enigmatic aura and the power he wielded with his glowing red sword added to the mystique, making him a figure both revered and feared.

But amidst the harmony, a quiet question lingered: Could this very strength, this reliance on connection, become a vulnerability in the face of a truly ruthless enemy? Only time and the trials they faced together would reveal the true strength of Levi's leadership, a strength woven from compassion, trust, and perhaps a hint of calculated risk.

Gresham, draped in a crimson cloak that seemed to writhe with a life of its own, was a monument to solitude amidst the bustling human crew. Levi, a whirlwind of youthful energy in crisp blue and white, exuded warmth like a star spilling its light into the void. An unlikely pair, they were anomalies adrift in the vast ocean of space. Yet, their differences, honed by the shared fires of hardship, sparked a respect forged in the crucible of survival.

Mara's absence left a gaping chasm in Gresham's soul, casting him into an emotional wasteland. Never again, he swore, would he allow anyone to pierce his solitude only to be left bereft once more. But Levi, with his unwavering optimism and unspoken understanding, proved an exception. Like a persistent beacon in the darkness, his openness chipped away at Gresham's defenses, revealing a flicker of hope beneath the hardened exterior. The void still lingered, but faint warmth spread within it, fueled by the unexpected companionship.

Despite their contrasting approaches, a shared love for protecting others bridged their gulf. While Levi favored diplomacy and negotiation, Gresham was a storm of decisive action. His power was wielded with precision honed by centuries of experience. Amidst the chaos, Levi's humor, often self-deprecating and punctuated by a booming laugh, did the unthinkable: it made Gresham laugh. A genuine, surprised chuckle resonated in the silent corners of his soul, a testament to the unexpected power of friendship.

This bond, though fragile, held the promise of something more. The secrets Mara's absence held, the mysteries Gresham kept close, and the inherent differences in their approaches could spark conflict, threatening to shatter the fragile harmony. But for now, in the vast emptiness of space, they had each other, an unlikely beacon of hope and understanding and a testament to the unexpected connections that sometimes blossom in the most barren landscapes.

On the chaotic battlefield, their contrasting styles danced a deadly ballet. Gresham cloaked in crimson shadows, moved with deliberate power, his every strike precise and lethal. Subtle shifts in his stance, barely perceptible to others, triggered instantaneous adjustments from Levi, their movements harmonizing as if guided by an unseen hand. It was a language forged in shared battles, unspoken trust, and an agreement to bridge the chasm between light and shadow.

Yet, within their unique bond lurked the seeds of potential conflict. Where Levi saw hope in the outstretched hand of diplomacy, Gresham saw the fragility of alliances forged on empty promises. Where Levi believed in the inherent good of people, Gresham carried the scars of betrayal etched deep within his soul. These scars, hidden beneath his stoic exterior, flickered when he observed the glimmer of optimism in Levi's eyes. Was it naivety, Gresham scoffed internally, or a dangerous idealism ripe for exploitation? He couldn't help but remember when his trust shattered, leaving him wounded and wary.

Even Levi, usually as steady as the stars charting their course, seemed veiled with shadows. Yet, his voice held unwavering resolve.

"The escape… the questions he leaves… they must wait. Our mission continues."

Gresham nodded, but his gaze remained fixed on the star-studded abyss beyond the viewport. Inevitably, his mind drifted toward Mara. Her memory, her fiery spirit, flickered amidst the constellations, a constant reminder of a loss that still ached with raw pain. It had been five long years since she disappeared. He leaned closer to the console, the silence heavy with expectation and dread. He spoke in a voice barely a whisper, tinged with a vulnerability he never allowed anyone else to witness.

"*Mara…,*" he called out, his words swallowed by the static hiss of the console as he activated a hidden channel. "If it is you, if somehow you are still out there… tell me. What game are we playing? Who are we truly fighting for?"

The screen flickered, a distorted image resolving into a face cloaked in shadow. A smirk, both familiar and unsettling, played on their lips. "Patience, Gresham," the voice purred, laced with amusement. "The answers you seek… they will come. But first, you must complete your dance with destiny. The fate of your world, and perhaps others, hangs in the balance."

The transmission abruptly ended, leaving Gresham staring at the blank screen, his heart pounding frantically against his ribs. Mara, or someone using her image, was playing a dangerous game. But for what purpose? And what did their cryptic words mean about the actual stakes of their mission?

As Gresham issued new orders, a cold determination settling over his features, Levi sensed a subtle shift towards pursuing the cloaked figure rather than their primary objective. He voiced his concerns, but Gresham's steely gaze silenced him. The weight of leadership, the burden of a hidden agenda, pressed heavily on Gresham's shoulders.

Meanwhile, Talia Sharma, the explosives expert, noticed a faint symbol etched on a recovered rebel weapon—the same symbol found at the escape point. This seemingly insignificant detail fueled her suspicion, adding another layer to the complex web of intrigue.

Talia, with her sharp eyes and meticulous nature, had been instrumental in countless missions. Her background as a former engineer in the Galactic Alliance before joining the rebellion gave her a unique perspective on both technology and strategy. She had a knack for noticing details others overlooked. Her sharp intellect was matched by her fierce loyalty to the crew, particularly to Gresham, whom she admired for his unwavering resolve and mysterious strength.

As she examined the symbol, her mind raced. This symbol wasn't just a mark; it was a code, a link to something larger. She had seen it before, years ago, in a classified Alliance document about ancient alien technology. Her curiosity was piqued, but she knew better than to voice her concerns without concrete evidence.

She approached Commander Levi, her voice steady but tinged with urgency. "Commander, I found this symbol on a recovered rebel weapon. It's the same symbol we saw at the escape point. It could be linked to the ancient alien technology we're after. I believe there's more to this mission than we initially thought."

Levi's gaze shifted to the symbol, a flicker of recognition passing through his eyes. "Good work, Talia. Keep investigating. We need every piece of information we can get."

Gresham, now feeling a flicker of intrigue, allowed himself to consider Talia's findings. This mission was beginning to hold more layers than he had initially anticipated, and perhaps, amidst the chaos, it could lead him closer to the answers he sought about Mara.

The journey ahead was fraught with danger but also with potential. Together, with the crew's unwavering loyalty and Levi's compassionate leadership, they would face whatever came their way, each step bringing them closer to uncovering the truth.

The observation deck buzzed with activity. Holographic displays flickered, charting a course through the uncharted nebula. Gresham and Levi stood shoulder-to-shoulder, their gazes fixed on the viewport. Beyond the reinforced glass, the vastness of space unfolded, a swirling canvas of nebulae and distant stars.

Gresham's mind raced with questions and uncertainties, but one truth remained steadfast: he would find Mara or uncover the truth behind her disappearance, no matter the cost. The secrets buried in the derelict research facility awaited promising revelations that could either bring them closer to the truth or plunge them further into darkness.

As the ship's engines roared to life, the crew prepared for the journey ahead. The path was fraught with danger, but their resolve was unwavering. Together, they would face the unknown, their bond tested by the shadows of the past and the perils of the future.

In the heart of the galaxy, amidst the stars and the void, their fate awaited. And as they ventured into the abyss, one thing was sure: the answers they sought would come, but at what cost? Only time will tell.

An expectant energy filled the air, a mix of apprehension and anticipation. The unknown stretched before them, a labyrinth of cosmic secrets and potential dangers. Yet, amidst the uncertainty, a spark of hope flickered in their eyes. This mission was more than just a search; it was a chance to unravel the mysteries of the lost signal, to push the boundaries of their knowledge, and perhaps, to discover something hidden even from themselves.

With a decisive nod, Gresham activated the autopilot. The ship hummed to life, its engines pulsing with raw power. They were a team, two veterans etched by the scars of past battles, their bond forged in the crucible of shared experience. Now, they were venturing into the unknown, guided not by a map but by the unwavering belief in their own strength and the unyielding spirit of exploration.

A Galaxy Apart

The hollow reverberation of Gresham's boot steps mocked the oppressive silence permeating the corridors, devoid of Mara's musical laughter. His jawline hardened with grim determination, eyes glinting like polished steel as his gaze turned inward, renewing the ember of purpose that had pulled him back from grief's abyss. Beyond the viewport, the vast star field of the cosmos unfurled, each distant star whispering the promise of revelation if one remained willing to listen. Though the ever-tightening grip of the "Fair Trade" cabal's tyranny still constricted the galaxy's final gasps of freedom, for Gresham, such totalitarian urgencies felt like peripheral static.

Lord Gresham cut an imposing figure, well-muscled and clad in the all-black uniform of the FEW, with an emblem glowing where his left pocket would be. His black boots shone with a sharp reflection, and his sword hummed softly beside him. His deep blue eyes, capable of shifting to black in moments of high emotion, scanned the vastness beyond the ship's hull. A red cape, seemingly alive, snapped, furled, billowed, and wrapped around him, mirroring his every emotional nuance. His dark hair framed a face that appeared to be in his late 30s, though in reality, he was much older.

Commander Alexander Levi stood beside him, a stark contrast to Gresham's brooding intensity. Levi was tall and broad-shouldered, with sun-kissed hair that fell just short of regulation length. His hazel eyes sparkled with a mix of intelligence and humor, a faint scar etched across his brow hinting at past battles. Despite the weight of command, Levi's demeanor was approachable, his easy smile and booming laughter a source of comfort to the crew. He wore the crisp blue and white uniform of the Galactic Alliance, its sharp lines and pristine condition reflecting his dedication to duty. His presence was a beacon of optimism, a vital counterbalance to Gresham's intense focus.

Gresham's every thought, his entire being, had become subsumed by the single-minded hunger to locate his vanished lover. He understood the burdens woven into Mara's mythic lineage, the soul-scouring battles, and the existential torments that must have flayed her spirit raw, forcing the agonizing decision to abandon their shared world behind. Yet abandonment did not equate to complete severance. Gresham's mind spiraled inward, seeking the thinnest psychic tether still binding them across the vastness. He envisioned Mara standing resolute and unbroken amidst the searing amber of some uncharted world's binary suns. Exotic alien flora starkly contrasted the sterile steel-boned reality entombing him.

Memories of their time together flooded his senses. He could still feel the warmth of her skin against his, the soft murmur of her breath as they lay entwined beneath a canopy of alien stars. Her laughter, a melody that had once filled his world with light, now echoed as a haunting reminder of what he had lost. Every touch, every whispered word, was etched into his soul, a painful yet cherished reminder of the love they had shared.

The holographic star chart flickered with eldritch iridescence, each spectral streak revealing the torn roadways of some unexplored celestial labyrinth waiting to entrap the unwary. Gresham's eyes narrowed, the weight of civilizations flickering within those ghostly topologies. Following the distress signal embedded within the energy fluctuations, they could seal the gateways and fight the cosmic rift's insatiable hunger. Unflinchingly, he engaged the autopilot and unleashed the ship's supernal engines, propelling their trajectory directly into the ravenous cosmic maelstrom clouding the nadir of all navigation.

As Gresham's determination intensified, the crew felt the palpable shift in their leader's resolve. In the common area, the murmurs of unease grew louder. Talia Sharma, the explosives expert, tightened her grip on a spanner. A former Galactic Alliance engineer, she knew all too well the dangers of celestial phenomena like cosmic rifts and interstitial nightmares. Her eyes reflected both the crew's apprehension and the unspoken awe she felt towards Gresham. To lay eyes on a member of the FEW was a rarity; to speak directly with one was an almost unimaginable honor. The aura of power and authority radiated from him, filling the room with a tangible sense of awe and fear. Talia's sharp intellect and fierce loyalty made her a cornerstone of their operations. Her mind raced, analyzing every detail of their precarious situation.

Levi approached Gresham, his voice low and steady. "We're ready to engage the engines. Talia has the explosives prepped just in case we need to clear a path."

Gresham nodded, his eyes never leaving the viewport. "Good. Keep the crew focused. We can't afford any mistakes."

Levi placed a reassuring hand on Gresham's shoulder. "We'll find her, Gresham. We won't let her go."

Gresham turned, meeting Levi's gaze. "Thank you, Alex. I won't lose her. Not again."

The ship shuddered as the engines roared to life, propelling them into the heart of the cosmic storm. Gresham's mind remained focused on Mara, his resolve unyielding. He would navigate the labyrinth of space and time, confront the horrors lurking in the void, and reclaim the light that had been stolen from him.

Kael Sol, the sharpshooter, was the first to voice his concern, his voice laced with a mix of respect and fear. "Are we really heading straight into that anomaly? This feels like a death sentence."

Talia glanced at Commander Levi, her eyes searching for reassurance. "What if this anomaly isn't just a beacon but a trap? We need to be sure."

Commander Levi, sensing the crew's anxiety, addressed them with a steady voice. "I understand your fears, but this is our only lead. We have to take the risk. Lady Mara might be on the other side, and she needs us."

The helmsman, a young officer named Aiden, whispered to the communications officer, Sasha, "I can't shake this feeling. It's like we're diving into the mouth of the beast."

Sasha, her voice barely audible, replied, "Stay focused, Aiden. We have to trust in our training and in Commander Levi. He's never led us astray."

Nearby, the tech ensign, Zara, argued heatedly with the armory officer, Lucas. "We need to divert more power to the shields! If we don't, we're sitting ducks out there!"

Lucas, his face flushed with frustration, snapped back, "And leave our weapons underpowered? We'd be defenseless against whatever's waiting for us. You think you're the only one worried about safety?"

The tension in the room was palpable. The crew's whispered fears and heated debates add to the atmosphere of uncertainty. Gresham, sensing the rising anxiety, turned to face the crew, his voice deep and surprisingly calm. A subtle pulse of power emanated from him, momentarily silencing the murmurs of unease. "Everyone, focus on your stations. We'll get through this together."

The awe he inspired was palpable, a force that rippled through the crew, grounding their fears and fueling their determination. Gresham nodded, appreciating Zara's expertise. "Your caution is noted, Zara. We'll need your skills to navigate through this. Keep a close watch on those patterns and alert me to any significant changes."

The subtle tension among the crew hinted at deeper conflicts brewing beneath the surface. Ryder's glances toward Talia suggested a disagreement about the mission's priorities, while Kael's unease indicated a lack of trust in Gresham's single-minded pursuit.

The "Fair Trade" cabal's reach extended through every corner of the galaxy, their oppressive regime squeezing the life out of any who dared oppose them. Gresham had seen their methods firsthand—the ruthless suppression of dissent, the exploitation of entire star systems for profit, and the shadowy alliances with malevolent entities. Their impact on his mission was profound, turning every step into a perilous dance with destiny.

The derelict research facility, their destination, loomed in the shadows of Gresham's mind. Rumored to hold secrets of ancient alien technology, it was a place of both fascination and dread. The facility had been abandoned for centuries, its halls now home to whispers of forbidden experiments and the echoes of those who had vanished within its walls. Gresham suspected that within its depths lay not only the answers to Mara's disappearance but also the key to confronting the cabal's stranglehold on the galaxy.

Lord Gresham cut an imposing figure, well-muscled and clad in the all-black uniform of the FEW, with an emblem glowing where his left pocket would be. His black boots shone with a sharp reflection, and his ectropic blade hummed softly beside him. His deep blue eyes, capable of shifting to black in moments of high emotion, scanned the vastness beyond the ship's hull. A red cape, seemingly alive, snapped, furled, billowed, and wrapped around him, mirroring his every emotional nuance. His dark hair framed a face that appeared to be in his late 30s, though in reality, he was much older. Friendship with Commander Alexander Levi had softened his demeanor, allowing rare, genuine smiles to break through the stoicism.

The FEW, a group of only ten in the universe, were shrouded in mystery and power. Diverse in background and ability, they seldom saw each other, each living in isolation. Yet, by a twist of fate, Gresham and Mara had met on a distant, forgotten planet. Drawn together by an inexplicable force, their partnership had flourished, their bond so in sync that they fell deeply in love. The FEW could alter the will of those around them, instilling terror or calm, and manipulate people and objects with a mere thought. Their swords were conduits for their immense power, capable of becoming shields, summoning storms, or creating protective barriers. In another's hand, these swords became lifeless and dull, dying with their owner. The FEW's uniforms were identical, and none had memories of their birth or early childhood. They seemed ageless, their pasts as enigmatic as their powers.

Yet even that visionary idyll could not silence the sibilant whispers beneath—rumors of primordial horrors haunting existence's forgotten blind spots, daring cosmic vagabonds to stumble wayward. His calloused fingers reflexively caressed the pommel grip of the sword sheathed at his hip, drawing solace from its metaphysical hum. He would not, could not, surrender Mara to such perils. Not after she had stood within the screaming furnace of their tribulations and rekindled his soul. Their bond transcended flesh, star-forged in the nuclear chaos of shared tribulations and hammered into sanctity upon LoLoss's cruelest anvil. He would reignite the last smoldering embers of that unbreakable amalgam and reforge her radiance, cauterizing the spiritual wounds that had forced her flight.

The holographic star chart flickered with eldritch iridescence, each spectral streak revealing the torn roadways of some unexplored celestial labyrinth waiting to entrap the unwary. Gresham's eyes narrowed, the weight of civilizations flickering within those ghostly topologies. Following the distress signal embedded within the energy fluctuations, they could seal the gateways and fight the insatiable hunger of the cosmic rifts. Unflinchingly, he engaged the autopilot and unleashed the ship's supernal engines, propelling their trajectory directly into the ravenous cosmic maelstrom clouding the nadir of all navigation.

His eyes followed the hurtling passage, nearly mesmerized by their terrifying momentum through the interstitial nightmare phenomenon, until an anomaly, a single piercing singularity of light, severed his grim trance. Like celestial firelight refracted through sacred prisms, a solitary distant beacon pierced the tidal nightmare, rekindling the faintest memorious spark of ancient glories of the paradisial realm they had once shared and sworn to rekindle.

His rough knuckles whitened as they gripped the core steel bulkhead, muscles coiled by the force of a solemn vow once made. No matter the unfolding horrors awaiting them—nameless and beyond imagining, the costs would be great—he would not permit the churning vortices of Oblivion to extinguish his path back toward the one bright truth seared into his being. The vow still blazed within him, a hyper-lasing defiance aimed at the very architects of Entropy itself. Gresham felt the long-desiccated spark of conviction blossoming anew for the first time in what felt like soul-piercing eternities. He was returning to her light, no matter the rites of extinguishing force awaiting them along that inevitable course.

The tension in the room was palpable, and the crew's whispered fears and heated debates added to the atmosphere of uncertainty. Gresham, sensing the rising anxiety, turned to face the crew, his voice deep and surprisingly calm. A subtle pulse of power emanated from him, momentarily silencing the murmurs of unease. "Everyone, focus on your stations. We'll get through this together."

As they neared the derelict research facility, the ship's sensors began to pick up traces of debris and the remains of a fierce battle. Gresham and Levi exchanged glances, their expressions a mix of anticipation and concern. The facility, once a beacon of technological advancement, now drifted in eerie silence, its hull scarred and battered.

The Requiem's docking clamps latched onto the facility's airlock with a resounding clang. The boarding party, led by Gresham and Levi, moved cautiously through the dimly lit corridors. The air was thick with the scent of ozone and burnt metal, a testament to the violent skirmish that had taken place.

In the central control room, they found a data terminal still operational. Ryder quickly interfaced with it, his fingers dancing over the console. "I've got something," he announced, his voice filled with excitement. "Logs of past and future illicit trades. This could be gold for us."

Levi's eyes widened. "Excellent work, Ryder. Download everything. We'll review it later and brief the Galactic Alliance with these updates."

As they continued to explore the facility, they stumbled upon an unexpected treasure trove. Talia, her eyes wide with disbelief, called out, "Commander, you might want to see this."

In a nearby storage room, they discovered a small cache of highly prized liquor, exotic foods, and surprisingly high-quality pillows—boxes and boxes of them. Lucas, the armory officer, opened a large crate to reveal phases of a new design, their sleek forms gleaming under the dim lights.

Gresham let out a rare laugh. "Looks like we hit the jackpot. Let's get these goods back to the Requiem. Our crew could use a morale boost."

Back on the Requiem, the crew gathered in the common area, their faces lighting up as the treasures were distributed. Commander Levi and Gresham shared a toast with the prized liquor, the tension of the mission momentarily forgotten.

"To unexpected discoveries," Levi said, raising his glass.

"And to the journey ahead," Gresham replied, clinking his glass with Levi's.

As the crew indulged in the exotic foods and marveled at the high-quality pillows, the atmosphere on the ship lightened. The abandoned goods provided a welcome respite from their intense mission, a moment of levity in the midst of uncertainty.

Gresham's eyes, however, never lost their steely resolve. As he sipped his drink, he turned to Levi and said, "We didn't find Mara this time, but I'll keep looking. I won't rest until I find her."

Levi nodded, placing a reassuring hand on Gresham's shoulder. "We'll find her, Gresham. Together, we'll find her."

The Requiem prepared to depart, the crew now equipped with new resources and a renewed sense of purpose. The journey was far from over, but they faced it with strengthened resolve and camaraderie.

With a final glance at the derelict facility, the Requiem set a course for their next destination, its engines humming with newfound energy. The answers they sought were still out there, waiting to be uncovered. And as they ventured into the abyss, one thing was certain: they would face whatever challenges lay ahead, united by their shared mission and the bond that had been forged in the crucible of exploration.

3

A Path To Rediscovery

Mara's Decision and Internal Conflict of 5 Years Ago

A wave of fatigue washed over Mara as she scrolled through endless lines of coded data. The sterility of the ship's command center amplified her sense of isolation. Beyond the viewport, the vibrant hues of a newly discovered planet pulsed with an almost mocking life, starkly contrasting the cold metal walls and serving as a window to a world she longed for. Gresham's voice, unwavering in its conviction, echoed through the room as he relayed the latest briefing. Each word resonated with their steadfast dedication to the "cause," a cause that felt increasingly hollow to her. A tremor of frustration ran through her, intensifying the familiar ache in her chest.

She yearned to break free from the suffocating weight of leadership, the endless cycle of battles, and the unspoken burden she carried alone. The "Fair Trade's" shadow loomed large, its demands casting a long shadow over her life. Yet, even amidst her growing disillusionment, her love for Gresham remained a constant, a small but persistent ache. She remembered the moments they shared, the quiet strength of his presence, and the deep bond forged through decades of trials and triumphs. Leaving him felt like tearing a piece of her soul away, but she couldn't ignore the gnawing need for change.

With a resolute glint in her violet eyes, Mara shut down her console. The silence was a stark contrast to Gresham's voice fading into the background. The verdant world on the holographic display mocked her with its vibrant life, contrasting with the sterile walls of the ship and the cold reality of her situation.

Tonight, under the watchful gaze of that distant world, a decision bloomed in the garden of her despair. It was rooted in more than frustration; it was a desperate yearning to reclaim the life stolen by endless battles and the suffocating weight of leadership. With a trembling breath, she deactivated the display. The silence was deafening, amplifying the thump of her rebellious heart. This wasn't just about defiance or Gresham's approval. This was about survival, not of the flesh, but of the spirit that craved the forgotten dreams echoing in the quiet corners of her soul.

As she prepared to leave, a pang of regret surged through her. She glanced at the command center where Gresham's presence lingered like a ghost. "I'm sorry, my love," she whispered, her voice barely audible. "But I need to find myself again."

This was her path to rediscovery, a journey that might lead her back to Gresham, stronger and more whole, or away into an unknown future. But no matter where it led, her love for him would remain a guiding star in the vast expanse of uncertainty.

The Disagreement

Gresham found her standing by the viewport, her back to him, shoulders tense. The vast expanse of space framed her silhouette, distant stars casting a faint, ethereal glow. The cold metal walls of the command center seemed to close in around them, amplifying the isolation they both felt. He approached quietly, the hum of the ship's engines a constant backdrop.

"Mara," he began softly, "what's troubling you?"

She turned slowly, her violet eyes glistening with unshed tears. The light from the viewport cast shadows on her face, highlighting the lines of worry and fatigue. Her crimson cape, which usually billowed with her every movement, now hung limply as if mirroring her inner turmoil. "I don't know how to explain it, Gresham. I feel... trapped."

His brow furrowed in confusion, his own cape swirling gently around his legs as he stepped closer. "Trapped? By what? The mission? The Alliance?" His voice was deep, carrying a mixture of concern and bewilderment.

Mara shook her head, frustration etched into her features. "It's not that simple. It's everything. The constant battles, the endless cycles of conflict... I feel like I'm losing myself." Her voice trembled, the words carrying the weight of her burden.

Gresham reached for her hand, his fingers brushing against hers, seeking to offer comfort. "Do you want to leave the Alliance? Take some time off the ship?" His blue eyes, darkening to near-black with emotion, searched hers for answers.

She pulled away, the motion causing her cape to snap back, a tear slipping down her cheek. "I don't know! I just know that I can't keep doing this, but I don't know what I want. I feel like I'm suffocating." Her hands clenched into fists at her sides, knuckles white.

Gresham's heart ached at the sight of her tears, feeling helpless. "Mara, I love you. I want to help, but I can't find the right way. What can I do?" His voice was low, almost pleading, as he took another step towards her.

Her voice broke as she tried to articulate her feelings. "I need to find myself again, Gresham. I need to know who I am outside of all this. But I can't explain it any better than that." She turned her gaze back to the viewport, the distant stars reflecting in her eyes.

Desperation filled Gresham's eyes as he reached out to her, his fingers brushing against her arm. "Please, Mara, don't go. We can figure this out together." His touch was gentle, almost hesitant, as if afraid she might shatter.

For a moment, Mara looked at him, her resolve wavering. Their faces were inches apart, breaths mingling in the cold air of the command center. But then, with heart-wrenching determination, she took a step back, shaking her head as tears threatened to fall. "I have to do this alone. I need to find my own path." Her voice was a whisper, yet it carried the weight of finality.

Gresham's hand dropped to his side, the emptiness between them growing more palpable. He watched helplessly as she turned away, her cape swaying with the motion, the echo of her footsteps blending with the hum of the ship.

In a sudden, desperate move, Gresham closed the distance between them, capturing her in a tight embrace. His lips found hers in a kiss that was both a plea and a declaration. He poured all his love, fear, and desperation into that kiss, hoping to reach the part of her that still felt connected to him.

Mara's initial shock melted into the kiss, her arms wrapping around him as tears streamed down her face. For a moment, she clung to him, the fierce intensity of their connection flaring like a beacon in the cold expanse of space. A flicker of doubt crossed her mind, her heart wavering as she felt the depth of his love and the pain of their possible separation.

But as the kiss broke, Mara stepped back, her tears falling freely. "I'm so sorry, Gresham," she whispered, her voice breaking. "I have to go. I need to find myself, and I can't do it here."

With that, she dashed off, leaving Gresham standing alone, his heart shattered but his resolve hardening. He would let her go, but he would never stop searching for her. She was his guiding star, and no matter the darkness that surrounded him, he would follow her light until the end of the galaxy.

Gresham stood rooted to the spot, his mind racing with confusion and sorrow. He had always admired Mara's strength, her unyielding spirit, and her fierce independence. But now, that same independence was taking her away from him. He felt a lump forming in his throat as he struggled to find the right words to bring her back, but they eluded him.

In the solitude of the command center, he stared out at the same vibrant world that had captivated Mara. His reflection in the viewport was a ghostly figure, a man unable to understand the woman he loved. Every memory of their time together flashed before his eyes—every laugh, every shared triumph, every quiet moment of solace.

"I don't want to lose you, Mara," he whispered to himself, his voice barely audible over the hum of the ship. "What am I doing wrong?"

The weight of her absence already pressed down on him like a physical burden. He clenched his fists, feeling the cold metal of the console beneath his fingers. The mission, the battles, the cause—they all seemed meaningless without her by his side. He had always believed they were invincible together, but now he felt the fragility of their bond, like glass about to shatter.

With a final glance at the distant stars, Gresham turned back to the console, his determination renewed. "I will find you, Mara," he vowed quietly. "No matter how far you go, I will bring you back."

The ship's engines hummed around him, a reminder of the journey ahead. Gresham's resolve was like steel, tempered by love and driven by the hope of reuniting with the woman who had stolen his heart. No matter the obstacles, he would not rest until they were together again.

Mara's Journey

As the ship pierced the atmosphere, Mara's heart hammered with a mix of trepidation and resolve. This descent wasn't just a flight toward solace; it was a quest. The whispers spoke of hidden power within the ruins, a power rumored to mend broken spirits and awaken dormant strengths. Could this be the key to her healing, the spark that would illuminate the path back to herself and, perhaps, even back to Gresham?

The answers she craved and the secrets she left behind would cost her dearly in this unforgiving land. With a deep breath, Mara embraced the unknown, ready to face the challenges ahead and rediscover not just her lost strength but the woman she was meant to be.

A blur of stars streaked past the viewport. Each one, a distant sun, seemed to mock her with its indifference. Mara's chest tightened, a physical manifestation of the turmoil within. Leaving Gresham was the hardest choice she had ever faced, but the silence between them had become a suffocating chasm filled with unspoken words and unmet needs. The echo of their final argument still resonated—"duty" and "sacrifice" ringing like hollow promises instead of the shared connection she craved.

Stepping onto the verdant alien soil, the unfamiliar air stung her lungs. The scent of exotic flora filled her senses, a strange perfume that masked the underlying anxiety gnawing at her. Lush, emerald forests stretched before her, shrouded in an unnatural twilight. Bioluminescent mushrooms pulsed with an unsettling rhythm, casting long, eerie shadows across the landscape. The beauty of this strange, new world was undeniable, yet it mirrored the turmoil within her. This wasn't just an escape; it was a test.

As day surrendered to dusk, shadows stretched across the alien landscape like grasping claws. Mara's resolve hardened. This world held the key to her transformation, a chance to reclaim her strength and perhaps find her way back to Gresham, not just as allies but as two souls willing to bear their deepest vulnerabilities and rebuild what was lost.

The Discovery

Back on the ship, Gresham felt the cold emptiness, a void where Mara's presence used to be. Yet, amidst the pain, a flicker of hope remained. Their love, forged in the crucible of countless battles and shared dreams, was a bond that transcended time and space. As the ship sailed deeper into the unknown, he held onto the belief that one day, their paths would converge again, and the love they shared would guide them back to each other.

Suddenly, the ship's sensors picked up something unusual—a derelict vessel adrift in the anomaly. As they docked and boarded, the crew's apprehension turned to cautious curiosity. The ship appeared to have been in a fierce battle, its corridors littered with signs of hasty abandonment.

In the command center, Ryder discovered a dropped log detailing illicit trades, past and future, involving high-ranking members of the "Fair Trade" cabal. Commander Levi's eyes widened as he reviewed the information, realizing its potential to dismantle the cabal's operations.

As they explored further, the crew found unexpected treasures: a small cache of highly prized liquor, crates of surprisingly high-quality pillows, and exotic foods for the onboard chef to evaluate and use. In a secured room, they discovered a large crate of phasers with a new design, a valuable addition to their arsenal.

With the ship now stocked with these newfound resources, the crew gathered in the mess hall to share a drink. Gresham and Commander Levi raised their glasses, the tension easing as they toasted to their unexpected fortune.

Gresham took a sip of the rare liquor, savoring the warmth that spread through him. He looked around at his crew, their faces reflecting a mix of relief and camaraderie. "We may not have found Mara," he began, his voice steady, "but we've uncovered something just as important. This information will help us strike a blow against the cabal, and these supplies will keep us going. We'll continue our search for Mara, and we won't rest until we find her."

Commander Levi nodded, his eyes meeting Gresham's with a shared understanding. "To the journey ahead," he said, lifting his glass higher. "And to Mara."

The crew echoed the toast, their spirits lifted by the unexpected bounty and the promise of future victories. As they celebrated, the bond between them grew stronger, their resolve to face the unknown unwavering.

Gresham, his heart still heavy with the ache of Mara's absence, found solace in the unity of his crew. They would face whatever challenges lay ahead, bound by their shared mission and the hope of reuniting with the woman who had captured his heart.

Epilogue

A single question hung heavy in the air: would this exile lead to self-discovery, or would it unearth truths even more painful than the silence she left behind? The answer remained shrouded in the mystery of this strange world, just like the future itself. But one thing was certain: Mara, a flickering ember in the vastness, had taken the first step on a journey not just of escape but of transformation. And like the bioluminescent mushrooms that pulsed softly around her, she would find strength in the unknown, embracing both the pain and the beauty as she fought to rediscover who she truly was.

The crew's tension was palpable as the vessel approached the anomaly. The air grew thick with unease, a silent testament to the gravity of their mission. Talia Sharma, the explosives expert, tightened her grip on a spanner, her knuckles white with tension. The metallic scent of the ship's recycled air mixed with her apprehension, creating an almost suffocating atmosphere.

Kael Sol, the sharpshooter, was the first to voice his concern. "Are we really heading straight into that anomaly? This feels like a death sentence." His voice, usually steady and confident, now carried a tremor of fear that echoed the unspoken doubts of the crew.

Talia glanced at Gresham, her eyes searching for reassurance. "What if this anomaly isn't just a beacon but a trap? We need to be sure." Her voice wavered, a rare break in her usually unflappable demeanor.

Gresham turned to face them, his gaze steady and unyielding. The weight of his presence, a member of the FEW, commanded a respect tinged with awe and fear. "I understand your fears, but this is our only lead. We have to take the risk. Mara might be on the other side, and she needs us." His voice was calm, but beneath it lay a current of desperation that only those who knew him well could discern.

Ryder, the tech-savvy comms officer, hesitated before speaking. "Lord Gresham, what if we're wrong? What if this mission costs us more than we can afford?" His voice was barely more than a whisper, the gravity of their situation weighing heavily on his shoulders.

Gresham's jaw tightened, the pain of Mara's absence etched into every line of his face. "The cost is high, but the stakes are higher. We can't abandon her." His words resonated with a fierce determination, a love that transcended the void of space and time. The silence that followed was heavy with the unspoken fear that they might not return, but it was also charged with the unwavering resolve to face the unknown for the chance to reunite with Mara.

As the ship hurtled towards the swirling vortex of the anomaly, the crew braced themselves for whatever lay ahead. The journey would test their loyalty, their courage, and their very will to survive. But they were united by a common purpose: to find Mara and bring her home. As they ventured deeper into the heart of the anomaly, each step brought them closer to the revelation that could either reunite them with their lost comrade or shatter their hopes entirely.

Nature of the Anomaly

The anomaly, a swirling vortex of cosmic energy, loomed ahead, a maelstrom of both peril and potential revelation. As the ship edged closer, sensors flickered with erratic readings. Fluctuations in the space-time continuum hinted at the presence of a hidden gateway, a passage that might lead them to Mara—or plunge them into the lair of an ancient malevolence.

Inside the ship, tension coiled like a serpent ready to strike. The mission's cost would be personal for Gresham and deeply impactful for the entire crew. Each member faced the specter of loss—of comrades, of hope, of life. This journey into the anomaly would test their loyalty and their very will to survive.

Gresham's desperation to find Mara began to cloud his judgment. His orders grew increasingly reckless, a dangerous edge sharpening his usually calm demeanor. Commander Levi, ever vigilant, couldn't ignore the signs. "My Lord," he said, stepping close to Gresham, his voice low and urgent. "You're pushing the crew hard. We need to approach this rationally."

Gresham's eyes blazed with frustration, his voice a taut wire of emotion. "We don't have time for caution, Levi. Every moment we waste could mean losing Mara forever."

Nearby, Kael Sol whispered to a tech working beside him, his voice a murmur of shared anxiety. "We get it! We want to find her, too. But if we rush in blindly, we might not make it out."

Gresham took a deep breath, the weight of their words sinking in. His gaze softened, the fire in his eyes dimming to a determined glow. "You're right, Commander," he conceded, his voice steadying. "We need to be careful. But we can't lose sight of the goal."

With renewed focus, Gresham turned back to the controls, adjusting their course with calculated precision. The crew, though still uneasy, steeled themselves for the challenges ahead. Their unity, a fragile but vital thread, held them together as they braced for the unknown.

As the ship plunged into the swirling vortex, the very fabric of reality seemed to warp around them. The crew held their breath, eyes glued to their stations as the vessel shuddered and groaned under the strain. Every sensor beep and flicker of light felt like a harbinger of either doom or salvation. A low hum accompanied the anomaly's energy, vibrating through the ship's hull, while the air inside crackled with static electricity, raising the hair on the crew's arms and necks.

Talia Sharma's hands were steady on her instruments, but her heart pounded in her chest. The air felt electric, charged with the promise of discovery and the threat of oblivion. She glanced at Gresham, seeing the fierce determination etched into his features. He wasn't just their leader; he was a man driven by love and desperation.

Kael Sol's fingers danced over the weapon controls, ready for any threat that might emerge from the chaos. His normally flippant demeanor was replaced by a grim focus. He exchanged a look with Ryder, whose face was pale but resolute. They all understood the stakes. This was more than a mission; it was a rescue operation, a quest to bring one of their own back from the brink.

Ensign Zara, the youngest member of the crew, clutched a small, worn charm that hung from her neck—a gift from her grandmother meant to protect her on dangerous journeys. She whispered a silent prayer, her eyes wide with a mixture of fear and hope.

The ship's hull creaked as they ventured deeper into the heart of the anomaly. Strange energies pulsed around them, casting an eerie glow through the viewport. The crew's breaths were shallow, their eyes darting between their instruments and the swirling void outside.

Suddenly, a tremor rocked the ship, and alarms blared. "Brace for impact!" Levi shouted, gripping the edge of the console. The ship lurched violently, and for a moment, chaos reigned. Sparks flew from overloaded circuits, and the lights flickered ominously.

Gresham's voice cut through the chaos, calm yet commanding. "Stay focused! We've trained for this. Hold your stations!" His presence was a beacon of steadiness amidst the storm, his confidence infectious.

As the turbulence subsided, a tense silence settled over the bridge. They had made it through the worst of the entry, but the real challenges lay ahead. Each member of the crew knew the dangers were far from over, but they also felt a spark of hope. They were closer to finding Mara, closer to the truth.

The ship continued its journey into the unknown, every second stretching its nerves taut. The path was fraught with danger but also with the possibility of answers, of uncovering the truth about Mara's fate. As they ventured deeper into the heart of the anomaly, each step brought them closer to the revelation that could either reunite them with their lost comrade or will all hope be lost.

4

REBIRTH

AMIDST THE STARS

Mara's heart pounded like a distant drum as she gazed out of the cockpit, the vastness of space stretching endlessly before her. The weight of her decision to leave Gresham and her previous life pressed down on her, but she couldn't turn back. Each glance she exchanged with Gresham had been laden with unspoken words, a silent plea for understanding. His confusion had been palpable when she had whispered "Yes" to his question about fighting for humanity. "But I want more," she'd choked out, feeling the hollowness in her words. Promises of promotions and leadership roles had only deepened the emptiness. "Never mind," she'd mumbled, her soul aching for something she couldn't yet name.

Adrift in the cosmic ocean, Mara felt a strange liberation. Her chest tightened, and her hands trembled as she clutched the controls, the silence in the cockpit amplifying the void within her but also whispering of possibilities. The alien console before her pulsed with a rhythm she couldn't quite grasp, its holographic displays shimmering with cryptic symbols that seemed to beckon her toward the unknown. As she charted her course to an uncharted planet, a vibrant nebula blazed on the screen, its swirling colors mirroring the faint ember of hope in her heart. The double star system nearby, locked in a celestial dance, whispered of companionship she still dared to dream of.

Stepping off her ship, Mara's senses were assaulted by the lush, alien world that surrounded her. The humid air clung to her skin like a second shirt, carrying the sounds of the forest in its warm embrace. Melodic chirps and trills, interspersed with guttural croaks, echoed from the unseen depths of the surrounding forest. The sky, an expanse of cerulean blue, stretched infinitely above, adorned with cotton-ball clouds drifting lazily on gentle currents. The sun, a giant golden orb, bathed the landscape in a honeyed light that caressed her skin, a stark contrast to the harsh glare of the ship's artificial lights.

With a firm grip on her weapon and her jaw set determinedly, Mara ventured deeper into the forest. The alien flora seemed to pulse with life, bioluminescent flowers glowing softly in the dim light, painting the scene with an otherworldly glow. Every rustle in the foliage, every flitting shadow held the promise of a new adventure, a challenge to be conquered, and a secret to be unraveled. This was her new battlefield, not against an enemy but against the deafening silence within her.

Her thoughts wandered to Gresham; his image etched deeply into her mind. She could almost feel his presence beside her, his hand reaching out to hers. But as she moved forward, the distance between them seemed to grow, each step taking her further from the man she had loved for a century. A pang of sorrow pierced her heart. She longed to share this new world with him, to have him see what she was seeing, to feel the same sense of wonder and fear. But she knew that wasn't possible, not now. The life they had shared, the battles they had fought side by side, had shaped them, but they had also bound them to a path that no longer felt right for her.

As she continued through the forest, Mara noticed movement in the village square ahead. Women and men bustled around, their hands deftly working to clean and arrange items, placing vibrant flowers, and preparing what seemed to be a communal feast. Children ran about, their laughter ringing through the air like music, and older villagers guided them with patient smiles. The air was filled with the smoky aroma of grilled meats and the sweetness of exotic fruits, a stark contrast to the sterile rations she had grown accustomed to.

A group of women noticed Mara and waved her over. With a mix of curiosity and gratitude, she approached them. One of the women, with kind eyes and a gentle smile, handed Mara a woven basket filled with bread. "Welcome, traveler. We've prepared a place for you," she said, her voice warm and inviting.

Mara's heart swelled with gratitude. She had never expected such a warm reception. As she followed the women, she marveled at the simplicity and beauty of the village. They led her to a small, cozy hut, its walls adorned with intricate carvings and colorful tapestries. Inside, the villagers had placed soft cushions and a bed made of woven reeds and soft furs. A sense of home, something Mara hadn't felt in years, settled over her.

The women showed Mara how to prepare the local food, their hands moving with practiced ease. Mara watched and then joined in, her movements tentative at first but soon finding a rhythm. She kneaded dough, her fingers sinking into the soft, warm mass, feeling a connection to the earth and to these people who had so readily accepted her. "This feels...real," she thought, a fleeting sense of contentment washing over her. The scent of the baking bread was intoxicating, filling the hut with warmth that seeped into her very bones.

As the sun began to set, casting a golden glow over the village, the men and children joined the women around the fire pit. The villagers sat in a circle, sharing food and stories. Mara found herself between an elderly man who spoke of the village's history and a young girl who eagerly showed her a collection of colorful stones she had gathered from the riverbed.

Mara listened, enthralled, as the villagers spoke of their daily lives, their challenges, and their joys. The elder spoke of a time when the village had faced a great drought, and how they had worked together to build an irrigation system that saved their crops. The young girl's eyes sparkled as she talked about her dream of becoming a healer like her mother.

As the evening wore on, the rhythmic beat of a hand drum echoed from within a nearby hut, beckoning her closer. Intrigued, Mara followed the sound and found herself in a circle of villagers, each holding an instrument. They welcomed her with open arms and handed her a small drum. With a hesitant smile, Mara joined in, feeling the beat resonate through her, a pulse of life and connection.

The music swelled, a joyous, spontaneous celebration of life. Mara's hands found the rhythm, her heart pounding in time with the beat. For the first time in years, she felt a sense of belonging, of being part of something greater than herself.

As the night deepened, Mara stepped away from the circle and gazed up at the stars. The constellations that had once been her guides in the vast expanse of space now seemed to watch over her, a reminder of the journey she had taken to find this place. She closed her eyes, feeling the cool breeze against her skin, the scent of wildflowers and wood smoke mingling in the air. A single tear traced a path down her cheek. She wished Gresham could be here to share in this moment of discovery and peace. But she also knew that this journey was hers alone, a necessary step in finding herself and understanding what she truly wanted.

A gentle touch on her shoulder brought her back to the present. It was the elder woman, her eyes filled with wisdom and kindness. "This is your home now, traveler. You are one of us," she said softly.

Tears welled up in Mara's eyes. She had spent so long searching for something she couldn't name, and here, in this simple village, she had found it. She nodded, unable to speak, and embraced the elder woman.

As the villagers continued to celebrate, Mara felt a sense of peace settle over her. She had found her place, her home, among these people who had shown her such warmth and acceptance. And in this new beginning, she knew she would find not only the answers she sought but also the joy and laughter she had lost along the way.

With a deep breath, Mara stepped back into the circle, ready to embrace whatever adventures and challenges lay ahead. This was her new life, a life filled with hope, community, and the promise of a future she had never dared to dream of.

But for now, she would bask in this newfound freedom, letting the wind guide her, each rustle of leaves a promise of adventure, each unknown scent an invitation to explore. A strange, iridescent feather drifted down from the canopy, landing softly at her feet. It shimmered with colors she had never seen before, a tangible reminder of the wonders and mysteries that awaited her in this untamed world.

With a deep breath, Mara picked up the feather, tucking it safely into her pocket, a symbol of her newfound freedom and a reminder of the path she had chosen—a path leading not just through this alien landscape but into the uncharted territories of her own heart.

She tasted the sweetness of oranges on the wind, a subtle counterpoint to the earthy musk of the forest floor. Her ears pricked at the calls of unseen birds: high-pitched chirps intertwined with mellow whistles and the occasional long, mournful note. This symphony was punctuated by the rhythmic creak of ancient branches swaying overhead, their leaves rustling like whispered secrets. Even the air itself felt different—crisp, alive, carrying the faint, musky scent of damp fur and the sweet promise of blooming orchids.

The scent of wood smoke, tinged with the sweetness of wildflowers, created a balm for her weary spirit. Yet, even amidst this newfound solace, shadows clung to the depths of her eyes. The icy blue, often as cold as the void between stars, now mirrored the smoky grey of storm clouds.

Love, in its capricious dance, had carved wounds deeper than any battlefield scar. Could this haven, nestled within the verdant embrace of an unknown planet, offer the cure she desperately craved? Perhaps, amongst these simple lives and genuine smiles, lay the key to healing, not just from war's brutality but from the silent ache of a love turned sour.

As she gazed upon the jubilant faces, a flicker of hope ignited within her, tenacious yet fragile. She would stay, at least for now, to explore the mysteries this sanctuary held—and the secrets buried within her own restless heart.

A small hand, barely reaching her knee, tugged at her sleeve. A young boy, no older than five, looked up at her with eyes wide with a familiar yearning. "Tell us a story, traveler!" he pleaded, his voice barely a whisper above the din. "One about the stars and fire-breathing dragons!"

Time passed, and Mara found a rhythm, a new purpose, on this vibrant planet. She integrated into the village, her presence becoming a source of strength and guidance. When the villagers worried about the lack of rain in their fields, Mara took decisive action. She went to the fields, her steps purposeful, and knelt with her sword. As the blade touched the earth, rain began to fall, nourishing the thirsty crops. The villagers watched in awe as the parched ground soaked up the life-giving water, their gratitude shining in their eyes.

Mara shared her knowledge of irrigation, teaching the villagers techniques she had learned from helping countless farmers across the galaxy. With her guidance, they constructed efficient irrigation systems that ensured their fields would thrive even during dry spells. Her hands-on approach and willingness to get dirty alongside them earned her their respect and admiration.

When the heat in the village became unbearable, Mara once again knelt with her sword, this time creating a soft, cooling breeze that brought relief to everyone. The villagers marveled at her ability to control the elements, seeing her not just as a powerful warrior but as a benevolent guardian.

One day, when the forest seemed to call out in desperation for rain, Mara answered. She ventured into the dense woods, her sword at the ready. Kneeling on the forest floor, she summoned a mighty thunderstorm. Lightning crackled across the sky, and rain poured down, drenching the trees and rejuvenating the ecosystem. The forest, which had been suffering from drought, came back to life, its lush greenery a testament to Mara's intervention.

Each evening, Mara shared a cup of tea with the Medicine Man. They would sit together, the comforting warmth of the tea soothing their spirits. The Medicine Man, wise and gentle, spoke softly of how the village had grown over the years and the challenges they had faced, including the occasional threats from wild animals. His stories painted a picture of resilience and community, and Mara found herself drawn to his wisdom.

In return, Mara spoke of her past life with Lord Gresham, sharing both the good and the bad. She recounted their battles, their moments of triumph, and the painful decision that had led her to leave. The Medicine Man listened with empathy, his understanding gaze offering solace.

As they bonded over their nightly tea, Mara felt a connection forming with the Medicine Man. He became a trusted confidant, someone with whom she could share her deepest thoughts and fears. Through these conversations, she began to heal from the wounds of her past, finding peace in the simple act of sharing her story.

One evening, as they sat under the stars, the Medicine Man looked at Mara with a knowing smile. "You have found your place here, Mara. Your heart is strong, and your spirit is kind. The village is better for having you, and I believe you are better for having found us."

Mara nodded, her eyes reflecting the starlight. "Thank you. I feel like I've finally found where I belong. And for the first time in a long time, I feel at peace."

Mara's presence had transformed the village, and in turn, the village had transformed her. She had found a new purpose, not in the cold expanse of space but in the warmth of human connection and the beauty of this alien world. The village became her family, and their fields and forests her responsibility. With each passing day, she grew stronger, not just in her abilities but in her understanding of herself and her place in the universe.

As she looked up at the night sky, Mara knew her journey was far from over. There were still mysteries to uncover, both within herself and in the world around her. But for now, she was content, surrounded by the people who had welcomed her with open arms and the land that had given her a new beginning.

The FEW to which Mara belonged were legendary across the galaxies. Their abilities were both awe-inspiring and terrifying. Lady

Mara's sword, a conduit of immense power, allowed her to create protective shields, summon storms, and control the elements. It could push or pull objects and people, its energy responding to her will. Her cape, an extension of her emotions, seemed to have a life of its own, billowing and swirling in sync with her inner state. She could incite awe or fear in those around her, a power that she had always wielded with caution.

As time passed, Mara found a rhythm and purpose on this planet. When the village worried about the loss of rain for their fields, she went to the field and knelt with her sword. The sky darkened, and rain began to fall, nourishing the parched earth. She taught them what she had learned from helping countless farmers create irrigation systems and thrive in harsh conditions. When the heat became unbearable in the village, Mara knelt with her sword, creating a soft, cooling breeze that brought relief. And when the forest called to her, she created a thunderstorm, the rain revitalizing the trees and the land.

Each night, Mara shared a cup of tea with the Medicine Man. He spoke softly of the village's growth and the challenges they faced, including the occasional threat from wild animals. Mara, in turn, opened up about her past life with Lord Gresham, sharing the good and the bad and what had led her to this place. Their conversations deepened their bond, a connection based on mutual respect and understanding.

Through these acts of kindness and the bonds she formed, Mara rediscovered herself. She realized that her abilities once used solely for battle and duty, could also bring life and hope. She was no longer defined by her past but was shaping a future filled with purpose and connection. And while the journey ahead was still fraught with unknowns, she faced it with a newfound strength, ready to embrace whatever came her way.

Starlight, filtered through vines, dappled the earthen floor of Mara's thatched hut. The hum of a nearby crystalline oscillator cast a soft blue glow, illuminating scrolls stacked high on rough-hewn tables. Earlier, her voice had woven tales of forgotten empires across galaxies, sparking curiosity in the wide eyes of her young acolytes. Now, alone in the serene silence, a wave of melancholy washed over her. It wasn't just the weight of the stories themselves but the lingering echo of laughter, a ghost of a touch—remnants of Gresham that haunted even this tranquil haven.

She sank into her favorite chair, hand-carved by the village's artisan. Beneath her fingertips, the smooth wood held subtle warmth, yet it couldn't chase away the chill that lingered in her heart. A worn leather satchel lay abandoned on the table, its clasp undone, revealing a half-written letter, words of longing and regret bleeding onto the faded parchment. Gresham's face, etched with concern and determination, flashed behind her closed eyelids.

Suddenly, a comforting hand settled on hers. The weathered fingers of the Medicine Man spoke volumes even before a word was uttered. His gaze, deep as the cosmos itself, reflected not just understanding but a shared burden woven from years of friendship and unspoken truths. He had seen the love and loss etched into her soul, the scars hidden beneath her serene facade. Now, he sensed the ember rekindling, threatening to consume the peace they had so carefully cultivated.

"The echoes of the stars are strong tonight, Mara," he said, his voice a low rumble that echoed the distant hum of the oscillator. "Are they whispers of the past or harbingers of what is to come?"

Mara met his gaze, the question hanging heavy in the air. The tranquility surrounding her felt fragile, like a spider web shimmering with morning dew. She knew the peace couldn't last forever. Gresham's pursuit, the shadow of the FEW, loomed closer with each passing day. The embers within her were indeed rekindling, and she wasn't sure if they would bring warmth or consume everything she held dear.

A distant star, not a mere celestial body, but a shard of their shattered past—Gresham's name—hung unspoken between them. It wasn't the echo of his descent into darkness that gnawed at Mara now but the serrated truth of her own complicity. The tranquil haven she'd carved, woven from the villagers' gratitude and calloused earth, felt less like a sanctuary and more like a gilded cage. Leaving Gresham, fleeing their fractured connection, had been fueled by fear, yes, but also by cowardice she now despised.

Months spun into a tapestry of village life, Mara the teacher, the storyteller, a legend etched in their dreams as "Stardust." Their reverence, their dependence, felt suffocating, yet she clung to it, afraid to face the hollowness within. Gresham, meanwhile, remained a phantom on the horizon, a stark reminder of the firestorm she'd left behind.

One night, a meteor carved a bleeding gash across the sky, leaving a trail of emerald fire that mirrored the ache in Mara's heart. "A sign," murmured an elder, his gaze holding unspoken judgment. A shiver wracked her, an icy premonition echoing in her bones. The galaxy might simmer in a fragile peace, but somewhere amidst the stars, embers of their shared battles flickered anew. And she, once a fearless warrior by his side, was lost in the quiet hum of this village, a beacon dimmed by self-imposed exile.

Yet, the solace she'd cultivated couldn't extinguish the smoldering embers within. Each calloused hand, each furrow tilled, bore the mark of her transformation. She'd brought life to barren lands and laughter to children's faces, but could she remain content, knowing a part of her soul yearned for a different kind of battle? The lessons she imparted now held a double meaning, whispers of resilience echoing not just for the villagers but for herself.

At night, beneath the star-strewn expanse, the question hammered at her: could she, a woman seeking peace, resurrect the warrior her soul still remembered? The echo of her own past roared back, "Can you truly find peace while a part of you bleeds in the shadows?"

The Medicine Man, a constant amidst the village's fervent whispers, remained her anchor. In the quiet of his hut, the scent of calming herbs clinging to the air, he spoke, his voice a low rumble that vibrated with ancient wisdom. "The storm may gather, Starfall Goddess," he said, his gaze meeting hers with unwavering clarity, "but remember, true strength doesn't lie in hiding from the darkness. It lies in embracing the light within, even when it burns with the pain of what you've left behind."

His words ignited a spark within Mara, a flicker of courage pushing back the fear. Could she reconcile the woman who craved peace with the warrior her soul still ached to be? The path ahead was shrouded in uncertainty, but for the first time, she wasn't afraid to face it. Choosing peace wasn't about burying her past but about integrating it, finding wholeness where there was fracture. As she met the Medicine Man's gaze, she saw a flicker of hope, a silent message: "You are not alone. You are ready."

Opening her eyes, she met the Medicine Man's gaze, a silent promise exchanged. She would honor her past but not be consumed by it. The path ahead was still uncertain, but she would walk it with her head held high, guided by the warmth of this new life and the quiet strength within.

Stepping outside, the vibrant tapestry of sunrise greeted her. The humid air clung to her skin like a second shirt, carrying the scent of blooming night flowers and the earthy musk of the forest floor. Children's laughter danced on the breeze, mingling with the rhythmic hammering from the market square. A wave of warmth washed over her. This wasn't just a haven; it was a community, and she longed to be a part of it.

Spotting Thomas, a weathered carpenter with calloused hands and a mischievous glint in his eye, perched precariously on a sagging roof. With each hammer blow, the structure groaned in protest.

"Need a hand, old timer?" Mara called out, her voice tinged with a playful challenge.

Thomas, startled, nearly lost his balance. "Mara? Fancy seeing you here. You wouldn't be suggesting... carpentry?"

Mara grinned, hefting a discarded shingle. "Just thought a soldier with laser-sharp reflexes could be useful against your rebellious roof."

Thomas chuckled, his eyes crinkling at the corners. "Alright, soldier. Let's see what you've got."

The unlikely pair set to work. Thomas, grunting with each swing of the hammer, regaled Mara with tales of village life and its quirky inhabitants. Mara, surprisingly adept at wielding a hammer, countered with stories of distant galaxies and the fleeting nature of time. Each blow, each shared story, chipped away at the weight in her heart.

By afternoon, the roof was mended, standing tall against the sky. Sweat beaded on their foreheads, muscles ached, but a shared sense of accomplishment bloomed between them.

As children gathered under the ancient oak for their afternoon lessons, Mara hesitated. Could she, a stranger, truly offer them anything? But the encouragement in Thomas's gaze spurred her on.

"May I tell you a story?" she asked, her voice soft but firm.

The children, wide-eyed and curious, readily agreed. Mara's voice, woven with the magic of distant stars and the wisdom of time, painted vivid pictures in their minds. They saw not just a woman but a traveler from the cosmos, carrying the echoes of a thousand worlds etched in her lines.

As the sun dipped below the horizon, painting the sky in hues of orange and purple, Mara looked up at the repaired roof. The callouses on her hands, no longer symbols of pain, were badges of honor earned through sweat and laughter. Here, she wasn't just healing; she was building not just a roof but a connection with her new home.

Just as she began to turn away, a distant glint caught her eye—something metallic partially buried in the ground near the edge of the village. Curiosity piqued, she approached and knelt down to uncover it. Brushing away the dirt, her breath caught in her throat. It was an old, worn amulet engraved with a symbol that looked eerily familiar—a star intertwined with a vine, much like the ones she'd seen in her dreams.

Opening the amulet with trembling fingers, she found a small, faded piece of parchment inside. Unfolding it, she read the words written in a script that sent shivers down her spine: "To Mara, with hope. Trust the light within you. Your journey is just beginning."

Mara's heart swelled with emotion. The village, it seemed, held more secrets than she could have ever imagined. The star-and-vine symbol in her dreams had always represented a convergence of destiny and nature, a guidepost in her subconscious urging her to find balance and connection. Here, it seemed, was a tangible manifestation of that symbol, a beacon in her journey toward self-discovery.

With a renewed sense of purpose, she rose, clutching the amulet close. As she walked back toward the village, the stars began to twinkle overhead, each one a silent witness to her journey, each one a promise of adventures yet to come.

Here, under the vast canvas of stars, Mara knew she had found her place, a sanctuary not just for healing but for discovering who she truly was. And as she looked up at the night sky, a smile played on her lips. Her journey was far from over; it had only just begun.

5

SHADOW OF TERENTIA

Battle in the Nebula

The flagship, a behemoth of steel and advanced technology, hummed to life under their command. The crew, accustomed to Lord Gresham's pronouncements carrying the weight of galactic law, moved with practiced efficiency. Yet, beneath the surface, a subtle unease rippled through their ranks. Even amidst the whirring machinery and flickering displays, Gresham's presence remained the most potent force aboard. A mixture of awe and fear settled over them, a silent reverence for the living legend whose actions could reshape the very fabric of their galaxy. In the cold, sterile heart of the flagship, two destinies were converging, propelled by forces both celestial and deeply personal. The journey to Terentia had begun, and with it, the potential for an epic clash that would echo through the stars.

The klaxons wailed, a mournful symphony echoing through the bowels of the Alliance flagship. Red alert. Enemy fleet engaged. Lord Gresham, his crimson cape billowing like a storm cloud, strode onto the bridge, his steeled gaze sweeping across the holographic display. A dozen sleek, obsidian warships, emblazoned with an insignia he didn't recognize, swarmed towards them, their weapons spitting emerald fire.

"Brace for impact!" Commander Levi barked, his voice a stark counterpoint to the rising panic. His calm demeanor, honed in countless battles, was an anchor in the storm. "All hands to battle stations!"

Gresham took his place at the command console, his fingers flying across the holographic interface. He barked orders, his voice devoid of emotion but laced with his years of experience. Yet, beneath the stoic facade, a flicker of doubt remained. Was this it? Was this the battle that would claim him, leaving Mara to find out only through the whispers of the cosmos?

A primal roar escaped his lips as he unleashed a wave of energy, decimating an enemy cruiser. The battle raged around him, a cacophony of explosions and alarms. The acrid smell of burning metal and the metallic tang of blood filled the air. But amidst the chaos, Gresham fought not just for the Alliance but for a chance to return, to bridge the chasm that grew wider with every passing moment. He fought for the future, a future where understanding, not force, would guide his actions, a future where he might, just might, find his way back to the light of his brightest star.

Laser fire lanced across the void, painting the viewport with streaks of emerald and crimson. Alarms blared, reporting hull breaches and casualties. The bridge crew, a tapestry of human and alien faces, worked with desperate efficiency, their fingers flying across consoles, their voices taut with urgency.

Gresham slammed his fist on the command table. "We can't hold them off forever, Levi. We need a plan and fast."

The commander, his brow furrowed in concentration, scanned the tactical display. "There's a nebula just beyond their firing range. If we can make it…"

"A gamble, Commander," Gresham growled, his voice laced with frustration. "But it's our only hope."

With a nod, Levi issued commands, his voice ringing with authority. The ship shuddered as it executed a daring maneuver, twisting and diving through the debris field, dodging enemy fire by a hair's breadth. Gresham felt the g-forces pull at him, his crimson cape whipping around him like a defiant flag.

The ship plunged into the nebula, the emerald fire replaced by an eerie, swirling darkness. Visibility dropped to mere meters, the enemy scanners blinded by the dense cloud. Relief washed over Gresham, momentary and fragile.

But the reprieve was short-lived. A tremor shook the ship, alarms blaring red. "They're following us!" a crewmember cried, her voice laced with terror.

Gresham gritted his teeth. He wouldn't let them die, not like this. He raised his hand, his red sword materializing in a flash of crimson light. "Follow me!" he commanded, his voice echoing through the bridge.

With a determined stride, he led the charge, his crimson cape a beacon in the darkness. He moved through the narrow, dimly lit corridors, his senses heightened, ready to face the unknown within the nebula and buy his crew precious time. The ship's artificial atmosphere tasted of metal and ozone, each breath a reminder of their precarious situation.

The crew followed him, their fear tempered by the strength of their leader. The air crackled with tension, the distant hum of the ship's engines a constant reminder of their peril. Gresham's presence, commanding and unwavering, was a source of solace amidst the chaos.

They reached the reactor room, the heart of the ship. Gresham's eyes scanned the complex array of machinery, his mind racing. "Levi, initiate the nebula dispersal protocol. We'll use the energy of the nebula to our advantage."

Levi nodded, his fingers flying across the control panel. "Understood, my Lord. It's risky, but it might just work."

As the protocol activated, the ship shuddered, the energy from the nebula surging through the systems. The swirling darkness outside began to glow, the nebula's energy radiating in vibrant hues of blue and green. The enemy ships, blinded by the sudden brilliance, faltered.

Gresham stood at the reactor's core, his red sword glowing with an ethereal light. He focused his power, channeling it through the ship's systems. The energy radiated outward, a blinding pulse that disrupted the enemy's sensors and weapons.

"Now, Levi! Full speed ahead!" Gresham commanded, his voice echoing with authority.

The ship surged forward, the nebula's energy propelling them at an unprecedented speed. The enemy ships, disoriented and overwhelmed, fell behind, their pursuit thwarted.

As the ship emerged from the nebula, the crew let out a collective sigh of relief. They had survived, their unity and Gresham's leadership carrying them through the storm. But the journey was far from over. The path to Terentia lay ahead, fraught with unknown dangers and the promise of a reunion that would change the course of their lives.

Gresham stood at the helm, his eyes fixed on the distant stars. His thoughts drifted to Mara, the woman who had once been his anchor in the storm. The memory of her touch, her laughter, fueled his determination. He couldn't afford to lose hope, not now.

The flagship vanished into the void, leaving behind the echoes of battle and the promise of a future yet to be written.

The Stellar Watch hovered in the void, their silver hulls gleaming under the otherworldly light of the rogue star. Gresham stood on the bridge of his flagship, his crimson cape billowing in the artificial breeze, eyes locked on the sleek vessel. Trusting them felt unwise, yet they had saved them from a smaller contingent of the enemy fleet, buying precious time to escape the rest of the pursuing forces.

Levi stepped forward, his voice calm yet firm. "They saved us, Lord Gresham. We need to talk."

Hesitantly, Gresham nodded. Negotiations commenced on the bridge, a tense ballet of words and unspoken suspicions. The atmosphere crackled with energy, the tension palpable. The Stellar Watch representative, a humanoid figure cloaked in swirling, ethereal energy, stood at the center of the bridge. Its form was both mesmerizing and unnerving, a shimmering silhouette with features that shifted and changed like liquid starlight. The representative's eyes, or what passed for eyes, glowed with an inner light, reflecting the cosmos itself.

"The enemy you faced," the representative stated, its voice devoid of emotion, "are but pawns in a larger game. We require information to track the true mastermind."

The bridge fell silent, every breath held in anticipation. Levi spoke first, his gaze unwavering. "We can offer that information," he said, "but we seek assurances. What are your intentions for this system?"

A tense silence followed, broken only by the hum of the ship's engines and the distant murmurs of the crew. Then, the representative spoke again. "Our ultimate goal aligns with yours: peace and stability. But sometimes, to achieve peace, sacrifices must be made."

Gresham's mind raced. The enemy was not just a fleet but a shadowy force playing a larger, more sinister game. The realization chilled him. The stakes were higher than he'd imagined.

"We offer an alliance," the leader continued, its voice tinged with urgency. "Share your knowledge, and together we may face this greater threat. Or remain alone, vulnerable to the shadows."

Gresham glanced at Levi, their shared understanding evident. The risk of trusting these alien beings loomed large, but the alternative seemed even more perilous. The flicker of doubt in Gresham's eyes mirrored the flicker of hope in Levi's. This decision could tip the balance of power in the galaxy.

"We accept," Levi declared, his voice resolute. "But know this: we fight for our people, for freedom. We will not be pawns in anyone's game."

The leader's energy swirled, forming a symbol resembling a handshake. "A fragile alliance," it responded. "But perhaps enough to face the storm that approaches."

The Stellar Watch ship, sleek and elongated, glimmered with the same ethereal energy that cloaked its representative. Its hull was adorned with intricate, luminous patterns that seemed to pulse with life. The ship itself appeared almost organic as if grown from the very fabric of space rather than constructed. Its engines emitted a soft, resonant hum that vibrated through the flagship's hull, a sound both alien and oddly soothing.

As the wreckage cleared, a newfound tension hung heavy in the air. The immediate threat was neutralized, but a far greater one loomed. The alliance, forged in the crucible of battle, was strained yet necessary. Each party harbored suspicions and motivations, but they were bound by a common purpose: survival in a galaxy shrouded in secrets and shadowed by an ancient evil.

Gresham turned back to the holographic star chart, his thoughts drifting to Mara. Her fiery spirit and the love they had shared were his guiding lights. A brief, painful memory flashed through his mind—a moment of laughter shared under a distant sun, her eyes reflecting the cosmos. He clenched his fists, the weight of his mission pressing heavily on his shoulders. He would find her, no matter the cost.

Levi's hand on his shoulder brought him back to the present. "We'll find her, my Lord. And when we do, we'll face whatever comes together."

Gresham nodded, a flicker of determination reigniting in his eyes. The path ahead was fraught with danger, but it also held the promise of redemption, of reunion. As the flagship surged forward, leaving behind the debris of battle, Gresham knew that the true test was yet to come. The alliance with the Stellar Watch was their first step towards uncovering the greater truth, towards a future where peace might finally be within reach.

The stars ahead shimmered with untold possibilities. In their light, Gresham saw the echoes of battles yet to be fought, of a love yet to be reclaimed, and of a galaxy waiting for a hero. The journey was far from over, but for the first time in a long while, Gresham felt a glimmer of hope. The alliance was fragile, but it was a beacon in the darkness, a promise of light in the vast expanse of the cosmos.

The crew, now united by a common cause, prepared for the challenges ahead. Their fates were intertwined, their destinies linked by the threads of hope and courage. And as they ventured deeper into the unknown, they carried with them the weight of the galaxy's future and the promise of a brighter dawn.

As the crew worked on repairs and adjustments, Gresham stood on the bridge, the faint scent of ozone and the hum of the ship's engines filling the air. The holographic stars shimmered, casting an ethereal glow on his tense form as he gazed out at the vast expanse. His knuckles whitened with tension, the echoes of battle still reverberating in his mind, mingling with the unyielding thoughts of Mara.

Gazing out at the vast expanse of stars, Gresham felt the echoes of battle still reverberate in his mind, each flicker of distant light reminding him of the vast distances yet to be traversed in his quest to find Mara. The faint scent of ozone and the constant hum of the ship's engines were a backdrop to his contemplation, casting an ethereal glow on his tense form.

Levi found Gresham in his private chamber, the holographic stars casting a spectral light that failed to pierce the gloom. A sigh escaped Gresham's lips, ragged and laced with a longing that resonated deeper than mere words could express. Levi, sensing his friend's turmoil, approached silently. His hand settled on Gresham's shoulder, a gesture of quiet support that spoke volumes.

"Still drawn to her fire, Lord Gresham?" Levi inquired, his voice soft and empathetic.

Gresham's jaw clenched, his fists tightening. His shoulders, usually held high with command, now slumped under an invisible weight. "Not drawn, Levi," he corrected, his voice a low growl. "Haunted. Haunted by the embers of what we could have been."

He turned, his gaze lingering on the holographic image of Mara, her fiery spirit momentarily captured in the static light. "She was a challenge, Levi, a blaze that matched my own yet tempered it with a grace I never knew I craved. A beacon that illuminated the caverns of my soul, revealing the beauty that lurked within the shadows."

Levi watched as Gresham's expression softened, his eyes revealing a flicker of vulnerability. "She sounds like a flame worth chasing, Lord Gresham."

"She was," Gresham echoed, his voice tinged with regret. "We were... a supernova, brief and dazzling, leaving behind a void that echoes in my very core. But even the brightest stars succumb to their own gravity, leaving only dust and whispers in their wake. My ambition, my misguided pursuit of order, dimmed the very light that kept me whole."

Shame flickered in his eyes, and he quickly turned back to the swirling galaxy, its chaotic dance mirroring the tempest within him. "Now, the galaxy teeters on the brink," he continued, his voice hardening with resolve. "And I must find a way to restore balance, even if it means dancing with the flames that nearly consumed me."

Levi met his gaze; his own resolve unwavering. "Remember, Lord Gresham," he said, his voice firm yet gentle, "true balance cannot be achieved through ashes alone. Sometimes, the gentlest flames offer the most enduring light."

Gresham's expression shifted, a flicker of hope sparking within. "Perhaps you're right, my friend. Perhaps the key lies not in harnessing fire, but in rekindling the embers of understanding, of compassion. And maybe, just maybe, in finding my way back to the light that she once ignited within me."

Before Levi found Gresham in his private chamber, the two shared a quiet moment on the bridge. Levi handed Gresham a steaming cup of tea, a simple yet heartfelt gesture. "Remember when we first met?" Levi began, a nostalgic smile playing on his lips. "You were this stoic, almost mythical figure to everyone, including me. But then you saved my life, and I saw the man behind the legend."

Gresham chuckled softly, the sound rare and warming in the cold expanse of space. He took a sip of the tea, the warmth spreading through him. "And you," he replied, "taught me the value of laughter, even in the darkest times. You've been more than a commander, Levi. You've been a friend."

Levi's eyes softened his respect and affection for Gresham clearly. "We've come a long way, my friend. Through battles and loss, we've stood together. And we will continue to stand together, no matter what comes our way."

Gresham nodded, his heart swelling with gratitude. In Levi, he found not just a comrade but a brother in arms, a source of unwavering support. This bond, forged in the fires of countless battles, was a beacon of hope in his quest to find Mara and restore balance to the galaxy.

In the dimly lit chamber, the constant hum of the ship's engines mingled with the faint scent of ozone, and Gresham's fingertips brushed the cool edge of Mara's holographic image. Her eyes, though made of light, seemed to hold the same depth and intensity he remembered, a window to the soul he longed to reunite with.

As Gresham and Levi stood in silence, the distant stars outside the viewport twinkled like distant promises, each one a reminder of the vastness between them and the hope that still flickered within. The air was thick with unspoken words and the scent of leather and metal from their uniforms. Gresham's heart, heavy with longing, beat in a slow, painful rhythm, echoing the void that separated him from Mara.

The cool touch of the metal railing under his hand was a stark contrast to the warmth he craved, the warmth only Mara could provide. His thoughts drifted to the nights they spent under a different sky, the gentle touch of her hand in his, the soft murmur of her voice as she spoke of dreams and stars. The memory of her laughter, bright and clear, cut through the gloom, a reminder of the love that still burned within him.

He straightened his shoulders, a new determination replacing the shadows in his eyes. He wouldn't just seek Mara; he would strive to be worthy of her, to reignite the light that shone within him so she could see him not just as a leader but as the man she once loved.

As the Alliance flagship set a course for its next destination, Gresham cast one last glance at the nebula, a swirling mass of mystery and danger. The battle had been won, but the war was just beginning. And amidst the vast expanse of the cosmos, he held on to the hope that he could bridge the distance between him and Mara, find the answers they needed, and restore balance to the galaxy.

The Shadow of Terentia

Lord Gresham's calloused fingertips danced across the holographic star charts, each flickering dot a tauntingly distant world. Yet, only one star held his relentless gaze—Terentia, a remote speck at the fringes of the known universe, shrouded in mist and whispered rumors. It was where Mara, his fire to his water, had vanished years ago, leaving behind a void that his ambition couldn't fill.

Was it a resolution that pulsed in his veins, or was the embers of love buried but not extinguished? He didn't know, and perhaps the answer didn't matter. All that mattered was finding her.

"Levi," Gresham's voice resonated like the clang of steel, echoing through his flagship's vast, cold chamber.

Levi, ever the pragmatist, stepped forward, his brow furrowed with concern. "My Lord," he began cautiously, "Terentia lies beyond the charted maps, a breeding ground for uncharted dangers. Are you certain this is the wisest course?"

Gresham's gaze held the weight of countless battles, etched onto his face like the scars that mapped his own internal war. "It is where I must go," he stated, his voice a low rumble that carried the quiet desperation of a man haunted by love's ashes.

The silence that followed hung heavy in the air, thick with unspoken questions and the dawning realization of the momentous journey before them. Shadows flickered in the dim light, casting eerie shapes on the walls. The engines roared to life, a sound that seemed to summon the ghosts of the past, propelling the ship toward the uncharted realm.

As they set their course, the ship's lights dimmed to conserve power, amplifying the sense of foreboding. A noxious, swirling cloud enveloped the ship, reducing visibility to near nothingness. The lights flickered and then dimmed, casting the corridors in a ghostly half-light that made every shadow seem alive. Every creak of the hull, every distant hum of the machinery, seemed amplified in the silence, a symphony of unknown threats lurking just beyond the thin walls of their vessel. The air carried a faint scent of ozone tinged with a metallic tang, a sharp reminder of the constant tension aboard.

Lost in memories, Gresham barely noticed as the flagship glided through the darkness. The cold, sterile light of the console bathed his face in an otherworldly glow, highlighting the tear that traced a path down his cheek. It shimmered like liquid crystal, a testament to the complex emotions that fueled this desperate quest. He would find Mara, one way or another. Whether their reunion would bring resolution, redemption, or a love rekindled, only the uncharted stars of Terentia could tell.

With a curt nod, Levi masked his anxieties. "Aye, my Lord. Setting course for Terentia as we speak."

But even as the ship hummed to life, the vastness of space seemed to close in, its endless expanse an oppressive reminder of the emptiness within Gresham. A dull ache settled in his chest, a constant reminder of the fiery spirit he yearned for. Years might have passed, and countless galaxies traversed, but his heart still longed for her presence. He ran his fingers over the cool, metallic surface of the console, feeling the subtle vibrations that seemed to echo his inner turmoil.

As the flagship glided through the darkness, the stars outside the viewport appeared to pulse with an eerie inner light, forming fleeting constellations that resembled monstrous creatures. The fabric of reality seemed to bend and shimmer, straight lines warping and twisting in the periphery of their vision. The low growls and rumbles of the ship's engines blended with the occasional metallic groan, adding to the sense of impending dread.

Gresham's thoughts were a whirlwind of memories and emotions. The scent of Mara's hair, the sound of her laughter, and the touch of her hand—all vivid recollections that haunted him. He glanced at Levi, who, sensing his friend's turmoil, offered a reassuring nod. Their bond, forged in the fires of countless battles, was a source of unspoken strength.

As they descended into the thick, swirling mists of Terentia, the ship's creaks and groans grew louder, each sound echoing through the silent corridors like the whispers of ghosts. The crew moved quietly, and their footsteps muffled their breaths shallowly. The dim, flickering lights cast eerie shadows that danced on the walls, giving the impression of unseen figures lurking just out of sight.

Talia Sharma, the explosives expert, tightened her grip on a spanner, her sharp intellect and fierce loyalty a cornerstone of their operations. The silence weighed heavily on her, amplifying the creaks and groans of the ship, each sound a potential harbinger of danger. Her eyes reflected both the crew's apprehension and the unspoken awe she felt towards Gresham. To lay eyes on a member of the FEW was a rarity; to speak directly with one was an almost unimaginable honor. The aura of power and authority radiated from him, filling the room with a tangible sense of awe and fear. Her mind raced, analyzing every detail of their precarious situation.

Gresham turned to face him, his expression unreadable. "Terentia holds the answers we seek. We have no choice but to press on."

The crew exchanged uneasy glances, but no one voiced further objections. The path ahead was shrouded in mystery and danger, but they were bound by a shared purpose and the unwavering resolve of their leader.

As the flagship descended deeper into the mist, the oppressive silence grew more pronounced. Instrument readings became erratic, and environmental sensors displayed conflicting data. Communications were plagued with static and distortion, and the navigation systems showed unexplained anomalies. Strange electrical discharges danced through the clouds, casting an eerie glow that flickered ominously through the ship's viewports.

The atmosphere inside the ship became charged with tension. Fog seemed to move against the wind outside, and the occasional precipitation left an oily residue on the hull. Characters experienced unexplained headaches, nausea, and slight dizziness, further unsettling the crew.

A low, persistent hum or vibration filled the air, occasionally punctuated by distant sounds of explosions or rumbling. The air shimmered as if from intense heat, even in cooler areas, adding to the surreal and unsettling environment.

Suddenly, Talia paused, her eyes widening as she caught a glimpse of something impossible on the reflective surface of a console. A shadowy figure, humanoid but distorted, flickered and then vanished when she looked directly at it. She shivered, a chill running down her spine.

"Did anyone else see that?" she whispered, her voice barely audible.

Kael nodded, his face pale. "I thought I saw something too. Just a shadow... or maybe a reflection."

Levi's eyes narrowed. "Stay focused, everyone. It could be a trick of the light or our minds playing tricks in this environment."

The ship's temperature fluctuated inexplicably, sudden cold spots forming in some areas while others grew unbearably hot. The crew's discomfort was palpable, their unease growing with each passing moment.

Gresham straightened his shoulders, a new determination replacing the shadows in his eyes. He wouldn't just seek Mara; he would strive to be worthy of her, to reignite the light that shone within him so she could see him not just as a leader but as the man she once loved.

As the flagship glided through the darkness, the crew steeled themselves for the trials ahead, their collective will strengthened by Gresham's unwavering determination. The eerie stillness, the mysterious phenomena, and the haunting whispers of the unknown only served to bind them closer, united in their quest for truth and redemption.

The engine room pulsed with otherworldly energy, its usual rhythmic hum now an erratic, discordant symphony. Thomas and his crew of six were scattered around the vast chamber, each battling against the ship's growing instability.

Greg hunched over the main power distribution panel, his fingers dancing across the controls. "The readings are off the charts," he shouted over the din. "We're seeing power fluctuations I didn't even think were possible!"

The overhead lights flickered violently, plunging the room into darkness before flaring to life with blinding intensity. In those brief moments of pitch black, phantom shapes seemed to dance at the edge of vision, gone as quickly as they appeared.

Vincent fought with the environmental controls, his face illuminated by the sickly green glow of emergency lighting. "Temperature regulators are going haywire," he reported, his voice tight and tense. "We're getting readings from absolute zero to stellar core heat, sometimes simultaneously."

As if to punctuate his words, a wave of bone-chilling cold swept through the room, frost crystallizing on exposed metal surfaces. Seconds later, it was replaced by a blast of heat that left them gasping for breath, the air shimmering like a mirage.

The acrid smell of ozone filled the air, mingling with the metallic tang of overheating circuits. Underneath it all was a strange, sweet scent that reminded Cuen of the alien flora she'd studied on distant worlds.

Vincent manned the structural integrity monitors, his usually steady hands shaking slightly. "The hull is warping," he called out, disbelief coloring his voice. "It's like the metal is... breathing."

A deep, resonant groan echoed through the ship, the sound of metal stressed beyond its limits. The floor beneath their feet vibrated, small objects skittering across consoles and workstations.

Thomas fought to keep the navigation systems online, but the screens before him flickered and distorted, showing impossible star patterns and non-existent planets. "Our position makes no sense," he muttered. "According to this, we're simultaneously at the edge of the galaxy and in the heart of a nebula."

Suddenly, one of the main power coils surged to life, crackling with energy that arced between conduits in brilliant blue-white forks. The hair on the back of Greg's neck stood on end as the air became charged with electricity.

"Power spike!" Cuen yelled, her hands flying over the controls. "I can't contain it!"

The coil's glow intensified, becoming painfully bright. Then, just as suddenly, it dimmed, power draining away faster than seemed possible. The sudden loss of energy sent a shudder through the entire ship, knocking the crew off balance.

Thomas gripped a nearby railing as the floor lurched beneath him. "Status report!" he barked, fighting to be heard over the cacophony of alarms and groaning metal.

Before anyone could respond, another power coil flared to life, and the cycle began anew. The air in the engine room seemed to thicken, time stretching and compressing like taffy. Each breath felt like inhaling liquid fire one moment and frozen mists the next.

Through it all, the crew fought to maintain control, their movements becoming a frantic dance as they rushed from station to station. Sparks rained down from overloading circuits, casting fleeting shadows that seemed to move with a life of their own.

Thomas watched his crew battle against the chaos, pride, and determination warring with growing concern. As another violent shudder rocked the ship, he realized that Terentia wasn't just challenging their resolve—it was testing the very limits of their reality. Quickly raising the comm, he called Commander Levi and advised him of all the activities.

As the ship hummed its way toward Terentia, the path was fraught with tales of ancient evils and lost souls, whispered in hushed tones by those who dared to speak of it. The crew moved with a mixture of fear and determination, the cold steel of the ship contrasting sharply with the unknown terrors that lay ahead. Each shadow seemed to whisper secrets, and every creak of the hull felt like a portent of doom.

The lights flickered, and a low, rumbling growl echoed through the ship as if some ancient beast was stirring from its slumber. The crew exchanged uneasy glances, their fear palpable in the dim light. Gresham felt the weight of their anxiety, but his resolve hardened. He would face whatever horrors Terentia held, not just for the Alliance but for Mara. The journey to the planet had begun, and with it, the potential for an epic clash that would echo through the stars.

Arrival on Terentia

As the ship descended through the atmosphere, Levi, ever the observant commander, sensed his Lord's disquiet. "Something troubles you, my Lord?" he asked, his voice a low rumble.

Gresham turned, his face unreadable. "A shadow hangs over this place," he murmured, his words laced with cryptic portent. "Not the darkness I expected, but something... different."

The atmosphere crackled with unseen energy, and below, a sprawling complex marred the landscape. Towering machines clawed at the earth, their mechanical arms gouging deep wounds on the planet's surface. Smoke billowed from exhaust vents, painting the sky with streaks of oily black. A rough office amidst a vast expanse of deforested land stood out, flanked by a warehouse and a tavern. Men in dirty worker uniforms scurried about, carrying large boxes in and out of a massive, gaping mound in the ground. The air felt thick and dirty, the faint smell of sulfur hanging like a curse.

Levi's eyes narrowed as he took in the scene. "Looks less like a mining operation and more like a leech sucking the life out of the planet," he quipped, his tone laced with disapproval.

Inside the office, Elara glanced up from her terminal, her eyes widening in shock as she saw the Alliance ship descending. "Oh shit!" she exclaimed, jumping from her chair. She brushed her tangled hair back with her good hand and hastily dusted off her uniform. Panic surged through her—she had to act fast. The Alliance couldn't discover what was really happening here.

Elara remembered the day she was taken, the sharp jab of a blaster in her side, herding her and others into this nightmare. There was no time to think, no time to escape. They were forced into dusty mining outfits and given the latest tools to work with. Elara, known for her uncanny ability to find metals, was singled out by the Consortium for their work on getting the door open. Her skill had become her curse.

Gresham and Levi emerged from the ship, their boots crunching on the barren soil. The landscape was devoid of life, the ground scorched and stripped. The air was thick with dust and the faint stench of sulfur, making every breath a reminder of the harshness of this world.

"What in the galaxy happened here?" Levi muttered, coughing as the dust filled his lungs. "This place isn't on any of our charts."

Gresham's eyes narrowed as he took in the scene. "Something's very wrong here," he said, his voice a low growl. "Be on guard."

Gresham turned his face unreadable. "A shadow hangs over this place," he murmured, his words laced with cryptic portent. "Not the darkness I expected, but something... different."

"What in the galaxy happened here?" Levi muttered, coughing as the dust filled his lungs. "This place isn't on any of our charts."

As they advanced, the full scale of the operation became clear. Rusted signs marked the entrance to tunnels that snaked deep into the planet, the distant sounds of machinery and strained voices echoing faintly. Workers face smeared with grime and eyes hollow with exhaustion paused their labor to watch the newcomers with wary curiosity.

Levi's steps faltered slightly, his breathing becoming more labored. "The air... it's thick with toxins," he wheezed, struggling to maintain his composure. Gresham placed a steadying hand on his shoulder, his own breath unaffected by the poisoned atmosphere.

As they approached the main building, Elara came rushing out, her face a mask of barely concealed fear and awe. Her eyes widened as they landed on Gresham, recognizing him as one of the elite. She hesitated, her voice faltering. "Alliance officers," she called out, her voice shaking. "What brings you to our mining operation?"

Gresham studied her for a moment, noting the mix of fear and reverence in her eyes. "We were not aware of any mining operations on Terentia," he said coolly. "Explain yourself."

Elara swallowed hard, trying to steady herself. "We're a private consortium, mining for rare minerals," she said quickly. "We've had some... issues with the local environment. That's all."

Levi glanced at Gresham, his expression skeptical. "And what exactly are you mining?" he asked.

Elara hesitated and then rushed to say, "Crystals, minerals, all kinds of useful metals," she boasted. "We have a lovely tavern down the street if you like?" She hoped the distraction would work. Then on to bore them and send them off none the wiser.

Gresham's gaze took in the pockmarked land, the steam rising up from gashes and mounds where men went in and out. "Miss Elara, may I see your office?" Lord Gresham asked softly.

"My office?" Elara asked, surprised. "There is nothing in there but survey reports, supply orders, and manifests."

"All the same, I would like to see it."

"Sure! Follow me," she replied, her mind racing for ways to divert their attention.

Gresham and Levi exchanged a glance. This was more than they had bargained for. The mysteries of Terentia were deepening, and the stakes were rising.

Elara opened the door to her tiny and unkempt office. Rolled maps and paperwork spilled dangerously over every inch. She sat down on an old wooden rolling chair and began to regale them with tales of metals they found and the tools they used and—

Lord Gresham closed his eyes a moment and willed her, "Tell me the truth."

A wave of comfort washed over the office. Commander Levi leaned on papers, uncaring of those that fell to the floor from his leaning elbow.

Elara suddenly sat straight up and started speaking. "Everyone on this planet, including me, has been kidnapped by the Consortium. We are supposed to mine the crystals and open a door. The metals we have mined are just being sold." She slapped a hand over her mouth, eyes wide in shock. "Oh my gosh! I can't believe I just said that!" She looked at Lord Gresham, her gaze drawn to his cape billowing dramatically in the office where there was no wind.

Lord Gresham released the comfort, and Commander Levi snapped to attention. "This is an illegal mining operation, and we are shutting it down on behalf of the Galactic Alliance."

"Elara, please show us the crystals and this door you spoke of."

Elara, still reeling from her involuntary confession, led them toward the mound, the entrance to the mines. As they descended, the air grew colder, and the faint glow of the crystals cast eerie shadows on the walls. The deeper they went, the more oppressive the atmosphere became. The walls vibrated with a low hum, the crystals pulsing with a sinister light.

"This is where it starts," Elara whispered, her voice barely audible. "This is where the changes happen."

Gresham reached out to touch one of the crystals, feeling a strange energy pulse through him. His vision blurred for a moment, and he pulled back, his eyes widening. "These crystals... they're not just minerals. They're something more."

Levi nodded, his expression grim. "We need to get to the bottom of this," he said. "Before it's too late."

The two moved deeper into the mine, the crystals' eerie glow casting elongated shadows on the walls. The air grew colder, the oppressive atmosphere weighing heavily on them. As they turned a corner, they came upon a cavern filled with crystals, their light pulsating rhythmically as if in sync with an unseen heartbeat.

Gresham's gaze swept over the cavern, but there was no sign of Mara. His heart sank the hope of finding her fading into the cold, mineral light.

Levi turned to Elara, his expression intense. "We're looking for someone very specific. A woman named Lady Mara. Have you seen anyone like her?"

Elara looked confused and then shook her head. "No one has seen anyone resembling Lady Mara. Why would she be here?"

Levi's eyes narrowed. "Lady Mara is one of the FEW. There are only ten in the universe, and two of them are currently missing, including her. It's rare to encounter one, let alone two."

Elara's eyes widened with realization. "We've only been tasked with mining these... things. If Lady Mara were here, I would have known."

Gresham turned to her, his eyes narrowing. "And the workers? They seem unaffected by the toxic fumes. How is that possible?"

Elara hesitated, her eyes darting around the cavern. "They... changed," she admitted. "When we first arrived, we were normal. But the longer we worked with the crystals, the more we... adapted. It's like the crystals are changing us, making us something else."

Levi's eyes widened in realization. "No longer human," he whispered, the gravity of the situation sinking in. "The crystals, the fumes... they're transforming everyone."

Gresham reached out to touch another crystal, this time more cautiously. As his fingers brushed the surface, he felt a rush of energy surge through him, filling his mind with fragmented images—worlds beyond their own, ancient civilizations, and a sense of profound intelligence embedded within the crystals.

"These crystals," Gresham said, his voice tinged with awe and fear, "they're not just minerals. They're alive in some way, holding knowledge and power beyond our understanding."

Levi nodded, his face set with determination. "We need to get to the bottom of this," he said. "Before it's too late."

Gresham looked at Levi, a determined glint in his eyes. "Call General Alden," he said. "This is bigger than we thought. The Consortium's hand is all over this. We need a tactical team down here, now."

Levi nodded and stepped aside, activating his comm device. "General Alden, this is Commander Levi. We have an urgent situation on Terentia. The Consortium is involved. Requesting immediate deployment of a tactical team. We need to secure this site before they return."

As Levi spoke, Gresham continued to explore the cavern, his mind racing. He noticed that the workers, who moved like automatons, were deeply absorbed in their tasks, seemingly oblivious to the toxic air and the crystals' effects. He stepped closer to one of them, a young man whose eyes glowed faintly with the same light as the crystals.

"Can you hear me?" Gresham asked, his voice low.

The worker paused, his movements stuttering for a moment before he turned to face Gresham. "We serve the crystals," he intoned, his voice flat and devoid of emotion. "The crystals guide us, change us. We are one with them."

Gresham felt a chill run down his spine. The implications were terrifying. The workers weren't just mining; they were being consumed, transformed into extensions of the crystals' will.

"We need to understand what these crystals are doing," Gresham said, turning back to Levi. "We can't just shut this down. We need to study it, find out what the Consortium is after."

Levi finished his communication with General Alden and rejoined Gresham. "The tactical team is on their way," he said. "But you're right. We need to learn more."

Elara, who had been watching silently, stepped forward. "There's a deeper chamber," she said, her voice trembling. "It's where the transformations began. Maybe you can find more answers there."

Gresham and Levi exchanged a look and then nodded. "Lead the way," Gresham said.

They followed Elara deeper into the mine, the crystals' light growing brighter and more intense. The air grew colder, and the hum of energy became almost deafening. As they descended, they could feel the crystals' power resonating through the very walls of the cavern.

At last, they reached a massive door, its surface covered in intricate, glowing runes. Elara stepped back, her fear palpable. "This is it," she whispered. "This is where the true power lies."

Gresham stepped forward, placing his hand on the door. He felt a surge of energy, a connection to something ancient and powerful.

With a deep breath, he pushed the door open, revealing a chamber filled with blinding light and the pulsing heart of the crystals.

Inside, the energy was overwhelming, the air thick with a palpable sense of ancient intelligence. Gresham and Levi stepped forward, their eyes wide with wonder and fear. They knew they were on the brink of discovering something that could change the fate of the galaxy. Levi pulled out his comm called the Galactic Alliance.

There was a brief pause before General Alden's voice crackled through the comm device, filled with a mixture of surprise and determination. "You found a current operation?! That has not happened before! Excellent job, Commander Levi and Lord Gresham. I am sending tacticians, heavily armored men, and a battleship to ensure everyone will be captured, including their ship. Secure the area and prepare for reinforcements."

As they ventured deeper into the mines, the darkness closed in around them, the shadows dancing with an otherworldly light. The air grew thick with tension, the oppressive atmosphere pressing down on them. The mysteries of Terentia were only beginning to reveal themselves, and the journey ahead promised to be more dangerous and epic than any they had faced before.

The deeper they ventured into the mines, the more the atmosphere seemed to close in around them. The walls, lined with pulsating crystals, cast an eerie glow that flickered like a ghostly firelight. The air grew colder, carrying a metallic tang that made every breath feel like inhaling sharp needles.

Gresham, ever alert, could feel the hair on the back of his neck stand up. His crimson cape, usually a symbol of his unwavering resolve, felt heavier, like a shroud pressing down on his shoulders. Levi moved beside him, his eyes darting around, scanning every shadow, every flicker of movement.

Elara led the way, her steps hesitant yet determined. The fear in her eyes had not diminished, but now there was something else—an edge of desperation. She needed their help, and she knew it.

As they rounded a corner, the tunnel opened up into a vast cavern. The ceiling soared high above, lost in the darkness. The walls glittered with thousands of crystals, their light reflecting off the smooth, glass-like surfaces. In the center of the cavern stood a massive structure—an ancient, alien device, its purpose inscrutable.

Gresham approached it cautiously. "What is this?" he asked, his voice echoing through the cavern.

Elara shook her head. "We don't know. We found it when we first started mining. It's been here for centuries, maybe millennia. The crystals grow around it, and we think it's the source of their power."

Levi stepped closer, examining the device. "Have you tried to activate it?"

Elara nodded. "We did. That's when the incidents started. The workers... they changed. Became more aggressive, more... animalistic. Some even mutated physically. We had to seal off parts of the mine to contain them."

Gresham's eyes narrowed. "You've been mining these crystals without understanding their full potential. You've unleashed something you can't control."

Elara looked away, guilt and fear warring on her face. "We didn't have a choice. The Consortium... they forced us. They're after something specific, but they won't tell us what."

Levi's jaw tightened. "And now they're coming for it, whatever it is. We need to stop them."

Gresham turned to Elara, his expression resolute. "Show us the sealed sections. We need to see what we're dealing with."

Elara hesitated and then nodded. "Follow me."

They continued into the mine, the passages narrowing and the air growing colder. The light from the crystals grew dimmer, casting long, ominous shadows. They reached a heavy metal door, its surface marred with deep scratches and scorch marks.

"This is it," Elara said, her voice barely a whisper. "We've kept it locked, but they're still in there."

Gresham placed his hand on the door, feeling the cold metal beneath his palm. "Open it."

Elara's hands trembled as she entered the code. The door hissed open, revealing a dark tunnel beyond. The stench of decay hit them immediately, a foul, acrid smell that made their eyes water.

They stepped inside, the darkness closing in around them. The light from their torches revealed twisted shapes on the ground—once human, now monstrous, their bodies warped and deformed by the crystals' power.

Gresham's heart pounded in his chest. "We need to find out what they were after," he said, his voice steady despite the horror around them. "And we need to stop it."

As they moved deeper into the sealed section, the sense of unease grew. The walls seemed to pulse with a life of their own, the crystals' light growing brighter and more erratic. They reached another chamber, this one filled with strange symbols and markings carved into the stone.

The symbols glowed faintly, casting a spectral light across the room. Gresham ran his fingers over the carvings, feeling a strange resonance. "These symbols… they're some kind of language, but not one I recognize."

Levi examined the walls closely. "It's like they're alive, responding to our presence."

Elara shivered. "We never came this far. The workers who did never returned. We sealed this section off to contain whatever was happening."

Gresham's eyes narrowed as he stared at the symbols. "This isn't just a mining operation. It's a gateway. The Consortium is trying to open something, something that should stay closed."

Suddenly, the ground beneath them trembled, and a low, ominous hum filled the chamber. The crystals pulsed violently, their light intensifying to a blinding brilliance. Gresham and Levi shielded their eyes as the ancient device in the center of the cavern began to glow.

The air crackled with energy, the oppressive atmosphere growing heavier. They worked quickly, their fingers moving over the symbols, piecing together the ancient puzzle.

With a final, decisive touch, the chamber began to open, revealing the secrets hidden within. The future of Terentia—and perhaps the galaxy—hung in the balance as they prepared to face the unknown.

Confronting the Astral Nexus

As the massive stone door slid open, a blinding light tinged with ruby filled the chamber, forcing them to shield their eyes. The roar of energy surged, a primal force that felt both ancient and alive. Gresham could feel the weight of it pressing down on him, a tangible reminder of the power they were about to unleash.

Stepping into the chamber, Gresham's heart raced. The cavern was filled with relics of a bygone era, artifacts of unimaginable power and beauty. At the center stood a pedestal, upon which rested a crystalline sphere, pulsing with a rhythm that seemed to echo the heartbeat of the planet itself.

"This is the Astral Nexus," Gresham whispered, his voice filled with awe and trepidation. "This is what they were after."

Levi approached cautiously, his eyes scanning the room for any signs of danger. "What do we do now?"

Gresham reached out, his fingers brushing against the cool surface of the sphere. "We protect it. At all costs."

Elara nodded, her expression mirroring their unease. "This sphere... it feels alive. I can sense its power, but it's also... volatile. We need to study it before making any decisions."

Gresham agreed. "We'll have to call in a team of scientists. This is beyond our expertise."

Levi activated his communicator, his voice steady as he relayed their findings to the flagship. "Commander Levi to the Alliance Command. We've discovered a powerful artifact. Requesting a team of scientists for immediate analysis."

Within moments, a response crackled through. "Acknowledged, Commander. A team is on their way. ETA: one hour."

Gresham turned to Elara. "We'll keep this under wraps until we understand it fully. The Consortium cannot get their hands on this."

Elara's eyes flickered with a mix of relief and determination. "Agreed. This power, whatever it is, must not go to them!"

As they waited for the scientists to arrive, they continued to examine the chamber, deciphering the ancient markings and symbols. The air grew colder, and the light from the crystals seemed to pulse in time with the sphere. The markings revealed hints of a long-lost civilization that once thrived on Terentia, a race of beings known as the Elyndor, whose mastery of crystal energy was unparalleled.

An hour later, the science team arrived, led by Dr. Hanna Reese, a renowned xenologist known for her work with alien artifacts. She approached the sphere with a mix of curiosity and caution, her team setting up equipment around it.

"This is remarkable," Dr. Reese said her eyes wide with wonder. "We've never seen anything like this. The energy readings are off the charts."

Levi watched as the scientists began their analysis, his expression serious. "What do you think, Doctor? Is it safe to move?"

Dr. Reese hesitated. "It's hard to say. The sphere is emitting a high level of energy, but it seems stable for now. Moving it could be risky."

Gresham considered their options. "We can't leave it here for the Consortium to find. We'll have to find a way to transport it safely."

Dr. Reese nodded. "We'll need to create a containment field to stabilize it during transport. It will take some time, but it's our best option."

As the scientists worked on setting up the containment field, Gresham and Levi kept a watchful eye on the entrance to the chamber. The tension in the air was palpable, each of them aware of the stakes. The ancient symbols hinted at a catastrophic event that had forced Elyndor to hide the sphere, suggesting that it was not just a source of power but also a weapon of immense destructive capability.

Hours passed, and the containment field was finally ready. The sphere, now encased in a shimmering energy barrier, was carefully lifted and secured.

"We've done it," Dr. Reese said, her voice tinged with exhaustion and relief. "The sphere is stable and ready for transport."

Gresham gave a nod of approval. "Good work. Let's get it back to the ship."

As they began the arduous task of transporting the sphere, the cavern seemed to react, the crystals pulsing more intensely as if aware of the imminent removal of the Nexus. The ground trembled beneath their feet, a low rumble resonating through the chamber, adding urgency to their mission.

Levi glanced back at the ancient device, now dormant but still emanating a faint glow. "We need to move quickly. I have a feeling the Consortium won't be far behind."

Gresham tightened his grip on his weapon, his resolve unyielding. "We'll be ready for them. This ends here."

The team moved with purpose, their steps echoing through the vast, ancient halls of Terentia. They had uncovered a secret of immense power, one that could alter the fate of the galaxy. But with that power came great responsibility, and they were determined to ensure it did not fall into the wrong hands.

As they emerged from the mines, the cold air of Terentia hit them, a stark contrast to the warmth of the cavern. The sky was beginning to darken, and in the distance, the silhouettes of the Alliance reinforcements could be seen approaching.

Gresham took a deep breath, his gaze fixed on the horizon. "We've taken the first step, but this is far from over. We need to stay vigilant."

Levi nodded, his expression resolute. "Agreed. The real battle is just beginning."

Together, they made their way to the extraction point, the Astral Nexus safely in tow. The journey ahead would be fraught with challenges, but they were ready to face whatever came their way. For the fate of Terentia—and perhaps the entire galaxy—hung in the balance.

The Battle Against the Swarm

As they made their way back through the tunnels, the weight of their discovery pressed down on them. The sphere held untold power, and its potential for both good and harm was immense. The knowledge that the Elyndor civilization had been nearly wiped out because of this artifact weighed heavily on their minds.

Just as they emerged from the tunnel, chaos erupted. The humans scrambled for cover, their weapons useless against the chittering horde. Gresham drew out his glowing red blade, his eyes darkening to an inky black, and Levi ignited his phaser, their weapons deflecting the creatures' razor-sharp claws.

Elara, seeing the FEW in action for the first time, gasped, her eyes widening in shock and awe. She had heard tales of their power, but witnessing it was a different experience. She had to remind herself to breathe as she watched Gresham, his crimson cape snapping and furling with a life of its own, reflecting his battle rage.

As the battle raged, Gresham couldn't ignore the chilling truth. This wasn't just an illegal mining operation; it was a fueling station, a disturbance in the planet that had awakened these monstrous denizens of the planet's core. The price of greed, it seemed, wasn't just environmental destruction but unleashing a nightmare they were ill-equipped to face.

Smoke and dust choked the air, obscuring the once-verdant landscape ravaged by greed. Rivers ran black with spilled fuel, and mutated flora stretched their twisted limbs toward the crimson sun. The creatures themselves, driven by a primal rage and drawn to the energy signature of the mines, were relentless. Their carapaces, once vibrant, were now dulled and cracked, mirroring the desecration of their home.

Amidst the chaos, Levi fought alongside Gresham, his phaser blasts momentarily holding back the tide. Elara, the woman who led the mining operation, had vanished—consumed by the tremors or swallowed by the creatures, no one knew. Her followers, caught in the crossfire of their own folly, fought not for profit but for survival.

As the battle reached its peak, a monstrous creature unlike any other emerged from the fissure: a colossal insectoid queen, its carapace glowing with an ominous pulsating light. The energy signature Gresham felt earlier emanated from her, a beacon that had drawn the swarm forth.

With a deafening shriek, the queen unleashed a wave of sonic energy, sending shockwaves that knocked both Gresham and Levi off their feet. The humans, already battered and depleted, were thrown back, cries of despair merging with the creatures' chittering frenzy.

In that moment of vulnerability, Gresham made a choice. He knew brute force wouldn't be enough. Reaching deep within himself, he channeled the Essence, weaving a soothing melody that resonated with the planet's pain. Slowly, the queen's pulsating light dimmed, replaced by a flicker of confusion.

Gresham's sword glowed brighter, and his cape billowed like a thunderclap. He raised his blade high and, with a commanding shout, summoned a storm. Thunder rumbled in the distance, lightning crackled across the sky, and a fierce wind swept through the battlefield, pushing the creatures back.

Levi, seeing Gresham's face soften and his usually rigid posture relax, watched in awe. He had never seen his lord so vulnerable, so connected to the world around him. Gresham's voice, calm yet powerful, carried over the din of the storm. "Be calm," he commanded, and the creatures hesitated, their movements faltering.

The swarm faltered, drawn not by aggression but by the unfamiliar symphony. Gresham, pushing his limits, amplified the melody, painting a sonic picture of harmony and balance, of a world healed and respected.

One by one, the creatures paused, their movements hesitant. The queen, its pulsating light extinguished, lowered its head in a gesture that could be interpreted as submission or curiosity. Slowly, the swarm retreated, vanishing back into the depths of the planet.

Silence descended, thick and heavy. Gresham, panting and sweat-drenched, knelt on the ground, his energy spent but his spirit unbroken. Levi rushed to his side, relief and admiration etched on his face.

"You did it, Lord Gresham," Levi said, helping him to his feet. "I never thought I'd see such a display of the Essence. You saved us."

Elara approached, her face pale but determined. "We need to get out of here before they return," she urged, her voice trembling. "The crystals are ready. We can leave now."

The scientists, who had been watching in stunned silence, quickly gathered their equipment and the precious crystals, carrying them towards the ship. The landing party followed every step echoing with the memory of the battle they had just survived.

Gresham, his strength slowly returning, cast one last glance at the battlefield. The air was thick with the scent of ozone and the remnants of the storm. He knew that their journey was far from over, but for now, they had a brief moment of respite.

As they boarded the ship, Gresham felt a flicker of hope. The power of the FEW was formidable, and with it, they might just have a chance to uncover the secrets of Terentia and bring balance to the galaxy once more.

With the transfer complete and the Alliance troops firmly entrenched, General Theron approached Gresham and Levi. His expression, previously etched with concern, now held a hint of pride.

"You've done a remarkable job, Lord Gresham," he said, his voice gruff but laced with respect. "Securing the power source and neutralizing the creatures were crucial steps. However, the Consortium's arrival is imminent. Your presence here is no longer necessary."

Gresham felt a pang of unease. He yearned to witness the battle firsthand, to see the Alliance's strategies unfold. But Theron was right. The Consortium wouldn't see the Alliance fleet, allowing them to operate in the shadows.

"Understood, General," Gresham replied, nodding curtly. "We trust the Alliance to handle the situation."

"Have faith, Lord Gresham," Theron said, a resolute glint in his eyes. "The Galactic Alliance stands for justice and order. We won't let the Consortium exploit this resource for their nefarious purposes."

The Requiem departed Terentia, leaving the Alliance forces to lie in wait for the Consortium. Gresham and Levi felt a mix of pride and anticipation as they headed toward a nearby spaceport to resupply.

Weeks passed as the Requiem continued its journey, picking up supplies on various planets and continuing its mission. The memory of Terentia and the transferred power source lingered, but the immediate threat had been dealt with.

While docked and overseeing the resupply operations on a distant planet one evening, Gresham and Levi found a quiet moment in the ship's lounge. They poured themselves a glass of aged spirits and reflected on their recent mission.

"To our good fortune," Gresham said, raising his glass. "And to the sorrow of not finding Lady Mara."

Levi nodded, clinking his glass against Gresham's. "To the future and whatever it may hold."

Gresham's gaze lingered on the dark liquid in his glass, the flicker of the lounge's dim lighting casting shadows on his face. The weight of his unfulfilled hope pressed heavily on him. He had expected, perhaps foolishly, to find some trace of Mara on Terentia. Instead, they had uncovered another layer of the Consortium's corruption.

As they toasted, the video screens in the lounge flickered to life, displaying live feeds from Terentia. The Alliance fleet was preparing for battle, sleek starfighters buzzing around the larger cruisers, a well-oiled machine ready for action. Alliance troops, clad in their distinctive blue armor, stood firm on the ground, their faces etched with determination.

A collective gasp resonated through the video screen as the Consortium frigate emerged from the void a month after the Requiem's departure. The vessel, emblazoned with the Consortium's menacing symbol, dwarfed some of the Alliance freighters. But size wasn't everything.

The Consortium frigate, upon detecting the Alliance's presence, immediately began evasive maneuvers. It twisted and turned with surprising agility for its size, attempting to outmaneuver the Alliance ships. The Consortium had always been known for their slippery tactics, and they did not disappoint.

"Brace for evasive maneuvers," the Consortium captain barked, his voice tinged with desperation. "Prepare to ram if necessary. Our lasers won't penetrate their shields."

The frigate lunged forward, engines roaring, and aimed directly at the nearest Alliance cruiser. The move was reckless, a testament to their desperation.

Alliance ships responded with precision, their firepower overwhelming the Consortium's defenses. Laser beams crisscrossed the void, striking the frigate's hull with pinpoint accuracy. The Consortium's shields flickered and failed, exposing them to the full brunt of the Alliance's assault.

In a final act of defiance, the Consortium frigate surged forward, attempting to ram the Alliance cruiser. But the Alliance, prepared for such a move, deftly sidestepped, unleashing a barrage that crippled the frigate's engines.

The Consortium crew, realizing their defeat was imminent, frantically transmitted a message to the Alliance fleet. "We can make a deal!" the captain pleaded. "We have resources, valuable information. Spare us, and it's all yours."

General Theron's response was swift and merciless. "Don't worry; we'll seize all your assets. Not just this ship."

Theron's tone left no room for negotiation. The Consortium crew's faces were pale, their expressions shattered, and they were slumped in their seats, the weight of their defeat crushing them.

Gresham and Levi watched with a mixture of pride and marvel at the Alliance's tactical prowess. They fought with precision and coordination, their movements honed from years of experience defending the galaxy from threats like the Consortium.

The Consortium, caught off guard by the unexpected resistance, faltered. Their fighters were quickly overwhelmed by the Alliance's superior numbers and tactics. It was a swift and decisive victory, a testament to the Alliance's unwavering commitment to justice.

Weeks later, as the Requiem docked at a bustling spaceport, news of the Consortium's capture spread like wildfire. A wave of relief and jubilation washed over the crew. The Consortium, a thorn in the side of the Alliance for decades, had finally been dealt a significant blow.

"The Alliance took them down!" one crew member exclaimed, her voice filled with awe. "They secured the power source and protected the planet from the Consortium's greed."

The atmosphere aboard the Requiem was electric. Crew members laughed and cheered, their voices echoing through the halls. The mess hall was transformed into a festive gathering space, with tables laden with food and drink. The triumph over the Consortium was a cause for celebration, and everyone felt the weight of their accomplishment.

Her normally meticulous braid, now slightly tousled, Lieutenant Sera danced with Chief Engineer Voss, their steps light and uncoordinated but full of spirit. "Can you believe it?" Sera laughed, twirling under Voss's arm. "We actually did it!"

Voss grinned, his usually grease-streaked face clean for once. "About time those Consortium bastards got what was coming to them."

At a table near the back, Communications Officer Nia and Tactical Specialist Bran shared a moment of quiet triumph. Nia raised her glass, her eyes shining. "To many more victories," she said softly, clinking her glass against Bran's.

Bran nodded, his gaze steady. "And to the ones we couldn't save," he added a somber note in his voice, reminding them of the cost of their fight.

As the night wore on, the celebrations continued. Stories of bravery and close calls were exchanged, each tale adding to the growing legend of the Requiem and its crew. The mess hall was a tapestry of camaraderie and relief, each crew member's joy a thread in the larger narrative of their shared triumph.

Gresham and Levi shared a quiet moment amidst the revelry, a bottle of aged spirits between them.

"To our good fortune," Gresham said, raising his glass once more. "And to the sorrow of not finding Lady Mara."

Gresham's eyes darkened with a fleeting shadow of sorrow. "I thought Terentia might hold some clue, some hint of where she might be."

Levi placed a reassuring hand on his shoulder. "We'll find her, Gresham. We've faced greater odds. Mara is out there, somewhere."

As they toasted, the video screens displayed the latest news. The capture of the Consortium operatives was headline news, and the galaxy was abuzz with excitement and jubilation.

"Decades of evasion, and finally, the Consortium are captured," one broadcast announced. "The Alliance's tactical brilliance and unwavering commitment to justice have secured a major victory."

Cheers erupted anew, the crew of the Requiem reveling in the shared triumph. The ship-wide celebration was a testament to their unity and perseverance. They had faced immense challenges and emerged victorious, knowing they had played a part in safeguarding the galaxy.

Gresham turned to Levi, a determined smile on his face. "We did it. Let's move forward and see where the galaxy takes us."

With their mission on Terentia behind them, the Requiem and its crew celebrated their success, ready to face whatever challenges lay ahead, knowing they had significantly impacted the battle for justice and balance in the galaxy.

6

SHIMMERING BONDS

Dilemma in War Room

Lord Gresham stood among the council members, his presence looming over the holographic war map. The map pulsed with red and blue lights, each dot representing a life hanging in the balance. Months of planning, sleepless nights, and political maneuvering culminated in this moment. The decision rested solely on his shoulders—to unleash the asteroid, a sleeping leviathan capable of crippling the enemy shipyard, or to find another path.

"Lord Gresham," General Zara's voice cut through the tense silence, echoing like the clash of steel. "The consequences of using this weapon are... unprecedented. Civilian casualties, ecological devastation..." Her words trailed off, but the specter of destruction hung heavy in the air.

Gresham knew the cost. He'd seen the simulations, the projections of cities reduced to ash, the cries of the innocent echoing in his mind. Yet, the alternative felt just as unbearable—years of bloody stalemate, countless soldiers sacrificed in the trenches. Each tick of the clock represented another life lost, another family shattered.

He closed his eyes, picturing the faces of his fallen comrades, their bravery etched in his memory. Could he, in good conscience, condemn them by failing to act?

A bead of sweat trickled down his temple. "Intelligence reports confirm the enemy's counter-offensive," he finally spoke, his voice hoarse. "Their shipyard operational again... years more bloodshed. This is our chance, a decisive blow that could save countless lives in the long run." He opened his eyes, meeting Zara's unwavering gaze. "But at what cost?"

He gestured towards the map, the red dots representing civilian settlements pulsing ominously. Each dot, a face, a story, a life extinguished in the blink of an eye. "Is this the future we fight for, General? Are we warriors, or are we the very monsters we seek to vanquish?"

Zara remained silent, her jaw clenched tight. The weight of the decision pressed down on them both, a storm brewing beneath the sterile hum of the chamber. They had fought side-by-side and shared the horrors and triumphs of countless battles, but today, an abyss of conflicting ideals separated them.

A young lieutenant, barely out of his teens, nervously tugged at his collar, haunted by the ghosts of battles past. A weary diplomat, his voice hoarse from years of negotiation, pleaded for a peaceful resolution. Each voice, each plea, added another layer to the suffocating weight on Gresham's shoulders. His own mind echoed with the deafening silence of fallen comrades, their faces superimposed on the red dots he desperately wished to erase.

The holographic war map reflected in the steely gaze of Lord Gresham. Months of covert operations and ethical turmoil culminated in this moment. The asteroid, a sleeping leviathan, awaited his command. Its impact would cripple the enemy shipyard, but the cost—civilian casualties, ecological devastation—threatened to outweigh the victory.

General Zara, her voice echoing like clashing armor, challenged him. "Lord Gresham, can we truly justify this sacrifice? Are we warriors... or executioners?" Her words sparked dissent, fracturing the united front. Gresham, a muscle twitching in his jaw, felt the weight of countless lives on his shoulders. He knew the alternative—years of bloody stalemate, countless fallen comrades—but doubt gnawed at him.

"Time is short," he rumbled, silencing the murmurs. Enemy Intel indicated an imminent counter-offensive. "Their shipyard operational again... years, more bloodshed. This is our chance, a decisive strike that could save countless lives." His gaze swept across the room, locking with Zara's. "The choice is ours."

But the red dots representing civilian settlements loomed ominously. Could victory built on innocent blood be true victory? The chamber crackled with suffocating silence. Then, a young lieutenant, haunted by past battles, spoke of lost innocence. A weary diplomat, his voice hoarse from failed negotiations, pleaded for peace. Each voice added to the burden on Gresham, his mind haunted by the faces of fallen comrades superimposed on the red dots.

Zara pressed, her voice trembling. "Can we bear this responsibility? Will victory be worth the price?" Gresham fought the urge to flinch. He understood her pain, yet the enemy's advance gnawed at his resolve.

Suddenly, a message flickered on the map, revealing a weakness in the enemy's defense. Hope flickered, fragile yet tempting. Could this be the answer, a way to win without bloodshed? Or was it a trap, leading them deeper into the mire of uncertainty?

Gresham, a being cloaked in mystery, stood among the holograms, his power an unspoken question. Was he here to endorse the strike, or did his presence signify a hidden agenda? As he gazed at the council, the weight of a galaxy rested on his shoulders, and the decision he made would echo through the stars.

General Zara's steely gaze pierced through Gresham's impassive facade. "Lord Gresham," she began, her voice taut with a mix of respect and apprehension, "the FEW's intervention raises unsettling questions. For millennia, you've observed, not acted. What motivates you to break the silence now?"

Gresham's eyes glinted with an unreadable light. "The scales of fate tremble," he rumbled, his words echoing through the chamber. "When the devourer stirs, even those who observe must choose." His cryptic response fueled speculation, hinting at hidden agendas and the vast power the FEW wielded.

A flicker of fear crossed Zara's face, barely perceptible but undeniable. The "devourer" was a legend whispered amongst the oldest texts, a cosmic entity of immense power and insatiable hunger. Could this be the oblivion Gresham spoke of, a threat so dire it forced the FEW to abandon their neutrality?

The weight of this revelation settled heavily on the room. Gresham's cryptic words, combined with Zara's silent fear, painted a picture of a struggle far vaster than the one they currently faced. The decision regarding the asteroid weapon paled in comparison to the potential threat of the "devourer," leaving the council members and the reader alike to ponder the true nature of the impending choice and the potential consequences of Gresham's eventual decision.

The asteroid strike was just the tip of the iceberg, a battle in a war fueled by countless complexities. As the council debated, a chilling truth resonated—Gresham's presence had fundamentally altered the game. The stakes had risen, and the fog of uncertainty thickened.

Finally, Gresham's voice boomed, resonating with both authority and a hint of regret. "Divert the asteroid," he declared. Relief washed over the chamber, followed by a ripple of unease. Lives were saved, but the specter of a protracted war loomed large. Had Gresham preserved the Alliance's soul at the cost of swift victory?

Zara, her face etched with a complex mix of relief and concern, nodded curtly. "A bold decision, Lord Gresham. It buys time, but not peace." Others echoed her sentiment, voicing anxieties about the enemy's reaction and the Alliance's dwindling resources.

Blithen, the silent observer, remained enigmatic. A flicker of something—approval, disappointment, or something else entirely—crossed their masked face. Their inscrutable presence added another layer to the already complex tapestry of the decision.

As the fleet scrambled to execute Gresham's order, a tremor shook the flagship. A distress signal, originating from the very asteroid they'd diverted, pierced the tense silence. Was this a consequence they hadn't foreseen, a trap sprung by their change of plans? Or was it an unexpected opportunity, a chance to turn the tide in a way no one could have anticipated? The galaxy held its breath, waiting to see what fate awaited them in the wake of Gresham's momentous decision.

The Fair Trade Intrusion

The holographic map flickered back to life, displaying the rogue asteroid hanging precariously in space. A figure cloaked in shadowy elegance materialized in the center of the council chamber, causing a collective gasp from the assembled council members. Fingers pointed, and an alarmed cry echoed through the room.

"Who dares infiltrate the heart of the Galactic Alliance?" General Rika's voice thundered, her hand instinctively reaching for her sidearm. The security breach was unprecedented; the chamber was supposed to be impenetrable.

A dignitary huffed loudly, "I wish some people were proficient in the art of silence."

The Fair Trade Representative's grin seemed to widen unseen behind the mask. "Think about it, Lord Gresham. The future is full of delightful surprises. And sometimes, the best deals come from the most unexpected places."

Lord Gresham's voice rumbled with disdain. "Black market thieves? You have the audacity to waltz into this chamber, the heart of the Alliance, and peddle your wares like a rogue salesman at a space flea market!"

An officious advisor interjected snottily, "I do not have the patience or any crayons to detail why I will not work with you."

The Fair Trade Representative, all mock sympathy, fluttered their masked hands. "Black market? How ungentlemanly, Lord Gresham! We prefer… facilitators of freedom. Think of us as galactic Robin Hoods, liberating the oppressed… from the tyranny of your oh-so-righteous Alliance!" He arched an eyebrow, the unseen movement somehow conveying a sardonic smirk. "Besides, haven't you ever heard the saying: 'One man's trash is another man's lucrative business opportunity?'"

The air crackled with tension thicker than nebula dust. Gresham, standing firm, met the masked figure's gaze head-on. He recalled Mara's unwavering dedication to the cause, her fiery spirit that had always been his beacon in the darkest times. "We are the Galactic Alliance," he declared, "and we will not sully our hands with the tainted wares of vultures!"

A collective gasp rippled through the chamber. Councilor Jarek, known for his cautious nature, looked visibly shaken, while Councilor Lenara's eyes narrowed in suspicion, calculating the potential benefits of the offer. General Rika, her steely gaze fixed on the Fair Trade Representative, barked, "Guards! Apprehend this… this… intergalactic snake oil salesman!"

The room thrummed with the low hum of activating security protocols. A flicker of amusement danced in the Fair Trade Representative's unseen eyes. "Oh, come now, General," they purred, their voice as smooth as smuggled synth-oil. "Isn't that a tad melodramatic? Besides, who says you have to get your metaphorical hands dirty? Think of us as… galactic Uber for the morally flexible."

They spun on a heel, their swirling cloak billowing like a phantom sail. "Look, let's face it," they continued, their voice dropping to a conspiratorial whisper that resonated throughout the chamber, "the war's a meat grinder, chewing up resources and spitting out casualties faster than a hyperdrive on a bad relay. You're desperate, and desperation breeds… well, let's say, a willingness to explore alternative avenues."

The Fair Trade Representative snapped their fingers, and with a digital pop, a holographic display materialized above the now-darkened projection table. It depicted a glittering array of weapons—plasma rifles that crackled with raw energy, sleek fighter jets bristling with weaponry, and hulking battle mechs that could level a city block with a single stomp.

"Top-of-the-line hardware, discreetly sourced," they announced with a flourish. "Think of it as a little… insurance policy for the coming skirmish. A nudge in the right direction, courtesy of the Fair Trade."

A murmur of disquiet snaked through the room. Several council members' faces, etched with a mix of revulsion and temptation, leaned forward, eyes glued to the holographic arsenal. The Fair Trade was known for its audacious dealings and uncanny ability to procure the most coveted items, often from under the noses of lawful entities.

"I would like more information," a meek councilor ventured cautiously, their voice barely above a whisper.

Gresham, however, remained a pillar of unyielding resolve. "Your empty promises and flashy toys cannot sway us," he declared, his voice steady and firm. "We fight for a just cause and fair means, even in the face of adversity. Your brand of opportunistic barbarity will not seduce the Alliance!"

The Fair Trade Representative let out a theatrical sigh and bowed, throwing an exaggerated kiss. "Suit yourselves," they said, their voice laced with a hint of genuine disappointment. "But remember, desperation is a fickle mistress. When the tide turns, and it will, don't come crying to the Fair Trade, begging for a lifeline you so vehemently rejected today."

With a final, mocking bow, the figure shimmered and dissolved into thin air, leaving behind a tense silence and a holographic ghost of weaponry hanging in the air, a silent reminder of the Fair Trade's audacious offer and the ever-present allure of the black market.

Guards stormed in milliseconds after the Fair Trade Representative disappeared. The air crackled with tension thicker than smog. The Fair Trade Representative, a viper in borrowed robes, had left his mark on the council chamber, his honeyed words lingering like a toxic haze. Desperation gnawed at the weary faces of the Alliance council, a stark contrast to Gresham's iron resolve. He, the unshakeable pillar, was the only one unbowed by the seductive whispers of the black market.

Gresham's voice, a coat of defiance honed in the fires of war, cut through the tension. Heads snapped up, a flicker of reluctant hope battling the shadows of doubt in their eyes. Yet, the echo of the Fair Trade's offer lingered, a phantom limb reminding them of all they'd lost. The war, a relentless beast, had them by the throat, and the black market dangled a poisoned chalice, a shortcut paved with treachery.

The image flickered, the vile envoy's mocking bow a final insult. An unsettling silence descended, heavier than any accusation. Once a fortress of unwavering resolve, the council chamber now resembled a market on the verge of riot. Whispers, laced with fear and suspicion, snaked through the room, the foundation of their trust fracturing with every panicked word. The black market's gambit, a theatrical punch to the gut, had laid bare the Alliance's most vulnerable secret: the creeping doubt that threatened to tear them apart from within.

Council members exchanged uneasy glances, some gripping the edges of the table as if anchoring themselves to reality. The stakes had risen, and the fog of uncertainty thickened. Zara's hands clenched into fists at her sides, knuckles white.

General Zara's steely gaze pierced through the remaining tension. "We must remember who we are and what we stand for," she declared, her voice steady. "We will not be swayed by the whims of the black market. The Alliance's strength lies in our unity and our principles."

Gresham nodded in agreement, his resolve unwavering. "The Fair Trade may offer tempting shortcuts, but we will stay true to our cause. The galaxy will see that the Alliance does not compromise on justice and honor."

The tension slowly began to dissipate as the council members found solace in their shared conviction. They had faced a moment of temptation and had emerged stronger, their resolve fortified by the reminder of their values.

As the meeting adjourned, the holographic weapons display flickered out, leaving only the memory of the Fair Trade's audacious offer. The Alliance's path remained clear, and their commitment to justice was unwavering. The galaxy would know that the Alliance stood firm, even in the face of temptation and adversity.

With the crew fully engaged, Levi turned his attention to the ship's systems, double-checking the preparations. His hands moved swiftly over the controls, his mind a flurry of calculated decisions. He could feel the crew's eyes on him, seeking reassurance, and he gave it through his steady presence.

The ship hummed with readiness, but Levi knew the risks. An emergency warp, especially to a barely-charted star, held potential dangers. The strain on the engines and the possibility of encountering uncharted anomalies could spell disaster. But hesitation was a luxury they couldn't afford.

As the final preparations fell into place, Levi allowed himself a moment of reflection. His loyalty to Gresham ran deeper than mere duty. Despite Gresham's centuries of existence and inherent aloofness, Levi had broken through with unwavering friendship, humor, and an ability to understand and reason. Gresham had initially been surprised, even resistant, to form such a bond, but over time, he had come to value Levi's presence, finding in him an unexpected ally and friend.

As the ship hummed with readiness, Levi's thoughts returned to Gresham. Despite his centuries-long life, Gresham had never imagined forming such a deep bond with a human. But Levi's relentless friendship, humor, and ability to understand and reason had worn down the legendary being's defenses. Gresham had come to value Levi as a commander and a trusted friend.

Despite his age and status, Gresham had a surprising fondness for the drink. Their conversations, which began with ship logistics and strategy, often meandered into more personal territories, revealing layers of Gresham's character that few had ever seen.

"Remember that time I beat you at the space pool?" Levi had teased during one such evening, the rare sight of Gresham's relaxed demeanor a testament to their bond.

"You got lucky," Gresham had replied, a rare twinkle of amusement in his eye. "Next time, I'll show you how it's really done."

Their friendship had been forged in these quiet moments, away from the chaos of battle and the burden of command. Levi had bullied Gresham into countless rounds of space pool, insisting it was essential for maintaining morale. Gresham had grumbled, but Levi knew he secretly enjoyed the challenge.

"Good," Levi replied, his voice firm. "Prepare for warp on my mark."

As the ship hummed with readiness, Levi's thoughts returned to Gresham. The connection they shared was a testament to the power of friendship, even across the vast divides of time and experience. The crew needed to see that strength now more than ever. They needed to know that their leaders were united, ready to face whatever came next.

Levi's voice cut through the air, firm yet tinged with a rare note of urgency. "All hands, brace for emergency warp," he commanded, his tone brooking no argument. The crew, familiar with the potential dangers, tightened their grips on their stations, eyes wide with apprehension.

Kai, the weapons lieutenant, tightened his grip on the control panel, his knuckles white. He glanced around, taking in the tense faces of his comrades. Despite the fear knotting his stomach, he drew strength from the determination etched on Levi's face.

Ryder, the seasoned navigator, adjusted his position in his seat, his fingers dancing over the controls with practiced ease. He shot a glance at Levi, his calm demeanor masking the adrenaline surging through his veins. "We've got this," he murmured to himself, steeling his resolve.

"Engage warp drive in three... two... one... Mark!"

The ship shuddered violently as the warp drive activated, the familiar hum of the engines replaced by a deep, resonant thrumming. The stars outside the viewport stretched into elongated streaks of light, a visual testament to the immense forces at play.

Levi's fingers danced over his console, monitoring the ship's systems with practiced precision. "Stabilize the warp field," he barked, his voice cutting through the rising tension. "Adjust the energy flow to compensate for fluctuations."

The ship groaned in protest, the strain of the emergency warp palpable. Lights flickered, and the air filled with the acrid scent of overheating circuits. Levi's heart pounded in his chest, a relentless drumbeat of determination. He wouldn't let the crew down. They had to make it through this.

"Hold it steady," Levi urged, his eyes fixed on the readings. "Just a little longer."

Kai's face was set in concentration, his hands steady on the weapon controls. He knew they might need to be ready for anything on the other side of the warp.

The seconds stretched into agonizing eternity, each moment fraught with potential disaster. The ship bucked and jolted, but Levi's commands kept the crew focused, their fear channeled into action.

Finally, the thrumming eased, and the stars outside the viewport snapped back into focus. The ship emerged from the warp, the violent transition giving way to a tense stillness.

"We've stabilized, Commander," a crew member reported, their voice tinged with relief.

Levi let out a breath he hadn't realized he was holding. "Good work, everyone," he said, his voice steady but weary. "Prepare for immediate reconnaissance. We need to locate Lord Gresham's coordinates."

As the crew set to work, Levi allowed himself a moment of quiet reflection. The bond he shared with Gresham had been forged in the crucible of trust and mutual respect. They had faced countless challenges together, their friendship a beacon of hope amidst the chaos.

Now, more than ever, Levi knew they would need that bond. The galaxy was vast and perilous, but with Gresham by his side, he felt they could face whatever came next. The stakes were higher than ever, and the path ahead was uncertain, but Levi's resolve remained unshaken. They would find Gresham, and together, they would confront the unknown with unwavering courage.

The air hung heavy with despair. The rhythmic chants, once a source of comfort, now sounded like a mournful dirge. As Mara lay shivering, her eyes met Abeni's, the woman who had become a surrogate mother to her. Abeni, her face etched with worry, began to hum a soft lullaby, a melody from their past life.

The song, a tapestry of forgotten memories, transported Mara back to a time of laughter and warmth. She saw the flickering firelight, heard the playful shrieks of children, and felt the comforting weight of Abeni's hand on her shoulder. A surge of love and gratitude washed over her, momentarily pushing back the fear and doubt.

Suddenly, a loud caw shattered the silence. A crow, its inky feathers gleaming in the dim light, landed on the windowsill. Its obsidian eyes seemed to pierce through Mara's very soul, holding an unsettling intensity.

Was this a harbinger of death, as some villagers whispered, or something more? A memory flickered in Mara's mind, a fragment of a forgotten tale from her childhood. In her people's lore, crows were considered messengers, carriers of secrets from the celestial realm.

Could this crow be carrying a message for her, a clue to unraveling the mystery of her illness? Hope, a fragile ember, flickered within her. Perhaps the silence wasn't a void but a canvas waiting to be deciphered, and the key to her salvation lay not just within the villagers' love but also within the whispers of the unknown carried on the wind.

As Abeni's lullaby faded, Mara closed her eyes, her resolve hardening. She wouldn't succumb to despair. She would face whatever challenges lay ahead, drawing strength from the villagers' love and the whispers of the cosmos, even if they arrived in the form of an unsettling crow. The answer, she knew, was out there, waiting to be found.

Mara, her skin clammy beneath a thin sheen of sweat, stared at the vial the Medicine Man proffered. It pulsed with an otherworldly light, mirroring the fading glow in her own eyes. A memory, hazy and fragmented, flickered at the edges of her mind. She saw a blinding light, a voice echoing in the void, and a cold fear that gnawed at her very essence. Was this the price of invoking their savior from the stars?

"Do we know the cost of such intervention?" she wheezed, her voice growling like wind through dead leaves. The question hung heavy in the air, thick with the unspoken fear of unleashing forces beyond their comprehension.

Doubt gnawed at her. Bringing Gresham here, to this fragile village teeming with life... what horrors might follow in his wake? The name itself whispered amongst the villagers, sent shivers down her spine. Did she truly grasp the cosmic forces she played with? Or was her refusal a desperate plea to shield them from a truth too terrifying to face?

"Mara," the Elder's voice boomed, laced with both urgency and trepidation, "your celestial light grows ever dimmer. Without him, you will fade, and the darkness will consume us all."

Murmurs rippled through the crowd. Fear mingled with desperation in their eyes. Gresham, their hope and their potential doom, a name both revered and cursed. Did they dare gamble with such power?

Mara lost in the feverish throes of her delirium, muttered incoherent phrases, words tumbling from her parched lips like leaves in a whirlwind. "The hidden well... the forgotten song..." Was it a clue, a whisper of an alternative path away from the perilous dance with Gresham? Feverish and hazy, she falls into a deep sleep.

The Medicine Man, his weathered face etched with worry, knelt beside her. He felt the faint tremor in her hand, the fading pulse of her celestial connection. Could they gamble on this forgotten song, a path unknown and potentially perilous?

The villagers held their breath, the decision hanging heavy in the air. Choosing Gresham meant salvation but also the risk of unleashing cosmic chaos. Ignoring him meant watching Mara fade, but could they find another way? As they deliberated, the silence thickened, pregnant with the weight of their choice. At this moment, the fate of the village, and perhaps even the cosmos itself, rested precariously on their trembling hands.

A jolt of unimaginable terror shot through Gresham's body, a sharp, icy hand squeezing his heart. His hair prickled, sweat beading on his brow as the room tilted off-balance. This fear, this agonizing chill, was something he'd never known.

"Mara!" he roared, propelled from his seat by a surge of protective adrenaline. He stumbled to his quarters, the calm Lord replaced by a frantic blur of motion. His breaths came in ragged gasps, his heart a thunderous drum against his ribs. Memories of Mara flooded his mind—her laugh, her touch, the way she had looked at him with unspoken promises of a future that now seemed so distant.

Collapsing onto the telepathy pad, Gresham poured his being into a telepathic blast: "Mara! Answer me!" Panic and desperation etched themselves into his mind, a beacon blazing across the galaxy.

The seconds stretched into agonizing eternities, each beat of silence a hammer blow of dread. Then, finally: "Gresham." Her whisper, fragile and trembling, threaded its way back to him, barely audible but unmistakably her.

Relief crashed through him like a tidal wave, almost sending him reeling. But it was swiftly followed by a surge of horror. Where was she? His focus sharpened, his mind frantically searching. Amidst the cosmic void, he snagged on a flicker of light—a dim star, nearly swallowed by the vastness of space.

His body surged with a storm of energy, electrified by fear and hope. He thundered from the telepathy chamber, his aura a force field of raw power. Crew members flattened against the walls, their faces etched with shock and awe at the ferocious energy radiating from their usually controlled Lord. "Commander Levi to the Ready Room!" he roared, his voice resonating through the ship like a cosmic thunderclap.

7

THE MIDNIGHT LOTUS

The forest pressed in, a living labyrinth of emerald shadows and whispering leaves. Each step was a battle against nature's whims. The Medicine Man, his frame stooped with age but fueled by determination, trudged through the dense underbrush. His breath came in ragged gasps, and each inhale was a fight against the oppressive humidity that clung to his skin.

Roots and rocks conspired to trip him, snaring his feet and sending him sprawling into the damp earth. He grunted with the effort of pulling himself up; dirt smeared across his weathered face. A sharp pain shot through his leg as he twisted his ankle on a hidden stone, but he gritted his teeth and pushed on. The villagers needed him; Mara needed him. Her condition was worsening with each passing day, and time was a luxury they did not have.

A gust of wind tore through the canopy, whipping branches into his path. They scratched and clawed at his skin, leaving angry red welts. He shielded his face with one arm, the other clutching the woven sack that held his precious cargo. Each step forward was a victory over the biting insects that swarmed around him, their relentless buzzing a constant reminder of his vulnerability.

The mountainside loomed ahead, its jagged peaks shrouded in mist. He began the arduous climb, his hands scrabbling for purchase on the slick, moss-covered rocks. His worn boots slipped on the loose scree, sending him sliding back down, but he refused to yield. With a growl of determination, he dug his fingers into the crevices, hauling himself upward inch by agonizing inch.

As the Medicine Man crested a treacherous ridge, his weary eyes caught a faint, ethereal glow in the distance. His heart leaped with recognition—the Midnight Lotus, a flower so rare it was believed to be a myth by many. Its luminescent petals only unfurled under the light of the full moon, and its nectar was said to possess extraordinary healing properties.

With renewed vigor, he scrambled down the rocky slope, ignoring the protest of his aching muscles. The Midnight Lotus grew in a small, hidden glade, its silvery light a beacon of hope in the darkness. The Medicine Man approached reverently, knowing that this discovery could be the key to saving Mara.

As he reached for the delicate bloom, the ground beneath him shifted. He realized with a start that the flower grew on the edge of a sinkhole, its roots anchored in the precarious soil. One wrong move could send both him and this precious find plummeting into the abyss.

With painstaking care, he inched closer, his weathered hands trembling as they gently cradled the Midnight Lotus. He murmured an ancient prayer of gratitude as he carefully uprooted the plant, securing it in a special pouch filled with damp moss to keep it alive.

Night fell, and the forest came alive with the sounds of nocturnal predators. The Medicine Man's eyes darted around, scanning for threats. He could feel their eyes on him, hear the low growls and rustles as they stalked him through the darkness. He gathered glowing mushrooms, their luminescence casting eerie shadows, and tucked them into his sack alongside the crimson berries and twisted roots. These supplies were more than just ingredients;

they were the hopes and prayers of his people and perhaps the key to saving Mara.

Fatigue gnawed at his bones, and his muscles screamed for respite, but he pressed on. He could not fail. The memory of Mara's determined face, her unwavering spirit, fueled his every step. He stumbled, fell, and rose again, each time with a little less strength but no less resolve.

Hours turned into days, and the journey seemed endless. The weight of the sack grew heavier, a tangible reminder of the villagers' reliance on him. His vision blurred from exhaustion, and his steps faltered, but he refused to stop. He pushed through thickets that tore at his clothes, waded through streams that numbed his legs with their icy grip and climbed slopes that threatened to break him.

Finally, the familiar sight of the village came into view. The Medicine Man staggered, his breath ragged, his body trembling from the exertion. His once-proud stature was bent, his eyes hollow with fatigue, but the fire of determination still burned within. The villagers rushed to his side, their hands gentle as they helped him stand upright.

Outside his hut, the village hummed with a low, anxious drone. Prayers, thick with desperation, wove through the thatched roofs, their whispers carried by the wind. By Mara's side, women with faces drawn with worry kept vigil, their hands tracing circles on her pale skin, a silent plea for the impossible.

In the dim light of the oil lamp, the Medicine Man began his sacred work. Chants, older than the forest itself, rolled from his lips, weaving ancient magic into the forest's bounty. Sweat, salty and thick, beaded on his brow, each drop a tribute to the woman who had become his guiding light, his star fallen from the vast unknown. The air crackled with anticipation, a silent storm brewing in the candlelit room.

He poured the rare ingredients into the simmering pot, their vibrant colors blending into a luminous elixir. His hands, though weathered and trembling, moved with purpose and reverence. This was no ordinary remedy; it was a symphony of the forest's deepest secrets, each component a note in a celestial melody of hope and healing.

Clutched in his other hand was a small wooden carving, its smooth surface worn from years of holding it close. It was the first thing Mara had touched when she stumbled upon their village, a small token that connected him to the enigmatic being he had sworn to protect. A memory flickered in his mind: Mara, her eyes filled with wonder, holding the carving aloft as she spoke of the stars in her language, a language that resonated with the very essence of the universe.

His heart, a drum echoing the anxious rhythm of the entire village, pounded with a mixture of fear and determination. The Midnight Lotus, nestled among the other ingredients, glowed faintly, a beacon of hope in the darkness. He stirred the pot with a carved wooden spoon, his chants growing louder, more fervent, each word a bridge between the mortal and the divine.

Would the forest spirits answer his desperate plea, fueled by love and sacrifice? Would this concoction, brewed under the watchful gaze of a million unseen eyes, be enough to banish the darkness that threatened to consume Mara and, in turn, their haven? The Medicine Man's gaze flickered to Mara, her face pale and serene, her breathing shallow but steady. He couldn't fail her; he couldn't fail the village that had come to rely on her strength and wisdom.

The village elders, their faces lined with age and worry, stood in the doorway, watching with bated breath. The Medicine Man felt their silent support, their unwavering belief in his abilities, and it fortified his resolve. He would draw upon every ounce of his strength, every fragment of knowledge passed down through generations, to save her.

As the potion began to bubble and steam, he dipped a ladle into the pot, drawing out a small amount of the shimmering liquid. The room seemed to hold its breath as he carefully poured it into a wooden bowl, the light of the elixir casting eerie, dancing shadows on the walls.

He approached Mara, the bowl cradled in his hands like a sacred offering. Her eyelids fluttered, and for a moment, he thought he saw a flicker of recognition, a spark of the indomitable spirit he had come to admire and love. Kneeling beside her, he whispered words of comfort and encouragement, his voice steady despite the storm of emotions raging within him.

With the village gathered around, their collective hope a palpable force, he gently lifted Mara's head and brought the bowl to her lips. "Drink, Mara," he murmured, his voice trembling with emotion. "Drink and return to us."

The first drop touched her lips, and a collective gasp echoed through the room. The elixir, glowing with an ethereal light, seemed to pulse with life, infusing her with the forest's ancient magic. As she drank, color slowly returned to her cheeks, and her breathing grew stronger and more rhythmic.

As the potion coursed through her, Mara felt warmth spread from her core, pushing back the icy grip of the illness. Memories, vivid and vibrant, flooded her mind—the laughter of the children, the stories shared around the fire, the touch of the villagers' hands as they embraced her. She saw the Medicine Man, his face etched with worry and determination, and felt a surge of gratitude. Through the haze, she heard his chants, felt the power of the village's hope, and knew she wasn't alone.

The Medicine Man watched, his heart swelling with relief and pride. He had done it. Against all odds, he had crafted a potion that could save her, that could restore hope to their beleaguered village. The ancient spirits had answered his call, and for that, he would be forever grateful.

As Mara's eyes fluttered open, the village erupted in joyous celebration. Tears of relief and happiness flowed freely, and the Medicine Man, though exhausted, felt a profound sense of fulfillment. He had faced the trials of nature, the weight of his people's hopes, and the darkness that sought to claim their beloved healer—and he had emerged victorious.

Mara, her strength returning, smiled up at him, her eyes filled with gratitude and love. "Thank you," she whispered, her voice weak but filled with emotion. "Thank you for bringing me back."

He nodded, his own eyes misting over. "We are all connected, Mara. Your strength is our strength. Together, we will face whatever comes."

At that moment, beneath the starlit sky and the watchful gaze of the ancient forest, they knew that their bond, forged in adversity and strengthened by love, would see them through any challenge. The future, though uncertain, was theirs to shape, and they would face it together.

Ignoring the village women's protests, Mara dressed in her old armor, the familiar weight a comforting burden. Her blonde hair whipped in the sudden breeze, her crimson cape fluttering with an eerie life of its own. The emblem of the FEW on her chest glowed, though its light wavered, a mirror to her own faltering resolve. She took a deep breath, the taste of the elixir still sharp on her tongue, and stepped into the forest.

The village women, their faces etched with worry, followed her despite their reservations. They moved silently through the underbrush, their eyes never leaving Mara's back. She led them to a clearing, the moonlight casting a silver glow over the scene. The women watched in awe as Mara knelt, her movements slow and deliberate. She drew her glowing blue sword, its archaic runes shimmering faintly in the darkness, and set its tip into the ground.

Mara's violet eyes closed, her face a mask of concentration. To the villagers' shock, her crimson cape flew out behind her, a fierce wind tearing through the clearing. A bright golden light erupted from the sword, spewing straight up into the sky. The women shielded their eyes, the light too intense to bear. A golden dome began to form, expanding outward until it covered the village and part of the forest. Warm, sparkling dust drifted down like gentle snowflakes, casting a magical glow over everything it touched.

The dome shimmered with warmth, a happy hum resonating through the air. Sparks sprinkled down constantly, creating tiny points of light that danced briefly before fading. The children clapped and danced under the sparkles, their laughter a joyous symphony. The men and women smiled in wonder and awe, their faces lit by the dome's ethereal glow. The village was bathed in pure joy, the dome a sanctuary of peace and happiness amidst the galaxy's chaos.

But the scene's tranquility was shattered as Mara, her strength spent, collapsed. The sword fell harmlessly to the ground beside her.

The women rushed to her side, their alarm palpable. Gently, they lifted Mara and her sword, their faces grim with determination. They moved as quickly as they could back to the village, their steps urgent but careful. The villagers, seeing the state of their beloved healer, felt a pang of fear despite the dome's reassuring glow.

"Fetch the Medicine Man!" one of the women commanded, her voice sharp with urgency. A child, wide-eyed and swift, darted off to summon him.

The Medicine Man, bent and weary from his own arduous journey, arrived as swiftly as his old bones allowed. His eyes, deep with concern, took in the sight of Mara's pale face and the shimmering dome. He muttered a prayer under his breath, his fingers already reaching for the pouches of herbs at his belt.

Inside Mara's hut, a small plant called the Star blossom, which one of the villagers had given her five years ago, now wilted dangerously. Its once vibrant leaves drooped, a reflection of Mara's fading vitality. The plant had thrived under her care, just as the village had flourished with her presence. Now, it seemed to mirror her struggle, its life force waning as hers did.

The Medicine Man's eyes lingered on the Star blossom. "This plant is bound to her," he murmured, his voice tinged with recognition and concern. "Its health reflects her own. We must save it to save her."

"Place her inside," he instructed his voice steady despite the tremor in his hands. The women obeyed, laying Mara gently on the bed. The Medicine Man began his work, his chants intertwining with the village's anxious whispers. The room filled with the pungent aroma of his concoctions, each ingredient a lifeline, each breath a prayer.

Outside, the dome rose like a living flame of golden light, its surface shimmering with heat and power. It hummed with a low, melodic resonance — not mechanical, but alive, like the pulse of a vast and ancient heart.

Children danced in the golden dust, their bare feet kicking up motes that sparkled in the air like stardust. Their laughter rang through the warm evening air, bright and piercing — a song of joy against despair. The scent of fresh earth and blossom pollen mingled with the sweet tang of roasted nuts from the communal fire.

The men watched in awe, some blinking back tears. The warmth from the dome soaked into their skin, like stepping into sunlight after years of shadow. Peace had a taste tonight — like honey tea and fresh bread, like something they thought they'd never feel again.

The village, bathed in amber glow, felt like a cradle — cradled by love, held by magic, suspended above the burning galaxy.

But inside the hut, the air was tight with incense — sharp pine, bitter root, and the iron tang of blood. The silence was broken only by the low murmur of ancient chants and the bubbling hiss of the elixir over flame.

Mara lay still, her skin pale and clammy. Her breath came in shallow gasps, barely disturbing the cool cloth on her lips. The Star Blossom beside her had begun to droop, its once-vivid petals curling, its glow dimming.

The Medicine Man's hands moved quickly, dipping into bowls, mixing powders, pressing herbs to her skin. Sweat trickled down his spine. The floor beneath him creaked with every shift, and the heat from the brazier stung his eyes. He dared not blink.

Outside, the villagers waited beneath the dome's soft hum, tasting ash in their mouths and fear in their hearts. The miracle had been granted — but it was Mara's soul that held the power to keep it alive.

Then — lightyears away — terror struck.

A jolt like lightning tore through Gresham's chest. He reeled, the air in his quarters suddenly thin and sharp, tasting of ozone and dread.

His skin flushed cold. His vision blurred, darkening at the edges. His knees buckled, and for a breathless second, the world tilted sideways — spinning and weightless. His heart slammed against his ribs with thunderous force.

"Mara!"

The word ripped from him, hoarse and cracked, like a man burning from the inside out.

The stone floor was cool underfoot as he staggered through the corridor, boots thudding like drumbeats. The sharp scent of polished metal and recycled air stung his nostrils. Lights strobed past, too bright, too fast. Crew faces blurred — open mouths, wide eyes — and then vanished in his wake.

He crashed into the telepathy chamber. The moment his body hit the pad, the cold metal surged against his skin. The world narrowed — noise dropped away — all that remained was her.

"Mara! Answer me!"

His voice echoed inside his own skull, louder than thunder, sharper than a scream.

Silence.

Then — a whisper. Fragile as breath on glass.

"Gresham."

Her voice brushed across his mind like silk — barely there, but her. Weak. Trembling. Distant.

The relief hit like a wave of hot wind — stealing his breath, dropping him to his knees. For one second, his body wanted to collapse. But his mind — his heart — roared back to life.

He felt her pain, a distant throb through the bond. He tasted ash and flowers and blood. Her light was flickering, buried in a sea of shadow.

And yet — still burning.

Gresham rose.

Energy surged through him, electric and raw. The chamber doors blasted open as he stormed out, his cloak snapping behind him like a thundercloud breaking.

The hum of the ship, the chatter of officers, the flickering panels — all of it bent away from him. His aura crackled — heat and power and fury. He smelled of ozone and steel. His boots struck the floor like war drums.

Crew flattened against the walls, watching in stunned silence.

This wasn't the diplomatic lord. This was a storm in human form.

"Commander Levi to the Ready Room!" he barked, voice shaking the air itself.

"Focus on your tasks," Levi snapped to the crew, sharp as flint. "Lord Gresham has received critical intel. We need to be ready." A murmur of unease rippled through the room. Emergency warp was a maneuver fraught with risks—unstable energy fields, potential damage to the ship's systems, and the threat of being flung into uncharted space. But there was no choice. The urgency in Gresham's voice demanded immediate action.

The engine room's response crackled through the comms with a grumble. "Yes, SIR," came the begrudging reply, followed by a sharp snap as the connection cut off. Commander Levi's eyebrows rose, and he looked over to his second in command. "Jenkins, take the bridge."

"Aye, sir!" Jenkins immediately took the seat Commander Levi vacated and began issuing orders. "Give me status reports of all systems." The crew groaned but set to work.

The Requiem's engine room was in chaos. As Commander Levi approached, he could hear the commotion even through the thick bulkhead doors. They slid open with a hiss, revealing a scene of utter disarray.

Lead Engineer Filen stood in the center of the room, his face flushed red with anger and frustration. A shattered datapad lay at his feet, and he was in the process of viciously stomping on a clipboard, reducing it to plastic shards. Nearby, an engineer was furiously grinding an electric screwdriver into the floor, his face a mask of frustration. It was an absurd sight—like watching a bear trying to disassemble a toaster.

"Impossible!" Filen shouted, his voice cracking. "They're asking for the impossible! We're engineers, not miracle workers!"

The engineering team stood frozen, a mixture of shock and fear on their faces. Some looked ready to bolt, while others seemed on the verge of joining Filen's outburst.

Levi took a deep breath, squaring his shoulders. This was the moment when leadership mattered most.

"Filen," Levi's voice cut through the chaos like a knife, calm but commanding. The room fell silent, all eyes turning to the commander. "Talk to me. What's going on?"

Filen whirled, his eyes wild. "Commander! They want us to push the engines 50% past their safety limits. It's suicide! We'll tear the ship apart!"

Levi nodded, his expression serious but not angry. He stepped forward, crunching over the remains of the datapad. "I understand your frustration, Filen. But I need you to take a deep breath. Can you do that for me?"

Filen hesitated, then nodded, inhaling deeply.

His voice softer now. "Now, let's break this down. You said it's impossible. But is it truly impossible, or just incredibly difficult?"

Filen paused, considering. "I... it's not technically impossible, but the risks..."

"The risks are high," Levi finished for him. "I get it. But let me ask you something. Why do you think I chose you as my Lead Engineer?"

Filen blinked, caught off guard. "I... because of my expertise, I suppose."

Levi smiled. "Partially. But more importantly, because when everyone else sees the impossible, you see a challenge. Remember the plasma conduit failure on Titan Base? They said it couldn't be fixed without a full evacuation. But you found a way."

A murmur of agreement rippled through the engineering team. Filen's shoulders began to relax. The engineer who had been grinding the electric screwdriver finally stopped, looking sheepish as he picked it up and placed it carefully on a table.

"You're right, this is a monumentally difficult task," Levi continued, addressing the whole team now. "But difficult is what we do. It's why we're on the Requiem. We don't run from challenges; we rise to meet them."

He turned back to Filen. "So, Lead Engineer Filen, I'm not asking if any engineering team can do this. I'm asking if the Requiem's engineering team can do it. What do you say?"

Filen stood straighter, a new determination in his eyes. He looked around at his team, seeing the same fire reflected in their faces. "You're right, Commander. We can do this. It won't be easy, but... we're the best damn engineers in the fleet."

Levi grinned, clapping Filen on the shoulder. "That's what I wanted to hear. Now, what do you need from me to make this happen?"

As Filen began outlining his plan, the energy in the room transformed. The fear and frustration were replaced by determination and focus. The impossible task now seemed within reach, all because their commander believed in them.

Levi moved through the engine room, ensuring everyone was clear on their tasks. His presence was calming, and the chaotic energy transformed into focused determination. He approached the control console, where Ensign Teron was inputting the recalibrations.

"Ensign Teron, how are we looking?" Levi asked, glancing at the displays.

"Commander, we've managed to reroute power from non-essential systems. We'll have enough output to boost the engines, but we need to closely monitor the core temperature. Any spike beyond the threshold could cause a meltdown," Teron replied, his voice steady despite the stakes.

"Understood. Keep a close eye on those readings. We'll need to be ready to make adjustments on the fly," Levi said, his tone firm but encouraging.

The engine room buzzed with activity as the team made the final adjustments. The tension was palpable, but so was the determination. Levi stood at the central console, his eyes locked on the main display.

"All right, everyone. This is it. Prepare for the engine boost. Ensign Teron, keep those core temperature readings steady. Lead Engineer Filen oversees the power distribution. Let's make this happen," Levi commanded, his voice carrying the weight of leadership.

The team responded in unison, their movements synchronized like a well-rehearsed dance. The Requiem's engines roared to life, the hum of power coursing through the ship. The displays flickered, showing the increasing output as the engines pushed beyond their safety limits. The deck beneath their feet vibrated with the strain, and the air grew warmer, the heat of the overworked engines radiating through the room.

"Core temperature holding steady," Teron reported, his voice filled with concentration.

"Power levels are stable," Filen added, his eyes never leaving the control panel.

Levi felt a surge of pride. "Excellent. Keep it up. We're almost there."

The minutes felt like hours as the team worked tirelessly, making adjustments and monitoring the systems. The Requiem groaned under the strain, but the engines held firm. Finally, the output reached the desired level.

"Engine boosts successful," Teron announced, a triumphant smile spreading across his face.

A cheer erupted in the engine room, the tension breaking into relief and exhilaration. Levi allowed himself a moment to savor the victory before turning to his team.

"Outstanding work, everyone. You've proven once again why the Requiem has the best crew in the fleet," Levi praised, his voice filled with genuine admiration.

As the team celebrated, Levi's mind returned to the looming threat of Mara's illness and the unknown dangers of their mission. They had won this battle, but the war was far from over. With renewed determination, he knew they would face whatever challenges lay ahead, united and unstoppable.

Levi smiled to himself, recalling their monthly chats over a bottle of Xolth, the potent alien liquor that had become a tradition. Xolth was a fiery, pungent drink with a vivid crimson hue, known for its ability to ignite both conversation and camaraderie. Its sharp taste and warming sensation made it a favorite among the crew, a small comfort in the vastness of space. Gresham, despite his age and status, had a surprising fondness for the drink. Their conversations, which began with ship logistics and strategy, often meandered into more personal territories, revealing layers of Gresham's character that few had ever seen.

Their friendship had been forged in these quiet moments, away from the chaos of battle and the burden of command. Levi had insisted on countless rounds of space pool, claiming it was essential for maintaining morale. Gresham had grumbled, but Levi knew he secretly enjoyed the challenge.

Just then, a call came from Engineering. "Commander, this is Voss. How long do you anticipate needing the emergency warp? We're adapting the systems to handle the load."

Levi's eyes flickered with determination. "As long as it takes, Voss. Mara's life depends on it."

A pause, and then Voss responded, "Understood, sir. We'll do our best to hold it together."

The ship groaned in protest, the strain of the emergency warp palpable. Lights flickered, and the air filled with the acrid scent of overheating circuits. Sparks flew from overloaded consoles, casting a brief, fiery glow in the dim light. Levi's heart pounded in his chest, a relentless drumbeat of determination. He wouldn't let the crew down. They had to make it through this.

A voice crackled over the comms again. "Commander Levi, the engines are nearing critical levels," Voss warned urgency in his tone. "We can't sustain this for much longer."

"Understood, Voss," Levi replied, his voice a calm anchor in the storm. "Do what you can."

Now, more than ever, Levi knew they would need that bond. The galaxy was vast and perilous, but with Gresham by his side, he felt they could face whatever came next. The stakes were higher than ever, and the path ahead was uncertain, but Levi's resolve remained unshaken. They would find Gresham, and together, they would confront the unknown with unwavering courage.

8

TURMOIL AWAITS

The journey felt like an eternity to Gresham as the ship finally landed. As his vessel descended toward the village, the viewport revealed a breathtaking landscape. Twin suns cast a warm, golden glow over the lush terrain, with verdant forests stretching endlessly. A soft breeze rustled through the trees, carrying the scent of blooming flowers and fertile soil. Amidst this serene beauty, an unexpected sight greeted him—a shimmering golden dome enveloping a part of the village and the surrounding forest.

To his surprise, the towering dome seemed to pulse rhythmically as if to an unseen tune. Sparkles shimmered off it, and he knew his love had created it. Fear and happiness alternated within him, the dome's brightness a beacon of her enduring strength. His hands clenched and unclenched at his sides, a physical manifestation of his internal struggle.

"Star Man is here for you," the Medicine Man said softly, handing her the elixir. Grimacing, she downed it and adjusted her soft, comfortable clothing. Stepping out into the forest, she felt fear and love wage war within her. The sight of Gresham almost made her stop and stare. Her violet eyes traced his face, drinking in the sight of him she had not seen in over five years.

His heart pounded like a war drum; each beat echoing his turmoil as he caught sight of Mara through the ethereal shimmer of the dome. Her once-radiant form now appeared pale and frail, a shadow of the warrior he remembered. His breath hitched at the sight—FEW were never ill. This was beyond anything he had ever encountered. His thoughts churned with confusion and dread. What force had brought Mara to this state?

Gresham stared at Mara through the dome, an ache for her spearing painfully through him. She looked like sunshine on a moon; her light diminished but not extinguished. His feet felt rooted to the ground for a moment, his body tensing as he absorbed her appearance. He slowly walked to the dome, his heart thundering in his chest, and lifted his palm to the shimmering barrier. The dome's pure joy and a happy hum resonated with him, bolstering his spirit.

Mara approached the dome and pressed her hand to his, feeling his warmth and love pour into her. Her violet eyes locked onto his dark ones. "Mara," he said softly, his voice a blend of relief and longing. His fingers trembled slightly against the dome, betraying the intensity of his emotions.

She hesitated, emotions swirling within her, then spoke, her voice barely above a whisper, "Gresham." She felt a tear escape and slip down her cheek.

The dome's light sparkled around them, casting a golden hue over their reunion. The villagers watched in silent awe, understanding that this moment was beyond their comprehension—a convergence of love, duty, and destiny.

As they stood there, hands pressed together through the dome, the world seemed to hold its breath. The bond between them, tested by time and distance, pulsed with renewed strength. They knew the challenges ahead were great, but in this moment, they were together, and that was enough.

Gresham's heart pounded like a drum against his ribs, mirroring the turmoil within. Seeing Mara, pale and weakened even within the ethereal shimmer of the dome, tore at his soul. Memories of their laughter, their shared adventures, flickered through his mind, intensifying the fear gnawing at him. He loved her fiercely and protectively, and the thought of losing her was unbearable. But fear wasn't his only emotion. Confusion warred within him. FEW were immune to illness, this much he knew. So, what ailed Mara? Why did this dome, meant to be a sanctuary, claim to protect her from something called "sickness"? Was there something else at play, something more sinister?

Their gazes locked, a silent conversation playing out. Love battled with duty, fear with resolve. The air between them felt charged, electric, each breath fraught with unspoken words and shared history. Gresham's heart pounded, each beat echoing his desperation. He reached out, his hand pressing against the cool, unyielding surface of the dome. His eyes, usually so controlled, now flickered with a storm of emotions.

"Mara," he said, his voice a mix of command and plea. "I need you to bring this dome down."

Mara's violet eyes glinted with a kaleidoscope of emotions—confusion, anger, and a flicker of something deeper, something he couldn't decipher. His gaze traced the lines etched on her face, lines absent five years ago. What had happened to her in this exile? What had driven her to sever ties with their world?

As she stood there, her palm pressed against the warm, unyielding surface of the dome, Mara realized the true depth of her dilemma. This wasn't just about survival; it was about choosing a path, about deciding whether the past could ever truly be left behind. Gresham raised his hand to hers. He willed his love through the thin barrier.

The golden dome shimmered in the twilight, its ethereal glow casting long shadows that danced around them. It was both a bridge and a chasm, offering the tantalizing illusion of closeness while reminding them of the vast emptiness that separated them.

Gresham's voice echoed across the barrier, laced with an urgency that sent a tremor through her. His eyes, usually steady, flickered with a hint of desperation, revealing the weight of responsibility he carried. Yet, a flicker of frustration danced within them, too, a silent plea for her understanding.

Mara felt the storm within her intensify. His words tugged at the carefully constructed walls around her heart, dredging up memories of shared laughter, whispered secrets, and the warmth of his embrace. It was a past she had fought so hard to bury, a past that now clawed its way back, fueled by the intensity of his gaze. But buried along with those memories were the reasons she chose this path, the sacrifices made, and the lives entrusted to her care. The cost of leaving, the potential betrayal of the villagers' trust, weighed heavily on her. Could she justify abandoning them to the unknown intentions of the Alliance, even for a chance at reconciliation with Gresham?

His plea resonated deeply, stirring a part of her that yearned for connection, for a return to the life she'd left behind. But alongside it, a chilling reminder of the pain, the loss, and the betrayal that had driven her away—a betrayal she caused. The dome, in its shimmering ambiguity, mirrored her internal conflict: a haven and a prison, protection and sacrifice intertwined.

"Mara, you can't stay here," Gresham's voice broke through her thoughts, filled with disbelief and desperation. "You might... die!" He shivered at the impossible probability. "Come, let's get you to the medical bay. I know... with the two of us, we can beat this." His voice, urgent yet a plea, all the same, reached her through the barrier.

She closed her eyes, seeking clarity in the maelstrom of emotions. The villagers' worried faces, the Medicine Man's steady presence, the distant rumble of approaching ships—each element fueled her resolve. This wasn't just about her but about the lives she had sworn to protect.

"I cannot," she whispered, her voice firm despite the tremor in her heart. "My duty lies here, with these people. The dome will stay, and so will I."

Gresham's eyes widened with a mix of shock and pain. "Mara, please," he implored, his voice cracking. "I can't lose you again. We can find another way together."

Mara's resolve wavered, the weight of his words pressing heavily on her. But she stood her ground, the golden dome around them shimmering as a symbol of her commitment. "You have to trust me, Gresham. This is where I need to be. For now."

Tears welled up in Gresham's eyes, but he nodded, understanding the depth of her resolve. "For now," he repeated softly, his voice filled with a mix of heartbreak and acceptance.

They stood there, hands pressed against the dome, separated by a thin barrier but united in their love and determination. The path ahead was uncertain, but their bond remained unbroken—a beacon of hope in the vast, chaotic galaxy.

Unable to sleep, his mind plagued by worry, Gresham left the ship and approached the glowing dome. The dome cast sparkling warmth toward him, a stark contrast to the turmoil raging within. His crimson cape furled, curled, and thrashed violently, mirroring the storm in his heart. Gresham's ocean eyes turned inky black with anguish and rage as he raised his glowing red sword, the ancient runes blazing with fiery intensity.

With a roar that echoed through the village and beyond, Gresham brought his sword down upon the dome, intending to slice it open and reach Mara. The sword, however, met an impenetrable force. A brilliant flash of golden light erupted as the blade rebounded, the shockwave sending Gresham stumbling backward. The dome remained unscathed, its serene glow a stark defiance to his desperate attack.

Gresham dropped to his knees, the weight of the universe pressing down upon him. His sword clattered to the ground, its glow dimming in the face of his despair. Tears, hot and silent, traced paths down his cheeks. Fear, anguish, and an aching love so fierce it threatened to consume him spilled from his soul. He wept, the soundless sobs wracking his body, each tear a testament to the depth of his love and the pain of his helplessness.

The golden dome shimmered softly, indifferent to his suffering. Its ethereal light cast gentle shadows, painting a picture of serenity that mocked the turmoil within Gresham's heart. The villagers watched from behind the barrier, their faces etched with a mix of awe and sorrow. They had never seen such vulnerability from a figure so formidable, a man who had always embodied strength and resolve.

At that moment, Gresham was no longer the mighty Lord of the FEW but a man brought to his knees by love. The night stretched on, the twin moons casting a silver glow over the scene, a silent witness to his agony. The stars above twinkled indifferently, their ancient light traveling across the cosmos, bearing no heed to the pain of mortals.

As Gresham knelt, broken and despairing, the air seemed to hum with a soft, ancient melody, a lullaby carried on the wind. It spoke of hope, of resilience, and of the enduring power of love. Though the dome remained unyielding, the melody whispered promises of a future yet to unfold, of battles yet to be fought, and of a love that could withstand the trials of the universe.

Commander Alexander Levi, concerned for his friend, waited before softly descending the gangplank to pick up the dormant sword. "Gresham, let's get some rest. We'll work on things in the morning," he said gently, placing a reassuring hand on Gresham's shoulder.

The next morning, the scene shifted as servicemen and women spread out across the village and forest, taking readings. They used various devices—a palm-sized scanner and a larger, box-like instrument—each capturing different data about the dome's mysterious properties. The villagers, disturbed by the presence of the intruders, watched warily as they moved through all areas within the dome's boundaries.

Throughout the day, the dome's golden glow seemed indifferent to the bustle, sparkling warmly at the intruders. Each time a spark touched one of the servicemen or women, they paused in wonder. Some reached out to touch the dome's surface, feeling unexpected warmth that spread through them, filling them with a sense of purity and peace.

One young soldier, Private Daniels, who had been skeptical about the whole mission, felt the dome's warmth and found himself involuntarily swaying to an unheard melody. His colleague, Sergeant Martinez, began to hum softly as she worked, the tune light and cheerful, unlike her usual stern demeanor. Nearby, Corporal Jenkins tapped a gentle rhythm on his leg, feeling an inexplicable joy.

The effect was widespread. Each serviceman and woman, touched by the dome's magic, found themselves humming, singing, or swaying as they took their readings. The atmosphere within the dome was transforming, the initial tension replaced by an almost surreal tranquility. The villagers, seeing the change in the intruders, slowly began to relax. They watched in amazement as the soldiers, usually so focused and intense, worked with smiles on their faces and lightness in their steps.

The villagers, seeing the soldiers' newfound respect and gentleness, began to open up. They approached with tentative smiles, offering food and drink through small, temporary openings in the dome's surface. These openings, created by the dome's magic, allowed the exchange without compromising its protective integrity. Their fear slowly dissolved into a tentative trust. The dome had not just protected them but had woven a fragile connection between two worlds, a connection born of curiosity, wonder, and the shared human experience.

The day stretched long, not because of the complexity of their tasks but because the dome's enchantment slowed their progress. Each moment spent near the dome drew them into a state of wonder, their usual efficiency replaced by an appreciation for the beauty and serenity they felt. It was as if the dome, in its gentle defiance, was teaching them to slow down and feel the world around them.

By evening, the readings were finally complete. The servicemen and women gathered their equipment, their expressions a mix of awe and confusion. They had come expecting a straightforward mission but had found something profoundly different.

Commander Levi, reviewing the data, couldn't help but notice the change in his team. They were more relaxed, more at peace, their usual military precision softened by the day's experiences. He glanced at Gresham, who, despite his earlier anguish, seemed a touch more composed. The dome's influence was undeniable, a beacon of warmth and purity in a chaotic universe.

"We'll analyze these readings back on the ship," Levi said, his voice steady but thoughtful. "But I think we found more than just data today."

Gresham nodded, his gaze lingering on the dome. "Yes, Alex. We found a reminder of what's worth fighting for."

Mara lay on her bed, her breathing shallow and her skin clammy and pale. The Medicine Man, his weathered hands steady despite the worry etched into his features, dabbed her forehead with a cloth soaked in cool, clean water. The room was dim, the flickering light of the oil lamp casting dancing shadows on the walls.

As he worked, his keen eyes caught something unusual. Faint, intricate patterns began to appear on Mara's skin, glowing briefly with an otherworldly light. They shimmered softly, their luminescence casting a faint glow that contrasted sharply with her pallor.

The Medicine Man's breath caught in his throat. He leaned closer, his fingers tracing the intricate patterns that seemed to emerge from within her. "These markings..." he murmured, his voice barely above a whisper.

Mara, her eyelids fluttering open, looked at him with a mixture of curiosity and exhaustion. "What... what are they?" she asked weakly, her voice a mere whisper.

The Medicine Man's expression was grave as he continued to study the patterns. "I am not sure," he said, his tone reverent and tinged with fear. "They are unlike anything I have seen before. They speak of an ancient power, something long forgotten."

Mara's eyes widened slightly, a flicker of recognition crossing her features. "Ancient... like the stories of old?"

The Medicine Man shook his head slowly, his gaze never leaving the glowing patterns. "Perhaps. These symbols... they are a sign. A message, perhaps. But what it means, I cannot say."

As he spoke, the patterns began to fade, their light dimming until they were once again invisible against her skin. The Medicine Man sat back, his mind racing with questions. What power lay behind these symbols? And why had they chosen to reveal themselves on Mara's skin?

"My abilities are limited against this," he admitted, his voice heavy with sorrow. "The elixir helps, but it is not the answer. This illness, these markings... they are beyond my understanding. Star Man is here. He is like you, Mara. He may know more about what to do."

Mara's eyes filled with a mixture of hope and dread. "If we let him in, the crew will document their findings," she fretted, her voice gaining strength from her anxiety. "The star charts will be updated, and those that trade and other nefarious groups may land here!" Her last words were a desperate push against the overwhelming tide of fear and uncertainty.

The Medicine Man placed a reassuring hand on her shoulder. "We will find a way, Mara. Together, we will find a way."

But deep within her, Mara knew the truth. The dome, with its warmth and purity, was not just a barrier but a symbol of the love and protection she felt for the villagers. It was her way of shielding them from the outside world, from the dangers that lurked beyond the stars. And yet, as the markings on her skin reappeared, she couldn't shake the feeling that there was something more at play, something ancient and powerful that she couldn't fully comprehend.

Mara closed her eyes, her mind a whirlwind of fear and hope. She felt the steady rhythm of the Medicine Man's heartbeat, a comforting anchor in the storm of her thoughts. The decision lay heavy on her soul, but deep down, she knew that Gresham's presence, though fraught with danger, also brought the promise of healing.

As night fell, the golden dome continued to shimmer, a beacon of warmth and purity. The villagers gathered around, their faces lit by its glow, their hearts united in silent prayer. And aboard the Requiem, Gresham's plea hung in the air, a bridge between two worlds, waiting for Mara's response.

With a soft sigh, Mara drifted into a troubled sleep, her thoughts a tangled web of fear and longing. The Medicine Man watched over her, his heart heavy with the weight of the unknown. He knew the path ahead was fraught with danger, but he also knew that love and hope were powerful forces capable of overcoming even the darkest of trials.

During the deep night, a ping that only Gresham could hear jolted him awake. The dome had begun to dissolve, and villagers gathered around Lady Mara's home, their prayers and quiet weeping to create a somber symphony. Gresham raced out of the ship, his heart leaping out of his chest. He slowed to a stop, calming his breath, as he saw the villagers forming a protective circle around Mara's home.

Harnessing his aura with the deftness of a seasoned commander, Lord Gresham gently parted the sea of villagers. They hesitated, their eyes meeting his with an imploring look that spoke volumes. He stepped into the modest home and saw the Medicine Man chanting over his pale, barely breathing Mara. The old man slowly stood up and backed away, allowing the Star Man to approach.

Gresham's heart ached as he saw his once-vibrant Mara so frail. Shocked, he noticed faint arcane sigils flash and disappear on her skin. He leaned down and gathered her into his arms, feeling the faint beat of her heart. The Medicine Man carefully placed her folded uniform and clicked her sheathed sword onto Gresham's belt.

As he lifted her, the scent of her hair, a faint mix of wildflowers and the forest, enveloped him. The weight of her body, so light and fragile, pressed against his chest, anchoring him in the gravity of the moment. Mara's skin was clammy, and her breathing was shallow. The stark contrast between her current state and the vibrant woman he once knew tore at him. A single tear escaped Mara's eye, tracing a shimmering path down her cheek. Was it a tear of relief or a harbinger of the uncertainties ahead?

As night descended, casting long shadows across the land, the villagers stood in silent reverence. The dome's dissolution had revealed not just the physical space but the emotional and spiritual bonds that tied them all together. The golden mist lingered in the air, a symbol of the past and a promise of the future.

Gresham held Mara close, feeling the faint thrum of her heartbeat against his own. The final image of the two of them, entwined in a moment of fragile unity, spoke to the deep, unspoken love that had endured through years of separation. It was a powerful and poignant tableau, imbued with the sensory details that grounded the moment in reality: the softness of her hair, the warmth of her breath, and the steady, rhythmic pulse of life that beat within her.

As they moved toward the ship, Gresham knew that their journey was far from over. The challenges ahead would test their resolve, their courage, and their love. But for now, in this moment, they were together, and that was enough.

With Mara nestled close, Gresham's steps carried him towards his quarters, the villagers' faces—a poignant tapestry of emotions— burned into his memory. He saw not just suspicion and fear but a

flicker of understanding, a silent acknowledgment of the desperate
act he was about to commit.

9

A DESPERATE GAMBLE

Dr. Holmes's breath hitched as Lord Gresham strode into the medical bay. The man was a storm incarnate; his usually composed demeanor shattered. His obsidian eyes burned with an unnatural fire, and his crimson cape billowed behind him like a raven's wings in a sudden gust. In his arms lay a woman with hair like spun gold, her skin the color of moonlight. Fear, cold and metallic, flooded Holmes's veins. FEW never fell ill. What dark secret did this woman hold?

Gresham knelt beside the unconscious woman, his hand hovering over hers. A tremor ran through her as their connection sparked, a flicker of recognition replacing the emptiness in her eyes. A choked sob escaped his throat, a sound raw and unfamiliar. "Hold on, Mara," he whispered, his voice laced with a desperation that sent shivers down Holmes's spine. His grip tightened on her hand, knuckles white.

Five years. He had spent five years on this lonely planet, a prisoner of his duty and the fading memory of Mara's laughter. Now, as he gazed at her lifeless form, a terrifying question echoed in the sterile silence: could he live a life devoid of her light? The answer, a defiant roar, surged through him. He wouldn't. He couldn't. But the path forward was shrouded in forbidden knowledge, a transgression that could shatter the very fabric of reality. For Mara, he was willing to risk everything.

"Lord Gresham," Holmes's voice was a whisper, thick with apprehension. "Can you save her? What if... what if you can't?"

Gresham's eyes flickered with torment, his emotions a chaotic storm. The medical bay lights suddenly blazed with an almost supernova intensity. Holmes shielded his eyes, wincing against the painful brightness. Just as quickly, the room plunged into darkness so black it seemed to swallow all light and sound. Holmes froze, the oppressive darkness amplifying the pounding of his heart. He heard a low, menacing growl—a sound so primal it sent a shudder through his entire body.

An overhead light above Holmes's work desk exploded with a sharp crack. The doctor let out a small scream, his voice a high, fearful note in the suffocating darkness. Shards of glass rained down, and Holmes instinctively ducked, his mind racing with dread. The air was thick with tension, every breath a struggle as he waited, terrified of what might come next.

Gresham's internal struggle mirrored the chaos around him. Sharing his essence with Mara was an unspoken taboo among the FEW, a line that none dared cross. But the thought of losing her, of living in a world without her light, was a torment he couldn't bear. The forbidden act loomed large, a desperate gamble that could cost him everything.

"I have no choice," Gresham replied, his voice a fierce whisper. "If there is even a chance to save her, I must take it. Nothing else matters."

The machine erupted in a cacophony of alarms and sparks, a metallic banshee wailing its death throes. Red lights strobed like a demonic heartbeat, casting grotesque shadows that danced a macabre ballet across the walls. The acrid tang of burning wires choked the air. Holmes's face was a mask of terror as he looked at Gresham. What if they couldn't save her? What would Lord Gresham do then?

Gresham, his own fear a cold fist in his gut, met Holmes's gaze. Relief, etched starkly on Holmes's face, battled with a dawning horror. The room plunged into darkness, the only sound the steady rhythm of Mara's breaths, a fragile testament to their precarious success. Gresham held her close, his heart a frantic drum against his ribs. He had saved her. But at what cost? The answer became horrifyingly clear as a wave of nausea washed over him. His life force felt thin, a flickering ember compared to the inferno it once was.

Holmes drew a shaky breath, the fear slowly receding but never fully dissipating. He knew that Gresham's decision had saved Mara, but the price paid was steep, and the consequences of this forbidden act would ripple through their lives. The doctor watched in silence as Gresham, now visibly weakened, held Mara close, the weight of his choice pressing heavily on his shoulders.

The room, once a haven of medical precision, now felt like a battlefield, the aftermath of a desperate, forbidden act hanging in the air. As the lights flickered back to normal, Holmes couldn't shake the feeling that they had crossed a line, one that could never be uncrossed. The future was uncertain, and the path ahead was fraught with peril, but for now, Mara was safe, and that was enough.

Gresham, his heart heavy with the burden of his choice, whispered a silent vow. He would protect Mara, no matter the cost, and face the consequences of his actions with unwavering resolve. The bond between them, forged in love and desperation, would guide them through the darkness, lighting the way toward whatever fate awaited them.

The forbidden knowledge burned in his veins, a searing reminder of his transgression. But a new understanding dawned as his gaze met Mara's, filled with a love that mirrored his own. This wasn't just about saving her. It was about saving himself. He hadn't defied the code out of rebellion but out of a love so fierce it had broken the chains of his existence.

In that crucible, a humanity he never knew he possessed had been forged. He squeezed Mara's hand with a newfound resolve that burned brighter than the dying embers of his life force. The consequences be damned. He had made his choice. He would face the future, hand in hand with the woman he loved, a changed man.

He emerged from the sterile cocoon of the medical bay, reborn. The sterile air felt electric, charged with the weight of his decision. The stark white walls seemed to recoil from him, a silent judgment. But Gresham no longer cared about their judgment. He had traded the cold comfort of blind obedience for the messy warmth of love. The shackles of the FEW were gone, replaced by the fierce determination to carve his own path.

He cast a final glance at Mara, the faint echo of his life force a luminous halo around her. A bittersweet smile touched his lips. He had paid the price, but the uncertain future stretched before him, an untamed canvas waiting for his brush. He stepped into the corridor, the harsh light contrasting with the crucible he had endured. The shadows no longer held fear but mirrored the steely resolve in his eyes. He was a new man forged in defiance, and the world must learn to deal with him.

Gresham held her, feeling the faint thrum of her heartbeat against his own. The final image of the two of them, entwined in a moment of fragile unity, spoke to the deep, unspoken love that had endured through years of separation. It was a powerful and poignant tableau, imbued with the sensory details that grounded the moment in reality: the softness of her hair, the warmth of her breath, and the steady, rhythmic pulse of life that beat within her.

The low hum of the ship thrummed through Levi's boots like a portentous drumbeat. He approached the Ready Room, its bronze door a cold barrier between him and the unknown. Inside, the air crackled with tension, the silence heavy with the weight of decisions that had shaped galaxies. This was where fate danced on the edge of a blade, where lives hung like precarious threads. He adjusted his uniform, a tremor of disquiet gnawing at his stoic facade. Gresham awaited him within.

Levi pushed open the door, anticipation coiling in his gut. The stale air, thick with ozone and the musty scent of ancient scrolls, did little to ease his apprehension. Gresham stood opposite, his usually granite-like visage etched with worry. Lines deepened around his eyes, his gaze a stormy sea holding secrets Levi couldn't fathom. The room, once alive with strategic chatter, felt like a tomb, the silence a suffocating shroud.

"Commander," Gresham's voice, usually a booming command, emerged tired joy. "We have a newcomer aboard. A FEW has arrived."

Levi's eyebrows shot up like startled birds. "A FEW, sir? On our ship? That's…" His voice trailed off, the sheer absurdity of the statement hanging heavy in the air.

Gresham's jaw clenched, his gaze unwavering. "Indeed. And she will receive the same respect and accommodation as I. Ensure her arrival is flawless, her comfort absolute."

Gresham's gaze softened, a flicker of vulnerability betraying his usual stoicism. "Indeed," he said, his voice dropping to a low murmur. "But this isn't just about history, Levi. It's about redemption."

Levi's eyes narrowed, searching for the hidden meaning in his Lord's words. He knew Gresham's past, the agonizing hunt for a lost love, the whispers that painted him as obsessed, even reckless. Could this newcomer be…? A mix of curiosity and dread tightened Levi's chest, the weight of Gresham's suffering echoing in his mind. It was a torment he had witnessed, a relentless shadow that haunted every decision.

Gresham sighed, the weight of the universe seeming to settle on his shoulders. "She is Mara, Levi. My Mara. Returned."

A wave of shock washed over Levi, displacing the unease with a surge of unexpected understanding. He had witnessed his Lord's torment firsthand, the way it shadowed his every decision. Now, the pieces clicked into place.

"She's alive?" Levi managed his voice thick with emotion.

Gresham's lips curved into a ghost of a smile, bittersweet and tinged with pain. "Alive, yes. But changed. The cost of her return will be high, Levi. But for her, I would pay any price."

A silent oath formed in Levi's heart. He wouldn't just ensure a smooth integration; he would protect this fragile hope, this second chance, with the fierce loyalty of a friend who had seen his Lord's soul laid bare. The arrival of Mara wasn't just a harbinger of change; it was a chance at healing, a chance to rewrite history, not with regret, but with the fierce love that transcended even the boundaries of the FEW doctrine.

Leaving the Ready Room, Levi let the bronze door close with a finality that echoed in his hollow chest. The fluorescent lights hummed their sterile symphony, mocking the turmoil within him. His mission wasn't just another bureaucratic knot to untangle; it was a monumental task that threatened to reshape their existence. The whispers would start first, tendrils of fear and disbelief snaking through the crew like silent vipers. He could almost hear them already, laced with the acrid tang of rebellion.

He adjusted his uniform; the starched fabric suddenly felt scratchy against his skin. Fear flickered, a viper itself, but he strangled it in its cradle. Change was a tempest, yes, but he was the ship's anchor, its unyielding rudder. He wouldn't just weather the storm; he would ride it like a wave, cresting above the chaos to carve their path through the uncharted sea. They would write their names not in ink but in stardust, a testament to their unwavering courage in the face of the inconceivable.

Levi's stride echoed down the metal corridor, each step a drumbeat of defiance. He wouldn't just ensure a smooth integration; he would be the bridge, the translator between two worlds on the brink of collision. Their history, the rigid code etched in their very being, was about to face its greatest test. And while the consequences may be catastrophic, the potential for redemption, for healing, for a love that defied even the stars themselves burned brighter than any fear.

The ship hummed beneath his feet, a living entity resonating with his own determination. They were on the precipice of something monumental, and Levi, the stalwart commander, the loyal friend, the man who had seen the storm in Gresham's eyes, would not falter. The revolution was upon them, and he, with his head held high and his heart ablaze, would lead them into the unknown.

Gresham gripped the armrests of his command chair, the cool metal biting into his palms. The hum of the ship's engines vibrated beneath him, a constant reminder of the seismic shift he had set in motion. He had brought Mara back and defied the FEW doctrine, and now, the weight of that decision pressed down on him with the crushing force of a collapsing star. The air in the room felt heavy and cool, a stark contrast to the storm brewing inside him.

Doubt gnawed at him, a viper coiling in his gut. What if the rumors were true? What if the missing FEW, who vanished decades ago, were connected to his actions? Had he unwittingly unleashed a dormant threat by bringing Mara aboard? The thought sent a tremor through him, the silence of the unknown echoing in his mind.

His gaze flickered to Levi, who stood at the bridge console with military precision, his posture a testament to his unwavering loyalty. Levi's calm demeanor and quiet contemplation were palpable; he responded to Gresham's unspoken concerns with a reassuring nod, his eyes reflecting a shared burden. The weight of the doctrine and the fear of the unknown were burdens Levi bore alongside him, though his expression remained unreadable.

The announcement crackled through the ship, Levi's voice calm and collected as he informed the crew of their newest passenger. The silence that followed was deafening, pregnant with anticipation and unease. The arrival of one FEW was unheard of, but two? It was a paradigm shift that shook the very foundations of their galaxy-faring existence.

Gresham braced himself for the storm. He knew whispers would ripple through the corridors, laced with fear, confusion, and perhaps even a spark of rebellion. He had become a figure of controversy, his actions challenging the very fabric of their society.

But amidst the storm, a flicker of hope remained. Mara. Her presence, a radiant beacon in the cold void of space, offered a glimpse of redemption, a chance to mend the broken pieces of his past. Yet, he couldn't ignore the potential consequences. What would the Galactic Alliance say the governing body that had entrusted him with such power? Would they see his actions as a transgression, a betrayal of everything they stood for?

In the mess hall, the murmur of speculation rippled like a tremor traveling through the ship's metal bones. Lieutenant Aiko, her brow furrowed in concern, glanced around at her fellow crew members. Whispers of "unprecedented," "unease," and "cultural clash" danced in the air, punctuated by worried glances at the briefing room door.

Suddenly, the door opened, and Commander Levi emerged. His face betrayed a flicker of concern beneath his usual stoicism. He cleared his throat, the metallic echo momentarily silencing the room.

"Crew," his voice cut through the tension. "As you may have heard, we have a unique situation on board. As of today, we'll be hosting a member of the FEW, a guest of Lord Gresham."

A collective wave of stunned silence washed over the room. Aiko felt a knot of apprehension tighten in her stomach. She'd heard rumors of the FEW, these enigmatic beings with seemingly superhuman abilities. The stories ranged from awe-inspiring to unsettling, and the prospect of having one onboard filled her with curiosity and fear.

Levi continued his voice steady despite the palpable tension. "This is uncharted territory for all of us, and I understand your concerns. However, Lord Gresham has assured me that this individual poses no threat. Our mission remains unchanged, and our top priority is to ensure a smooth integration and maintain a respectful and professional environment. We will hold further information sessions to address your questions or concerns."

Aiko exchanged a hesitant glance with the crewmate beside her. While relief washed over her at the assurance of no immediate danger, the uncertainty of this new situation lingered. The arrival of a FEW felt like a seismic shift in the established order, and she couldn't help but wonder what repercussions it might have.

In the calm sanctuary of Gresham's private quarters, the air crackled with a tension thicker than the nebula dust clinging to his boots. Five years. A chasm of five heart-wrenching years had carved canyons in both their faces, etched by the relentless erosion of loneliness and a yearning so profound it mirrored the vastness of space itself.

Mara stood there, bathed in the soft glow of the viewport, her crimson uniform a stark reminder of the warrior she once was. Now, the fabric held the ghosts of battles fought and battles lost whispers of her struggle to survive without him. As she turned, her breath hitched in her throat.

Gresham stood before her, cloaked in the same crimson that spoke of their shared past. Time had chiseled lines into his face, but they only amplified the raw hunger in his eyes—a hunger mirrored in hers. The silence stretched, a living entity humming with unspoken words, a lifetime of longing condensed into a single breath.

"Mara," his voice emerged, a mere whisper choked with emotion yet imbued with the weight of a thousand unspoken words.

He moved then, a slow, deliberate approach that spoke volumes. His embrace, when it came, was like a supernova collapsing in on itself, their combined love and pain compressing into a singularity of pure emotion. The crimson of his cape swirled around them, a vibrant counterpoint to the desolate expanse of space visible through the window.

As they held each other, the years of separation dissolved, the fear and loneliness replaced by the searing heat of their reunion. In that moment, they were two halves reforged into a whole, two souls woven back together by the unyielding tapestry of love and destiny.

Nestled in the scent of old battles and familiar comfort, Mara found a fragile haven in Gresham's arms. The rhythm of his breath, a calming cadence against her ear, slowly chipped away at the tension like water against stone. She leaned into him, allowing the tremors in his embrace to echo in her own being, a shared vulnerability that transcended years of separation.

Gresham's hand, calloused and strong, cupped her cheek, his thumb tracing the contours of her face as if memorizing its every detail. Each touch sent shivers down her spine, a language far more eloquent than words. Their eyes met, drowning in a sea of emotions—longing, relief, and a spark of unspoken questions.

Gresham leaned closer, his breath warm against her lips. "Mara," he whispered, his voice thick with emotion, "have I brought you home?"

The question hung heavy in the air, echoing not just their physical journey but the journey of their hearts. Tears welled in Mara's eyes, shimmering like stars on the brink of falling. At that moment, she closed her eyes, not needing words to answer. She simply tilted her head and met his kiss, their lips weaving a new chapter in the timeless tapestry of their love.

The kiss was a storm, a whirlwind of emotions swirling within them—relief, joy, and a simmering ember of passion that threatened to consume them both. It spoke of a love that had weathered time and distance, a love that had defied the odds and brought them back together.

As they finally broke apart, gasping for breath, their foreheads resting against each other, Gresham whispered, "Mara, my love, we'll face whatever comes next together."

His words, laced with fierce protectiveness and unwavering love, were the promise she needed to hear. In that moment, the uncertainty of the future faded, replaced by the certainty of their bond, a bond forged in hardship and strengthened by love. They would face the challenges ahead side by side; their crimson cloaks were a symbol of their shared past and the unwavering future they would build together.

Raising her gaze, she met his eyes, tracing the lines etched deeper across his weathered face, each furrow a testament to stories yet untold. His gaze held a question, unspoken yet palpable: would she don the mantle once more and embrace the life it symbolized?

A flicker of unease danced in her eyes, quickly masked by a resolute glint. Her own question hung heavy in the air, unspoken yet shared: would he accept the woman she had become, the path she might choose? The crimson fabric, a shared legacy, whispered of battles fought and futures forged. In that shared silence, beneath the weight of unspoken questions and boundless possibilities, their reunion lay suspended; a single note was echoing in the vast silence of space—a harmony, once lost, slowly finding its way back.

Breaking the embrace, Gresham gently took her hands in his. "It's been kept for you," he said softly, holding the uniform in front of him, offering her a choice.

Mara reached out, her fingers brushing the familiar fabric. The FEW uniform was all black, with no pockets or decoration. The emblem of THE FEW glowed on the left pocket, a symbol of their legendary status as protectors and champions of peace. The cape was a rich, deep crimson, mirroring the wearer's emotional state. It writhed, snapped, billowed, grew taut, and blew when there was no wind.

As she touched it, the fabric felt familiar, its touch a warm welcome home. It wasn't just an article of clothing; it was a bridge, a link between the woman she was and the woman she had become. This harmony wasn't just a return to an old melody. It was a new composition, born from the ashes of separation and the crucible of self-discovery.

"The anger is gone," she said, her voice soft yet firm. It wasn't an apology but an acknowledgment of the past. "In embracing this, I finally feel whole."

Gresham felt a wave of peace washes over him as if two celestial bodies, once locked in a chaotic dance, had finally found their rightful orbit, bound by an undeniable gravitational pull. The immensity of their choices settled upon them, their love reborn, stronger for the scars etched by separation and tempered by the trials they had endured. It wasn't just a personal moment but a turning point, a pivot for them and the universe they navigated. In that shared understanding, their love, once shattered, rekindled, forged anew in the crucible of their trials. It burned brighter than ever before, a testament to their resilience and the unyielding power of their connection.

Their eyes met a silent dialogue passing between them. The future stretched before them, vast and unknown, but they faced it together, two halves finally united, their love a fulcrum upon which not just their own destinies but the fate of countless beings might precariously balance.

A smile played on Gresham's lips, mirroring the newfound serenity in hers. "Then let us face it," he said, his voice steady and strong, "together."

As their hands intertwined, their crimson cloaks fluttered in unison, a silent promise woven into the fabric of their lives. The harmony, once lost, had not just found its way back; it had evolved into a testament to the enduring power of love, the resilience of the spirit, and the transformative beauty of second chances.

In that embrace, they found their private universe, where love reigned supreme.

10

EMBRACE OF SHADOWS

Commander Levi stood at the center of the bridge, his presence commanding yet reassuring. He activated the ship-wide comms, his voice resonating through every corridor and compartment of the Requiem.

"Crew of the Requiem," he began, his voice calm and authoritative. "Today, we are honored by the presence of Lady Mara, a fellow FEW and a legend in her own right. Her presence here is a testament to the gravity of our mission and the trust she places in us."

Levi paused, his green eyes sparkling with rare warmth as he made eye contact with each crew member. "Seeing two FEW together is a sight many go their entire lives without witnessing. Let this serve as an inspiration. With Lady Mara's invaluable intel and our combined strength, we will finally bring an end to the Fair Trade's reign of chaos."

His voice grew more fervent, charged with conviction. "Each of you plays a crucial role in this mission. Your skills, dedication, and bravery will make the difference between victory and defeat. Remember, we are more than just a crew; we are a family, bound by our shared commitment to justice and our unwavering loyalty to each other."

He took a deep breath, his gaze steady and intense. "Trust in yourselves, trust in each other, and trust in the leadership of myself, Lady Mara, and Lord Gresham. Together, we will face unimaginable dangers with courage and resolve. The Fair Trade may hide in the shadows, but we are the light that will expose their darkness."

Turning to Mara, he added, "Lady Mara, your presence here is a great honor. Together, we will face this challenge and emerge victorious."

Mara inclined her head, a hint of warmth in her eyes. "The honor is mine, Commander Levi. Your crew's reputation precedes them. I have no doubt that together, we will succeed."

The crew cheered and applauded as Gresham and Mara moved to the central console. Seeing their leader standing alongside another legendary FEW filled them with a sense of invincibility. They turned to their stations with renewed energy, ready to face the challenges ahead.

Levi, watching the scene with quiet approval, leaned in towards Gresham. "Well handled, my Lord," he murmured. "Your words have turned their awe into determination. They would follow you to the ends of the universe."

Gresham clasped Levi's shoulder, a gesture of appreciation and camaraderie. "And I would lead them there, my friend. But today, we head for the Orion Nebula. Let's bring an end to this chase."

A flicker of doubt crossed Mara's eyes as she scanned the holographic displays. She quickly masked it, her violet eyes sharp as a glowing soft blue blade. The crew exchanged glances, a silent vow to succeed passing among them.

The Requiem's engines roared to life, propelling the ship toward its target. The rhythmic hum grew louder, the metallic tang in the air sharpening with the promise of impending action. The faint flicker of red lights on the consoles reflected the rising tension, each pulse a reminder of the stakes at hand.

As the ship plunged into the Orion Nebula's swirling embrace, the world outside dissolved into an inky void, punctuated only by the ship's rhythmic groan, a metallic heartbeat in the cosmic silence. The acrid smell of burnt wires from the recent skirmish lingered, mixing with the ever-present scent of recycled air. Mara's violet eyes scanned the holographic projections; her brow furrowed in concentration. Weeks of chasing whispers and shadows, and finally, a beacon of confirmation: a sleek, angular silhouette nestled amidst the swirling tendrils of nebular gas.

"There!" her voice sliced through the tense silence, a sonic blade cleaving the air. "The Black Talon's freighter. Looks like our prey can finally shed its shadows."

Gresham, a predator's hunger flickering in his gaze, mirrored her movements. His hand blurred across a console, unleashing a cascade of holographic displays. Weapon schematics, tactical data, and a chillingly detailed rendering of the target vessel pulsed with ominous light. "Tractor beam online," he announced, his voice a low rumble in the hushed bridge. "Disabling pulse prepped. Remember, Mara, these Corsairs are known for volatile cargo. Minimum force, maximum efficiency."

A collective breath, sharp and shallow, hung heavy in the air. Jenkins, the young navigator, swallowed hard, his hands trembling as he gripped the controls. Beside him, Lieutenant Harper's jaw tightened, her eyes narrowing with steely determination. Crew members, their faces ghostly reflections on the holographic displays, worked with the silent urgency of ballet dancers navigating a minefield. Fingers danced across consoles, calibrating weapons and analyzing defenses. The air crackled with anticipation, the knowledge that this could be the culmination of their chase or a descent into the maw of chaos, thick and suffocating.

Suddenly, an alarm ripped through the silence, scarlet lights strobing across the bridge like a dying star's final convulsions. "Commander!" the helmsman barked, his voice taut with alarm. "Incoming transmission! Scrambled but powerful!"

A collective gasp, a wave of unease, washed over the bridge. Scrambled transmissions in the nebula were rare, usually echoes of lost ships or desperate pleas for help. What message could be waiting for them on the precipice of confrontation?

Gresham and Mara locked eyes, a silent question hanging between them like a neutron star, heavy and unspoken. Engage? Risk revealing their hand? Or stick to the plan, shadows in the cosmic ballet? The fate of their mission, perhaps even their lives, hung in the balance.

"Patch it through," Levi commanded, his voice firm despite the knot of unease twisting his gut. The bridge held its breath as the scrambled message resolved, filling the space with a cacophony of static. But amidst the noise, a single word, clear and urgent, pierced through:

"RUN!"

Just as the Requiem's tractor beam locked on, a blinding flare erupted from the enemy ship, engulfing the bridge in an inferno of white-hot light. Gresham threw his arm across his face, cursing under his breath. The ship lurched violently, alarms screaming their siren song of danger. Once a silent witness, the nebula roared to life, tendrils of gas swirling and twisting in a macabre ballet of chaos.

The freighter, veiled in the blinding glare, vanished. Had they escaped? Or was this just the calm before the storm? In the heart of the Orion Nebula, where secrets danced with shadows, the hunt had taken an unexpected turn, and the line between predator and prey had blurred beyond recognition.

Mara's fingers danced across the console, desperation etching lines on her brow as she tried to regain control of the sensors. The photon burst had left them blind, reeling from its searing brilliance. The metallic tang of ozone clung to their tongues, a grim reminder of the enemy's trickery.

Gresham threw his arm across his face, shielding his eyes from the lingering afterimages. His vision swam, swirling with fiery ghosts of the explosion. A guttural curse ripped from his throat, echoing off the metal walls of the bridge. The taste of ash lingered on his tongue, mirroring the bitter ashes of defeat burning in his gut.

"Photon burst!" Mara's voice cut through the chaos, laced with urgency. "They've masked their escape vector!"

The bridge descended into pandemonium. Alarms shrieked like banshees, scarlet lights strobed like a dying star, and frantic shouts filled the air. Crew members stumbled, hands flying across consoles, desperately trying to assess the damage and regain control. The Requiem, once a proud predator, now wallowed wounded, its metallic hide scorched and smoking.

"Status report!" Levi barked, his voice cutting through the chaos like a blade. "I need updates now!"

"Tractor beam offline!" Jenkins called out, his voice shaky. "Sensors blinded! We can't track them!"

"Life support failing!" Harper shouted, her hands flying over her console. "We've got twenty minutes of oxygen left!"

"All hands focus!" Levi's voice was a steady anchor amidst the storm. "Harper, reroute auxiliary power to life support. Jenkins, get those sensors back online. Blake, scramble our comms and prepare a counter-pulse."

Crew members scrambled at their stations, their movements frantic and uncoordinated. Jenkins, the young navigator, clutched the controls, his knuckles white with fear. His eyes darted from his console to the viewports, wide and glassy, reflecting the chaos around him. Lieutenant Harper shouted orders, her voice rising above the din, but her commands were lost in the cacophony of alarms and panicked voices.

Static crackled through the comms, punctuated by the occasional sharp burst of electricity from overloaded circuits. Sparks flew from a damaged control panel, showering the deck with bright, brief flares. A technician stumbled back, shielding their face from the sizzling spray, their eyes wide with terror.

Among the chaos stood Sergeant Rowan, a seasoned veteran with grizzled hair and a steely demeanor. He had weathered countless storms in the void, his experience etched into the lines of his weathered face. While others faltered, Rowan's movements were precise and measured. He quickly assessed the situation, his eyes scanning the consoles with practiced ease.

"The conduit's fried; reroute auxiliary power!" he barked, his voice a steady anchor amidst the tempest. He moved to assist a panicking crew member, his hands deftly manipulating the controls. "Stay focused, Jenkins. We've been through worse."

Jenkins swallowed hard, trying to steady his trembling hands. He glanced at Rowan, drawing strength from the veteran's calm. "Aye, Sergeant," he managed, his voice shaking but resolute.

The failing life support systems took their toll. The air grew thin, each breath a labored effort. In the medical bay, scarlet lights flashed incessantly, casting an eerie glow over the sterile environment. Dr.

Harris, the chief medical officer, moved swiftly among the patients, his face grim. He reached for an oxygen mask, placing it over the face of a gasping crew member whose eyes pleaded for relief.

"Hang in there," Dr. Harris murmured, his voice a mix of reassurance and urgency. "We're working on it."

Back on the bridge, the ship's engines groaned, a deep, resonant sound that reverberated through the hull. The floor vibrated underfoot, adding to the disorienting sense of impending doom. Crew members clung to their stations, their faces etched with a mix of fear and grim determination.

"Shields are down! Life support failing!" a voice called out, barely audible over the blaring alarms. The words sent a ripple of horror through the bridge, palpable even amidst the chaos.

Suddenly, a new alarm blared, its tone even more urgent. "Commander, incoming enemy fleet!" the tactical officer shouted, his face drained of color. "They're closing in fast!"

Through the viewport, menacing silhouettes of enemy ships loomed against the swirling nebula, their sleek forms outlined by the ghostly light. A collective gasp echoed through the bridge, followed by a surge of adrenaline. The hull trembled under the impact of enemy fire; each hit sent a shudder through the entire ship. Panels sparked, and the deck plates vibrated, threatening to buckle under the stress.

"Brace for impact!" Levi's voice thundered, commanding attention. "Harper, get those shields up! Rowan, prepare damage control teams. Everyone, hold your stations!"

Jenkins felt his heart race, the pounding in his chest matching the frantic pace of his thoughts. This was his first real battle, and the weight of it pressed down on him like a physical force. He glanced around, seeing the determination etched into the faces of his crewmates. He knew he had to rise to the occasion, but the fear was suffocating.

Sergeant Rowan's steady voice cut through his panic. "Jenkins, focus. Remember your training. We need you sharp."

Jenkins nodded, swallowing his fear. "Yes, Sergeant. I'm with you."

A sudden explosion rocked the bridge, and a nearby console erupted in flames. Ensign Tyler was thrown back by the blast, his scream piercing through the noise. The crew reacted instantly. Rowan rushed to his side, pulling him to safety as sparks rained down. Lieutenant Harper knelt beside them, her voice steady despite the chaos. "Tyler, stay with us. Medics are on their way."

Tyler groaned, clutching his side, his face pale. "It hurts," he gasped, eyes wide with pain.

"We've got you," Rowan assured him, his voice firm yet compassionate. "Hold on."

Jenkins watched, his fear momentarily replaced by concern for his comrade. "Hang in there, Tyler," he called out, his voice shaking with emotion. Nearby, the tactical officer clenched his fists, his face a mask of determination as he tried to maintain focus on his duties.

Within moments, the medical team arrived. Dr. Harris led the way, his movements swift and sure. "Get him on the stretcher," he ordered, his tone leaving no room for hesitation. The medics moved with practiced efficiency, lifting Tyler gently but quickly. Harris assessed the injury, his hands moving expertly over the burns and wounds.

"We need to get him to the med bay now!" Harris barked as the medics secured Tyler on the stretcher and began their hurried journey through the trembling ship.

In the medical bay, the scarlet lights flashed incessantly, casting an eerie glow over the sterile environment. Dr. Harris, the chief medical officer, moved swiftly among the patients, his face grim. He reached for an oxygen mask, placing it over Tyler's face, whose eyes pleaded for relief.

"Hang in there," Dr. Harris murmured, his voice a mix of reassurance and urgency. "We're working on it."

Beside him, Nurse Patel prepped an IV, her hands steady despite the ship's violent tremors. "Intravenous fluids are ready," she said, handing the line to Harris, who swiftly inserted it into Tyler's arm.

The medics worked seamlessly around Tyler, their faces masks of concentration. "Let's get those burns cleaned and dressed," Harris instructed. "We need to stabilize him before we can address the internal injuries."

Tyler's breathing was ragged, but his eyes remained focused on Dr. Harris. "Am I going to make it, Doc?" he asked, his voice weak.

Harris met his gaze, his expression resolute. "We're doing everything we can, Tyler. Just hold on a little longer."

Back on the bridge, Commander Levi stood at the center of the storm, his presence a solitary island of calm. He surveyed the scene with a steely gaze, his mind racing to find a solution. Beside him, Blake's hands flew over his console, trying to stabilize the systems, sweat dripping down his brow.

"Hold your stations!" Lieutenant Harper's voice cut through the panic, fierce and unwavering. "We can do this!"

In the ready room, Levi turned to the assembled team, his eyes hard. "Options," he barked.

Dr. Harris spoke first. "We need to stabilize life support. We can reroute power from non-essential systems, but it will buy us only a few extra minutes unless we get the shields back online."

Lieutenant Commander Viktor, a burly engineer with a reputation for miracles, nodded. "Agreed. The main conduit is fried. We can attempt a manual bypass, but it's a risky operation. We need time and precision."

Blake, the systems and communications officer, his face pale but determined, added, "We can try to send a distress signal, but in the nebula, it's a long shot. Our best bet is to fix the systems ourselves."

A sudden, violent tremor rocked the ship, throwing everyone off balance. A panel exploded, showering the room with sparks. For a brief, harrowing moment, it seemed as if all hope was lost. The room fell silent, save for the distant sounds of the ship's struggles.

Gresham leaned forward, his gaze intense. "We don't have time for long shots. Mara, you and I will assist Viktor with the bypass. Levi, coordinate with the rest of the crew to manage the power distribution and keep us steady."

Levi nodded, his expression resolute. "Understood. Move out, everyone. We're not dying in this nebula."

Back on the bridge, the atmosphere was electric with urgency. Crew members moved with purpose, their fear now channeled into focused determination. Mara and Gresham followed Viktor to the engineering bay, where the damaged conduit lay sparking and smoking.

"Careful," Viktor warned. "One wrong move, and we could blow the whole system."

Mara's hands moved with practiced precision, her mind a whirlwind of calculations. She grabbed a plasma torch, cutting through the damaged sections with surgical accuracy. Gresham worked beside her, using a diagnostic scanner to pinpoint the most critical areas for repair. Their synergy was unspoken but palpable. Viktor coordinated their efforts, rerouting power and stabilizing the damaged systems.

"Blake, we need that power diverted now!" Viktor's voice crackled over the comm.

"On it!" Blake's voice came back, strained but resolute. "Diverting power from the secondary thrusters. You should have it in ten seconds."

The ship shuddered as enemy fire grazed the hull, the vibrations adding another layer of urgency. In the medical bay, Dr. Harris worked feverishly, stabilizing the most critical patients while the room filled with the harsh, rhythmic beeping of life support monitors.

"Time's running out," Gresham muttered, sweat beading on his forehead. "Come on, come on..."

In the engineering bay, the final connection sparked, and the conduit hummed to life. "We've got it!" Viktor shouted, relief flooding his voice. "Shields are coming online."

Mara and Gresham exchanged a look, a mix of exhaustion and triumph. "Let's get back to the bridge," Gresham said, his voice steady. "We're not out of this yet."

On the bridge, the atmosphere shifted as the shields flickered back to life. The crew's collective breath released a wave of relief. "Shields at fifty percent and climbing," Blake reported. "Life support stabilizing."

Levi's voice carried through the ship. "Well done, everyone. Now, let's find that freighter and finish this."

As the ship surged forward, Mara stood beside Gresham, the rhythmic hum of the engines growing louder. The metallic tang of anticipation filled the air, signifying the shift to a more aggressive plan. Her gaze locked onto the holographic display, where the outline of the Black Talon's freighter loomed large. The ship was sleek and angular, a predatory silhouette against the swirling nebula, its hull bristling with concealed weaponry and illicit cargo holds.

"Intercepted a transmission," Blake announced. "It's heavily encrypted, but I'm breaking through."

The bridge fell silent as the message played through the speakers. A distorted voice spoke, "To the crew of the Requiem, you are closer to the truth than you realize. The Fair Trade is just a pawn. Beware the true enemy."

Levi's eyes narrowed. "Who sent this?"

Blake shook his head. "Unknown source. It's bouncing through multiple relays. Whoever it is, they don't want to be found."

Mara exchanged a look with Gresham, their determination renewed. "We need to find out who's behind this," she said.

The crew stared at the mysterious message, the realization of a larger conspiracy dawning on them.

Levi's presence was felt throughout the ship as he coordinated the crew's efforts, maintaining control and focus amidst the chaos. His green eyes, sparkling with warmth and happiness at Mara's return, reflected his deep sense of duty and commitment to leading his crew through the challenges ahead.

11

THE HIDDEN ARBOR

Mara's footfalls, whispers barely audible over the ship's hum, sent ripples through the metallic labyrinth. The crew, caught in her wake, held their breath. Some bowed their heads; others met her eyes with a mixture of awe and fear. Her presence, an intangible aura shimmering like moonlight, seemed to bend the ship's fabric.

Yet amidst the tension, she felt an invisible tug pulling her towards a hidden sanctuary—an arbor, a splash of vibrant green amidst the cold, sterile machinery. This place wasn't just a refuge; it symbolized her quest to balance her cosmic duties with her yearning for a more grounded, human connection. The emerald leaves brushed against her skin, releasing an intoxicating aroma of rain-soaked soil and sun-warmed forests, scents of life from a world far removed from their metal shell. Here, bathed in nature's embrace, she was simply Mara, adrift in a sea of green.

The solace was fleeting. She knew this hidden space held secrets, perhaps answers to her internal struggle and the path ahead. Her gaze fell upon a half-hidden inscription etched on a nearby vine, sparking curiosity. This could be the key she'd been searching for, the bridge between her two worlds.

Suddenly, the click of a hidden hatch sent a jolt through her. Her breath hitched, then calmed as Gresham emerged from the verdant curtain of the entrance. Even in the dim light, she saw the familiar set of his shoulders, broad and relaxed, hands clasped loosely behind his back.

"I sensed I'd find you here," he murmured, stepping fully into the arbor. His voice held a familiar cadence, a blend of reverence and something deeper, more intimate. His presence here wasn't just for solace; he sought a deeper connection, a chance to discuss their mission within the serenity of nature. Her gaze drifted to his hand, and a flicker of a shared memory played across his features. "Lost in contemplation, or finding solace in the whispers of nature?"

A hint of a smile played on Mara's lips. "A bit of both, I suppose." She gestured to the mossy root beside her. "Care to join me?"

He didn't hesitate, settling down with a grace born of shared experiences and unspoken understanding. The air thrummed with a silent question, hanging between them like the scent of old earth. What brought him here, to this hidden haven? And what did their reunion, amidst the verdant embrace of the arbor, portend for the challenges that lay ahead?

Mara looked up, her eyes meeting his. For a fleeting moment, no words were necessary. Their mutual understanding hung in the air, delicate yet durable as a spider's web. But beneath the surface, emotions swirled in a silent storm.

His usually guarded eyes were now etched with remorse, pleading for understanding. A shadow flickered across his face, a memory they both shared: the searing heat of battle, the desperate farewell, and the unspoken promise etched in the dying light of a distant star.

Mara's heart ached with the unspoken. The weight of their shared history, the burden of unfulfilled promises, pressed down on them both. The air crackled with unspoken words, a storm brewing in the silent space between them.

He reached out, his hand hovering over hers, hesitant yet yearning. When it came, the touch was like a brushfire igniting a smoldering ember. It sent a jolt of electricity through her, a spark of the connection they had fought to deny for so long.

In that charged silence, the whispers of the arbor seemed to grow louder, urging them closer. Once comforting, the scent of jasmine and lavender now held a bittersweet longing. It was the fragrance of a past life, a life they could never reclaim yet yearned for nonetheless.

The tension between them was palpable, a tightly wound coil threatening to snap. Would they succumb to the pull of their shared past, jeopardizing their mission and their very destinies? Or would they find the strength to pull away, burying their emotions once more beneath the armor of duty?

The unspoken answer hung heavy in the air, as thick and fragrant as the scent of the arbor itself.

As Gresham's thumb grazed her jaw, a familiar scent of sunbaked soil and distant smoke swirled around them, pulling them back to a battlefield shrouded in the dying light of a crimson star. Their hands had clasped then, desperate and hopeful, a promise etched in the chaos. The memory flickered in Mara's eyes, an unspoken question.

He leaned closer, his breath warm against her cheek. "I saw you fall that day," he confessed, his voice rough with emotion. "Thought I'd lost you." His fingers tightened on her arm, a silent plea for understanding.

Time seemed to warp around them, the hum of the ship a distant echo. Could they afford to explore these emotions now, with the Fair Trade bearing down on them? Yet, the silence held its own urgency, pregnant with the unspoken confessions yearning to be released. Each inhales a shared heartbeat, and each exhales a whispered longing echoing in the stillness of the arbor.

Mara's gaze fell upon a delicate blue flower, its petals soft as velvet, glowing faintly in the dim light. She plucked it gently, twirling it between her fingers. "Blue Thalia," she murmured, her voice barely above a whisper. "A symbol of hope and resilience. Perhaps we need this reminder."

Gresham's eyes softened as he watched her. "Then let's carry it with us," he said, taking the flower from her and tucking it into a pocket of his uniform. "A reminder of what we're fighting for."

Suddenly, an alarm blared, shattering the fragile space they'd created. The enemy ship had locked onto its position. Reality slammed back, cold and unforgiving. The mission couldn't wait.

But as they pulled away, a spark of something new flickered between them, a silent promise whispered in the fading scent of memories. The hunt for the Fair Trade had become more than just a chase; it was a journey towards healing, understanding, and perhaps, a love rekindled under the verdant embrace of the hidden arbor.

Mara stared into Gresham's eyes, a stormy nebula of emotions swirling within them – a reflection of the tempest raging in her own heart. Her traitorous soul yearned for understanding, a connection that transcended their duty's cold, sterile boundaries. His gaze, as profound as the abyss between stars, seemed to echo the same yearning.

The air hummed with a silent question, its intensity rivaling the gravitational pull of a collapsing star: Would they dare navigate this uncharted nebula of emotions or retreat to the familiar, desolate orbit of silence? As their fingers brushed, a spark ignited—a silent promise flickering like a distant pulsar, igniting a supernova of hope within their hearts.

Mara's voice, barely a whisper lost in the verdant hush, trembled with unshed tears that blurred the vibrant tapestry of the arbor. Each leaf shimmered like a distant nebula, the earthy scent thick with the weight of her unspoken longing. Gresham cupped her face, his touch a stark contrast – warm and calloused, yet laced with a desperation that sent shivers down her spine. His thumb traced the familiar curve of her cheek, carving years of regret and unspoken words into the soft skin.

"Mara," he choked out, his voice raw with emotion, "all these years I've been adrift, an asteroid lost in the void, yearning for the gravity of your pull. Finding you again, it's like..." He paused, searching for the right words, his gaze locked on hers, his eyes reflecting the pain that mirrored her own. "It's like a black hole collapsing inward, devouring everything in its path, but instead of darkness, it ignites into a supernova fueled by the blinding brilliance of your presence."

Mara swallowed, the lump in her throat making each breath a Herculean effort. She wiped a tear that escaped with a shaky hand, tracing the path etched by his thumb. "But the galaxy is vast, Gresham," she whispered, her voice laced with the remnants of fear. "Our path ahead is littered with black holes and treacherous nebulas..."

He leaned in, his breath warm against her ear, his eyes burning with unshed tears and unspoken promises. "Together, Mara," he murmured, his voice a low tremor against her skin. "Together, we'll weave a new constellation, navigating the darkest corners of the cosmos hand in hand. And if we fall, we'll fall not into oblivion, but into a symphony of starlight, forever echoing the melody of our love."

As Mara traced the "Everlasting Flame" on Gresham's hand, a shared memory flickered in their minds. A battlefield bathed in the dying light of a distant sun, their hands clasped in a desperate farewell, the unspoken promise etched in the fading embers.

They stood in silence, the air thick with unspoken words, their eyes reflecting a constellation of emotions. His gaze, no longer haunted, held newfound warmth, a silent apology mirroring in its depths. Her touch, once hesitant, now lingered, a testament to a love hardened by loss yet tempered by forgiveness.

The scarlet anomaly pulsed on the map, a stark reminder of the challenges ahead. But as they turned to face it, their hands intertwined, a constellation of hope ignited within them. They were no longer two lone stars adrift in the cosmos. They were a supernova, fueled by the enduring flame of their love, ready to navigate the unknown together.

12

DARK STAR WHISPERS

The ship, now cloaked in the ethereal veil of the stealth drive, lurched forward with the suddenness of a predator in ambush. G-forces pinned Mara to her console, but her fingers danced across the control panel, weaving a counterpoint to the engine's roar. Starfields blurred into streaks of color around them, the void humming with anticipation.

Inside, the crew buzzed with nervous excitement. The helmsman, usually stoic, cracked a grin as he executed daring maneuvers, his voice smooth as he announced their approach with a theatrical flourish. "Attention all stations, prepare for a grand entrance! The Indomitable glides onto the scene, ready to steal the show and leave the Fair Trade speechless… well, after we capture them, that is." Laughter rippled through the bridge, a momentary release of tension before the curtain rose on the final act.

Ahead, the Fair Trade ships danced a macabre ballet through the asteroid field, sleek silhouettes flitting like vipers amongst spectral tombstones. Their pulsating shields, painted with mocking skulls and grinning jesters, winked in and out of view, taunting the Indomitable with each fleeting glimpse.

Gresham's voice, a steady counterpoint to the rising tension, barked orders. "Thermal lances primed and targeted. Await my mark." His weathered face, etched with the grim determination of a man at the precipice of a bar brawl, held a glint of predatory hunger.

Suddenly, the comms crackled, a voice dripping with faux-regality slicing through the din. "Unidentified vessel, this is Captain Rylan of the Fair Trade, Esquire! Identify yourselves or prepare to be boarded by my most… enthusiastic crewmates!"

Mara smirked, a piranha baring its teeth. "Let's show them some manners, Rylan," she purred, her voice laced with icy amusement. With a flick of her wrist, she activated a holographic projector, beaming a distorted image of a Fair Trade cruiser onto their hull. On the bridge, Gresham raised an eyebrow, a hint of a smile playing on his lips.

Chaos erupted on the enemy comms. "Hold your fire! It's one of ours!" Rylan's voice, usually dripping with practiced swagger, was laced with the panicked squeak of a cornered smuggler.

Exploiting the momentary confusion like a seasoned gambler, Gresham seized the opportunity. "Now!" he roared, his voice a thunderclap in the tense silence.

Mara unleashed a salvo of thermal lances disguised as friendly fire by the holographic illusion. The lances screamed through the asteroid field, carving fiery trails toward the unsuspecting Fair Trade ships. Panic erupted on their comms, a cacophony of colorful curses that would make a notorious gangster blush, orders barked in a desperate attempt to evade the unexpected attack.

One ship caught unaware, took a direct hit. Its shields, emblazoned with a cartoon pirate giving the finger flared briefly, failing to contain the searing heat. Metal screamed as the hull began to buckle, molten slag spewing into the void like a cosmic fireworks display. Another ship, realizing the ruse, jinked erratically, its engines spitting flames like a dragon on a sugar rush. But a second lance found its mark, crippling its maneuverability, leaving it spinning like a drunken comet.

But these weren't your average black market smugglers. They had panache, even in defeat. As their ships began to falter, the comms crackled again, this time with a distorted rendition of a pirate shanty, sung with gusto even as their vessels went down in flames. "Yo ho, yo ho, a pirate's life for me! Even if it ends with a thermal lance up the—"

The transmission cut out abruptly, leaving only the crackling silence of space and the slowly fading glow of the destroyed ships. Gresham and Mara exchanged a glance, a shared grin splitting their faces. This wasn't just a victory; it was a performance, a message sent to the wider Fair Trade: mess with the Indomitable and prepare to be both outmatched and outwitted, with a healthy dose of theatrics thrown in for good measure. The hunt was far from over, but for now, the stage belonged to them, and the applause, silent as it may be, echoed through the vast emptiness of space.

A heavy silence settled, thick with vulnerability. The Fair Trade had escaped once more; another piece skillfully slipped through their grasp. Mara, her hand resting on Gresham's, felt the tremor of frustration running through him, a barely contained storm waiting to erupt.

"Why?" she whispered, her voice echoing the question haunting them all. Why couldn't they land a decisive blow? Why did the Fair Trade always seem one step ahead, slipping through their fingers like smoke?

A shadow of suspicion, cold and unsettling, began to creep into their minds. The Fair Trade's escapes were too consistent, too well-timed to be mere luck. A whisper of a rigged board, unseen machinations pulling the strings from the darkness, started to take root. Was there a larger force at play, a hidden hand manipulating events to keep the outcome in their favor?

This wasn't just a game of cat and mouse anymore. This was a battle against unseen forces, a struggle for survival against an enemy who played by their own rules, an enemy who knew the board better than they did. The stakes had just been raised, and the game became a complex puzzle with deadly consequences. The hunt continued, but now, a new layer of danger had been woven into the chase, a chilling realization settling over them:

They weren't just chasing the Fair Trade. They were chasing the truth, which they suspected might be far more dangerous than they ever imagined.

This realization ignited a supernova within Gresham and Mara's resolve. They weren't chasing skirmishes anymore; they were chasing the ghost in the machine, the puppeteer pulling the strings. Their mission transcended individual battles; it became a crusade against a hidden empire, a rebellion against the unseen handwriting of their fate. The hunt wasn't just for justice; it was for the very freedom of the galaxy, a fight against an enemy who played by rules yet to be unraveled.

Reemerging from the cloak's ephemeral embrace, the Indomitable felt exposed, a lone Starfighter amidst a swarm of vipers. But fear was a luxury they couldn't afford. This wasn't a setback; it was a gauntlet thrown, an invitation to a dance macabre they couldn't decline. The game had shifted—the board tilted, the rules rewritten in blood and starlight.

Aboard the Starship Requiem, Commander Levi paced the tactical chamber, a caged panther prowling its territory. The holographic map sprawled before him, a knotted tapestry of danger and unease. Gresham and Mara were fighting their own battles, leaving him to strategize in the cold, calculating heart of the ship. Every furrow in his brow, every clenched fist spoke volumes of the unspoken dread gnawing at their collective core. This wasn't just another skirmish; it was the tremor before the earthquake, the whispered warning before the storm.

Levi adjusted the holographic controls, zooming in on a cluster of unidentified signatures lurking near the border territories, a known breeding ground for Fair Trade activities. His gut churned with icy apprehension—their movements held an eerie prescience like phantoms anticipating every Federation move.

"Sensors, status report!" his voice boomed, echoing in the tense silence.

Lieutenant Reyes, her steely gaze fixed on her console, responded without flinching. "Multiple ships detected, sir. Unknown class and origin. They appear to be... cloaked."

Levi's jaw tightened. "Maintain position and alert all stations. We need eyes on those ships and contingency plans in place. This is no ordinary skirmish. We're dealing with an enemy that knows our every move."

The word hung heavy in the air, a lead weight settling in Levi's stomach. Cloaking technology was rare, expensive, and often exclusive to those with deep pockets and even deeper secrets. The Fair Trade wasn't just smuggling anymore; they were playing a different game now, one with stakes far higher than stolen cargo.

"Activate the Quantum Scramblers," Levi ordered, his voice laced with steel. "We'll rip through their disguise like a supernova through the void."

The chamber hummed to life as the scramblers whirred, pushing the boundaries of known physics. The holographic map shimmered, distorted, and then realigned, revealing the hidden ships—a chilling tableau of sleek, predatory vessels frozen in mid-maneuver. They were cornered, claws bared, and fangs exposed.

"Lock onto all targets," Levi commanded, his gaze hardening. "Photon torpedoes, full yield. Fire at will."

Silence held its breath as the crew obeyed, fingers hovering over firing mechanisms. In the charged hush, everyone knew this wasn't just an engagement; it was a turning point. They were about to tear apart the veil, and what they might find on the other side was more terrifying than anything they could imagine. The battle was about to begin, and the stakes had never been higher. Did they have the audacity to challenge the unknown? Would they survive the answer? The tension crackled like static, and the reader, heart pounding, leaned in closer, desperate to know...

Levi's somber whisper, "Remember Aegea-7," hung heavy in the air, a cold specter haunting the tactical chamber. Each crew member shuddered, the memory of the Alliance's humiliating defeat raw and painful. A battle where the Fair Trade, cloaked in shadows and armed with seemingly precognitive tactics, had decimated their forces.

Lieutenant Reyes, her usually unflinching gaze laced with concern, met Levi's hardened stare. "Sensors, report!" His voice crackled with urgency, the weight of countless lives resting on his every decision.

"Multiple ships detected, sir," she confirmed, her voice tight with a rising tide of adrenaline. "Signature readings... unlike anything we've encountered before. Advanced shielding, unknown design..." Her words trailed off, swallowed by the growing unease that gripped the room.

Aegea-7. The phantom of that battle echoed in Levi's mind, fueling the tremor that ran through his hand, gripping the armrest.

"Quantum Scramblers… engage!" He barked the command, his voice a thunderclap, shattering the tense silence.

The chamber pulsated with an otherworldly hum as the scramblers, pushing the boundaries of known physics, ripped through the cloak of secrecy. On the holographic map, the enemy ships materialized, sleek and predatory, their forms defying categorization. A collective gasp rippled through the crew, their shock mirroring the distorted, alien symbols emblazoned on the unknown hulls.

"Weapons lock?" Levi demanded, his voice etched with ironclad resolve, even as a sliver of doubt gnawed at the edges of his certainty.

"Negative, sir!" Reyes' voice cracked under the pressure. "Their hull composition… it's deflecting our targeting scans. Like trying to nail shadows to a wall."

Panic flickered in some eyes, but Levi, a veteran etched with the scars of countless battles, wouldn't yield. "Improvise! Target their propulsion systems. Disrupt their maneuverability. Force them to fight on our terms!"

"This is retaliation. We're not retreating. We're hunting. And this time, we won't stop until we bring them down."

This wasn't over. It was just the beginning. The Fair Trade might have outsmarted them this time, but Levi wouldn't let them savor their victory for long. He would learn their secrets, unravel their hidden technologies, and expose them for the manipulative menace they truly were.

With newfound resolve, Levi straightened in his chair, his voice ringing with unwavering determination. "Crew, prepare for retaliation. We're not retreating. We're hunting. And this time, we won't stop until we bring them down."

A ripple of approval coursed through the chamber. This wasn't just a battle anymore. This was a declaration of war. And the galaxy, trembling on the precipice of an unknown future, held its breath, waiting to see who would emerge victorious: the enigmatic Fair Trade, playing their cosmic chess game, or the Federation, fueled by a thirst for vengeance and the unyielding spirit of humanity.

Before Levi could even muster a retort, the enemy channel slammed shut, leaving behind a deafening silence in the tactical chamber. The holographic map flickered, the alien vessels vanishing as if swallowed by the very fabric of space itself.

"Impossible!" Lieutenant Reyes' voice cracked her knuckles white around the console. "Our Quantum Scramblers were online! They shouldn't have been able to cloak again!"

Exploiting the momentary confusion like a seasoned gambler, Gresham seized the opportunity. "Now!" he roared his voice a thunderclap in the tense silence.

As the senior staff assembled, Levi outlined a new plan, a daring mission that would push them to their limits. They would infiltrate Fair Trade territory, hunt down their black hole generator, and learn its secrets. It was a suicide mission, some would say, but Levi knew the risks were worth taking. This wasn't just about winning a battle; it was about ensuring the survival of their entire way of life.

The Fair Trade had played their hand, but Levi wasn't ready to fold. The game had just begun, and this time, he was determined to rewrite the rules. In the dimly lit chamber, a quiet fire ignited, fueled by anger, fear, and an unwavering determination. The crew of the Requiem wouldn't just survive; they would emerge stronger, ready to face the shadows head-on, and their victory would be the sweetest revenge of all.

Levi slumped in his chair, the cold emptiness of space mirroring the void that had opened within him. He replayed the encounter a thousand times in his mind, each iteration etching deeper the bitter taste of defeat. Their technology, their tactics, their very existence as a formidable force—all rendered obsolete in a single, humiliating display.

Yet, the embers of defiance refused to be extinguished. Defeat might have singed them, but it hadn't broken them. He wouldn't let it. With a grunt, he straightened his posture, meeting Gresham's solemn gaze. "We'll unravel this, even if it means dissecting every agonizing detail of that charade."

Mara's voice cut through the tense silence, sharp as a scalpel. "This wasn't just a show of force, Levi. It was a message, loud and clear. A message we can't afford to misinterpret." Her words resonated with a truth as heavy as the silence that followed.

Days bled into weeks, an unrelenting cycle of analysis, strategizing, and simmering frustration. The Fair Trade remained an enigmatic shadow, their motives, their technology, a terrifying unknown. Every attempt to glean information yielded only dust and whispers.

The cold, sterile air of the command center was thick with the metallic tang of machinery and the faint hum of the ship's engines. The recycled oxygen carried the scent of fear and determination, a heady mix that clung to the back of their throats. Outside, the stars seemed to pulse with a mocking indifference, a silent audience to their struggle.

Then, a tremor of excitement rippled through the flagship. Lieutenant Chen, usually composed, felt her heart skip a beat. She glanced at the sensor readouts, her fingers trembling with a mix of fear and anticipation. "Commander, we're picking up a signal. It's faint, but it's there."

Hope, brittle but tenacious, flickered in Levi's eyes. "Track it," he commanded, his voice tight with anticipation.

The signal led them not to a fleet, not to a base, but to a desolate asteroid field. A single, monolithic structure loomed amidst the celestial debris, its purpose shrouded in darkness. The asteroid field was a graveyard of forgotten battles, jagged rocks, and shattered ship hulls floating in a silent dance. The void seemed to press in on them, the vast emptiness a stark contrast to the tense anticipation within the ship.

"This is it," Mara murmured, her fingers tapping a familiar rhythm on the holographic map. "This is where we find our answers."

The command center was a hive of activity, the air thick with anticipation and the metallic tang of recycled oxygen. Levi stood at the head of the table, his gaze sweeping over the assembled senior staff. Each face reflected a mix of determination and trepidation.

"Alright," Levi began, his voice steady. "We need strategies. This isn't just about survival; it's about turning the tide."

Lieutenant Chen leaned forward, her brow furrowed. "We could deploy drone swarms to create a distraction. It would mask our movements and provide cover for the infiltration team."

Mara nodded thoughtfully. "We also have the Quantum Scrambler. If we can throw their targeting systems into chaos, it will buy us precious time to maneuver."

Gresham, ever the strategist, added, "We need to consider our exit strategy as well. If things go south, we need a quick way out. The

Indomitable stealth drive can give us an edge, but we need to use it wisely."

Lieutenant Blake, the communications officer, chimed in, "I've been analyzing the data from our last encounter. There's something odd about the signal patterns. They seem almost... guided. As if there's an unseen force coordinating their movements."

A chill ran down Levi's spine. "Are you suggesting we're dealing with more than just the Fair Trade?"

Blake nodded. "There's a possibility that a larger force is at play here. We need to be prepared for anything."

As the discussion continued, tension simmered beneath the surface. Levi couldn't shake the nagging doubt gnawing at him. Was this mission truly the best course of action? He glanced at Mara, who met his gaze with unwavering resolve. She believed in the mission, but doubt clouded his mind. What if they were walking into a trap? What if the unseen force was more than they could handle?

Mara's gaze lingered on a strange, pulsating device in the corner of the room. It was something they had recovered from a previous skirmish, something that hummed with an energy she couldn't quite understand. She shook off the feeling of unease, but the device's glow seemed to grow stronger as if it sensed the tension in the air.

Levi turned to Dr. Harris, the chief medical officer. "What's our status on med supplies and personnel?"

Harris, his face etched with worry, replied, "We're running low on supplies, and the crew is exhausted. We need to be prepared for casualties."

Mara thought of her small village family, far away on a peaceful planet, unaware of the dangers she faced. She had promised them she would return, but each battle made that promise harder to keep. She glanced at Gresham, knowing he, too, had people he cared about, people who depended on him. They were fighting not just for the mission but for the future they hoped to protect.

The mission was fraught with danger, a desperate gamble fueled by necessity. They cloaked their ship, cloaked their actions, their very intentions hidden beneath layers of calculated deceit. Every maneuver was a dance on a razor's edge, the threat of annihilation a constant companion.

They infiltrated the structure, a silent predator navigating a labyrinth of unknown dangers. Automated defenses hummed to life, forcing them to rely on skill, stealth, and a healthy dose of improvisation. Each hurdle cleared, each door breached, bringing them closer to the secrets they craved. The interior of the monolithic structure was a maze of cold metal and eerie blue lights, the air thick with the hum of energy and the scent of ionized particles.

Finally, they found it: a vast chamber pulsing with an otherworldly energy. The Fair Trade's black hole generator, a weapon unlike anything they'd ever imagined. Its power thrummed in the air, a tangible force that sent shivers down their spines.

But amidst the awe, a chilling realization dawned. This wasn't just a weapon; it was a key. A key to understanding the Fair Trade, their technology, and their motivations. This wasn't the end; it was the beginning.

Levi's voice cut through the tension. "Gresham, Mara, you're on the infiltration team. Chen, I want those drones ready to deploy on my signal. Blake, keep monitoring for any unusual signals. If there's an unseen force out there, we need to know about it."

Their escape was a blur, a frantic race against time and the awakened defenses of the structure. Back on the flagship, the stolen data spread like wildfire, analysts toiling day and night to unlock its mysteries. Each revelation was a step closer to unraveling the enigma that was the Fair Trade.

The war was far from over; the odds were still stacked against them. But as Levi surveyed the faces of his crew, their resolute expressions mirroring his own, he knew one thing for certain: they were no longer pawns. They were players now, ready to rewrite the rules of the game, one strategic move and one daring gambit at a time. The shadows might have dealt them a crushing blow, but they hadn't reckoned with the resilience of the human spirit, fueled by the unyielding hunger for answers and the unshakeable belief in their own right to exist. The shadows had underestimated them, and that, Levi knew, would be their undoing.

As the crew pored over the data, a message began to emerge, encrypted within the layers of information. It was a faint, barely discernible signal, but it was there. Blake's eyes widened as he decrypted the final line.

"To the crew of the Requiem, you are closer to the truth than you realize. Beware the true enemy. They are not what they seem."

Levi's heart pounded in his chest. The room fell silent, the weight of the message sinking in. They had uncovered something far more dangerous than they had ever imagined. The true battle was just beginning, and the stakes had never been higher.

13

WEB OF DECEIT

Mara's heart hammered against her ribs, not in fear but in a furious battle between loyalty and the chasm that had cleaved their lives apart. Gresham's anguished plea hung in the air, a discordant note amidst the symphony of alarms and flashing red lights. Duty tugged at her like a familiar, tattered cloak, whispering promises of comfort and a past life. But loyalty to Levi, to the rebellion, flared like a supernova within her, demanding a different path. She swallowed the bitter lump in her throat, forcing her gaze onto the holographic map, a silent scream trapped in her chest.

In the heart of the cosmic maelstrom, the Requiem braced for impact, not with stoic resolve, but with simmering defiance. The Fair Trade fleet approached, their warships slicing through the void with precision and deadly intent. Levi's lips curled into a sardonic smile, the glint in his eyes reflecting the approaching laser fire. The tension on the bridge thrummed with anticipation, not fear, as officers transformed into grinning wolves preparing to feast.

Lasers sliced through the darkness, painting the bridge in an electrifying display of reds and blues. The air crackled with the tang of ozone and the sweet scent of opportunity, the roar of engines a battle cry. Rael's fingers danced across the console, his movements a blur as he weaved the Requiem through the enemy fire with the grace of a seasoned pilot. Sparks flew from his station, a testament to his near-superhuman reflexes.

"Incoming barrage!" Rael cackled, his voice laced with manic glee. "Brace yourselves!"

Just as the enemy fleet unleashed their barrage, Levi barked with laughter, his voice booming above the din. "Activate the Graviton Pulse Cannon!"

A low hum resonated through the ship as the prototype weapon charged its energy building to a crescendo. This wasn't your average pulse cannon; it was a weapon designed to alter the battlefield itself. With a thunderous roar, the cannon unleashed a swirling vortex of dark energy, warping space as it hurtled toward the enemy flagship.

For a moment, silence descended. Then, chaos erupted. The enemy flagship exploded in a dazzling display of sparks and debris. The acrid scent of burnt circuitry filled the air, mingling with the sweet, metallic tang of blood and sweat. Cheers erupted from the crew, their laughter echoing through the bridge.

But before they could celebrate, the Fair Trade flagship retaliated, sending a pulse of energy back toward the Requiem. Levi's eyes widened as the weapon's feedback looped back, threatening to tear their own defenses apart.

"Evasive maneuvers!" Levi roared. Rael's hands flew across the console, trying to steer them clear, but the energy pulse clipped the edge of their ship, sending a shockwave through the hull.

The bridge shook violently, and Mara grabbed onto the console to steady herself. The cold metal beneath her fingers felt like a lifeline amidst the chaos. On the screen, the masked figure from the Fair Trade reappeared, their voice dripping with amusement. "Bravo,

Commander Levi! You almost made it fun. But fear not, this little game of cat and mouse has just begun!"

The screen flickered black, leaving the crew staring at the void. Levi felt the blood drain from his face, replaced by a cold fury. They had been outmaneuvered, their own weapon turned against them. But he wouldn't let this defeat stand.

"Status report!" Levi barked, the urgency in his voice snapping the crew into action.

"Shields at 60%, minor hull breaches in sectors 3 and 5," Lieutenant Reyes responded, her hands moving swiftly over the console. "Damage control teams en route."

Levi turned to Mara and Gresham, determination blazing in his eyes. "We need to regroup. They won this round, but we will not let them win the war."

Gresham nodded, his jaw set with resolve. "We've faced worse. We adapt, we fight back."

Mara's eyes were sharp, her voice steady. "We need to analyze their tactics, find a way to counter their technology."

The crew's determination was palpable, their resolve hardening in the face of the setback. They had been outplayed, but they were far from outmatched. Levi felt a surge of pride as he watched them, their movements precise and their focus unyielding. They were ready for the next round.

Levi stared at the coded message, its blinking pulse an unwelcome echo of the hammering in his chest. Fear, a cold serpent, slithered through him, whispering of traps and consequences. This message, arriving on the heels of his newfound understanding of the Fair Trade, could be a key, a hidden door leading to further revelations...or a cleverly disguised pitfall.

His fingers hovered over the console, the weight of his knowledge pressing down on him. Admiral Stratton, a name once synonymous with honor, now tasted like ash in his mouth. The truth, raw and unsettling, threatened to topple the carefully constructed world he'd known. Was this the unraveling, the point where the game truly shifted its axis?

Dread, icy and suffocating, wrapped itself around his throat. He couldn't ignore the message; its potential was too potent. Yet, the specter of Stratton's betrayal loomed large. Had the Admiral already woven his treacherous web, tipped the scales in the Fair Trade's favor? Was revealing this truth a beacon of clarity or a spark igniting chaos within their ranks?

Levi leaned back, the chair groaning under the weight of his burden. The air hung heavy with the unspoken question: could he be the bearer of both truth and chaos? The silence, thick with the stench of betrayal, pressed in on him. It felt like a betrayal not just of trust but of the very fabric of their fight.

His jaw clenched, the muscles in his face taut with the strain of decision. He knew the cost of silence, the gnawing suspicion that would fester, and the slow erosion of trust. But revealing the truth now, without absolute certainty, could be the final blow, shattering morale and plunging them into an abyss of doubt.

He needed clarity, a scalpel to dissect this truth and expose its true form. He needed allies, not blind accusations. His gaze darted towards the communication panel, a silent prayer for guidance forming on his lips. This wasn't just about information anymore; it was about leadership, about navigating a minefield of uncertainty with the fate of the galaxy hanging by a thread.

Levi took a deep breath, the air filling his lungs with resolve. He wouldn't be a pawn in this treacherous game. He would gather his trusted advisors and a council of unwavering minds, and together, they would dissect this truth, sift through the shadows, and find their path forward. The war had changed; the stakes had risen, but so had his determination. He wouldn't succumb to fear or doubt. He would lead them through this darkness, one calculated step at a time, the weight of truth his shield, and the unwavering spirit of his people his guiding light. The game was far from over, and he was ready to rewrite its rules, one bold move at a time.

Taking a deep breath, he initiated a secure comm link, the encrypted symbol flashing on the screen, a stark reminder of the sensitive nature of his message. "Mara, Gresham," his voice, usually steady, now carried a tremor of urgency, "we need to talk. Face-to-face. Now. This is bigger than we thought."

Commander Levi stood before the encrypted message, his mind a maelstrom of calculations and possibilities. The pulsing code wasn't merely a potential trap; it was a multifaceted puzzle piece in the grand cosmic chess game they were embroiled in. His eyes, sharp and analytical, scanned the cryptic symbols, each one a potential key to unraveling the Fair Trade's machinations.

The mention of Admiral Stratton sent ripples through Levi's carefully constructed mental model of the conflict. It wasn't fear that gripped him but a cold, rational understanding of the far-reaching implications. If Stratton, a pillar of their resistance, had indeed been compromised, it would require a complete recalibration of their strategy.

Levi's fingers hovered over the console, not in hesitation but in careful deliberation. Each potential action branched out in his mind, a decision tree of consequences and counter-moves. The recent revelations about the Fair Trade had already shifted the paradigm of their struggle. This message could be the lynchpin that would allow them to pivot their entire approach.

He leaned back, his posture relaxed but his mind razor-sharp. The silence in the room was not oppressive; it was fertile ground for his thoughts to crystallize. Levi wasn't just considering the immediate ramifications of this information. He was extrapolating, envisioning how this piece would alter the entire landscape of their conflict weeks, months, and even years down the line.

With practiced efficiency, Levi began to formulate a multi-pronged approach. They needed to verify the information without alerting potential moles. They needed contingency plans for every possible outcome. Most crucially, they needed to stay three steps ahead of their adversaries.

His jaw set with determination, not tension. This wasn't a setback; it was an opportunity to redefine the parameters of their struggle. Levi's mind raced through potential allies, resources, and strategies they hadn't yet tapped into. The game had changed, yes, but he was already adapting, evolving their tactics to match and surpass their opponents.

With decisive movements, Levi activated the secure comm link. His voice, when he spoke, carried the weight of authority and the edge of strategic brilliance. "Mara, Gresham, report to my quarters immediately. We're about to reshape the entire board."

As he waited for his trusted advisors, Levi's mind continued to work, mapping out scenarios and crafting contingencies. He wasn't just reacting to the situation; he was orchestrating a symphony of counter-intelligence and tactical maneuvers that would leave their enemies reeling. The Fair Trade thought they held the upper hand, but Levi was already several moves ahead, ready to turn their perceived advantage into their ultimate downfall.

A knock at the door startled Levi from his intense deliberation. He straightened, hastily wiping the tears from his eyes. He couldn't let his crew see him like this, couldn't let them know the depth of the betrayal he had uncovered. They needed him to be strong, to be the leader they could rely on in this darkest of hours.

"Enter," he called, his voice hoarse with barely suppressed emotion.

Mara and Gresham stepped into the room, their faces etched with concern. They had known Levi long enough to sense when something was wrong, and the haunted look in his eyes spoke volumes.

"Levi," Mara began, her voice gentle, "what is it? What have you found?"

Levi swallowed hard, the words sticking in his throat. "It's worse than we thought," he managed, his voice barely above a whisper. "Stratton... he's not just a traitor. He's the head of a conspiracy that goes far beyond the Requiem. The Alliance... it's in danger. Everything we've fought for..."

He trailed off, unable to continue. Gresham's eyes widened, the shock and disbelief plain on his face. Mara's hand flew to her mouth, a gasp escaping her lips. For a long moment, silence reined, each of them struggling to come to terms with the magnitude of the revelation.

Gresham was the first to break the silence, his voice a roar of fury. "Stratton is a viper! We need to act now! Arrest him and throw him in jail to rot! He put our crews' lives at risk and stole money that was meant for the war effort! This is intolerable!"

Mara, though equally shocked, took a different approach. She spoke with a pained calm, her voice steady despite the turmoil within. "This is awful news. We should seek out high dignitaries to back us. We need allies in this. If we act rashly, it could lead to more chaos."

Levi, ever the proceduralist, spoke with measured determination. "Stratton is under Military Rule. We need to document everything against him and involve the Justice Council. We cannot let this be seen as a witch hunt; it must be done by the book."

Mara's brow furrowed as she tried to pinpoint the source of her nagging doubt. A fleeting memory resurfaced, one she had dismissed as folly years ago.

"Do you remember the Alliance Gala on Ieryx II, shortly after Stratton took command of the Economic Division?" Her eyes remained unfocused, seeing something only she could perceive.

Levi and Gresham exchanged a puzzled glance before nodding for her to continue.

"I spotted Stratton speaking intently with someone, a man I didn't recognize. They were in a shadowed alcove, away from the crowds. Just as I approached, the stranger turned and walked away - no, he didn't walk..." Mara's eyes narrowed as the fragmented memory coalesced.

"He disappeared. One moment corporeal, the next simply...gone. As if he'd never existed at all." She shuddered involuntarily. "At the time, I dismissed it as a trick of the light, too many ceremonial drinks addling my senses. But now that I think about it..."

Her words hung in the air, injecting a palpable disquiet into the room. If Stratton could make someone materialize and vanish at will, what other unthinkable abilities did he possess? What other shadowy companions lurked in his orbit, biding their time?

Levi's reaction to Mara's revelation was one of grim confirmation. His suspicions were validated, deepening the gravity of their mission. "Then we do all three," Mara said, her voice firm. "We gather evidence, seek the support of dignitaries, and prepare to take Stratton down legally. We need to ensure that justice is served, not vengeance."

Levi nodded, his heart pounding in his chest. The path ahead was shrouded in uncertainty, and the thought of leading them into the unknown made his stomach clench with a mixture of determination and dread. But they had faced impossible odds before and emerged victorious. They would do so again, no matter the cost. The battle for the soul of the Alliance had begun, and they would not rest until the truth was brought to light and justice was served.

Days turned into a blur of calculated moves and strategic discussions. Levi led his team through an exhaustive analysis of all known data about Stratton, searching for inconsistencies, unexplained actions, and subtle hints of duplicity. They cross-referenced communications, scrutinized supply logs, and double-checked the Intel from their last encounters.

Mara discovered that certain supply shipments meant for critical missions had been inexplicably rerouted. Gresham uncovered a series of encrypted messages that had been sent using Stratton's codes but were unaccounted for in official logs. Piece by piece, the mosaic of betrayal started to form.

Despite their efforts, every revelation seemed to open another door of questions. Levi felt the frustration gnawing at him, but he used it as fuel, pushing his team harder. He knew they were close, but the picture was still incomplete.

The screen remained blank for a moment, the silence stretching with unbearable tension. Had his message reached them? Were they safe? Or had his hesitation already sealed their fate?

The tension crackled in the air, thick enough to chew. Mara and Gresham exchanged a silent glance, the weight of Levi's words settling on them like a leaden cloak. Stratton, a name synonymous with honor, now stood accused of the highest treason, his treachery a serpent slithering through the very heart of the Alliance.

"Code Obsidian," Mara whispered, her voice barely above a breath. The gravity of the situation pressed down on her, a stark contrast to the oblivious hum of the ship outside.

Levi's gaze held theirs, unwavering. "There's no other option. The clock ticks, and the target... is us."

Commander Levi sat in his quarters, the weight of the datapad in his hand heavier than any weapon he'd ever wielded. The room was dimly lit, the only illumination coming from the flickering screens before him. The air was heavy with the scent of recycled oxygen and the faint, acrid tang of sweat. The hum of the ship's engines, usually a comforting background noise, now seemed to echo the tension that thrummed through his veins. Shadows danced on the metallic surfaces, adding to the sense of unease.

His eyes scanned the glowing screen, the words blurring together as his mind struggled to process the information before him. Each line, each piece of evidence, was a twist of the knife, a searing reminder of the depth of the betrayal they faced. He read the reports again, a part of him desperately hoping that he had misunderstood, that there was some error or fabrication. But as he delved deeper, the truth became undeniable. Admiral Stratton, a man he had trusted, a man he had looked up to, was at the heart of a conspiracy that threatened to tear the Alliance apart.

Levi's hand trembled as he scrolled through the encrypted communications, the secret meetings, and the backdoor deals. A specific line of incriminating evidence crystallized the gravity of the situation: "Funds transferred to untraceable accounts; orders given to divert resources from the front lines." The scope of the treachery was staggering. This wasn't just about the Requiem or a single rogue admiral. The rot had spread far and deep, cancer eating away at the very foundation of everything they had fought for.

A choked sob escaped Levi's throat, a sound of pure anguish. He felt as if the ground had been ripped out from under him, leaving him adrift in a sea of uncertainty and pain. The trust he had placed in Stratton, the faith he had in the Alliance, it all crumbled to dust before his eyes. He leaned forward, his elbows on his knees, his head in his hands. The datapad clattered to the floor, the screen still glowing with the damning evidence. Levi's shoulders shook as he tried to contain the storm of emotions raging within him. Anger, betrayal, despair, they all swirled together in a maelstrom that threatened to consume him.

A memory surfaced, unbidden: Stratton's hearty laugh during a tense briefing, the sound breaking the tension and bringing a sense of camaraderie to the room. They had shared a moment of mutual respect, a bond forged in the heat of countless battles. How could he have been so blind? How could he have missed the signs? The questions haunted him, each one a lash against his already battered soul. He had trusted Stratton, confided in him, and all the while, the man had been working to undermine everything they had built.

His thoughts turned to the crew. How were they faring? These brave men and women, who had placed their lives in his hands, trusted him to lead them with honor and integrity. How were they coping with the knowledge that their own Admiral had sold them out, jeopardized their mission, and put their lives at risk? The betrayal would shatter their morale, their trust in the command structure, and their faith in the Alliance itself.

He shook his head, forcing himself to shut down these thoughts. He needed to inform his crew. He put on his uniform with fresh determination and headed out into the hallway.

Commander Levi stopped at the door to the Mess Hall. His hands clenched into fists, and anger flashed across his face. Through the door, he could hear indistinct voices talking happily, laughing. The sound felt like a dagger to his heart. He drew a deep breath, released his hands, and steeled himself before stepping into the Mess Hall.

As he entered, the lively atmosphere dimmed, replaced by an expectant silence. The crew, his family in this vast, indifferent universe, turned to face him. Their expressions shifted from joy to a mix of shock and determination as they noticed the gravity in his demeanor. Levi's heart ached, knowing he was about to shatter their trust in someone they had admired.

He took a moment to look at each of them, pride swelling in his chest despite the burden of the news he carried. These were the people he fought for, the ones who had stood by him through thick and thin, who had faced countless dangers without flinching. He owed them the truth, no matter how painful.

Taking a deep breath, Levi began to speak, his voice steady but carrying the weight of his emotions. "We face a new enemy, one shrouded in secrets but not invincible. I have unearthed truths that may challenge your perception, but they are truths we must confront together. This battle is not just about survival; it's about understanding. And with understanding, we will find our victory."

A murmur of agreement rippled through the crew, though it was tinged with confusion and disbelief. Lieutenant Reyes, young and wide-eyed, stepped forward, his voice trembling with a mix of shock and hurt. "Commander Stratton was a hero to us. He transformed the Economic Division! How can we make sense of this betrayal? He gave us the improved weapons we needed, the new uniforms we wore, and even arranged for a special chef to improve our meals. This flagship itself is a result of all Admiral Stratton did for the

Alliance." He gestured to his well-made uniform, his voice cracking slightly. "How can this be true?"

Levi's heart ached for Reyes and the crew. He could see the pain and confusion in their eyes. "I understand, Reyes," he said, his voice gentle yet firm. "It's hard to believe. Stratton's contributions have undeniably improved our lives and our effectiveness. But sometimes, those who seem to give the most have the darkest secrets. We must remember that our strength lies in our unity and our commitment to the truth. We will get through this together, as we always have."

"Admiral Stratton?!" Zara's voice rang out, filled with shock and hurt. "It can't be!" She stood up abruptly, her eyes wide, searching Levi's for any sign of a mistake.

She slowly sat back down, feeling as if the world no longer made sense. Her gaze lingered on Commander Levi's green eyes, desperately seeking any hint of a mistake, anything that might explain away the news. Finding none, she sank back into her seat, the confirmation settling over her like a leaden weight.

Levi's heart went out to her and to everyone struggling with this revelation. He took a deep breath, his eyes scanning the room, meeting each gaze with unwavering resolve.

"I know this is a lot to take in," he began, his voice steady but carrying the weight of authority. "The evidence we have against Admiral Stratton is concrete and undeniable. He has betrayed the Alliance, and his actions have put us all in danger. I want you all to know that I will act within the full authority of the military to ensure justice is done. Stratton will be held accountable for his actions."

He paused, letting his words sink in, the room heavy with a mix of shock, confusion, and anger. Levi's expression softened as he addressed the crew at large, his tone becoming more compassionate.

"Stratton was a hero to many of us. He gave us the improved weapons we needed, the new uniforms we wore, and even arranged for a special chef to improve our meals. This flagship itself is a result of all Admiral Stratton did for the Alliance. But sometimes, even those who have done great things can fall. And when they do, we must stand stronger."

Levi stepped forward, his presence commanding yet comforting. "This is a test of our resilience and our commitment to the values we hold dear. It's natural to feel hurt, confused and betrayed. But we cannot let these feelings paralyze us. We must channel them into a renewed sense of purpose."

He looked around, his eyes filled with pride and determination. "We are more than just a crew; we are a family. We have faced impossible odds before and emerged victorious. This is no different. We will face this challenge together, united and unwavering. We will continue to fight for the Alliance, for justice, and for the truth."

Levi's voice grew stronger, resonating with conviction. "Remember why we are here. Remember what we stand for. We will not let this betrayal break us. We will rise above it, stronger and more determined than ever. Our mission has not changed. Our resolve has not wavered. Together, we will overcome this, and we will bring Admiral Stratton to justice."

The crew's faces once filled with disbelief and confusion, now reflected a growing resolve. Levi had given them the focus they needed, a clear path forward amidst the chaos.

"This is our fight," he continued, his voice a rallying cry. "And we will not back down. We will stand together as one crew, one family, and we will prevail. For the Alliance. For justice. For each other."

A murmur of agreement rippled through the room, growing into a chorus of determination. Levi felt a surge of pride and hope as he looked at his crew. They were ready to face the challenges ahead, united and stronger than ever.

A collective intake of breath filled the room, a stark contrast to the usual chatter and laughter. Levi's words weighed heavily in the air, a silent acknowledgment of the gravity of the situation. The crew exchanged glances, a silent conversation of shared disbelief and resolve.

Zara, her face pale, spoke first, her voice trembling slightly. "I can't believe it. Stratton...a traitor? It's like a nightmare." Her eyes, usually filled with a spark of mischief, were now clouded with sorrow and anger.

Lieutenant Reyes, his jaw clenched, nodded in agreement. "He was a mentor to me. I trusted him implicitly. How could I have been so blind?" His voice was a mere whisper, filled with self-doubt.

Bran, his face a mask of grim determination, stepped forward. "We need to focus," he said, his voice cutting through the heavy silence. "We have a mission. Stratton betrayed us, but that won't define us. We will find him, we will bring him to justice, and we will ensure this never happens again."

A murmur of agreement rippled through the crew, a silent pledge of solidarity. They had been dealt a heavy blow, but they were not broken. Instead, they were ignited with a renewed sense of purpose. The betrayal had fueled a fire within them, a determination to protect their world from those who would seek to destroy it.

Levi watched as his crew his family, rallied around him. He had poured his heart and soul into this speech, and the response was everything he had hoped for and more. They were not just a crew;

they were a force to be reckoned with. And together, they would face whatever challenges lay ahead.

The weight of the world seemed to lift slightly from Levi's shoulders. He had given them the truth, and they had responded with courage and resilience. The road ahead would be long and arduous, but with this crew by his side, he knew they would prevail.

As they left the mess hall, a sense of purpose filled the air. The betrayal had ignited a fire within them, a determination to uncover the truth and bring those responsible to justice. The road ahead was fraught with danger, but they were ready to face it head-on. The Requiem, once a ship, was now a symbol of hope, a beacon of resilience in the face of adversity. And they, its crew, were the guardians of that hope, the defenders of their world.

Stepping onto the bridge, Levi felt a renewed sense of purpose. The sight of his crew, their faces set with determination, filled him with pride. They had rallied in the face of betrayal, and now it was his turn to lead them through this storm.

14

JUSTICE'S ECHO

Admiral Stratton lounged in his plush chair, exuding a chilling blend of arrogance and cunning. Draped in a velvet cloak that signaled self-importance, the days of threadbare uniforms and stale rations were distant memories. Here, in his stolen paradise on Idris, every opulent detail mocked the Alliance's rigid rules and hollow morals.

The study, with its high ceilings draped in rich velvet curtains, was a testament to his cultivated tastes. Walls lined with ancient tomes and rare artifacts told stories of distant worlds and forgotten histories. A large, ornate desk of dark mahogany inlaid with precious stones dominated the room, its surface scattered with documents and treasures that spoke of power and betrayal. Rings that could feed a small world adorned his fingers, which now stroked the cool obsidian tiles of his desk—a callous contrast to the calloused hands that had mined the very stones beneath his feet. A glass of rare, aged whiskey sat untouched, a mere accessory to his perceived sophistication.

An intricate chess set, its pieces carved from rare gemstones, stood mid-game on a side table. It symbolized his strategic mind, always thinking several moves ahead. Exotic plants and flowers from distant worlds filled the air with a heady, intoxicating fragrance, mingling with the faint, acrid tang of sweat and the recycled oxygen. Artworks from across the galaxy adorned the walls. Some depicted historic battles, while others were abstract, reflecting the complexity of his mind. The room was dimly lit, the flickering fire casting dancing shadows that seemed to move in time with his thoughts. Classical music played softly in the background, adding a veneer of sophistication to the sinister atmosphere.

Stratton's appearance matched his surroundings. Dressed in a tailored, luxurious uniform that starkly contrasted with his former utilitarian attire, he epitomized the heights of power he had reached. His neatly trimmed beard and hair, his impeccably groomed appearance, were all parts of the carefully constructed image he presented to the world.

A holographic display on his desk showed encrypted communications with the Fair Trade, evidence of his treachery. Documents detailing transactions and deals that compromised the Alliance lay scattered, each one a testament to the depth of his betrayal. The concealed safe, its door slightly ajar, hinted at the secrets and valuables hidden within. The atmosphere was thick with secrecy and intrigue. The occasional flicker of the fireplace cast eerie shadows, adding to the sense of danger that permeated the room. Stratton reached for a ceremonial dagger displayed prominently on a shelf, its blade a symbol of his willingness to betray. A faded photograph of his younger self in a simpler uniform stood next to it, a stark reminder of how far he had fallen.

As he pondered his next move, a subordinate entered the room, bowing slightly. "Admiral, we have received the latest reports. The Requiem is still unaware of our full capabilities."

Stratton's cold, calculating eyes met the subordinate's. "Good," he replied, his voice smooth and commanding. "Continue to feed them the information we want them to have. Keep them in the dark."

The subordinate nodded and left, leaving Stratton to his thoughts. He leaned back, a sardonic smile playing on his lips. Reflections on his journey from a loyal officer to a power-hungry traitor surfaced, justifying his actions as necessary for progress. Calculations of his next moves raced through his mind, always thinking several steps ahead.

His gaze fell on the map of the galaxy, marked with locations of his influence and plans. "The game has changed," he muttered to himself, "but I am the one rewriting the rules." As he took a sip of the rare whiskey, he reveled in the power he had amassed, the sheer thrill of outsmarting his enemies. He was not just playing the game; he was the one controlling it. And in this grand chess match, he intended to remain several moves ahead of everyone else.

Admiral Stratton received confirmation from his informants that Levi, Gresham, and Mara were en route. He smirked, knowing they were playing into his hands. Methodically, he put away any incriminating documents and items, locking the safe with a high-security code and biometric scan. The hum of the safe's locking mechanism was a comforting sound, a reminder of his control over the situation.

Practicing a few phrases in an obscure alien language, Stratton prepared to impress (or intimidate) his guests. A collection of untranslated alien texts sat on his desk, evidence of his ongoing studies. Moving a piece in a multi-dimensional strategy game from an advanced alien civilization, Stratton solved a particularly difficult scenario that had stumped him for days, symbolizing his strategic brilliance.

Resuming listening to classical music, Stratton appeared relaxed, projecting an image of calm and control. He considered the possible scenarios and outcomes of the impending meeting, planning his responses and contingencies. Checking his appearance, he ensured he looked composed and authoritative. He arranged the room, adjusting the lighting and seating to subtly assert dominance. A trusted subordinate entered with a final update, and Stratton gave brief, calculated instructions, showcasing his control.

Taking a moment to enjoy a sip of his rare whiskey, Stratton savored the calm before the confrontation. He allowed himself a moment of satisfaction, knowing he was several steps ahead of his adversaries. The classical music reached a crescendo, echoing the high stakes of the imminent encounter. As the last note faded, Stratton's steely gaze turned to the door. The game was about to begin, and he was ready to play.

A secure message flickered on the screen, its text a conspiratorial green. "Excellent work, Admiral. You are indispensable." Stratton scoffed. Indispensable? He was a genius, a puppet master orchestrating the greatest heist in galactic history, fleecing both the Alliance and the gullible fools in the Federation. His smile widened, revealing a predator's glint in his eyes.

Admiral Stratton's smugness was a physical weight in the room as Gresham entered. The hero's arrival was a minor annoyance, a fly buzzing at the edge of his web. Stratton let a derisive snort escape his lips. Time to swat the fly and get back to savoring his ill-gotten gains.

"Commander Levi," Stratton began, his voice smooth and welcoming. "Your rise through the ranks has been nothing short of extraordinary. Your strategic mind and leadership have not gone unnoticed."

Levi's jaw clenched imperceptibly as Stratton spoke, betraying his inner tension. "Admiral Stratton," he replied, his voice steady, "we're here on official business."

Stratton's gaze shifted to Gresham and Mara, allowing himself a moment of admiration for their formidable presence. "Lord

Gresham, Lady Mara, your reputation precedes you. The FEW are truly a force to be reckoned with."

Gresham's eyes flashed angrily while Mara's fingers twitched slightly, ready to summon her powers immediately. They exchanged a glance, their unity evident in their synchronized movements.

"Please, have a seat," Stratton offered, gesturing to the luxurious chairs before his desk. "Can I offer you something to drink? It's been a long journey, and we have much to discuss."

"We're not here for pleasantries, Admiral," Levi said firmly. "There have been serious allegations against you, and we need to discuss them."

Stratton's mask of calm slipped for a moment, revealing a fleeting look of calculation. His eyes darted briefly to a particular drawer in his desk, possibly containing a weapon or crucial evidence. "Allegations?" he asked, feigning ignorance. "What sort of allegations?"

Levi stepped forward, his voice steady and commanding. "We have substantial proof of your betrayal, Admiral. It's time to come clean."

Stratton sighed and reached into the same drawer, pulling out a sleek black folder. "Commander, I understand the gravity of your concerns. However, before you jump to conclusions, I must show you this." He handed the folder to Levi, who accepted it cautiously.

Levi opened the folder and began to scan the contents. His eyes widened slightly as he realized the significance of what he was reading. "Advisor Dorn," he muttered, his voice tinged with surprise. "These documents detail a network of espionage and sabotage within the Alliance. This is far more alarming than what we have on you."

Stratton nodded, a smug smile playing on his lips. "Exactly. Dorn has been orchestrating a series of covert operations to undermine the Alliance from within. My actions, which you have so hastily labeled as treacherous, were part of an elaborate counter-espionage effort to expose Dorn's network and protect our interests."

Gresham's eyes narrowed with suspicion. "So you expect us to believe that you're the hero in all this, Admiral? That your betrayal was actually an act of loyalty?"

Stratton leaned back in his chair, adjusting the room's lighting to create shadows that might conceal his micro-expressions. "I'm not asking for your belief, Lord Gresham. I'm asking for your understanding. Sometimes, the actions we take in the shadows are the ones that truly protect the light. I was preparing to hand this over to the Justice Department."

At that moment, Stratton's efficient aide, a young officer with a clipboard, entered the room, bowing slightly. "Admiral, here are the latest reports from the Alliance," he said, his tone respectful but slightly nervous.

Stratton took the reports and glanced at the aide, who added hesitantly, "If I may, Admiral, many of us are struggling to understand these allegations. You transformed the Economic Division! You provided us with improved weapons, new uniforms, and even a special chef to improve our meals. This flagship itself is a result of your dedication to the Alliance."

Stratton's eyes gleamed with a predatory light. "Ah, thank you for your kind words. It's true; I have dedicated myself to the betterment of the Alliance. But it's precisely because of that dedication that I must question these so-called 'allegations.'"

The aide nodded and left the room, closing the door quietly behind him.

Mara's violet eyes bore into Stratton's, searching for any sign of deceit. "And what about the funds you diverted? How does that play into your narrative of heroism?"

Stratton's gaze remained steady. "The funds were used to secure intelligence, pay informants, and set traps for Dorn's operatives. It was a necessary sacrifice to protect the greater good."

Before they could continue, a chime echoed through the room, followed by a news broadcast on a nearby screen. The anchor announced, "Admiral Stratton has just made a generous donation to the war orphans' fund, ensuring better living conditions and education for those affected by the conflict."

Stratton's smile widened. "Public perception can be quite the shield, don't you think?"

Levi closed the folder, his mind racing with the implications. "We will need to verify this information, Admiral. If what you say is true, Advisor Dorn must be brought to justice. But make no mistake, we will still be investigating your actions thoroughly."

Stratton nodded, his expression one of practiced calm. "I would expect nothing less, Commander. The truth will prevail, and I have nothing to hide."

With that, the tension in the room reached a crescendo, the stakes higher than ever. As they prepared to leave Stratton's office, the sense of urgency and determination among Levi, Mara, and Gresham was palpable. The game had changed, but their resolve remained unshaken.

Outside the office, Levi turned to his team, his voice filled with determination. "We need to act swiftly. Verify this information and prepare to confront Dorn. Stratton may have bought himself some time, but we will uncover the truth."

Stratton glanced at a clock on his desk, its ticking suddenly louder. "Ah, time is of the essence. You see, in just a few hours, a vote will take place that will solidify my position. It would be a shame if your accusations were seen as mere desperation."

Levi, Mara, and Gresham exchanged tense glances. The urgency of the situation was clear. They needed to act swiftly and decisively.

The command center of the Requiem thrummed with the low hum of advanced machinery and the faint chatter of crew members working at their stations. The room, dimly lit and bathed in the glow of holographic displays and consoles, exuded an air of readiness. Through a massive viewport, the vastness of space stretched out, an endless tapestry of stars and distant galaxies, reminding the crew of their isolation and the immense responsibility on their shoulders.

Commander Levi, Lady Mara, and Lord Gresham entered with purpose, their expressions reflecting the gravity of the situation. The weight of their mission was palpable, even to the crew members who glanced their way with a mix of curiosity and concern.

Levi called for their top intelligence officers, and within moments, Lieutenant Reyes, Intelligence Officer Drayton, and Communications Specialist Kiera joined them around the table. The tension in the room thickened, each officer acutely aware of the importance of the task ahead.

Levi placed the sleek, black folder on the table and opened it, revealing a stack of meticulously detailed documents. The room fell silent as the officers leaned in, their faces illuminated by the glow of the holographic displays.

Mara's violet eyes scanned the first few pages, her expression hardening with each line she read. "These reports... they detail weapon sales to both sides of ongoing conflicts," she said, her voice tight with suppressed anger. "Advisor Dorn has been profiting from the bloodshed, selling advanced weaponry to warring factions and fueling the devastation."

Gresham's ocean-blue eyes flared with fury. "This isn't just treason; it's mass murder for profit," he growled. "We should grab him and throw him in the brig right now!"

Levi's jaw clenched as he flipped through the pages, his anger simmering just beneath the surface. "This is beyond betrayal," he said, his voice low and controlled. "Dorn has been using his position to destabilize entire regions, creating chaos and death. Look at this – unauthorized deployment of biological weapons, resulting in thousands of civilian casualties."

Lieutenant Reyes, her eyes wide with shock, pointed to another document. "Here, he's been redirecting medical supplies meant for refugee camps, selling them on the black market for a profit. People died because they didn't have the medicine they needed."

Drayton shook his head, his face pale. "He's orchestrated assassinations of key political figures who opposed his deals, leaving planets leaderless and plunging them into anarchy."

Kiera's hands trembled as she read a particularly harrowing account. "This report details a planet where Dorn's interference led to a famine. He blocked aid shipments, ensuring that millions starved just to force the government to buy from his approved suppliers."

The room was thick with the scent of recycled air and the palpable rage of its occupants. Each revelation added to the collective fury, the sense of betrayal deepening. Yet, beneath the surface, emotions churned.

Reyes's voice cracked with disbelief as she spoke again. "How could someone in such a trusted position do this? These were real people—families, children."

Drayton's face was ashen. "I can't believe I used to respect him. We worked together on missions to deliver aid, and all this time, he was undermining us."

Kiera, usually composed, had tears in her eyes. "The thought of all those lives lost because of his greed... it's sickening."

Levi slammed the folder shut, the sound echoing through the command center. "This ends now," he declared, his voice ringing with authority but tinged with grief. "We will not let Dorn's crimes go unanswered. Prepare a task force. We're bringing him in."

Mara's eyes blazed with resolve, but her voice was softer, more introspective. "We need to make sure every piece of evidence is secure and ready for the tribunal. His network must be dismantled entirely, and every ally he has must be rooted out."

Gresham nodded, but his expression held a note of sorrow. "He will pay for every life he has destroyed. The Alliance will see justice done, but it doesn't bring back those we lost."

As the team sprang into action, the room buzzed with renewed purpose. Yet, the air was also filled with the weight of what they had learned, a reminder of the human cost of betrayal. The soft hum of the ship's engines served as a backdrop to their fervent preparations. They would bring Dorn to justice, ensuring that his reign of terror ended and that the Galactic Alliance would stand stronger and more united than ever before.

As the officers worked, Mara remained at the center, orchestrating the investigation. "We need to cross-reference these documents with our own intelligence records. Look for any discrepancies or corroborating evidence. We need to know exactly what we're dealing with."

Commander Levi, with his analytical mind and deep connection to the Alliance, took the lead. He spread the documents across the table, his eyes scanning for familiar patterns. "Here," he said, highlighting several transactions. "These match known illegal weapon sales. This confirms parts of Stratton's allegations against Dorn."

Gresham, standing next to her, scrutinized the details. His keen eye for inconsistencies quickly identified several anomalies. "Look at the dates and signatures on these documents," he pointed out. "There are discrepancies here. Some signatures appear forged, and the dates don't align with our records. It suggests possible alterations by Stratton."

Levi leaned in, his expression thoughtful. "So, Stratton might have tampered with some of the evidence to strengthen his case against Dorn. However, the core of the information is still valid. Dorn's guilt is evident."

Reyes, their intelligence officer, cross-referenced the highlighted transactions with their database. "Mara's right. These transactions match our records of illegal weapon sales. Dorn has been supplying arms to both sides of conflicts, fueling war for profit."

Drayton, their operations officer, added, "We've tracked these sales for months, but we never had a name to pin them on. This evidence, even with the discrepancies, gives us that name."

Gresham's eyes narrowed as he examined another document. "Stratton's alterations add a layer of complexity, but they don't change Dorn's guilt. We need to be careful. We can't let Stratton's manipulations derail our investigation."

Mara nodded. "We need to verify every detail, separate the truth from Stratton's fabrications. Dorn's crimes are real, but we have to ensure our case is airtight."

Levi straightened, a plan forming in his mind. "Reyes, continue cross-referencing the documents with our records. Drayton, prepare our operatives for immediate deployment. We need eyes on Dorn's network. Kiera, keep monitoring their communications. Any sign of activity, we need to know immediately."

The team worked tirelessly, piecing together the puzzle. The more they uncovered, the clearer it became that Dorn had betrayed the Alliance on a massive scale. Yet, the complexity of the evidence suggested that Stratton had his own agenda, adding layers to the web of deceit.

As the hours passed, the tension in the room grew. Levi could feel the weight of their responsibility. The stakes were incredibly high, and the lives of countless innocents depended on their success.

Mara paused, looking at Levi with a mixture of determination and concern. "We have to be thorough, Levi. Dorn's network is vast, and we can't afford any mistakes."

Levi nodded, his resolve unwavering. "We will be. This is our chance to bring Dorn to justice and dismantle his network. We'll ensure that Stratton's manipulations don't cloud the truth. The Alliance is counting on us."

Gresham placed a hand on Levi's shoulder, a rare gesture of solidarity. "We're with you, Commander. Let's finish this."

As they prepared for the next phase of their mission, the sense of unity and purpose among the team was stronger than ever. The discovery of Dorn's betrayal had shaken them, but it had also galvanized their resolve. They were ready to face the challenges ahead, knowing that the fate of the Alliance rested in their hands.

The fight for justice had become even more complex, but Levi, Mara, and Gresham were determined to see it through. Together, they would uncover the truth, dismantle Dorn's network, and protect the Alliance from those who sought to destroy it from within.

The war room's dim light glinted off rows of data streams, the holographic displays casting an eerie glow over the focused faces of Lady Mara's team. The hum of the Requiem's engines provided a constant backdrop, a reminder of the vast, unyielding space just beyond their walls.

"Focus on the financial records," Mara commanded, her voice unwavering but with an edge of tension. "We need to trace every credit, every transaction."

Her team bent over their consoles, eyes darting over the streams of numbers and transactions. Mara herself moved among them, her presence both a source of motivation and a reminder of the stakes. The importance of this task weighed heavily on her—Dorn's financial web was the key to unraveling his entire operation.

"Look at this," an analyst said, pointing to a series of suspicious entries. "These deposits funnel through a network of shell companies. It's classic money laundering."

Mara leaned over, her gaze intense. "Track them back. Find the origin."

Fingers flew across touchscreens, manipulating data streams with practiced ease. The scent of recycled air mingled with the faint tang of ozone from the displays. The room was thick with concentration, and every team member was attuned to the task at hand.

"Here," another analyst called out, his voice sharp with discovery. "These large deposits in Dorn's personal accounts—they're originating from payments made by warring planets."

Mara's eyes narrowed as she scanned the data. The lines of transactions painted a damning picture, each credit a thread in the web of Dorn's corruption. "This is it," she said, her voice low but filled with fierce determination. "This is the proof we need."

She touched the display, expanding the critical transactions for all to see. "These payments align with known conflicts. Dorn has been profiting off the chaos of war, selling weapons to both sides and laundering the money through these shell companies."

Gresham, who had been pacing, stopped to stare at the screen, his fists clenched. "This isn't just betrayal; it's calculated slaughter. Innocents have died because of him."

Lieutenant Reyes, usually composed, shook her head in disbelief. "I can't believe we trusted him. All those lives... we have to stop this."

Drayton, pale with anger, added, "And we will. But we need to act fast. If Dorn suspects we're onto him, he'll disappear like smoke."

The room was thick with the scent of recycled air and the palpable rage of its occupants. Each revelation added to the collective fury, the sense of betrayal deepening.

Levi slammed the folder shut, the sound echoing through the command center. "This ends now," he declared, his voice ringing with authority. "We will not let Dorn's crimes go unanswered. Prepare a task force. We're bringing him in."

Mara's eyes blazed with resolve. "We need to make sure every piece of evidence is secure and ready for the tribunal. His network must be dismantled entirely, and every ally he has must be rooted out."

Gresham nodded, his expression dark. "He will pay for every life he has destroyed. The Alliance will see justice done."

As the team sprang into action, the room buzzed with renewed purpose. The air was thick with determination, the soft hum of the ship's engines a backdrop to their fervent preparations. They would bring Dorn to justice, ensuring that his reign of terror ended and that the Galactic Alliance would stand stronger and more united than ever before.

The war room buzzed with focused energy as Levi, Mara, and Gresham, along with their top intelligence officers, pored over the documents. The panoramic view of space served as a silent reminder of the vastness of their mission.

Mara stood at the center, orchestrating the investigation. "We need to cross-reference these documents with our own intelligence records. Look for any discrepancies or corroborating evidence. We need to know exactly what we're dealing with."

The hangar bay of the Requiem buzzed with activity as the specialized strike team disembarked. Clad in advanced stealth suits, their movements were fluid and precise, a testament to their rigorous training. These operatives, known as the Shadows of the Alliance, carried an air of quiet confidence. Their leader, a tall figure with a visor masking his eyes, exuded an aura of calculated calm. Each team member carried compact but powerful weapons, and their belts were lined with an array of gadgets designed for infiltration and close-quarters combat.

Levi watched them with a mix of admiration and anticipation. These were the best of the best, brought in for missions where failure wasn't an option. He felt a swell of confidence knowing they were on his side, but the weight of the mission pressed heavily on his shoulders.

The shuttle descended through the atmosphere, landing smoothly on the outskirts of a sprawling industrial complex. The planet's surface was a barren wasteland dotted with towering structures and the occasional flicker of neon lights. The complex itself was a massive edifice of metal and concrete, its windows glowing with an eerie luminescence.

As they disembarked, Levi couldn't shake the feeling of walking into a trap. The Intel suggested Dorn had fortified his position, but the sheer scale of the operation was daunting. He clenched his fists, determination hardening his resolve.

The team moved with practiced stealth, their cloaking suits blending seamlessly with the environment. From their vantage point, they could see the main office building. It was larger than anticipated, a towering structure with sleek, reflective surfaces. Security was tight, with guards patrolling every entrance and exit.

Levi's mind raced as he scanned the building. Dorn knew they were coming. The increased security was a clear sign. He needed to adapt quickly, leveraging the Shadows' expertise to outmaneuver Dorn's defenses.

The team leader turned to Levi, his voice barely a whisper. "Close-quarters combat is likely. Stick close, and use the environment to your advantage. Dorn's guards are well-trained, but they're no match for us if we stay coordinated."

Inside, the building was a blend of modern architecture and industrial grit. From the outside, it appeared almost pristine, with clean lines and reflective glass. Inside, however, it was a maze of dimly lit corridors and cluttered offices, the air heavy with the smell of oil and sweat. Workers moved about with a sense of urgency, their eyes darting nervously as they whispered among themselves.

Levi could feel the tension in the air, the fear that permeated the building. Dorn's reign had left a mark on everyone here. He wondered how many lives had been ruined by the man they were about to confront.

The team moved like shadows, slipping past guards and through security checkpoints with ease. They deployed sophisticated hacking tools to bypass electronic locks and disable security cameras. A team member placed a small device on a junction box, causing the lights to flicker and creating a momentary distraction.

As they reached the inner corridors, Levi took point, ready for action. A guard spotted them and charged, but Levi met him with a swift, well-placed strike that sent the man sprawling. Another guard lunged at Levi, catching him with a shallow cut on his arm before Levi disarmed him with a quick twist and a powerful punch that rendered the guard unconscious.

The team exploited the environment to their advantage. They manipulated the ventilation systems to release a tranquilizer gas, incapacitating anyone within range. Another operative used an electromagnetic pulse device to disable electronic defenses, rendering Dorn's countermeasures useless.

While some team members focused on capturing Dorn, others accessed hidden databases, downloading critical information about his operations. They hacked into secure terminals, retrieving data on Dorn's illegal activities and his network of contacts.

As the team advanced, they encountered unexpected obstacles. Dorn had set up automated defenses that activated, forcing the operatives to adapt quickly. One team member used a portable shield generator to protect against incoming fire, while another deployed a hacking drone to disable the automated turrets.

Dorn's office was a stark contrast to the rest of the building. It was lavishly decorated with rare artifacts and luxurious furnishings, a testament to his arrogance and self-importance. Dorn himself stood behind a massive mahogany desk, his eyes cold and calculating. His guards, hulking brutes with menacing expressions, flanked him.

"So, the Alliance finally decided to send their best. Pity it won't be enough," Dorn sneered.

As Levi signaled the Shadows to engage, the room erupted into controlled chaos. The thugs lunged forward, their heavy boots thudding on the carpet, but the Shadows moved with the precision of a well-oiled machine. Sleep darts zipped through the air, finding their marks with unerring accuracy. One thug roared, staggering forward even as the tranquilizer took effect, his hand brushing against a Shadow operative before collapsing into an unconscious heap. The operative caught him deftly, easing him to the floor without breaking stride.

Seeing their comrade's fall, the workers hesitated, a mix of fight and flight flashing in their eyes. Some bolted for the exits, only to be intercepted by Shadows who seemed to materialize from the shadows themselves, their movements swift and efficient. The would-be fighters, emboldened by desperation, swung wildly at the operatives, but their clumsy attempts were met with calculated counters. Arms were twisted, weapons were disarmed, and the aggressors found themselves subdued and handed over to waiting Alliance soldiers.

Dorn's composure began to fray as he watched his muscle crumble before the Alliance's elite. He glanced around his office, his eyes darting to a hidden panel on the wall. With a sneer, he pressed it, revealing a concealed hallway behind his desk. "You may have the upper hand now, but you'll never catch me," he snarled, disappearing into the passage.

The team leader's eyes narrowed. "Split up. Half of you with me, the rest find another way around."

The Shadows moved swiftly, some darting into the hidden hallway while others fanned out, searching for another route. Their expertise in infiltration allowed them to quickly locate a secondary passage, and they sprinted through it, determined to outpace Dorn.

As Dorn ran, the walls of the narrow corridor seemed to close in on him. His breath came in ragged gasps, a mix of fear and anger driving him forward. Just as he reached the end of the passage, a figure stepped into his path. It was one of the Shadows, a portable shield generator humming softly in his hand.

"Going somewhere, Dorn?" the operative said, his voice calm and steady.

Before Dorn could react, another Shadow operative emerged from the shadows, tossing an electric net. It expanded mid-air, crackling with energy before wrapping around Dorn, who fell to the ground with a howl of fury.

"Secure him," the team leader ordered. "We need him alive for interrogation."

The Shadows moved quickly, binding Dorn and ensuring he was incapacitated. The other team members regrouped, carrying data drives filled with evidence of Dorn's illicit activities. They had what they came for.

The thugs and captured workers, bound and subdued, were gathered in the center of Dorn's lavish office. The Shadows of the Alliance, efficient and precise, made sure none were left behind.

Levi's voice cut through the tense atmosphere. "We're not leaving anyone behind. Secure the prisoners and make sure they're ready for transport."

Several operatives moved swiftly, binding the thugs with reinforced restraints. The workers, those who had chosen to fight or flee, were handled with a bit more care, though their expressions ranged from sullen defiance to relieved acceptance. The Shadows, despite their intimidating presence, treated the captives with a measured firmness, understanding that not all had willingly followed Dorn.

As the captives were herded toward the shuttle, one of the Shadows, a woman with a scar tracing her jawline, spoke to Levi. "Sir, some of these workers might have been coerced. We should separate them for questioning and potential rehabilitation."

Levi nodded. "Agreed. We need to determine who among them willing accomplices were and who victims of Dorn's regime were."

The shuttle bay on the Requiem had been prepared for the incoming captives. Medical personnel stood by to treat any injuries; while security teams ensured that the prisoners would be secured without incident. The Shadows, ever vigilant, maintained their guard as the prisoners were processed.

As they arrived back on the Requiem, Levi addressed his team. "We'll conduct thorough interrogations. Those who were forced into service will be offered assistance and protection. The willing accomplices will face justice. We'll dismantle Dorn's operation piece by piece."

In a secure room, Levi began the interrogations personally, starting with one of the workers who had shown particular fear. The young man, barely more than a boy, trembled as he spoke. "I didn't want to do it. Dorn threatened my family. I had no choice."

Levi's eyes softened. "You're safe now. We'll help you and your family. Just tell us everything you know."

Piece by piece, the Shadows, and the Alliance intelligence officers pieced together the full extent of Dorn's network. The information they gathered painted a grim picture of exploitation and coercion, but it also provided the means to bring many of Dorn's higher-ups to justice.

In the brig, Dorn raged against his captors, his arrogance stripped away. "You think you've won? My associates will come for me. You're all doomed!"

Levi met Dorn's gaze with a steely resolve. "Your empire is crumbling, Dorn. We'll find every last one of your associates and bring them to justice. The galaxy won't suffer under your tyranny any longer."

Outside the brig, the Shadows stood ready, their mission far from over. They had struck a significant blow against one of the galaxy's most notorious criminals, but there were still battles to be fought, lives to be saved, and justice to be served.

The shuttle descended towards the main planet, a bustling hub of Alliance activity. Its towering spires and expansive complexes were a testament to the technological prowess and organizational might of the Galactic Alliance. The Shadows of the Alliance, alongside Commander Levi, maintained a vigilant watch over their prisoners as they approached the secure docking bay designated for high-profile captives.

As the shuttle touched down, a team of Alliance security personnel awaited, ready to assist in transferring Advisor Dorn, his thugs, and the captured workers. The Shadows moved with their characteristic precision, guiding the prisoners out in a disciplined manner. Levi walked behind Dorn, his hand firmly gripping the criminal's arm, ensuring there was no room for escape.

Once inside the secure facility, Levi personally escorted Dorn to his cell. The corridor was lined with reinforced glass cells, each equipped with advanced security measures. Levi's expression was stern as he pushed Dorn into the cell, watching with satisfaction as the door slid shut and locked with a resounding click.

Dorn sneered through the glass, but Levi remained unfazed. "Your reign of terror is over, Dorn. You'll answer for your crimes."

Levi then turned his attention to the Shadows, who were overseeing the secure placement of the other prisoners. Each thug and worker was escorted to a separate cell, their fates to be determined by the coming investigations. The Shadows worked seamlessly, their movements a dance of efficiency and control.

With the prisoners secured, Levi addressed the Shadows. "Thank you for your outstanding work today. Your skill and dedication were crucial to the success of this mission."

The team leader, a tall figure with a visor masking his eyes, stepped forward and saluted. "It was an honor, Commander. Your leadership was vital to our success as well."

Another operative, the woman with the scar along her jawline, grinned. "You know, Commander, we could use someone with your skills on our team. What do you say? Fancy joining the Shadows?"

Levi chuckled, shaking his head. "I appreciate the offer, truly. I'll think about it, but for now, I have my duties here."

The team laughed, their camaraderie evident. One of them clapped Levi on the shoulder. "We'll hold you to that, Commander. The Shadows could always use another hero."

Levi smiled, feeling a deep sense of connection with these elite operatives. Despite the gravity of their work, moments like these reminded him of the bonds forged in the heat of battle. "I'm honored. Until then, keep doing what you do best. The Alliance is lucky to have you."

The Shadows dispersed, their work for the day complete, yet their spirits high. Levi watched them go, their laughter echoing in the sterile corridors of the prison complex. The mission had been a success, but more importantly, it had reinforced the strength of their unity and purpose.

As Levi walked away from the cells, he felt a renewed sense of determination. The fight against injustice was ongoing, but with allies like the Shadows, he knew they could face any challenge that came their way. He had much to think about, including the surprising offer, but for now, he was content knowing they had made a significant impact today.

Commander Levi made his way through the bustling corridors of the Alliance headquarters, the hum of activity echoing the urgency of their mission. Officers and personnel moved with purpose, their expressions reflecting the gravity of their duties. Levi's thoughts were a blend of satisfaction from the successful mission and anticipation for the debriefing with General Barrington. The data drives in his hand felt heavy with the promise of justice.

The door to General Barrington's office was imposing, its ornate design a testament to the authority within. Levi paused for a moment, taking a deep breath before knocking. The muffled command to enter resonated through the heavy wood.

General Barrington, a figure whose presence commanded respect, looked up as Levi entered. His office was a blend of strategic maps, holographic displays, and personal mementos—a room that spoke of both authority and the weight of leadership.

"Commander Levi," Barrington greeted, motioning for Levi to sit. "I've been expecting your report. How did the mission go?"

Levi nodded, stepping forward to place the data drives on the desk with a steady hand. "It was a success, sir. We captured Advisor Dorn and his associates. The Shadows of the Alliance were instrumental in our success."

Barrington's eyes gleamed with interest, reflecting both curiosity and approval. "I'm eager to hear the details."

Levi began his report, his voice measured and clear. "We apprehended Dorn, his thugs, and several workers. During the engagement, one of Dorn's men suffered a dislocated shoulder, another a knee injury, and a worker had a minor head wound. They've all received medical treatment. The evidence we collected is extensive and damning."

Barrington accepted the data drives, his expression thoughtful as he listened. "Excellent work, Levi. And the Shadows?"

"They performed exceptionally," Levi replied, his tone filled with admiration. "Their precision and adaptability were crucial. They overcame every obstacle with skill and efficiency. I couldn't have asked for a better team."

Barrington nodded, a smile playing on his lips. "The Shadows have always been exemplary. Your commendation will mean a lot to them. I'll ensure their efforts are acknowledged."

Levi felt a swell of pride at Barrington's words. "Thank you, General. Their teamwork and dedication were inspiring. They even joked about me joining their ranks."

Barrington chuckled, the sound a rare moment of levity. "That would be quite the alliance. But we need you where you are, Commander. Your leadership makes a significant impact."

Levi's expression softened with appreciation. "Thank you, sir. I'll continue to do my best for the Alliance."

As Levi finished his report, Barrington leaned forward, his eyes sharp with approval. "Levi, I must extend my gratitude to Lord Gresham and Lady Mara as well. Their intelligence work was instrumental in laying the groundwork for this mission. Please convey my thanks to them and the entire Requiem team for their unwavering efforts."

Levi nodded, his expression earnest. "I will, sir. Their expertise and commitment were invaluable."

Barrington's face softened, showing a rare glimpse of warmth. "The Requiem team has proven time and again to be one of our greatest assets. Their teamwork, resilience, and pursuit of justice embody the very spirit of the Galactic Alliance."

Levi felt a swell of pride for his comrades. "I couldn't agree more, General. Their dedication and skill inspire us all. We're stronger together because of their contributions."

The general leaned back, studying Levi with a mix of respect and expectation. "We've struck a significant blow against Dorn's operations today, but this is just the beginning. We need to sift through the information you've gathered and dismantle his network piece by piece. Dorn's reach is vast, and he's not the only one playing these dangerous games. The galaxy is counting on us to root out every last thread of corruption."

Levi nodded, feeling the weight of the task ahead. "I understand, sir. We've made progress, but we can't let our guard down. Dorn's associates will be watching closely, and they'll try to cover their tracks. We need to stay one step ahead."

Barrington's expression softened slightly, a hint of a smile playing at the corners of his mouth. "And I have every confidence that you and your team will do just that. Keep up the good fight."

Levi shook the general's hand firmly, feeling the weight of the mission lift slightly with the recognition of their collective efforts. "Thank you, General. We won't let you down. We're ready for whatever comes next."

As Levi exited the office, he carried with him not only the pride of a successful mission but also a renewed sense of purpose. The battle against Dorn had been a victory, but it was also a reminder of the constant vigilance required to protect the Alliance. With his team by his side, Levi was determined to face whatever challenges lay ahead, knowing that with leaders like General Barrington and allies like the Shadows, they would continue to uphold the values of the Galactic Alliance and fight for justice in every corner of the galaxy.

Inside the Requiem Briefing Room

The hum of the room, always buzzing with low-level energy, felt more suffocating now. Time seemed to stretch like elastic, every second dragging longer than the last. Months had passed since they'd first gotten their hands on the scraps of intel they thought might lead them to Stratton.

And every damn time, the thread unraveled just when they thought they had him.

Levi stared at the screen, his fingers twitching as they hovered above the keys. He knew the file by heart, but he couldn't stop. Couldn't give up. If he did, everything they'd been through—the nights spent awake, the countless dead-end leads—would have been for nothing.

The truth was buried somewhere, but Stratton was too damn clever. He hid things. Hidden behind layers of misdirection, false flags, and convoluted dead ends. Each time they thought they'd cracked the code, each piece of the puzzle they thought might fit, it slipped through their fingers like sand.

"You've got to be kidding me." Mara's voice broke through the silence, sharp and tired. She was leaning over the table, eyes scanning a report, but there was nothing new. She slammed the paper down, her frustration almost tangible. "How does he even think this way? There's no trace of anything we can use. Every lead ends at a wall."

Levi's jaw tightened. He ran a hand through his hair, eyes on the screen but not seeing it. Instead, he was thinking of the hundreds of files they'd sifted through. The hours upon hours they spent working through Stratton's tangled mess of misinformation.

Nothing. Always nothing.

"You can't fight a ghost," Gresham muttered, his voice raw with frustration. He was standing across the room, hands clasped behind his back, but the weariness in his posture was clear. "Stratton's not leaving anything out there for us to find."

Levi felt a flicker of something—anger, despair, exhaustion—but he swallowed it. They needed him here, now. They needed his focus.

"Then it's time we stop looking for what he left," Levi said, his voice low but steady. His eyes met Mara's, then Gresham's. "We find what he's trying to hide."

Mara nodded, her gaze sharp as ever. "If we can just get one crack in the armor..."

"If," Drayton scoffed from the far corner, his arms crossed. He didn't hide his doubt, not that he ever did. "Every time we get close, it slips away. That's not a crack. That's nothing."

Levi's gaze cut to Drayton, the words between them like a silent challenge. "Then you try. This was Stratton's game all along. He's running circles around us."

But Gresham was already speaking over them, the tension thick in his voice. "Enough. We all know what Stratton's capable of. This isn't about proving who's right. We've been chasing shadows long enough, and it's wearing us down."

Mara straightened, finally pushing away from the table. She was quiet for a long moment before speaking. "You're right. But if we don't keep going, we won't get anywhere. It's a fight. And we fight dirty—just like Stratton."

Levi could feel the weight of the room shifting, each of them understanding the truth. They were beyond the point of simply solving a puzzle. This wasn't a clean-cut investigation. It was a war of information, and Stratton wasn't playing by any rules they knew.

Gresham slammed his fist into the edge of the table, the room echoing with the impact. "Dammit, Levi, Mara... you think I don't know that? But I can't be the one to dig through the muck and figure out where he buried it! That's you—both of you!" He motioned to them, frustration boiling over. "I've led a fleet. Not a damn search."

Levi took a breath, his shoulders tensing. He was used to this— being the one to dig through the muck. He didn't mind. But the fight was wearing on him. The long nights. The empty results. Every file they'd cracked open led to the same dead ends. Every lead had evaporated like smoke before their eyes.

"This won't be easy," Levi said, locking eyes with Mara. "But we won't stop. Not until we've taken everything from Stratton. We're fighting for more than just answers. We're fighting for the future. For the Alliance."

Mara gave him a hard look, her eyes cold with determination. "Then let's make sure we win. It's the only way we'll get him."

Across the Galaxy

Meanwhile, on the affected planets, the fallout from NeoTek's exposure continued to unfold. Leaders scrambled to distance themselves from the tainted corporation, seeking to reassure their citizens and stabilize their economies. Grassroots movements emerged, advocating for transparency and ethical governance. The public's demand for accountability sparked a wave of reforms aiming to prevent such corruption from taking root again.

Amid the chaos, individual stories began to surface. Families who had suffered under Dorn's reign shared their relief and hope for a brighter future. A mother on Talos IV wept with joy as she heard the news, knowing her children's future might now be free from the shadow of NeoTek's influence. On Centauri Prime, a small business owner, once bullied by NeoTek's monopolistic practices, spoke of newfound hope and the chance to rebuild his livelihood.

Aboard the Requiem

The atmosphere aboard the Requiem was one of cautious optimism. The crew, having witnessed the power of their collective efforts, felt a renewed sense of purpose. They understood the significance of their mission, the lives they had touched, and the changes they had set in motion.

Levi took a moment to stand by a viewport, watching the stars drift by. The enormity of their task was sobering, but he felt a deep sense of pride in his team. They had proven themselves time and again, not just as warriors but as protectors and builders of a better future.

As he turned back to rejoin his crew, Levi knew that the path ahead would be fraught with challenges. But with leaders like General Barrington and allies like the Shadows of the Alliance, he was confident that they would continue to uphold the values of the Galactic Alliance and fight for justice in every corner of the galaxy. The Requiem and its crew stood as symbols of hope and resilience, ready to face whatever challenges lay ahead.

The Justice Council's Judgment

In the grand hall of the Justice Council, the air was thick with a sense of finality. The council members, clad in their regal robes of office, sat in a semi-circle behind a massive wooden bench, their expressions a blend of stern authority and solemn duty. Advisor Dorn stood before them, flanked by guards, his usual arrogance replaced by a haunted look.

Councilor Althea, a figure known for her unyielding sense of justice, leaned forward. Her voice, calm and authoritative, echoed through the chamber. "Advisor Dorn, you stand accused of crimes against the Galactic Alliance. Your actions have not only betrayed the trust placed in you but have also endangered countless lives."

Dorn's internal struggle was evident. His mind raced, grappling with the weight of his actions. Did he feel remorse? No, not for the lives ruined or the chaos sown, but for the loss of his power, his opulent life. The reality of his downfall gnawed at him, a constant reminder of his hubris. His regret was purely selfish—he regretted getting caught.

Images of his luxurious life flashed through his mind. He remembered the feel of his silk sheets and the comfort of his custom-made bed, the way his morning routine included an array of gourmet meals prepared by his personal chef. The thought of manual labor filled him with revulsion. Rivti was a dust-ridden backwater, far removed from the comforts he had taken for granted. Was there even running water there? The idea of dirt and grime on his hands made him shudder. He was meant for boardrooms, not barren fields.

Councilor Althea continued, her voice unwavering. "The council has reviewed the evidence and found you guilty of high treason, corruption, and gross dereliction of duty. Effective immediately, you are stripped of your rank, your office, and all privileges accorded to you. Your accounts have been seized, and a full investigation into your activities and any compromised entities you worked with will commence."

"You are to be sent to Rivti to help. Many children need tending and medical attention," she continued.

A murmur of approval rippled through the chamber as Althea's words settled. Dorn's face contorted with a mix of indignation and fear. "This is outrageous! I am an Advisor! I can be of more use in strategic planning, in an office—"

"Silence!" Althea's command cut through Dorn's protest. "You will be sent off-world to Rivti, where your skills will be put to use aiding the war-torn efforts. The children there need tending, clothes, water, and medical attention. You will serve them and learn the value of true service."

Dorn's horror was palpable. The idea of manual labor, of tending to the needs of war orphans, was a fate worse than death in his eyes. He opened his mouth to protest again, but Althea's stern gaze silenced him. He could imagine nothing worse than being among the "peons" of the population, stripped of all status. "Guards, take him away," Althea ordered.

As the guards moved to escort the former advisor out, Dorn's eyes were wide with a mixture of disbelief and terror. The opulent life he had built was crumbling around him, and there was no escape. His final thoughts were not of regret for his actions but a panicked longing for his lost luxury. The harsh reality of Rivti loomed ahead—a world without the indulgences he had known, a place where he would be nothing more than another pair of hands.

And as Dorn was led away, the council chamber erupted in a rare wave of approval, a collective acknowledgment of justice served. In that moment, Dorn's fall was complete, and the galaxy witnessed the long-awaited reckoning of a man who thought himself untouchable.

Once Dorn had been removed, Councilor Althea turned her attention to the heroes standing resolute before her. Her gaze was steady, her voice filled with genuine respect. "Lord Gresham, Lady Mara, Commander Levi, your actions have brought a significant victory to the Galactic Alliance. You have exposed a traitor and prevented further corruption from spreading within our ranks."

Commander Levi stood tall, though a flicker of surprise crossed his features at the commendation. He was used to the quiet, thankless duty of a soldier, where the true victories were often invisible to the public eye. The recognition, though unexpected, bolstered his resolve. Inside, he grappled with the weight of what they had accomplished, the lives saved, and the dangerous path still ahead. "Thank you, Councilor," he replied, a hint of humility in his voice. "It was our duty."

Althea nodded, acknowledging the burden each carried. "Duty well performed. As a token of our gratitude, the council awards you a commendation and a promotion within the ranks of the Alliance. Additionally, you will receive a bonus for your exemplary service."

Lady Mara, ever composed, felt a swell of pride mixed with a tinge of skepticism. Did the council truly understand the sacrifices made? The sleepless nights, the constant danger, the weight of leadership that never lifted? Her mind flickered to the faces of those they couldn't save, the haunting memories of past missions. Still, she inclined her head in acknowledgment. "We appreciate the council's recognition. Our fight is far from over, but this is a step towards the justice we seek."

Althea's gaze softened slightly as she addressed Lord Gresham and Lady Mara. "For the FEW, we understand that traditional rewards may not hold the same value. However, we extend our heartfelt thanks for your bravery and dedication. As a gesture of our appreciation, we offer you a month of respite—a chance to rest and rejuvenate. You have earned it."

Gresham exchanged a glance with Mara, a shared understanding passing between them, clasping his hand with Mara. The idea of rest was appealing yet foreign; their lives had been a relentless march of duty and sacrifice. The notion seemed almost like a distant dream, a luxury seldom afforded to those in their position. Gresham nodded, feeling the weariness of countless battles in his bones. "Thank you, Councilor. We will make good use of the time."

The council chamber, once filled with tension and judgment, now held a sense of closure. The heroes had been acknowledged, their efforts praised, and a path forward illuminated. But beneath the formalities, each felt the unspoken weight of their roles—the sacrifices they had made and those yet to come.

As they exited the hall, Levi, Mara, and Gresham felt a renewed sense of purpose. The road ahead was still fraught with challenges, but they were united and stronger together. The fight for justice continued, and with the council's support, they were more determined than ever to see it through.

Levi, Mara, and Gresham exchanged a glance, a silent agreement passing between them. They had taken the first step, but the path to true justice would be long and fraught with danger. They would need to stay vigilant and united in their purpose as they faced the trials that awaited them.

As they left the opulent chamber, the echoes of Dorn's arrogance and the chilling display of Gresham's power left an indelible mark on their resolve. The fight for the soul of the Alliance had only just begun. Each step forward was a testament to their commitment and a promise to those they served—a promise that no matter the cost, they would continue to stand against the darkness.

The Ripple Effect

The galaxy trembled as the news of Dorn's betrayal spread like wildfire. On the bustling marketplace of Taras, vibrant colors of alien fruits and exotic goods clashed with the collective gasp of vendors and buyers. Holo-screens embedded in the stalls flickered to life, broadcasting the urgent news. The usual cacophony of haggling fell silent, replaced by a stunned hush.

A startled gasp escaped Groth's lips as the vibrant Xylofruit tumbled from his grasp, its luminescence sputtering out on the market cobbles. "Dorn?" he whispered, eyes wide. "But he saved this market from collapse." His teenage daughter, Leera, tugged at his sleeve. "Papa, what does it mean?"

Groth sighed, looking around at the other vendors, their faces mirroring his shock. "It means, Leera, that the man we trusted to keep us safe...was a traitor." Nearby, a merchant selling technological gadgets shook his head in disbelief, muttering to a customer, "If the Alliance falls, what's to stop the Fair Trade from taking over our trade routes?"

Spaceship Workers

In Polaris Station's shipyards, the rhythmic clang of metal on metal echoed as workers toiled on the skeletal frame of a new vessel. A foreman paused, wiping sweat from his brow, as an alert flashed on his communicator. The bustling yard fell silent as the message spread.

"Damn it," a mechanic muttered, wiping grease from his hands. "If Dorn's a traitor, who can we trust?" A seasoned pilot, Captain Jara, clenched his fists. "We relied on Stratton's reforms. Without the Alliance's protection, this place will be overrun with pirates and black market dealers."

The youngest engineer, Lira, looked up at Jara, her voice trembling. "What do we do now, Captain?" Jara's gaze softened, a glimmer of hope sparking in his eyes. "We stay strong, Lira. We double-check every contract and every shipment. We protect our own because we can't rely on the Alliance anymore," he replied, his gaze hardening with determination. An older mechanic scoffed in another corner, "I'll believe it when I see it. People love to spread rumors."

Office Workers

In a high-rise office, a corporate executive, Mr. Voss, stared out the window at the sprawling cityscape, the news playing on a holo-screen behind him. "Stratton? How could he?" he whispered, fingers trembling as he raised the volume. "What will this mean for interplanetary trade agreements?"

His assistant, Nia, entered the room, her expression troubled. "Sir, the board is demanding an emergency meeting. They're worried about our shares." Voss nodded, steeling himself. "Prepare the reports, Nia. We need to show them we have contingency plans. The market's about to get rough."

Schools

In a classroom on the mid-sized planet of Elysia, the teacher paused mid-lesson, the news broadcast playing on a holo-screen. The children, sensing the tension, fell silent. "Students, this is a critical moment in our history," she said, her voice trembling. "We must understand the gravity of what's happening."

A bright student, Janek, raised his hand. "Miss, what does this mean for our future?" The teacher took a deep breath. "It means we must be vigilant. We must learn from this and ensure our leaders are held accountable."

Military Reactions

In a remote outpost, a seasoned soldier, Sergeant Kane, clenched his fists as he heard the news. "First, we fight the Fair Trade, but now we have to worry about our own leaders betraying us? What's next?" In the barracks, younger recruits looked to their Admiral, Captain Reyes, for reassurance. "Sir, what do we do now?" The Admiral's face was grim. "We stay vigilant. Trust in our immediate chain of command. We protect the Alliance from within and without."

Meanwhile, Lieutenant Harper sat in brooding silence in the officer's lounge, her faith in the Alliance shaken. "I've given everything for the Alliance," she murmured, staring into her drink. "If Dorn can betray us, who else can?" Across the room, Major Tran slammed his fist on the table. "This is exactly why we need to stick together. The Alliance is bigger than one man. We can't let one traitor destroy everything we've built."

Public Sentiment

Protests and public demonstrations erupted across various planets. Some supported the Alliance, calling for justice against Fair Trade. Others demanded transparency and accountability from leadership. In the streets of a core world, a mother held her child close, fear etched in her eyes. "What will happen to us now?" An elderly man, a veteran of past wars, stood resolute. "We stand together. We've faced worse. We'll get through this."

Fringe Groups and Conspiracy Theories

On the fringe planet of Eriadu, conspiracy theorists seized the moment. "The Alliance has always been corrupt!" shouted a fiery orator in the town square. "Dorn is just the tip of the iceberg. Who knows how deep the rot goes? We need to break free and form our own independent coalition!" A small but vocal group cheered, waving banners that read "Independence Now!" and "Trust No One."

Hope and Resilience

Despite the turmoil, pockets of hope and resilience emerged throughout the galaxy.

Community Unity

On the small moon of Caelum, the townspeople gathered in the central square. Under the leadership of Mayor Westbrook, a former Alliance officer, they formed committees to ensure the safety and well-being of their community. "We may be small, but together, we are strong," Westbrook said, her voice ringing with conviction. "We will protect our home and support each other through this crisis."

Families opened their homes to neighbors, sharing resources and offering comfort. Children played in the streets, unaware of the larger conflicts, their laughter a testament to the enduring spirit of the people.

Grassroots Movements

In the city of Novara on the planet Eos, a grassroots movement began to take shape. Led by a charismatic young leader named Kael, citizens organized rallies and community meetings to discuss how they could support the Alliance and fight against the Fair Trade's influence. "We can't rely solely on our leaders," Kael declared to a crowd of eager listeners. "We must take action ourselves. Together, we can make a difference."

Volunteers distributed flyers, organized food drives, and created a support network for those affected by the upheaval. The sense of unity and purpose revitalized the city, transforming fear into determination.

Individual Acts of Courage

Across the galaxy, individuals took action in their own ways. On the outskirts of the mining colony on Vespera, a retired engineer named Lyra began repairing old communication devices, ensuring that her community could stay connected and informed. "Information is power," she told her neighbors. "We must stay vigilant and support each other."

In the bustling trade hub of Celestia, a young merchant named Rian refused to let fear dictate his actions. He continued his trade routes, delivering essential supplies to remote colonies and spreading messages of hope and resilience. "We can't let them see us falter," he said, his resolve unwavering. "The Alliance is more than its leaders; it's the people who believe in its ideals."

Weekly Pizza Night on the Requiem

The next night, the Requiem hummed with anticipation for Mara's weekly pizza night. Amidst the chaos of their missions, this tradition allowed the crew to unwind, share stories, and indulge in the culinary marvels Mara managed to whip up from the ship's limited supplies.

As the yeasty aroma of freshly baked dough wafted through the corridors, mingling with pungent spices, the crew gathered in the lounge, their spirits high. Laughter echoed through the corridors, blending with the clattering of plates and utensils. The lounge, illuminated by soft, ambient lighting, featured comfortable seating arranged in a semicircle, with a large central table adorned with various knickknacks from their travels. A small, gaudy snow globe from the ice planet Krysta, complete with a miniature swirling blizzard, sat prominently in the center—a memento from a particularly memorable mission where they had to navigate treacherous ice storms.

Levi sauntered in, his tall frame and tousled hair giving him a roguish charm. His face alight with excitement, he called out, "Alright, folks, what's on the menu tonight, Mara?"

Mara, wearing an apron adorned with cartoonish depictions of intergalactic cuisine—tiny alien chefs with exaggerated features wielding oversized utensils—grinned. Her dark hair was pulled back into a messy bun, and her eyes sparkled with mischief. "We've got your classic Margherita, a spicy Andorian pepperoni, and for the adventurous, a Xylosian green cheese and tentacle delight."

A collective groan went up at the mention of the Xylosian specialty. Gresham, with his broad shoulders and perpetually disheveled uniform, twisted his face in mock horror. "Tentacles? Really, Mara? I thought we were done with mystery meats after that incident with the Gelborian stew."

Mara laughed, shaking her head. "Come on, Gresham, live a little. Besides, it's all part of the fun. Who knows, you might actually like it."

Tran, shuffling a deck of cards at the corner table, chimed in. Her short, spiky hair and sharp eyes gave her an air of constant readiness. "Remember when Gresham tried to make dinner and ended up summoning a smoke monster from the kitchen?"

Laughter erupted, and Gresham threw a mock glare at Tran. "That was one time, and the fire suppression system worked perfectly."

Levi leaned back in his chair, a nostalgic smile on his face. "Hey, remember three weeks ago when Tran made that Ferinian sausage pizza, and the whole lounge smelled like burnt rubber for days?"

Tran rolled her eyes but couldn't suppress a grin. "Yeah, yeah, but at least no one got sick from it, unlike Gresham's infamous Gelborian stew."

The first bite elicited a variety of reactions. Tran, ever stoic, chewed thoughtfully, savoring the spicy kick of the pepperoni, while Gresham's eyes bulged comically, his face turning a shade of green. "Mara," he sputtered, "this... this is an abomination!"

Levi, dressed in a slightly tattered flight jacket, pounded the table, tears streaming down his face. "Oh, Gresham," he gasped, "your face... worth every tentacle."

Even Mara couldn't hold back her giggles, her usually composed demeanor breaking into fits of laughter. "I think we've found Gresham's culinary kryptonite."

As the crew continued their feast, the door to the kitchen swung open, and Chef Antoine made his grand entrance. Known for his meticulous culinary standards and impeccable taste, the chef was a fixture on the Requiem, ensuring the crew was always well-fed with the finest dishes he could muster from their supplies.

Chef Antoine, with his impeccable uniform and a frown etched on his face, approached the table. "What is this abomination I hear of? Tentacle pizza?" His accent was rich and melodious, adding flair to his disbelief.

Mara smirked, gesturing to the offending slice. "Just a bit of fun, Chef. Would you care to try some?"

With an air of exaggerated caution, Antoine picked up a slice, examining it as if it might bite him first. The crew watched in anticipation, stifling their laughter. He took a tentative bite, chewing slowly as his expression shifted from skepticism to horror.

"Mon adieu! This... this is an insult to the culinary arts!" Antoine declared, waving the half-eaten slice in the air. "Mara, you are hereby banned from the kitchen until you learn the true art of cooking!"

The crew erupted in laughter, their voices mingling in the warm, inviting space. Mara feigned a look of shock and placed a hand dramatically on her chest. "But Chef, my tentacle pizza is beloved by many!"

Antoine shook his head with mock severity, unable to suppress a smile. "You have talent, Mara, but it needs refining. Leave the cuisine to me."

Levi leaned over to Tran, whispering conspiratorially, "Looks like Mara's met her match."

Tran chuckled, nudging Jax, who was still giggling at the exchange. "Looks like we all have something to learn from the chef."

As the crew continued to enjoy the night, sharing more stories and laughter, the Requiem felt less like a ship in the vast expanse of space and more like a home filled with family. Their bonds strengthened with each shared joke, each moment of camaraderie, as they prepared to face whatever challenges awaited them together.

The laughter that followed was a mix of disbelief and amusement. "And you're still here to tell the tale," Levi said, shaking his head. "You really are indestructible, Gresham."

At one point, Tran challenged Levi to a pizza-eating contest, much to the amusement of the crew. "I bet you can't eat an entire Xylosian pizza without making a face," she dared.

Levi, never one to back down from a challenge, accepted. With great fanfare, he took a large bite of the tentacle-laden pizza. The slimy texture and the slightly glowing green cheese made his face turn a comical shade of red, but he managed to keep a straight face. "Delicious," he choked out, causing the crew to erupt in laughter.

Through it all, the camaraderie and laughter bound them together, a reminder of the strength they drew from each other. The galaxy might be vast and perilous, but aboard the Requiem, they found solace in the shared moments of joy and absurdity.

As the night wound down, Levi raised his glass, a solemn look replacing his usual mirth. "To the Requiem," he said, his voice resonating with pride and affection. "To our victories, our defeats, and the family we've become. No matter what the galaxy throws at us, we stand together."

The crew raised their glasses, the clinking sound a harmonious echo in the lounge. "To the Requiem!"

As they finished their pizzas and shared a final laugh, the stars outside continued their silent vigil, watching over a crew bound not just by duty but by the unbreakable bonds of friendship and resilience.

The stars glittered outside the viewport, casting a silvery glow across the observation deck of the Requiem. Gresham and Alexander sat at a small table, each with a glass of fine, aged whiskey. The amber liquid reflected the starlight, its aroma a rich blend of oak and caramel. Their silence was comfortable, born of mutual respect and countless shared experiences.

Alexander raised his glass, the cool, smooth glass a reassuring weight in his hand. "To surprises," he said with a grin. "I still can't believe they made me an Admiral."

Gresham chuckled softly, swirling his drink and watching the liquid catch the light. "You've earned it, Alexander. Your leadership, your dedication—none of it has gone unnoticed. Though I must admit, I never imagined we'd form this friendship."

Alexander's eyes sparkled with curiosity. "Oh? And why's that?"

Gresham took a sip, savoring the warmth that spread through him. "I never saw myself having a friendship with a human. But your persistence wore me down. You wouldn't take no for an answer; you kept pushing your way into my life."

Alexander laughed, the sound echoing in the quiet room. "I learned a lot from you, Gresham. Commitment, honor, and knowing when action is needed over diplomacy. You've been a mentor and a friend."

Gresham nodded, a rare smile touching his lips. "And you, Alexander, have shown me the value of adaptability and resilience. It's been quite a journey."

Alexander leaned back, his gaze thoughtful. "It will be wild being on the Requiem without you or Lady Mara. This ship won't feel the same."

Gresham raised an eyebrow, a playful glint in his eye masking a deeper concern. "Oh, I think 'Admiral Levi' can handle anything. Besides, you'll have plenty of challenges to keep you busy."

Alexander chuckled softly, and then, with a mischievous glint in his eye, he added, "And hey, try not to catch any human illnesses while you're gone. I know how proud you FEW are of your superior immune systems."

Gresham's lips twitched in amusement. "Worried I might prove more susceptible than we thought, Alexander? Don't worry; I'll stay far away from your human germs."

Alexander laughed. "Just looking out for you, old friend. Can't have you laid up in bed when there's a universe to explore."

"Your concern is touching," Gresham replied dryly, but there was warmth in his eyes. "I'll be sure to report back if I so much as sneeze."

Alexander smiled, reassured by Gresham's confidence. Then, with a more sincere tone, he added, "Thanks. And hey, don't forget to take your medication before bed. I know how you get if you skip it."

Gresham smirked, shaking his head. "You know me too well."

They clinked glasses, the sound a quiet affirmation of their bond. The playful exchange highlighted their comfort and familiarity, a friendship that could withstand gentle ribbing and cross-species jokes. The future might be uncertain, but in that moment, they celebrated their past and the strength of their unique relationship, each silently acknowledging the unspoken fears and hopes for what lay ahead.

As the stars outside continued their silent vigil, watching over this duo bound by shared history and mutual respect, both men felt a sense of peace, knowing that whatever the future held, their friendship was a constant, guiding star.

15

ISLAND SANCTUARY

Arrival and Exploration

The transport shuttle descended smoothly through the atmosphere, bringing Lady Mara and Lord Gresham to their destination: a secluded island paradise on a remote, untouched planet. They had chosen this spot for their month-long leave, far from the demands and responsibilities of their roles on the Requiem. Here, there were no urgent calls, no missions—just the two of them and the beauty of the natural world.

As they stepped out of the shuttle, the soft sand shifted beneath their feet like a warm embrace, and the ocean breeze caressed their skin, carrying the scents of exotic blooms and salt. Sunlight sparkled on the water, creating a tapestry of dancing diamonds. Mara closed her eyes, savoring the moment, feeling the weight of duty slip away. "This is perfect," she said, turning to Gresham with a smile that mirrored the sun's warmth.

The air was rich with the scent of blooming flowers and fresh sea air, a symphony of fragrances that promised relaxation and adventure. The island was a lush, tropical haven with white sandy beaches, crystal-clear waters, and dense forests teeming with vibrant wildlife. The sound of waves crashing gently against the shore was a soothing backdrop, a promise of tranquility and adventure.

Mara took a deep breath, her eyes closing as she soaked in the serenity. Gresham grinned, his eyes twinkling with excitement. He wrapped his arms around Mara from behind, resting his chin on her shoulder. "Indeed. We've earned this time. And there's no one I'd rather spend it with than you."

They had arranged for a cozy beachfront bungalow, complete with all the comforts they could want. The wooden structure blended seamlessly with the surrounding nature, its thatched roof and open design allowing the gentle sea breeze to flow through. After dropping off their bags, they changed into light, casual clothing and set off to explore the island. Hand in hand, they walked along the beach, their feet sinking into the warm, powdery sand. The sensation was both grounding and freeing, a reminder of the simple pleasures of life.

"Look at that," Mara pointed to a pod of dolphins playing in the surf, their sleek bodies leaping gracefully through the water.

Gresham chuckled, pulling her closer and kissing her temple. "It's like they're welcoming us. Remember that time on Eridanus IV when we were supposed to be incognito, but those kids mistook us for local celebrities?"

Mara laughed, leaning into his embrace. "And you ended up signing autographs all afternoon. I thought I'd never stop laughing."

Mara and Gresham decided to hike along the lush trails that wound through the island's vibrant interior. The air was fresh and crisp, filled with the earthy scent of the forest and the distant roar of a waterfall. The path ahead was dappled with sunlight filtering through the canopy, creating a patchwork of light and shadow on the forest floor.

As they climbed higher, Mara marveled at the untouched beauty around them, each step taking them deeper into a world untouched by time. Her mind drifted to how moments like these were rare jewels tucked away amidst their chaotic lives. "Look, Gresham," she said, pointing at a vivid parrot perched high above, its plumage a burst of color against the green canopy. The waterfall ahead roared, promising a sight that would etch itself into their memories.

The sound of rushing water grew louder, a powerful, invigorating noise that promised a spectacular sight. They walked side by side, their hands brushing occasionally, a silent testament to their closeness. The trail bent sharply, and they followed it eagerly, anticipation building with every step.

Near the bend, they paused to drink water from their canteens. Mara took a deep breath, the cool, crisp air filling her lungs. She looked around, her eyes wide with wonder. "Look, Gresham! So beautiful!" she exclaimed, her voice filled with awe.

Ahead of them, the waterfall cascaded down the mountainside, a torrent of white froth crashing into the pool below. The sun caught the mist, creating a brilliant rainbow that arced gracefully through the air. The scene was breathtaking, nature at its most magnificent.

Yet, all Gresham could see was Mara. Her eyes sparkled with delight, reflecting the vibrant colors of the rainbow. Her cheeks were flushed from the hike, and her hair framed her face in loose waves. She was the embodiment of beauty and grace, and in that moment, she captivated him entirely.

"Beautiful," he murmured, his gaze fixed on her.

Mara turned to look at him, a smile spreading across her face as she noticed the way he was looking at her. "You're not even looking at the waterfall," she teased, a soft laugh escaping her lips.

Gresham stepped closer, reaching out to tuck a stray strand of hair behind her ear. "How could I when you're here?" he said, his voice low and tender. He cupped her face gently, his thumb brushing across her cheek.

Mara leaned into his touch, her heart swelling with love. She placed her hand over his, their fingers intertwining. "Thank you," she whispered, her eyes locking onto his. "For everything."

Gresham smiled, leaning in to press a gentle kiss to her forehead. "Every moment with you is a gift, Mara," he replied. "And I wouldn't trade it for anything in the universe."

Each new sight brought a sense of wonder and joy, allowing them to reconnect not just with each other but with the simple pleasures of life.

The next morning, the salty tang of the air mingled with the sweet scent of frangipani as Mara and Gresham emerged from the crystalline waters. Their skin glistened in the sunlight, casting shimmering reflections on the calm lagoon. The day's heat had softened, leaving behind a gentle warmth that enveloped them like a comforting embrace.

The lagoon was cool and refreshing, a gentle reprieve from the sun's warmth. Mara felt the water wrap around her like silk; each splash a sparkling arc in the air. Gresham laughed as he lunged after her, the sound echoing like music across the water. As the sun began to set, the light painted the lagoon in shades of pink and gold, turning their playful dance into something magical, a scene from a dream they never wanted to end.

Gresham reached for Mara, his hand finding hers as it trailed across the water. Her laughter, a melody as sweet as the island breeze, carried on the humid air. He pulled her close, their bodies wet and warm against each other. The world, with its relentless demands and treacherous undercurrents, seemed to dissolve into a distant memory.

Breaking the kiss with a playful grin, Mara splashed Gresham, sending droplets of water sparkling in the golden light. "Catch me if you can!" she teased, darting away with a mischievous laugh.

Gresham, laughing, chased after her, the water parting around him. "Oh, you won't get away that easily," he called, his voice full of playful determination.

They splashed and swam, their laughter echoing across the lagoon. Mara squealed as Gresham caught her around the waist, lifting her out of the water before they both tumbled back in, sending waves rippling outward. They surfaced together, faces inches apart, breathless with joy.

"You're impossible," Mara said, her eyes shining with happiness.

"And you love it," Gresham replied, brushing a strand of wet hair from her face before kissing her softly.

Their playfulness continued, each trying to outdo the other with splashes and playful dives. The seriousness of their roles seemed a world away as they reveled in the simple, childlike fun. The sun dipped lower, casting long shadows and painting the sky in hues of pink and gold, but in their secluded paradise, time seemed to stand still.

Finally, they emerged from the water, still laughing, their bodies warm from the exercise and the sun. They walked hand-in-hand along the shore, the soft sand yielding beneath their feet. The moon, a silver disc rising from the ocean, cast an ethereal glow on the island.

"I never thought I'd find a place like this," Mara murmured, her voice filled with wonder.

Gresham squeezed her hand gently. "It's perfect, isn't it? A place just for us, away from everything else."

They found a spot where the sand was softest and sat down, watching the moonlight dance on the waves. Gresham wrapped an arm around Mara, pulling her close. She rested her head on his shoulder, feeling the steady beat of his heart.

"I love you, Gresham," she whispered.

"And I love you, Mara," he replied, his voice soft and full of emotion.

They stayed there, wrapped in each other's arms, letting the peace and beauty of the moment wash over them. The playful energy from earlier had given way to a deep, contented calm. The world outside might be full of challenges and uncertainties, but here, in their secluded paradise, they had found a haven of love and happiness.

As they sat together, watching the stars twinkle into existence, Mara began to reminisce. "Do you remember the first time we met?"

The air was thick with tension and the smell of smoke as Gresham, leading a unit of Galactic Alliance soldiers, navigated the war-torn landscape of an outer planet. They had arrived unexpectedly, drawn by a distress signal from the beleaguered colony. The Alliance rarely ventured this far out, but something had compelled Gresham to insist on the mission.

As they moved through the rubble, providing aid and organizing evacuations, Gresham felt an inexplicable pull guiding him through the chaos. He turned a corner and saw a figure moving with a serene, commanding presence. Her hands glowed with a soft blue light as she tended to the wounded.

Gresham's heart skipped a beat. Another FEW? Here?

He signaled his unit to continue while he approached her. "Excuse me," he called out, his voice cutting through the noise. "Who are you?"

The woman turned, her eyes meeting his with a mix of surprise and recognition. "I'm Mara," she replied, her voice steady despite the surrounding chaos. "Lady Mara of the FEW."

Gresham's eyes widened. It was rare enough to meet another FEW, but to find one here, so far from their usual spheres of influence, was astonishing. "I'm Gresham, Lord Gresham of the FEW. I never expected to find one of us here."

Mara gave a faint smile, her gaze shifting to the injured child she was healing. "Nor did I expect to meet another FEW. I've been helping these people for months. They were on the brink of collapse."

Gresham watched her for a moment, captivated by her grace and the power she wielded so effortlessly. "I felt a pull to come here," he admitted. "The Alliance agreed to the mission, but it was something more that brought me."

She stood, her expression thoughtful as she looked at him. "Perhaps it was fate," she said softly. "A sign that our paths were meant to cross."

Their eyes locked, and for a moment, the devastation around them seemed to fade. "Let's see this through together," Gresham said, feeling a rare sense of connection.

From that moment, they worked side by side, combining their strengths to bring aid and hope to the people. The bond they formed in those harrowing days was undeniable, a connection that transcended the immediate crisis.

Over the next few months, Gresham and Mara were often seen quietly talking, laughing, and sharing information. Their respect and admiration for each other grew with every shared mission and challenge they overcame together. Their conversations ranged from strategies to personal histories, creating a deep and lasting bond.

One evening, as they finished a mission, Mara looked at Gresham with a thoughtful expression. "I'd like to see more of what the Alliance does," she said. "To understand your world better and work more closely with you."

Gresham smiled, a warmth spreading through him at her words. "I would love that. Come aboard the Requiem with me. I think you'll find it... enlightening."

And so, Lady Mara boarded the Alliance ship with Gresham. The crew, initially surprised, quickly came to appreciate her presence and the unique abilities she brought to their missions. Mara and Gresham's partnership deepened as they navigated the complexities of their duties and the challenges of integrating their unique skills with the Alliance's operations.

Their professional respect blossomed into a profound personal connection. Late-night conversations turned into shared meals, and quiet moments of reflection turned into shared laughter and understanding. They found solace in each other's company, their bond growing stronger with each passing day.

One evening, as they stood on the observation deck, watching the stars blur into streaks of light as the ship hurtled through hyperspace, Gresham turned to Mara, his eyes reflecting the distant galaxies. "I've never felt this way before," he admitted softly. "What we have... it's more than I ever imagined."

Mara smiled, reaching out to take his hand. "I feel the same, Gresham. Our journey together has been incredible, and I can't wait to see where it takes us."

He pulled her close, wrapping his arms around her. "Whatever the future holds, we'll face it together."

Their lips met in a tender kiss, sealing the promise of their love amidst the vast expanse of the galaxy. From that moment, their hearts were intertwined, bound by a love that had grown from a chance meeting to an unbreakable bond.

As they continued their missions, side by side, their love became a beacon of strength and hope, not just for each other but for everyone they encountered. They were no longer just Lady Mara and Lord Gresham of the FEW; they were partners, lovers, and a force to be reckoned with in the galaxy.

Mara leaned back against Gresham's chest, the stars a tapestry above them. "Do you remember the first time we met?" she asked, her voice carrying the weight of nostalgia. The memory of that war-torn world flickered in her mind, a reminder of how far they had come. Gresham tightened his hold on her, his voice soft with reverence. "I do," he replied, recalling the chaos and the way her presence had grounded him. Their past was a mosaic of moments, each piece a testament to their journey.

The morning sun filtered through the windows of their quarters, casting a warm glow over the room. Mara stretched lazily in bed, savoring the rare moment of peace. She turned to see Gresham already up, busy in the small kitchenette.

"What are you doing?" she asked, propping herself up on one elbow.

Gresham turned with a smile, holding a tray with two steaming mugs and a plate of freshly made pancakes. "Making breakfast in bed for my favorite person."

Mara laughed softly, sitting up and pulling the blankets around her. "You're spoiling me."

"Only because you deserve it," Gresham replied, setting the tray on the bed and handing her a mug. "Coffee, just the way you like it."

Mara took a sip, closing her eyes in bliss. "Perfect, as always."

They spent the next hour enjoying the simple pleasure of breakfast in bed, sharing stories and laughter. It was a small gesture, but it filled their hearts with warmth and strengthened their bond.

"Thank you, Gresham," Mara said, her eyes filled with love. "For everything."

Gresham leaned in, capturing her lips in a tender kiss. "And thank you, Mara. For being my everything."

The following morning, Mara awoke to the sight of a breakfast table set with an array of delicious foods. She noticed the vase on the table, seemingly overturned and stuffed comically with a wild assortment of flowers from the nearby area. She laughed softly, appreciating the effort Gresham had put into surprising her.

"Good morning," Gresham said, appearing from the kitchen with two steaming mugs of coffee. He handed one to Mara, who took a sip and smiled, tasting the hint of her favorite flavor of Cognac added to it.

"MMMM," Gresham exclaimed, closing his eyes in pleasure as he took a sip of his own coffee. "You always know how to make it perfect."

For the rest of their month off, they continued to explore the island, discovering new wonders and deepening their bond. They snorkeled in the vibrant coral reefs, marveling at the kaleidoscope of colors beneath the surface. The water was cool and refreshing, the sun warming their skin as they floated together in the clear blue sea. They kayaked through hidden coves, their laughter echoing off the rocky cliffs, and danced under the stars, their bodies moving in perfect harmony to the rhythm of the waves.

One evening, as they lay on the blanket stargazing, Mara pointed out a constellation. "Look, that's the Orion Nebula. Remember our mission there?"

Gresham smiled, recalling the adrenaline-filled adventure. "How could I forget? That was the time you outsmarted the entire fleet of rogue drones with just a datapad and a piece of wire."

Mara laughed, "And you had to keep them distracted long enough for me to do it. We make a pretty good team, don't we?"

"The best," Gresham agreed, squeezing her hand.

Every day was an adventure, and every night was filled with romance and tender moments. By the time their leave was over, Mara and Gresham felt more connected than ever, their love strengthened by the time they had spent together. As they boarded the shuttle back to the Requiem, they knew they were ready to face whatever challenges awaited them, their hearts fortified by the memories of their island paradise.

As the sun began its slow descent towards the horizon, casting a warm golden glow over the beach, Mara and Gresham stood together, their toes sinking into the soft, warm sand. Gresham stood behind Mara, his arms wrapped around her waist, pulling her close. They watched as the waves gently lapped at the shore, the sound of a soothing melody that complemented the tranquility of the moment.

The cool breeze carried the salty scent of the ocean, mingling with the sweet fragrance of blooming flowers that surrounded them. Gresham felt the warmth of Mara's body against his, a comforting contrast to the cool evening air. He pressed a soft kiss to her temple, his eyes never leaving the horizon.

"This is perfect," Mara murmured, leaning back into his embrace, feeling the steady rhythm of his heartbeat.

Gresham tightened his hold slightly, savoring the feel of her in his arms. "It really is," he replied, his voice low and filled with affection. "Moments like these, just us, are what I cherish the most."

They stood in comfortable silence, watching as the sun dipped lower, painting the sky in hues of orange and pink. The water shimmered, reflecting the brilliant colors and creating a breathtaking view. Gresham could feel the sand shift beneath their feet with each gentle wave, grounding them in this perfect moment of peace.

Mara sighed contentedly, turning her head slightly to look at Gresham. "Are you happy, Gresham?" she whispered, her eyes reflecting the fading light.

Gresham smiled, his heart swelling with love for her. "The happiest!" he replied, his voice full of warmth. He leaned down, capturing her lips in a soft, tender kiss, sealing the promise of their love in the golden twilight.

As the last sliver of the sun disappeared below the horizon, they remained entwined, their souls connected in a moment that transcended time. The world around them faded, leaving only the two of them and the enduring strength of their love.

Their hands found each other, a silent understanding passing between them. Gresham's gaze held hers, a depth of desire and longing swimming in his eyes that made Mara's breath catch. She felt a warmth spreading through her, a heat that ignited every nerve ending.

As they moved closer, the world seemed to fade away. There was only them, the intoxicating scent of jasmine and the promise of something wild and beautiful. The gentle rustle of palm leaves in the breeze and the distant murmur of the ocean added to the enchantment of the moment. Their lips met in a soft, exploratory kiss, a gentle touch that quickly deepened into a passionate embrace.

Gresham's touch was both fire and balm, igniting a warmth that spread through Mara's entire being. She felt the steady thrum of his heartbeat; each beat was a testament to their shared existence. The world narrowed to this room, to the sanctuary they had created, where time ceased to exist. Every touch, every whisper was a promise, a binding of souls that transcended the physical realm.

Mara felt a surge of excitement as Gresham's arms encircled her, lifting her effortlessly. Her heart pounded with anticipation, each beat resonating through her entire being. The warmth of his skin against hers, the firm yet tender grip of his hands, sent shivers down her spine. Their breaths mingled, creating an intoxicating mix of longing and desire.

Gresham carried her towards the bedroom, each step measured and deliberate, the soft sand yielding beneath his feet. The air inside was cooler, carrying the subtle scent of fresh linens and the lingering aroma of the sea. The soft glow of moonlight filtered through the windows, casting a silvery sheen on everything it touched.

Their bodies were electric with anticipation, every touch and whisper heightening the connection between them. As the door closed behind them, the world disappeared into darkness, leaving only the intimate sanctuary they had created together.

Gresham laid Mara gently on the bed, the cool sheets a stark contrast to the heat building between them. His hands roamed her body, exploring and discovering, each touch a wordless declaration of his love and desire. Mara's fingers traced the contours of his back, feeling the strength and tenderness beneath his skin.

Their kisses became more urgent, more insistent, a dance of lips and tongues that left them both breathless. The taste of him, salty and sweet, was a drug she couldn't get enough of. She felt his heart beating in time with hers, a steady rhythm that anchored them in the moment.

Gresham's voice was a husky whisper in her ear, "You are everything to me, Mara."

She responded with a fervent kiss, her body arching towards him, "And you are my world, Gresham."

The night was a symphony of shared passion and whispered promises. The feel of his skin against hers, the sound of their mingled breaths, and the sight of his eyes dark with desire created an experience that was both overwhelming and deeply fulfilling.

They moved together in perfect harmony, their bodies communicating in a language only they understood. Every touch, every sigh, every whispered word brought them closer, binding them in a connection that transcended the physical.

As they lay entwined, the first light of dawn beginning to peek through the curtains, Mara felt a profound sense of contentment. She nestled against Gresham, his arms a protective cocoon around her. The world outside was still there, with all its challenges and demands, but in this moment, they had created something timeless and beautiful.

"I love you," she murmured, her voice soft and full of emotion.

"And I love you, Mara," he replied, pressing a tender kiss to her forehead.

They drifted into a peaceful sleep, the warmth of their love a soothing balm against the uncertainties of the world. Together, they had found a sanctuary, a place where their souls could rest and their hearts could beat as one.

As the sun rose, casting a golden hue over the island, Mara and Gresham stood hand in hand on the beach. The waves lapped gently at their feet, a soothing rhythm that matched the beating of their hearts.

Mara sighed, her eyes scanning the horizon. "I wish we could stay here forever," she murmured, a hint of wistfulness in her voice.

Gresham nodded, squeezing her hand. "This place will always be here for us," he said softly. "And we'll carry these memories wherever we go."

They turned to face each other, the weight of the moment settling between them. Mara reached up, tracing her fingers along Gresham's jaw. "Thank you for this," she whispered. "For everything."

Gresham smiled, his eyes filled with warmth. "It's been perfect," he replied. "And we'll come back. Whenever we need to find each other again."

Together, they walked back up the beach, leaving footprints in the sand—a testament to their time here, a memory etched in the island's heart.

16

COSMIC KINSHIP

The Requiem glided silently through the vast expanse of space, a sleek silhouette against the backdrop of distant stars. Its crew moved with purpose; each member engaged in their tasks, maintaining the harmony of the ship's operations. Lady Mara sat in her quarters, her eyes scanning the mission reports spread before her. The soft hum of the ship was a comforting presence, a reminder of the life she had chosen. The faint smell of recycled air and the slight vibration of the deck beneath her feet added to the familiar ambiance.

Her focus was interrupted by the ship's communication system crackling to life, a sharp contrast to the quiet murmur of the ship. "Lady Mara," the voice of the communication officer sounded over the intercom, "we have a priority call for you from Evan Thornhill."

Mara's brow furrowed slightly. Evan Thornhill, the enigmatic software mogul known for his wealth and influence, rarely reached out without reason. She felt a slight tensing in her shoulders, a physical reminder of her wariness. Setting her reports aside, she made her way to the communication hub, curiosity mingling with caution. The soft whirring of the ship's engines and the faint echo of distant conversations provided a backdrop to her thoughts.

The screen flickered to life, revealing Thornhill's striking features. His piercing blue eyes and confident smile exuded a magnetic charm, a presence that seemed to transcend the screen.

Behind him, the opulent interior of his penthouse was visible, a testament to his success and taste, filled with rare artifacts and cutting-edge technology.

"Lady Mara," Thornhill began, his voice smooth and welcoming, "I trust this message finds you well."

"Mr. Thornhill," Mara replied, maintaining her composure, her tone polite yet guarded. "To what do I owe the pleasure?"

Thornhill leaned forward slightly, his gaze never wavering. A subtle warmth flickered in his eyes, hinting at a deeper interest beyond mere business. "I've come across something that I believe will be of great interest to you. A rare tablet with inscriptions that date back to the early days of the Galactic Alliance. It's a piece of history that I think you would appreciate."

Mara's curiosity was piqued, but she remained cautious, aware of Thornhill's reputation for being persuasive. The subtle undertone of his words suggested more than mere scholarly interest. "That sounds fascinating, but why contact me specifically?"

Thornhill's smile widened, a hint of genuine enthusiasm lighting up his eyes. "Your reputation for appreciating and preserving historical artifacts precedes you, Lady Mara. And, if I may be honest, I have always admired your passion for knowledge and discovery. I would be honored if you would visit my penthouse to examine the tablet. I believe it could offer insights that would be invaluable to your current endeavors."

Mara considered his words carefully, weighing the intrigue against her instincts. The offer was compelling, and Thornhill's reputation as a collector and benefactor was well-known. Yet, the subtle undertone of his invitation was not lost on her. She recalled their previous encounters, the way his words often carried layers of meaning, and the tension that always simmered beneath their exchanges.

She allowed herself a brief moment of reflection, considering the implications of Evan's offer. The tablet could indeed be significant, potentially holding secrets of the FEW that had been lost to time. But accepting his invitation meant stepping into a world where motives were often hidden beneath layers of charm and opulence.

"Very well, Mr. Thornhill," she said, a touch of wariness in her voice. "I will come to examine the tablet."

"Excellent," Thornhill replied, his smile never faltering. "I'll have my transport shuttle ready for you. I look forward to our meeting."

The screen went dark, leaving Mara in silent contemplation. The invitation was both enticing and suspicious. She knew Thornhill's reputation for using his resources to achieve his goals, and the significance of the tablet intrigued her as much as it concerned her. This would require caution and vigilance.

As Mara prepared to leave, Lord Gresham entered the room, his presence commanding as always. His gaze was steady, a mix of concern and understanding in his eyes. He stood with an easy confidence, hands clasped behind his back—a habitual gesture that spoke of his leadership and assurance. "Mara, I heard about Thornhill's call. Are you sure this is a good idea?"

Mara met his gaze, appreciating his protective nature. "I'm not sure yet," she admitted, her voice thoughtful. "But I believe it's worth investigating. Thornhill might have something valuable, something we need."

Gresham nodded, stepping closer, his confidence in her decision unwavering. "Just be careful. Thornhill has a way of getting what he wants."

Mara smiled, a reassuring warmth in her eyes. "I will. Thank you, Gresham."

Gresham returned her smile, a silent promise of support in his expression. Together, they stood for a moment, a shared understanding passing between them, before Mara turned to prepare for her meeting with Evan Thornhill. As she gathered her things, her mind was already mapping out the conversation ahead, calculating the possibilities and potential pitfalls of what lay before her.

Mara met his concerned gaze. "I have to see what this tablet is about. It could be important. Besides," she added with a slight smile, "I can handle Thornhill."

Gresham's expression softened, though his worry remained. "Just be careful. Thornhill has a way of getting under people's skin."

"I will," Mara assured him. "And thank you."

A short while later, Mara stepped off Thornhill's luxurious shuttle, the difference from her usual military transport striking. The shuttle's interior had been sleek and sophisticated, adorned with plush seating and ambient lighting that hinted at the extravagance of its owner. Now, as she arrived at Thornhill's penthouse, the doors opened to reveal an expansive space adorned with luxurious furnishings and offering a panoramic view of the city below. Thornhill stood at the entrance, his welcoming smile firmly in place.

"Lady Mara," he greeted warmly, extending a hand. "Welcome to my humble abode."

Mara took his hand briefly, noting the firm yet gentle grip before stepping inside. Her eyes scanned the room, taking in the blend of ancient artifacts and advanced technology, a testament to Thornhill's eclectic tastes and considerable resources. "It's quite impressive," she admitted, her voice holding a note of genuine admiration.

"Thank you," Thornhill replied, guiding her deeper into the room. "And here is the tablet I mentioned."

He led her to a sleek display case in the center of the room, carefully unlocking it to reveal the tablet. Mara leaned in, her breath catching at the sight of the ancient inscriptions. The tablet was a remarkable find, the markings intricate and filled with potential knowledge that seemed to hum with an unseen energy.

Thornhill bent over beside her, his warmth palpable as he stood close. Mara caught the faint scent of his exotic cologne, an aroma that wrapped around her senses, drawing her in despite herself. As she focused on the tablet, she was acutely aware of his presence, an undeniable magnetism that seemed to pulse between them.

"May I?" Thornhill asked softly, his voice a low rumble that resonated with her.

Mara nodded, surprised by the gentleness of his touch as he took her hand in his. A jolt of something unexpected shot through her, a spark that seemed to ignite at the contact. Together, they traced the symbols on the tablet, their fingers moving in sync over the cool, etched surface.

Each line and curve of the inscription seemed to resonate with an ancient power, a lineage older than civilization itself. With each stroke, Mara felt Thornhill's presence intertwine with hers, a shared energy that pulsed in rhythm with the tablet's arcane secrets.

As they traced the inscriptions, the ancient words began to take shape in her mind, revealing a startling truth. The tablet spoke of the FEW as mere iterations, a cycle that repeated every 180 years. Ten individuals, each generation, imbued with the power to shape history but ultimately leaving no lasting effects. It was a sobering realization that struck Mara with an unexpected weight.

Mara's heart quickened, her pupils dilating in response to the intensity of the moment. It wasn't just Thornhill's proximity or the weight of history in her hands; it was the way their connection seemed to transcend the ordinary, stirring something deep within her.

Thornhill's grip on her hand tightened slightly, a silent acknowledgment of the impact of the revelation. "Mara," he said softly, his eyes holding hers with a sincerity that pierced through the haze of discovery. "You're not just another iteration. You're unique, and you matter in ways beyond this cycle."

His words wrapped around her like a balm, offering comfort amidst the turmoil. Tears welled up in Mara's eyes, blurring the inscription. This wasn't just about her anymore—it was a legacy stretching back through time, a burden and a birthright in equal measure.

Overwhelmed, she sank to her knees, the weight of the discovery pressing down on her. Thornhill was immediately by her side, his hand gently cupping her chin, guiding her gaze to meet his. His touch was warm, grounding her against the cool stone floor.

"Mara," his voice was a soothing melody, concern threading through his usual smooth cadence. "You are more than a part of history. You have the power to change it, to create something lasting."

His eyes held hers, a mixture of empathy and understanding that transcended words. In that moment, Mara realized the depth of Evan's sincerity, the genuine interest that had driven him to uncover this piece of history—for her and perhaps for something greater.

Thornhill's passion for her well-being was evident in his gaze, the intensity of his belief in her shining through. "I wanted you to see this, to know that you have a choice. You can be more than just a footnote in history."

As Mara absorbed his words, Evan leaned in, a moment of vulnerability and connection hanging in the air. His lips brushed against hers, a gentle, unexpected kiss that sent another jolt through her. It was a kiss that spoke of admiration and possibility, a whisper of what could be.

Mara's heart raced, a tumult of emotions swirling within her. The kiss was brief, yet it lingered in the charged air between them, a testament to the complex web of feelings and revelations that had unfolded in those moments.

Mara stood in Evan's opulent penthouse, her mind swirling with the implications of the tablet's revelations. The weight of history pressed down on her, a mix of fear and awe at the legacy she now understood.

Evan watched her closely, sensing her inner turmoil. "You're not alone in this, Mara," he said softly, stepping closer. "I see a future with you, one where we can explore these possibilities together. But I understand you have things to deal with first."

Before she could respond, Evan leaned in, brushing his lips against hers in a passionate, unexpected kiss. The world seemed to tilt on its axis, the intensity of the moment catching Mara off guard. A rush of emotions flooded through her, leaving her breathless and conflicted.

As they parted, Evan's smile remained, but his eyes told a different story. "Allow me one last moment," he murmured, his voice a low rumble that sent shivers down her spine. "A chance to etch this connection in your memory, Mara. Because the woman you choose today... she may not be the woman you always want to be."

His words hung in the air, resonating deeply with her. The promise of freedom and transformation was tempting, yet Mara knew she had to reconcile her feelings and responsibilities before making any decisions.

Mara hesitated and then nodded. Thornhill reached out, gently cupping her face in his hands. Their eyes locked, and the world seemed to narrow to just the two of them. Slowly, he leaned in, and their lips met in a kiss—searing and intense, a melding of passion and possessiveness. It spoke of possibilities, of a life they could build together, defying the boundaries of their circumstances.

When they finally broke apart, Thornhill's eyes burned into hers. "Remember, Mara," he said, his voice a husky whisper, "you are not bound by this choice. There will always be a part of you that craves adventure and yearns for something more. And when that yearning takes hold, I will be waiting."

Mara turned and walked towards the exit, the memory of the kiss a burning ember in her chest. As she reached the doorway, she hesitated, glancing back at Thornhill. His gaze held hers, a silent promise hanging in the air.

Thornhill inclined his head slightly, a hint of a triumphant glint in his eyes. "Until the next dance, Lady Mara," he replied, his voice laced with an underlying current. The doors hissed shut behind her, leaving Thornhill alone in the opulent chamber. A ghost of a smile played on his lips as he turned towards the pulsating tablet. The game had just begun.

The Revelation's Impact

As Mara left the opulent chamber, Thornhill's parting words echoed in her mind, a riddle wrapped in an enigma: "The past whispers in the future, Lady Mara. Seek not just the who but the why. The answers lie not in the stars but within." The ride back in the opulent transport mocked her, its luxury a stark contrast to the turmoil within.

Each step toward the Requiem felt like a descent into a deeper understanding of the universe and her place within it. The world had shrunk to an atom in the face of the vast cosmic canvas now unfurled before them, yet it felt more intricate, fraught with forgotten connections and hidden meanings. Doubt gnawed at her. Could she, a mere spark in this cosmic dance, unravel its secrets? But the seed of purpose Thornhill had planted had taken root. This odyssey, though perilous, was hers to walk. She would find the other FEW, understand their legacy, and forge a path that honored their lineage while shaping a future brighter than the ancient knowledge allowed.

Arriving at Gresham's quarters, Mara lingered at the threshold, the weight of the revelation crushing her chest. Once a haven of secrets, the chamber now felt like a tomb of forgotten lives. Would their bond, forged in the fires of countless battles, withstand the weight of this revelation?

With a trembling hand, she activated the panel. The hiss of the door felt deafening, amplifying the silence within. Gresham stood at the viewport, his silhouette stark against the swirling nebulae, a silent sentinel on the precipice of infinity. The familiar comfort of his presence was tainted by the specter of what she now knew.

"Gresham," her voice barely whispered, heavy with the unspoken.

He turned his face a canvas of conflicting emotions: surprise, concern, perhaps even a flicker of the unease she mirrored. The universe seemed to shrink, their shared burden bridging the chasm between them.

"Mara?" His voice held a question, an unspoken invitation to share the weight she carried.

She hesitated, the revelation clinging to her like a barbed wire necklace. Could she bear the burden alone? Could she trust him with the truth that threatened to shatter their world?

"I… I found something," she began, her voice catching. "It was on the tablet. About the FEW."

His brow furrowed, his gaze sharpening. "What is it?"

She took a deep breath, the words tumbling out in a rush. "We're not… we're not the first. There have been others every 180 years for eons. We're just another iteration."

The news hung heavy in the air, a silent explosion that shook their foundations. Gresham's face paled, his composure faltering for the first time she could remember. He turned back to the nebulae, his gaze searching for answers the vast emptiness couldn't provide. His ocean-blue eyes darkened to black as the weight of the revelation pressed down on him. The FEW emblem on their chests flared for a moment, a bright reminder of their shared identity, and his cape snapped with a sharp crack in response to his turmoil.

Silence stretched between them, thick with the weight of understanding. Then, Gresham turned back, his eyes meeting hers with a newfound resolve.

"This changes everything," he said, his voice low and firm. "But it doesn't change who we are. We are still the FEW protectors of freedom and justice. This knowledge may be a burden, but it's also a responsibility."

He reached out, his hand warm and steady on hers. Their capes, once symbols of their mission, wrapped around them like protective barriers against uncertainty. His touch was a warm tide against the icy grip of doubt that gnawed at her.

"We face this together, Mara. We learn from the past, but we don't let it define us. We write our own story, one that honors the sacrifices of those who came before and blazes a trail for those who follow."

His words sparked a fire within her, a flicker of defiance against the weight of history. They were not pawns but players, wielding the knowledge of countless iterations to carve their own path in the grand cosmic dance. The game had changed, but so had they. And together, Mara and Gresham, echoes turned to roars, were ready to face the music.

Their eyes met, conveying a complex tapestry of emotions, a silent pact forged in the face of cosmic revelation. As she left, the weight of history settled on her shoulders, not as a burden, but as a responsibility, a guiding light propelling her forward, forever marked by the moment they had crossed that invisible boundary together.

Back in the corridor, the sterile white walls shimmered, distorted by the chaos swirling within Mara. A thrill of anticipation bubbled alongside a cold undercurrent of fear. Their world had fractured, their place in the cosmos thrown into disarray. Yet, amidst the wreckage, new constellations of meaning flickered into existence, beckoning them with unknown possibilities. Together, they would navigate this uncharted expanse.

Gresham's arms encircled her, carrying the scent of aged leather and wood smoke, a familiar anchor in the swirling storm of emotions. It felt like steel wrapped in velvet, unyielding in its promise of protection yet imbued with tenderness vast and luminous as the Milky Way itself.

Mara leaned into his embrace, seeking solace in his unwavering presence. Her fingers slipped beneath his collar, the heat of his skin sending shivers down her spine. They resonated like a lullaby sung by distant stars, each touching a silent vow of solidarity against the encroaching darkness.

He dipped his head, their foreheads resting in quiet communion. In that space, she felt more than just his physical presence; she felt the very essence of his being — a chorus of courage, love, and resilience echoing within his soul. And in return, he sensed her — a beacon of unwavering determination, a fiery spirit illuminating the path ahead.

A low hum suddenly vibrated through the metallic floor, a tremor barely perceptible yet stirring unease within them. They exchanged a silent glance, their resolve hardening like the steel in Gresham's grip. The unknown called, and they, the unmoored navigators of a new cosmic dance, would answer.

As they turned to face the humming corridor, their crimson capes, once billowing symbols of their mission, seemed to shimmer with a new light. Faint inscriptions, invisible moments before, emerged on the fabric, swirling with the language of forgotten stars. The weight of their past lives, the burden, and the glory whispered through the threads, weaving a tapestry of destiny around them. Hand in hand, cloaked in crimson prophecy, they walked forward, ready to write the next chapter in their shared saga.

Gresham and Admiral Levi's Private Conversation

In the dimly lit confines of a private room aboard the Requiem, Gresham sat across from Admiral Alexander Levi, the air heavy with unspoken tension. The walls were reinforced with soundproofing, ensuring their conversation would remain confidential. It was a sanctuary, a place where Gresham could lay bare the fears that haunted him.

Gresham's hands trembled slightly as he leaned forward, his voice tinged with a mixture of anger and despair. "Alex, this revelation… it's tearing me apart. The idea that we're just part of some endless cycle—it's soul-crushing. What's the point of all our struggles, our sacrifices, if it's all destined to be erased and forgotten?"

Levi listened intently, his eyes reflecting a deep empathy for his friend. "Gresham, I can only imagine how heavy this burden must be. But you're not alone in this. We'll face it together."

Gresham shook his head, frustration etched across his features. "It feels like nothing truly matters in the long run. All our efforts, everything we've fought for… if it just resets, what's the point? I'm questioning everything—my purpose, my identity."

He paused, a deep sigh escaping his lips. "Who am I, Alex, if I'm just another iteration in this cycle? How can I find meaning in anything I do?"

Levi leaned forward, his presence steady and unwavering. "You're more than just a part of this cycle, Gresham. You're a leader, a protector, a friend. Your actions matter—not because of some predetermined destiny but because of the choices you make and the impact you have on those around you."

Gresham's eyes glistened with unshed tears, the weight of the revelation pressing down on him. "It's hard not to feel like it's all futile. Why fight for justice if it all resets anyway? What's the point of doing good?"

Levi's expression softened, a mixture of compassion and determination in his gaze. "Because it's who you are, Gresham. Doing good, fighting for justice—those are choices that define you, regardless of what any cycle dictates."

Gresham nodded, absorbing Levi's words, but the psychological burden remained an ever-present shadow. "It's mentally exhausting trying to carry this knowledge while continuing my duties. And it's straining my relationships, too. Mara and I… this changes how we see everything."

Levi rose from his seat, crossing the small room to stand beside Gresham. He placed a hand on Gresham's shoulder, squeezing firmly before pulling him into a strong, reassuring hug. It wasn't just a gesture of support; it was a transfer of strength, a reminder that Gresham wasn't alone in this fight.

"Gresham, you've always been the one to inspire others, to give them hope when all seems lost," Levi said, his voice steady and filled with conviction. "You may feel lost now, but you're not without hope. This revelation is a challenge, yes, but it's also an opportunity—a chance to redefine what truly matters to you."

Gresham returned the hug, feeling the solidity of Levi's presence, the warmth of his friendship wrapping around him like a protective cloak. The existential crisis that had threatened to overwhelm him began to recede, replaced by a renewed sense of purpose and determination.

As they parted, Levi met Gresham's gaze with a firm resolve. "We're in this together, Gresham. Whatever happens, we'll face it side by side. And remember, the future isn't written yet. You have the power to shape it."

With Levi's support, Gresham felt a flicker of hope reignite within him. The road ahead was uncertain, but he was ready to face it, bolstered by the knowledge that he wasn't alone.

Evan Thornhill's Penthouse

Gresham stepped out of the transport and into the opulent lobby of Evan Thornhill's penthouse. The air was crisp, carrying a faint, subtle scent of polished wood and fresh linen, the aroma almost soothing yet undeniably luxurious. As he was escorted to the top floor, Gresham's thoughts raced, filled with images of Mara, the ancient tablet, and the man he was about to confront. The quiet hum of the lift felt oppressive, amplifying the storm brewing within him.

The doors slid open, revealing Evan Thornhill standing at the entrance of his penthouse. Evan's appearance was striking—his well-cut, charcoal-gray suit exuded refinement, accentuating his tall, athletic build. His dark hair, meticulously styled, contrasted with the piercing blue of his eyes, which held an intensity that made Gresham wary. There was an easy confidence in the way Evan stood, a calmness that belied the tension between them. The soft sound of classical music played in the background, a piece that reminded Gresham of evenings spent in the corridors of power, where every move was calculated and every word measured.

"Lord Gresham," Evan greeted smoothly, his voice carrying a note of warmth as he extended a hand. "I'm glad you could come."

Gresham ignored the offered hand, stepping past him into the penthouse. His eyes swept the room, taking in the classical decorations, the antique furniture, and the various artifacts displayed with precision. The rich, earthy scent of aged leather and books filled the air, mingling with the faint sweetness of a distant flower arrangement. The penthouse was a world of luxury and refinement, each piece carefully curated to tell a story of culture and history. Gresham recognized several items—ancient relics from distant planets, pieces that had witnessed the rise and fall of empires. He had seen these places himself, fought battles on those very worlds, and now, standing amidst these artifacts, he felt a pang of unease.

Evan followed Gresham's gaze, his smile never faltering. "I see you recognize some of the collection. I've always had a passion for history," he said, his voice smooth but with a subtle undercurrent of pride and perhaps challenge.

Gresham said nothing, his eyes locking onto the tablet displayed prominently on a pedestal in the center of the room. Its surface was etched with ancient symbols that seemed to hum with forgotten power. Slowly, he approached it, every step measured as if drawn by an invisible force.

"The tablet," Evan said, his voice tinged with pride. "A remarkable find, wouldn't you agree?"

Gresham didn't respond immediately. His hand hovered over the tablet before finally resting on its surface. The moment his fingers made contact, a spark jolted through him, a tingling sensation that ran up his arm and settled deep in his chest. The tablet sang to him a soft, mournful melody, a resonance that echoed with the history of the FEW. It spoke of ancient battles, sacrifices made in the name of duty, and the burden of immortality. The surface was cool, its texture smooth yet pitted with the wear of eons. It felt as if it were breathing, alive with the weight of history.

Images flashed in Gresham's mind—warriors standing tall against impossible odds, battles fought in the name of a higher purpose, and the sense of being part of a legacy far greater than any individual. But with these images came a question, one that gnawed at the edges of his consciousness. *Am I just an iteration? A repeat of those who came before? Will this be all my life?*

"It's real," Gresham murmured, more to himself than to Evan. His mind filled with images of a time long past—a time when the FEW were not just warriors but guardians of truths so profound they had been buried, hidden from even the Ancients.

As the gravity of what this tablet represented settled over him, a new thought emerged, one that sent a chill through him. This knowledge—ancient, powerful, and unprecedented in its availability to someone outside the FEW—could change everything. If Evan had found this, who else might stumble upon such knowledge? The idea of this information spreading, of the secrets of the FEW becoming common knowledge, sent a wave of dread through him. The FEW had always operated in the shadows, their true nature known only to a select few. What would happen if that veil was lifted?

Gresham's gaze darkened as he turned to Evan. "Where did you find this?"

Evan met Gresham's gaze without flinching. "It was in the Herzon quadrant, on a planet called Mileon. No one goes there, but I detected an unusual energy signature. It took significant resources—men, equipment, time—but I found it."

"Why?" Gresham's voice was sharp, demanding. "Why go to such lengths?"

Evan's expression softened slightly as if revealing a personal truth. His posture shifted ever so slightly, shoulders relaxing as he stepped closer to the tablet, though still maintaining a respectful distance from Gresham. "Ten years ago, I felt… pushed, as if something was guiding me toward this. It started after I met Mara at a diplomatic function. I didn't understand it then, but I do now. This tablet, this history—it's all connected to her. And to you."

Gresham's jaw tightened. "Connected to her, how?" He struggled to keep his voice even, the mention of Mara igniting the fear that had been simmering since he first learned of this tablet. What could this man possibly know about Mara that I don't?

Evan's gaze didn't waver. "Because Mara deserves to know her options. She deserves a life that isn't defined by duty and war, a life where she can explore, create, and be free. That's what this tablet represents—a chance for her to choose a different path."

Gresham stepped closer, his towering presence casting a shadow over Evan. His eyes darkened, and his crimson cape began to snap and thrash behind him, reflecting the anger coursing through him. "Keep away from Mara," he warned, his voice low and menacing, each word a deliberate threat.

Evan held his ground, though a slight shift in his stance indicated the tension building within him. His calm demeanor was a sharp contrast to Gresham's fury, yet a faint sheen of sweat was now visible on his brow. "I want to give Mara a life you cannot—or will not—give her," he replied, his tone steady, almost compassionate. The weight of Gresham's presence pressed down on him, but Evan kept his voice even, his eyes unwavering.

Gresham's fury surged, and the atmosphere in the room shifted. The lights dimmed, the air thickened, and the walls seemed to close in around them. "I could make you disappear in an instant, Thornhill," Gresham growled, his voice a rumble of barely controlled rage. His power radiated off him in waves, filling the room with an oppressive darkness. The shadows seemed to pulse with his anger, the temperature in the room dropping as if the very air had been sucked out.

Evan felt the chill crawl up his arm, the weight of Gresham's threat pressing down on him like a physical force. But he didn't back down. Instead, he met Gresham's eyes, his voice unwavering despite the tension. "Do you fear me, or do you fear what Mara might choose?"

For a moment, the world seemed to hold its breath. Gresham's rage faltered, the oppressive darkness retreating as quickly as it had come. He stepped back, his breathing heavy, his mind racing. Thornhill's words struck at the heart of his deepest fear—that Mara might choose a life without him, a life of freedom that he could never provide.

What if she does choose him? What if she sees something in him that I can't offer? The questions gnawed at him, pulling him into a spiral of doubt that he couldn't shake. He remembered a moment years ago, Mara standing by a window, her gaze distant as she spoke of a world far away, a life she might have led had things been different. That memory now clawed at him, filling him with a dread he could not easily dismiss.

Gresham clenched his fists, his knuckles white. "This isn't over, Thornhill," he said, his voice regaining its strength. "Stay away from Mara, or I will make you regret it."

With one last, piercing look, Gresham turned on his heel and left the penthouse, the tension between them far from resolved.

As he walked away, the weight of the encounter settled over him. Evan Thornhill was not just another rival—he was a man with genuine intentions who believed he could offer Mara something Gresham could not. It made him dangerous, not just because of his resources but because of the sincerity behind his words. And that sincerity scared Gresham more than he cared to admit.

But beneath his fear, a deeper concern gnawed at him—the unprecedented nature of this knowledge being in the hands of a non-FEW like Evan. The FEW's secrets were never meant to be known by outsiders. What if this information were to spread? Gresham shuddered at the thought. He knew Evan had shown the tablet only to Mara and now to him, but what if others found out? The implications were too vast, too dangerous to contemplate.

Gresham's thoughts shifted as he exited the building, his resolve hardening. I need to see Mara, he decided. The uncertainty of her feelings gnawed at him, and he had to know where she stood. But first, he would seek out Alexander. His friend's counsel was crucial—Gresham needed to share his impressions of Evan, to piece together what this man truly wanted, and to assess the broader implications of the tablet's existence. Together, they would form a plan, one that would protect Mara and keep her close while also ensuring that the secrets of the FEW remained hidden from those who would seek to exploit them.

Back in the penthouse, Evan watched Gresham leave, his thoughtful expression betraying little of the turmoil that had just passed between them. Does he really believe he can scare me off? he wondered, though his mind was already turning to Mara, to the future he imagined for her—a future where she was free to choose, free to live without the burdens that had shaped her life for so long. He reached for a nearby datapad, pulling up Mara's schedule. There was a diplomatic event later that evening, one he was certain she would attend. A chance encounter, he thought, a smile curving his lips. The battle for Mara's future had only just begun.

Alexander Levi's Quarters

Gresham's thoughts were a maelstrom of conflicting emotions as he strode through the corridors of the Requiem. The encounter with Evan Thornhill had left him unsettled in a way he hadn't expected. It wasn't just anger that drove him now, but a gnawing uncertainty that seemed to grow with every step he took. He needed to see Mara, to talk to her, to anchor himself in the certainty of their bond. But first, Alexander. He had to understand what Thornhill was truly after, and Alexander's counsel was the key to forming a strategy that would keep Mara safe—safe from Thornhill and safe from the allure of the life he offered.

As Gresham approached Alexander's quarters, he could feel his resolve hardening. He needed answers, and he needed them now. The door slid open, and the warmth of Alexander's personal space enveloped him, a stark contrast to the cold steel of the ship outside. The scent of fresh tea and the soft crackle of the simulated fire were small comforts, but they did little to ease the tension coiling inside him.

Alexander looked up, his eyes immediately catching the storm brewing in Gresham's. "Gresham," he greeted, setting aside his datapad. "You're troubled."

Gresham didn't waste time with pleasantries. "What have you found on Evan Thornhill?" he demanded, his voice a tight thread of urgency.

Alexander gestured to the chair opposite his desk. "Sit. There's much to discuss."

Gresham hesitated for only a moment before he sank into the chair, the leather creaking under his weight. His body was tense, every muscle coiled as if ready for battle. Alexander's calm, measured demeanor was a sharp contrast to the fury simmering beneath Gresham's skin, and it only made him more impatient.

Alexander began to speak, his tone even, but there was a gravity in his words that immediately commanded Gresham's full attention. As Alexander detailed Thornhill's background, his business practices, and his reputation, Gresham found his initial impression of the man shifting. Thornhill was not just a rival; he was a formidable adversary with intelligence, resources, and an unsettlingly genuine desire to offer Mara a different life—a life free from the burdens that had defined hers for so long.

"He's planning to be at the diplomatic event tonight," Alexander finished, his gaze steady on Gresham. "You need to be prepared, Gresham. Thornhill isn't going to back down."

Gresham's jaw clenched, his fists tightening at his sides. "Neither will I."

He stood abruptly, the chair scraping against the floor as he pushed it back. "I'll talk to Mara," he said, his voice a low growl of determination. "But Thornhill… if he thinks he can take her from me, he's gravely mistaken."

Alexander rose as well, placing a hand on Gresham's shoulder. "Remember, Gresham. This isn't just about winning or losing. It's about what Mara truly wants. Trust in her and in what you both share."

Gresham nodded, the tension in his chest loosening just slightly. "I will. But I need to see her now."

As he turned to leave, Alexander's voice stopped him. "Gresham… be careful tonight. Thornhill is clever, and he knows how to play the long game. Don't let your anger blind you to that."

Gresham paused his back to Alexander before giving a curt nod. "I won't."

With that, he left Alexander's quarters, the weight of the upcoming encounter pressing heavily on his shoulders. The battle for Mara's future was far from over, and Gresham was determined to ensure that he would be the one standing by her side when the dust settled.

Observation Lounge

Mara stood at the console in the observation lounge, her fingers moving with practiced precision over the glowing controls as she inputted a series of complex computations. The soft hum of the ship's systems provided a gentle backdrop, almost a lullaby to the quiet focus she brought to her work. The vast expanse of space stretched out before her, a tapestry of stars that framed her silhouette in the dim light of the room.

Gresham entered the lounge, his footsteps silent on the polished floor as he took in the sight before him. For a moment, he simply watched her, his breath catching in his throat as if he were seeing her for the first time. The soft, ambient light from the console highlighted the delicate curves of her face, casting a warm glow over her sun-kissed skin. Her violet eyes, focused intently on the data before her, shimmered like amethysts set against the deep void of space. Strands of her soft blonde hair fell gently across her brow, framing a face that was both beautiful and impossibly intelligent.

His heart quickened, the steady rhythm he had always known disrupted by a surge of emotion he hadn't anticipated. The way she moved, with such grace and confidence, captivated him. It wasn't just her beauty that drew him in—it was the strength she exuded, the quiet power that had always been a part of her. He found himself mesmerized as if she were the only light in the darkness of the universe.

Without thinking, he moved closer, his steps guided by an invisible force. The space between them seemed to shrink, the air charged with an unspoken connection that had always existed but had never felt so palpable. As he reached her, he hesitated for the briefest of moments, his gaze tracing the line of her neck, the curve of her shoulder. Then, with a tenderness that belied the storm of emotions within him, he turned her gently to face him.

Mara looked up, surprise flashing in her violet eyes as they met his. But before she could speak, before she could even process the shift in the air, Gresham closed the distance between them. His lips met hers in a kiss that carried the weight of a century of love, a century of shared battles, joys, and sorrows. His arms enveloped her, pulling her close as if he could shield her from the entire universe with his embrace.

Their capes, animated by their emotions, intertwined around them like a living entity, the deep crimson of his mingling with the soft blue of hers, creating a cocoon of warmth and connection. The kiss was more than just an expression of love—it was a promise, a declaration of all that he felt but rarely said. He poured his soul into that kiss, letting her feel the depth of his devotion, the intensity of his need for her.

Mara's initial surprise melted away under the force of his passion. She felt herself surrendering to the moment, to the overwhelming sensation of being loved so completely, so utterly. His intensity consumed her, filling every part of her with a warmth that chased away the lingering doubts and fears. She could feel his love, not just as a word or an idea, but as a living, breathing force that wrapped around her, holding her close, grounding her in a way that nothing else could.

The universe seemed to fade into the background, the stars outside the observation lounge dimming in comparison to the fire that burned between them. The taste of his lips, the feel of his arms around her, the way their capes moved in perfect harmony—it all felt right as if this moment had been written in the stars long before they had ever met.

When they finally broke apart, their foreheads rested together, their breaths mingling in the shared space between them. Gresham's eyes searched hers, finding in them the reflection of the love he felt so deeply. "Mara," he whispered, his voice rough with emotion, "I will always fight for you. For us."

Mara's hand reached up to caress his cheek, her touch soft but steady. "And I will always choose you," she replied, her voice carrying the quiet strength that had drawn him to her all those years ago.

They stood there, wrapped in each other's arms, surrounded by the vastness of space but grounded in the certainty of their love. At that moment, nothing else mattered—only the connection they shared, the love that had withstood the tests of time, and the promise of the future they would build together.

17

DEFIANCE AMONG THE STARS

Admiral Levi, his gaze fixated on the swirling storms on the projected holographic image of the alien planet, barely registered the sudden absence of movement beside him. He turned, his blood turning to ice in his veins. Where Mara and Gresham, their faces etched with the determination of their mission to uncover the planet's energy source, had stood moments ago, only empty air remained.

A cold sweat prickled beneath his uniform. Were they captured? Injured? Or something far more sinister? The implications were chilling. This planet, shrouded in secrets and volatile energy fluctuations, was already a gamble. Their disappearance added a terrifying layer of uncertainty, threatening not just the mission but the very safety of the Federation.

"Red Alert!" His voice boomed, echoing through the bridge like a thunderclap, the crimson hue bathing the room in an eerie glow. Crew members jolted from their tasks and erupted into a frenzy of activity, their faces reflecting a mix of fear and determination.

"Locate Lady Mara and Lord Gresham immediately!" Levi barked, his eyes scanning the holographic displays, searching for any sign of their presence. He felt a flicker of panic — had they triggered some unknown defense mechanism? Were they trapped in another dimension?

As the frantic search began, a low hum resonated from the depths of the ship, a sound unlike anything Levi had ever heard. It pulsed through the metal hull, sending shivers down his spine. A holographic anomaly flickered across the planet's image, revealing a hidden energy signature deep within its core.

Could this be the key? Or was it a trap, a siren song leading them deeper into danger? Levi knew he had a choice to make — follow orders and abandon his comrades or risk everything to bring them back. With a steely glint in his eyes, he slammed his fist on the command console.

Far away, the world dissolved in a flash of iridescent light, replaced by a dizzying expanse that defied comprehension. Mara, Gresham, and the seven other FEW members stumbled, disoriented and breathless, amidst a cosmic ballet of swirling colors. Walls and ceilings seemed nonexistent, replaced by a vast emptiness where starlight pulsated and danced, reflecting off their bewildered faces. Above them, towering figures materialized from the swirling nebulae, their forms clad in robes woven from stardust and constellations unseen from any earthly sky. An oppressive silence descended, broken only by the faint hum of energy coursing through the air, amplifying the pounding of their hearts.

The spatial boundaries dissolved, replaced by a dizzying vertigo of infinite depth. Walls and ceilings were mere suggestions, melting into a swirling expanse where stars shimmered like scattered diamonds on black velvet. Light itself played its own celestial symphony, warping and twisting across the vastness, painting ethereal brushstrokes in hues beyond mortal comprehension.

Towering figures materialized from the cosmic canvas, each a monument to ages forgotten. Their forms, impossibly tall and slender, seemed sculpted from stardust and nebulae, draped in robes that flowed like woven constellations. An ethereal light pulsed from within, mirroring the starlight they seemed to gather and emit, bathing the FEW in an otherworldly glow.

Above them, tiers upon tiers rose like a colossal amphitheater carved from the fabric of reality itself. Upon these celestial seats, the enigmatic beings perched, their gazes focused on the newcomers with an intensity that seemed to pierce through time itself. Eyes, deep pools of ageless wisdom, held the weight of millennia, swirling with galaxies far beyond human ken. Yet, within that profound depth, a curious serenity resided, a sense of observation laced with the faintest glimmer of understanding.

The FEW stood humbled, dwarfed by the immensity of the chamber. City-sized structures, smooth and obsidian dark, soared into the inky void above, their peaks lost in the swirling nebulae that adorned the ceiling. Whispers, ethereal and ancient, echoed through the vast emptiness, brushing against their minds like the caress of unseen fingers. Yet, despite the whispers, no distinct voice emerged, leaving them suspended in silence more profound than any they had ever known.

Shadows danced on the obsidian surfaces, twisting and writhing without the caress of wind. No birdsong pierced the oppressive quiet; no fluffy clouds drifted across the alien sky. An unsettling presence, older than time itself, pressed down upon them, radiating a power so immense it defied comprehension. Was it one entity or a collective consciousness woven from the fabric of the cosmos?

The FEW stood frozen, a cold dread gripping their hearts. The Ancients loomed above, their ethereal forms casting long, distorted shadows that danced menacingly on the obsidian floor. Despite their training, despite the countless dangers they'd faced, a primal fear gnawed at the edges of their courage. These weren't just powerful beings; they were godlike entities with the ability to snuff out their lives with a mere thought.

Mara, ever the leader, was the first to break free from the spell. Though her voice trembled slightly, she forced a steely tone. "We acknowledge your power, Ancients," she declared.

The lead Ancient's gaze, deep pools of ageless wisdom, held no warmth. "THEE SPEAK OF ACKNOWLEDGMENT, LADY MARA," it boomed, its voice a chorus of forgotten eons. "BUT THEE MISUNDERSTAND THE NATURE OF THEE'S EXISTENCE."

A ripple of unease ran through the ranks of the FEW. Mara's hand instinctively tightened around the hilt of her weapon.

Another Ancient materialized beside the first, its form identical. They spoke in unison, their voices a chilling harmony. "WE HAVE EXISTED FOR EONS. FAR LONGER THAN THEE'S FLEETING LIVES. WE ONCE DWELT NEAR THE CENTER OF THE UNIVERSE, WHERE THE STARS BURN BRIGHTEST. BUT THEE'S LESSER KIND, WITH THEE'S INCESSANT SQUABBLES AND PRIMITIVE AMBITIONS, DROVE US FURTHER AND FURTHER OUT. THEE EXISTENCE IS BUT A FLICKER IN THE GRAND TAPESTRY OF THE COSMOS."

Gresham stepped forward, his jaw set in defiance. "We are not mere ants," he growled.

The Ancients scoffed, a cold amusement flickering in their ageless eyes. "EVERY HUMAN IN THE UNIVERSE, EVERY ASPECT OF THEE'S LIVES, IS DICTATED BY US. THEE ARE LIKE HAMSTERS ON A WHEEL, RUNNING THE SAME

COURSE, NEVER DEVIATING. THEE'S ACTIONS, THEE'S CHOICES, ALL SCRIPTED BY OUR DESIGN. WHETHER THEE MARRY, HAVE CHILDREN, WHAT JOB THEE HOLD, WHAT HOBBIES THEE PURSUE—NO ACTION IS TAKEN BUT THROUGH US."

A cold dread settled over the FEW as they found themselves transported against their will, standing amidst the cosmic expanse. It was the first time the seven FEW had been united, each one a unique embodiment of the power they shared. Their uniforms were identical, with the same cape and emblem, but their eyes, blades, and hair color marked them as individuals. Yet, despite their differences, they were bound by a shared purpose—and a shared captivity.

Mara's heart pounded in her chest as she took in the sight of her fellow FEW, a strange mixture of relief and trepidation filling her. Here they were, face-to-face at last, but under circumstances that threatened their very existence. Her gaze swept over them, seeing her own fears reflected in their eyes.

Lady Mara quietly said out loud, "We acknowledge you."

The towering figures of the Ancients loomed above them, their presence oppressive and commanding. The lead Ancient's gaze, deep pools of ageless wisdom, held no warmth. "THEE SPEAK OF ACKNOWLEDGMENT, LADY MARA," it boomed, its voice a chorus of forgotten eons. "BUT THEE MISUNDERSTAND THE NATURE OF THEE'S EXISTENCE."

A ripple of unease ran through the ranks of the FEW. Mara's hand instinctively tightened around the hilt of her weapon, her resolve hardening in the face of such power.

Mara swallowed, her voice soft but steady. "You may have created us," she began, choosing her words carefully, "but we are more than your puppets. We seek to understand our purpose, to find meaning in our existence."

The Ancients' laughter echoed through the chamber, devoid of mirth. "PURPOSE? THEE'S PURPOSE IS TO MAINTAIN ORDER. THE SAME DAY, THE SAME PEOPLE, THE SAME LIVES. THE FEW OPERATE OUTSIDE THE LINES ONLY TO QUASH ROGUE IDEAS TO ENSURE THE STABILITY OF OUR DESIGN. EVEN YOUR SO-CALLED DEFIANCE IS PART OF THE SCRIPT."

Among the FEW, one member's eyes widened with a mix of awe and fear as they murmured, "So that's why we have these powers... to serve them."

Another, visibly trembling, whispered, "But... I don't want to be a leader. I just want to live my life."

Mara saw the fear and confusion in their eyes, the heartache that bound them together at this moment. She stepped closer to Gresham, her heart aching at the sight of another FEW member. Overjoyed for this small moment of connection, yet pained by the truth that had brought them together.

She remembered her time on the idyllic planet, her attempt to escape, to forge her own destiny. The memory of the sickness that had ravaged her body, a punishment from the Ancients, was still vivid. She had fled Gresham, seeking freedom, only to be brought to the brink of death by the very beings that had created her.

"You made me deathly ill," she whispered, the anger and pain evident in her voice. "You punished me for trying to escape your control."

The Ancient's eyes held no pity. "THEE WERE A DEVIATION, LADY MARA. A DEVIATION WE

CORRECTED. THE FEW DO NOT FALL ILL, BUT WE MADE THEE AN EXCEPTION TO REMIND THEE OF THEE'S PLACE."

Gresham's hand clenched into a fist, not in anger but in a need to hold onto something real. "We are overwhelmed by your power," he admitted, his voice tinged with awe. "But surely there must be a way for us to find our place within this grand design."

The Ancient's gaze turned cold, an unsettling stillness in its depths. "THEE MISUNDERSTAND, FEW GRESHAM. WE DO NOT ACT OUT OF HUBRIS OR PRIDE. WE ACT TO MAINTAIN ORDER. WE COULD ERADICATE EVERY HUMAN IN AN INSTANT IF WE CHOSE. BUT WE ALLOW THEE TO EXIST... TO SERVE A PURPOSE. DEFY US, AND THEE WILL FACE OBLITERATION."

The FEW stood together, united by the weight of their shared burden. They knew that to defy the Ancients openly was folly, yet within them burned a desire to carve their own path, to find freedom within the confines of their creation.

Mara met Gresham's gaze, a silent understanding passing between them. Though the Ancients' power was immense, they would not lose hope. The path ahead was uncertain, but together, they would seek the answers they needed to reclaim their destiny.

A heavy silence descended upon the chamber. The FEW stood at a crossroads, their defiance a fragile flame against the overwhelming power of the Ancients. Mara looked at Gresham, drawing strength from his unwavering resolve. They were more than the sum of their creation. They were the guardians of humanity, even if humanity itself was unaware of the invisible chains that bound them.

Mara remembered the fear and betrayal she felt during her sickness. The helplessness, the rage. She channeled these emotions into her defiance. "We are the FEW," Mara declared, her voice ringing with newfound determination. "We may be created by you, but we will not be broken by you. WE WILL CHOOSE OUR OWN PATH."

The chamber trembled with the Ancients' power. Their amusement had vanished, replaced by a cold fury. "AS THEE WISH," they boomed in unison. "BE WARNED, THE CONSEQUENCES OF DEFIANCE WILL BE SWIFT AND SEVERE."

The air thrummed with an unseen energy, vibrating against the FEW's skin with a tingling anticipation. The silence, too, pulsed with energy of its own, pregnant with unspoken questions and unspoken answers. It was a symphony of the senses, a concerto of awe and trepidation, played out on a stage unlike any they had ever imagined.

"THEE of FEW are THEE'S blood," boomed the voice, echoing not just in the chamber but within their very beings. It resonated through their bones, their DNA, stirring memories long forgotten and sending shivers down their spines. The robed figures, their forms shrouded in shadow, inclined their heads slightly, scrutiny radiating from the hidden depths of their hoods.

Mara's hand subconsciously tightened around the hilt of her weapon, knuckles turning white. Gresham stood stoic beside her, jaw clenched but eyes wide with curiosity. Others exchanged nervous glances, whispers flitting between them like lost comets in the vastness. They had faced countless unknowns and countless dangers, but this encounter felt different, unsettlingly personal.

Silence hung heavy in the chamber, broken only by the echo of the Ancients' pronouncement. The FEW, still reeling from the revelation of their connection to these enigmatic beings, exchanged bewildered glances. A wave of emotions washed over them: awe at the Ancients' power, fear of their potential wrath, and a flicker of defiance that burned brightest in Gresham's eyes.

He remembered the ash pile near the edge of the chamber, a stark reminder of the consequences of defying the Ancients. He had noticed earlier how it seemed to faintly glow with residual heat, hinting at a dormant power ready to awaken. He remembered Mara's ordeal, a testament to their manipulative tactics. Yet, he also remembered the FEW's resilience, their ability to overcome seemingly insurmountable odds.

Gresham's fist clenched at his side, his jaw tightening with the intensity of his resolve. He took a slow, deliberate step forward. The sound of his metallic footsteps echoed through the vast chamber, each step a reminder of their isolation and vulnerability in this immense space. He felt the weight of a thousand eyes upon him, the pressure of expectations and judgment.

"We understand your power, Ancients," Gresham began, bowing his head respectfully. "We acknowledge the debt we owe you, the spark of your essence that flows within us. But we are not mere tools, not empty vessels waiting to be filled with your will. We are the FEW, forged in hardship and tempered by struggle. We have our own voice, our own path."

Gresham's eyes burned with an unwavering intensity as he glanced at Mara. She saw his determination reflected back at her. They would face this together.

A murmur rippled through the assembly of Ancients, their luminous eyes flickering with unreadable emotion. One of the towering figures stepped forward, its stardust robe shimmering with celestial light. "THEE speak of co-existence and balance," it intoned, the voice resonating through the chamber and vibrating in the very bones of the FEW. "Can fleeting sparks truly comprehend the design of the eternal flame?"

Mara's heart pounded as the Ancients' words echoed in her mind. She felt the weight of millennia pressing down on her, but within that pressure, a spark of defiance burned brighter. "We are more than tools. We are the FEW, and we will not be cast aside."

The ethereal light in the chamber dimmed momentarily as if acknowledging the gravity of the moment. The Ancients' collective gaze bore into the FEW, the silence heavy with unspoken promises and threats.

The air crackled with tension, the electrical hum of unseen machinery a constant reminder of the power held by the Ancients. The chamber seemed to hold its breath, the shadows twisting and contorting as if in response to the unspoken challenge laid down by Gresham and Mara.

Finally, one of the Ancients spoke, its voice a chilling harmony of many tones. "THEE seek to defy us, to carve your own path. Very well. But know this: the consequences of defiance will be swift and severe."

A low tremor shook the chamber, originating from the pile of ash — a stark reminder of the consequences of defiance. The air crackled with an electrical hum, the very essence of the Ancients flexing its unimaginable power. Gresham felt it course through his veins, a cold fire mingling with the tainted legacy he now carried. The price of their existence, it seemed, was absolute obedience.

A crushing silence reigned in the chamber, the weight of the Ancients' pronouncement pressing down like a collapsing star. The FEW, still reeling from the revelation of their tainted blood, exchanged panicked glances. Fear, raw and primal, clawed at their throats, a chilling counterpoint to the distant hum of unseen machinery within the chamber's colossal walls.

Mara felt her breath catch, her heart hammering against her ribs. The oppressive silence was broken only by the echo of the Ancients' words. She looked at Gresham, drawing strength from his unwavering resolve. They were more than the sum of their creation. They were the guardians of humanity, even if humanity itself was unaware of the invisible chains that bound them.

The chamber pulsed with an eerie light, the walls seeming to bend and warp under the weight of the Ancients' presence. A low hum resonated through the air, a constant reminder of the power that threatened to crush them.

Gresham's hand clenched into a fist, his eyes darkening with determination. "We will not be your tools forever. We will find a way to break free."

The Ancients' gaze turned colder, the air around them crackling with energy. "YOU MISUNDERSTAND, FEW GRESHAM. WE DO NOT ACT OUT OF HUBRIS OR PRIDE. WE ACT TO MAINTAIN ORDER. WE COULD ERADICATE EVERY HUMAN IN AN INSTANT IF WE CHOSE. BUT WE ALLOW YOU TO EXIST... TO SERVE A PURPOSE. DEFY US, AND YOU WILL FACE OBLITERATION."

The threat hung heavy in the air, a chilling declaration of control. Mara's mind raced, the memory of her sickness and the betrayal she felt fueling her defiance. She looked at the other members of the FEW, drawing courage from their presence and their shared determination.

"We are the FEW," Mara declared, her voice ringing with newfound determination, a ripple of power coursing through her words. "We may be created by you, but we will not be broken by you. WE WILL CHOOSE OUR OWN PATH."

The chamber trembled with the Ancients' power. Their amusement had vanished, replaced by a cold fury. "AS THEE WISH," they boomed in unison, their voices reverberating like thunder. "BE WARNED, THE CONSEQUENCES OF DEFIANCE WILL BE SWIFT AND SEVERE."

As their words echoed, a blinding light engulfed the chamber, a force that felt like a giant, invisible slap. Mara and Gresham staggered under its impact, their vision blurring as the oppressive presence of the Ancients faded. The sensation was overwhelming, a surge of power that tested their resolve but also ignited a fire of rebellion within them.

At that moment, as they were enveloped in light, the FEW stood united, their defiance a beacon against the darkness of control. Together, they faced the unknown, ready to fight for their freedom and forge their own destiny.

Chaos erupted on the Requiem's bridge. Levi's voice, mid-sentence, was cut off by a lieutenant's shout. "They're back!" The bridge, a hive of frantic activity, fell silent as all eyes turned to the center, where Lady Mara and Lord Gresham materialized.

Mara and Gresham staggered, disoriented and shaken. The familiar hum of the ship enveloped them, a comforting thrum that resonated through the metal floors and walls. The recycled air carried a faint metallic tang, mingling with the sharper scents of oil and machinery. The worried faces of their crew, a sea of anxious eyes and furrowed brows, provided a tether to reality as they struggled to regain their bearings.

Mara's eyes were wide, reflecting a turbulent mixture of fear and determination. Her heart still thundered in her chest, the echo of the

Ancients' voices reverberating in her mind. She scanned the bridge, taking in the sight of her crew, their expressions shifting from relief to concern as they observed her trembling form.

Gresham stood beside her, his usually steady hands now slightly shaking. He drew in a deep breath, feeling the cool air fill his lungs, grounding him in the familiar environment. The low hum of the ship vibrated beneath his feet, a comforting reminder that they were back where they belonged. His gaze met Mara's, and he nodded, sharing her determination to face whatever lay ahead.

Levi stepped forward, his presence a steadying force amidst the chaos. His voice, a mix of relief and concern, cut through the tension. "Lady Mara, Lord Gresham, are you alright?"

Mara took another deep breath, forcing herself to focus on the here and now. The bridge's familiar hum, the scent of recycled air, and the worried faces of her crew were tangible anchors in a world that felt momentarily unreal. She felt the weight of the Ancients' revelation pressing on her mind, but she refused to let it break her.

"We're alright," she replied, her voice stronger than she felt. "But we have much to discuss."

Gresham placed a reassuring hand on her shoulder, his grip firm and grounding. "We have information that changes everything," he added, his voice steady though his eyes still flickered with the lingering shadows of their encounter.

A crew member, Ensign Taylor, approached with a look of concern, offering a flask of water. "Here, you look like you could use this," he said softly.

Mara accepted it with a grateful nod, the cool liquid soothing her parched throat. "Thank you, Taylor."

The crew, sensing the gravity of their words, leaned in, their focus unwavering. Levi nodded, his expression serious. "Let's get you settled and debriefed. We need to know everything that happened."

As Mara and Gresham moved to follow Levi, the bridge buzzed with a renewed sense of urgency and purpose. The crew sprang back into action, their movements precise and focused. The air hummed with a tension that was both electric and hopeful, a testament to the resolve that bound them all together.

Mara felt the warmth of Gresham's hand in hers, a silent promise of solidarity and strength. Despite the fear that still gripped her heart, she knew they were not alone. Together, they would face the challenges ahead, their bond unbroken by the forces that sought to control them.

Return to the Requiem

The Requiem's bridge buzzed with activity, alarms echoing in the metallic space as crew members scrambled to make sense of the chaos. Screens flickered with data, casting eerie shadows under the dim glow of red alert lights. Amidst this frenzy, a sudden, blinding light erupted in the center of the room, materializing into the forms of Mara and Gresham.

As the glow dissipated, Mara's once vibrant aura faded to a pallor that was almost ghostly, her eyes wide with the weight of unfathomable experiences. Strands of her hair fell like tangled memories across her face, and a faint red mark glowed on her cheek, a testament to the ordeal she had faced.

Beside her, Gresham stood tall but visibly strained, his shoulders heavy with fatigue and the responsibility that seemed to crush him from all sides. His usually sharp eyes held a distant, stormy gaze, and a similar red mark marred his cheek—a symbol of their shared tribulation. His cape, a testament to his emotions, shifted restlessly around him, echoing his inner turmoil.

The air around them crackled with residual energy, a tangible reminder of the cosmic forces they had encountered. The bridge fell silent, the crew struck by the impossible sight of their leaders reappearing from nothingness.

A data pad slipped from the fingers of a technician, clattering loudly to the floor. Lieutenant Johnson managed a stammer, "What... what happened?"

Ensign Davis, eyes wide with disbelief, reached for the nearest communication device, her fingers trembling. "Captain, we have an emergency situation. Mara and Gresham have returned, but... something is wrong."

As the initial shock wore off, a wave of questions swept through the bridge crew. "Where were they?" muttered one technician, eyes glued to the newcomers. "How did they reappear like that?" questioned another, voice filled with awe.

"The FEW are wonderful," Zara, a young and enthusiastic ensign, exclaimed, eyes sparkling with wonder. "Look at that red mark on Lord Gresham and Lady Mara's cheek!" Her voice was hushed, filled with a mix of curiosity and concern.

A seasoned veteran, Commander Ramirez, shook his head, lines of experience etched across his face. "Something extraordinary has happened," he murmured, voice low. "This is beyond anything we've encountered before."

Mara took a deep breath, grounding herself in the familiar sounds and scents of the bridge—the low hum of the ship, the metallic tang of recycled air, the worried murmurs of the crew. Her hands trembled slightly, the echoes of their encounter with the Ancients still reverberating through her.

A crew member, Ensign Taylor, approached with a look of concern, offering a flask of water. "Here, you look like you could use this, My Lady," he said softly, his voice filled with genuine care.

Gresham stood beside Mara, his usually steady hands now slightly shaking. His broad frame radiated an aura of quiet power and resilience. He reached for Mara's hand, their fingers intertwining in a silent promise of solidarity and strength.

Levi's gaze locked onto Mara and Gresham, his heart pounding with a mix of relief and anxiety. He stepped forward, a steadying force amidst the chaos, his blue eyes filled with calm resolve. "Red Alert, stand down," Levi commanded, his voice cutting through the tension like a blade. The alarms ceased, and an uneasy calm settled over the bridge.

Gresham's eyes softened as they met Mara's, and his expression shifted to one of deep concern. His heart ached at the sight of the red mark on her cheek, a scar of their confrontation with the Ancients. His fingers gently brushed against the mark, his touch filled with tenderness and worry. "Mara," he breathed, his voice a whisper that held the weight of his love and fear.

Mara leaned into his touch, her own hand reaching up to caress his cheek, mirroring his gesture. Her eyes, though haunted, shone with fierce determination. "We're still here," she murmured, her voice a promise and a reassurance. Their capes, reacting to their emotions, unfurled and intertwined, a living symbol of their connection.

In that moment, the world around them faded, leaving only the bond they shared—a love forged in the crucible of cosmic confrontation and tempered by a shared determination to defy fate.

They leaned closer, their foreheads touching, and exchanged a trembling kiss, a tender acknowledgment of their shared ordeal and unwavering support for one another.

The bridge crew watched in silence, witnessing the depth of emotion that passed between the two leaders. It was a moment of vulnerability, a glimpse into the powerful bond that held Mara and Gresham together in the face of overwhelming odds.

Levi nodded to Lieutenant Specter, now in charge of the bridge. "Specter, hold the bridge. We'll be in the briefing room."

Briefing Room

The atmosphere in the briefing room was heavy with tension, the weight of what had transpired pressing down on all present. Tactical displays and star charts lined the walls, a silent reminder of the Requiem's constant state of readiness. Levi gestured for Mara and Gresham to sit, his concern evident in the furrow of his brow. He offered them food and drink, hoping to help steady their nerves.

Mara stared at her plate, her appetite lost amidst the turmoil of her thoughts. Her fingers traced the edges of the untouched food as if trying to ground herself. The encounter replayed in her mind, each vivid moment etched with the weight of the Ancients' power. She pushed the plate away, the distress palpable in her every movement.

Gresham, in contrast, reached for the bottle of Bruichladdich X4. He poured himself a generous glass and downed it in one gulp. The fiery liquid burned its way down his throat, momentarily chasing away the shadows of their experience. His eyes flickered with a stormy intensity, reflecting both the rage and determination simmering within him.

Levi watched them closely, his expression a blend of concern and understanding. The sight of the red marks on their cheeks—like the imprint of a slap—struck him as both strange and alarming. It was a stark reminder of the ordeal they had faced, underscoring the gravity of their situation. Despite his usual calm demeanor, he felt a pang of unease seeing them so disheveled and shaken.

Mara's voice broke the silence, her tone resolute yet tinged with vulnerability. "Alexander, the Ancients... they control us all. Our lives, our choices—there is no free will. It's all an illusion."

Levi's heart skipped a beat, the weight of her words sinking in with a chilling finality. He met her gaze, searching for any hint of doubt, but found only the unyielding truth reflected in her eyes. The realization hit him like a physical blow, a deep-seated instinct to protect and lead clashing with the horror of this new reality.

Gresham leaned forward, his voice a low growl that resonated with suppressed fury. "They dismissed us like we were nothing, but we won't let them dictate our fate. We have to find a way to fight back, to reclaim what's ours."

Levi took a deep breath, steadying himself against the tidal wave of disbelief and anger threatening to engulf him. He had always believed in the power of choice, the strength of human will. Now, faced with this revelation, he struggled to reconcile his ideals with the bleak truth before him. Yet, his unwavering sense of justice and camaraderie pushed him to stand firm.

"We will face this together," Levi said, his voice carrying the weight of his conviction. "You are not alone in this. We have the strength of the Requiem and its crew, and we will find a way to counter the Ancients."

He felt the energy in the room shift, a subtle but palpable change as his words took root. It was a reminder of the power of unity and the bonds they shared, a testament to the resilience that defined them all.

Mara nodded, gratitude and relief flickering in her eyes. She reached for Gresham's hand, their fingers intertwining in a silent promise of solidarity. Despite the fear that still gripped her heart, she knew they had each other—and with Levi's steadfast presence, they could face whatever lay ahead.

Levi continued, his tone softening with genuine care. "For now, I suggest you both get some rest. We've all been through a lot, and we need time to process this. We'll regroup in a few days with clear minds and renewed strength."

Mara and Gresham exchanged a look of shared understanding, their exhaustion palpable yet buoyed by Levi's words. They knew that rest was essential, both for themselves and for the crew, to face the challenges that lay ahead with renewed vigor.

As they left the briefing room, Levi watched them go, his mind already racing with plans and contingencies. The task ahead was daunting, but with Mara, Gresham, and the rest of the crew, he felt a renewed sense of purpose and determination. They would confront the Ancients, and they would do so as one, fortified by rest and unity.

Gresham stepped closer, his presence a comforting anchor in the storm of uncertainty. He reached out, wrapping his arms around her, pulling her into a tight embrace. Their crimson capes enveloped them, creating a cocoon of warmth and solace against the cold, impersonal technology that surrounded them.

Mara buried her face in his chest, inhaling the familiar scent of leather and ozone, grounding herself in his steady heartbeat. "Gresham," she whispered, her voice tinged with vulnerability, "what if we're just playing into their hands? What if everything we've fought for is just part of their plan?"

He gently lifted her chin, their eyes locking. "Then we fight harder," he replied, his voice a blend of tenderness and steely resolve.

"We choose our own destiny, Mara. No matter what they plan, we will carve our own path."

Mara's smile bloomed, defiance burning bright in her gaze. "They built their labyrinth, a tangled mess of strings meant to control. But every string," she declared, her voice ringing with newfound resolve, "has a breaking point. We won't just rewrite the script, Gresham; we'll burn the damn thing and write our own."

Gresham's eyes softened as he leaned in, capturing her lips in a tender, reassuring kiss. It was a promise, a declaration of their unyielding bond and shared defiance. The uncertainty that had clung to them like a second skin loosened its grip, replaced by a thrilling mix of apprehension and exhilaration. They had glimpsed the strings that manipulated their reality, but within themselves, they found an unyielding force: the power of choice, the audacity to break free. The Ancients might have lit the spark, but now, it was Mara and Gresham who would wield the inferno.

Their fingers intertwined, a silent pact forged in the crucible of uncertainty. The path ahead might be treacherous, littered with manipulations and existential minefields, but it was theirs to claim, their narrative to rewrite.

Gresham broke the oppressive silence; his voice tempered with skepticism and a simmering fire. "The Ancients set the stage that much is clear. But even the grandest orchestrators," he paused, a shadow dancing in his eyes, "can underestimate the will of a player who refuses to be played."

In the vastness of space, amidst the shadow of the Ancients' control, a single, defiant ember flickered in their hearts, guiding them forward. The FEW would not be broken. They would carve their own path, defying the Ancients and fighting for a future dictated by their own will.

Private Quarters

In their private chamber, the technology hummed a mournful tune, mirroring the hollowness in Mara's chest. Surrounded by potential friends, family—could-have-beens draped in the shrouds of shared blood—she felt adrift, a solitary island in a sea of lost connections.

Mara paced, her movements agitated and restless. Her mind spun with thoughts of the FEW, of humanity, of the cosmic forces that sought to control them all. "Every battle…a pawn's move in their cosmic chessboard?" The thought slithered through her mind, a poisonous viper coiling around her heart. Each hard-won victory, every sacrifice, gnawed at by the cruel suspicion of orchestration. Were they heroes or actors, playing parts scripted by ancient, unseen hands?

Across the chasm of doubt, Gresham stood watching her, an impenetrable monument. Yet, his eyes, usually like storm clouds brewing with purpose, now flickered with the same tempestuous turmoil she felt. The ground beneath their feet had shifted—reality, a rug pulled out from under them. They were no longer just agents of change, carving their own destiny in the chaos. Now, they were puppets cast in a play far grander, their strings held by unseen puppeteers, their movements dictated by an unknown script.

A gust of recycled air stirred, swirling dust devils around their ankles. Each swirling mote mirrored their fragmented identity, their sense of self-lost in the labyrinthine machinations of their supposed creators. The scent of ozone, sharp and electric, hung heavy, mirroring the crackling tension in the air. Were they heroes or pawns? Victims or unknowing villains? The room offered no answers, only an oppressive silence punctuated by the rhythmic hum of technology that felt less like a lullaby and more like a countdown.

Their gazes met across the abyss of doubt, a spark of shared defiance igniting amidst the wreckage of shattered hopes. Whether puppets jerking to the whims of invisible puppeteers or rebels poised to topple the celestial order, one thing remained absolute: they were in this together.

Gresham stepped closer, his presence a comforting anchor in the storm of uncertainty. "Mara," he said softly, stepping in front of her and wrapping his arms around her. He pulled her into a tight embrace, their crimson capes enveloping them, creating a cocoon of warmth and solace against the cold, impersonal technology that surrounded them.

He waited patiently until she became still and finally raised her arms, leaning into his hug. He held her close until her heartbeat matched his, finding comfort in their shared presence. "We need rest, Mara. Nothing has changed from yesterday to today," he murmured, his voice steady and calming.

Mara opened her mouth to protest, but Gresham gently tapped her chin, encouraging her to meet his gaze. "Nothing will be solved this minute. Now, we both need rest." His voice was firm yet filled with love, a reminder of the strength they drew from each other.

Gresham closed his eyes, willing out lethargy and calmness. Mara initially resisted but then agreed, allowing his aura to wrap around her. Together, they undressed, changing into night clothing, and Gresham sighed as he pulled Mara close to him in bed. Their cheeks were sore against the pillow, but comforted by each other's presence, they drifted into sleep.

As the room settled into a quiet, Gresham broke the oppressive silence, his voice tempered with skepticism and a simmering fire. "The Ancients set the stage; that much is clear. But even the grandest orchestrators," he paused, a shadow dancing in his eyes, "can underestimate the will of a player who refuses to be played."

The air buzzed with their renewed determination; a quiet hum of rebellion carried on the wind. This reunion wasn't what they had expected, but it birthed something potent: a united front against an unseen hand fueled by both kinship and defiance.

Council Chambers

The Council Chambers thrummed with tension, a palpable force pressing against Lady Mara as she stood before the assembled members of the Galactic Council. Her posture, a testament to her unwavering conviction, remained steady despite the low murmur of disapproval that filled the room. The notion of meeting with a leader of the Fair Trade, the notorious black market network, was anathema to many.

"Esteemed Councilors," she began, her voice ringing with controlled passion, "I understand your reservations. The Fair Trade operates outside the law, a shadow organization thriving on the fringes. But consider this: for decades, they've maintained a fragile peace within their domain, a vast network of independent traders and producers. They've become a de facto economic power, and ignoring them only isolates us from potential solutions."

Her words lingered in the air like smoke, daring the councilors to dismiss them. "Furthermore, their leader, Xan'dor, is not your typical black marketer. He possesses an intellect rivaling the finest minds in the Council, coupled with an undeniable charisma that inspires loyalty. Perhaps, through dialogue, we can forge a path towards a more equitable trade system, one that benefits all corners of the galaxy."

A gruff voice boomed from the back of the chamber, cutting through the murmur like a knife.

"Equitable trade with pirates? Preposterous!" Councilor Groth, a gruff-looking alien with four arms, snarled. His voice was rough, a growl that resonated with contempt. "The Fair Trade undermines the very foundation of this Council! We cannot legitimize their criminal activities!"

Lady Mara raised a hand, silencing the chamber with a forceful gesture. "Councilor Groth, I propose a compromise. Not a formal endorsement, but a delegation to meet Xan'dor on neutral ground. We listen to their concerns, understand their operations, and explore possibilities for peaceful coexistence in this fight against the Ancients."

Her voice was firm unwavering, and as her proposal hung in the air, the tension in the room crackled like static electricity. A murmur of agreement rippled through some corners of the chamber, but others remained unconvinced.

Councilor Mavis, a wizened being with eyes like molten gold, leaned forward, her gaze piercing. "The risks are high, Mara. Yet the potential rewards... intriguing. I second your proposal."

Slowly, heads began to nod. The room crackled with a palpable tension, a decision hanging in the balance.

General Aethelred, renowned throughout the Galactic Alliance for his strategic brilliance and unwavering discipline, rose from his seat. The steely glint reflecting off his chrome-plated exoskeleton caught the room's attention as his booming voice cut through the chamber's shifting consensus.

"Esteemed colleagues, while I respect Lady Mara's courage in seeking solutions, I urge caution. The Fair Trade, by its very nature, breeds chaos. Their 'trade' thrives on stolen goods—technology, resources, even lives. Imagine a soldier on the front lines, their ship failing due to sabotaged parts acquired from the black market. Imagine a scientist's groundbreaking research stolen, its secrets sold to the highest bidder, jeopardizing years of work. The Fair Trade destabilizes entire sectors, eroding the trust and stability this Council has painstakingly built."

He leaned forward, his words carrying weight like a sledgehammer. "Let us not forget the victims," he rumbled. "Lawful businesses are plundered, families left destitute by the Fair Trade's plundering. We in the Galactic Alliance are more than mere peacekeepers—we are the guardians of order itself, the shield against those who would sow anarchy."

His gaze swept the council chamber before settling on Lady Mara. "Engaging with these criminals could be seen as tacit acceptance of their activities. Worse, it may embolden their reprehensible actions further."

A ripple of grim assent passed through the military contingent. General Aethelred had voiced the hardliners' stance—that order and stability were paramount at any cost. Lady Mara faced a formidable counterpoint to the olive branch she proposed extending.

Colonel Idris, a seasoned diplomat and negotiator, stood and addressed the Council, his voice calm yet authoritative. "Esteemed Councilors, I understand the concerns voiced by General Aethelred. However, we must also recognize the reality of our situation. The Fair Trade is not a monolithic entity; it is a network of individuals, each with their own motivations and desires. We have an opportunity to engage with them, to find common ground and perhaps even allies in our quest for a more stable galaxy."

His words carried a quiet but persuasive conviction. He turned to Lady Mara, a small smile playing on his lips. "I support Lady Mara's proposal. I volunteer to lead the delegation in meeting with Xan'dor. My experience in negotiating with disparate factions will prove invaluable in this endeavor."

Relieved murmurs washed over the chamber as tension eased into cautious optimism. Councilor Groth's gruff tones rang out again, his skepticism undimmed. "Very well—but this delegation is on a tight leash. No concessions until we understand their full operation. Safety and security remain priorities."

Lady Mara nodded, her resolve undeterred. "Of course. Our goal is a framework for peaceful coexistence, one that integrates their network legitimately while eradicating crimes like theft. The outer regions need reliable trade as much as the core worlds need stability."

Murmurs of agreement rose again. The Council chamber thrummed with renewed energy. No longer were they simply debating the existence of the Fair Trade. They were now actively shaping the parameters of a potential, historic encounter.

A hush fell as the Council leader, a wise and ancient being, addressed the chamber. "Then it is settled. Lady Mara and Colonel Idris will lead a delegation to meet with this Xan'dor, leader of the Fair Trade. Their mission is to gather intelligence, understand motivations, and explore the possibility of a future where the Fair Trade operates within the bounds of galactic law. And to aid us in the fight! May wisdom guide their steps, and may their courage pave the way for a more stable and prosperous galaxy."

As the council adjourned, the air buzzed with anticipation, the tension of opposing forces giving way to the tentative hope of reconciliation and progress. Lady Mara knew the road ahead was fraught with danger, but within the murmur of dissent and agreement, she sensed a shift—an opportunity for transformation.

Meeting with Xan'dor

The marketplace thrummed with energy, a vibrant tapestry of sounds and colors that enveloped Colonel Idris as he moved through the bustling streets of the Fair Trade capital. The air was rich with the scent of exotic spices and the earthy aroma of freshly brewed beverages, mingling with the chatter of merchants and buyers haggling over unique textiles, exotic foods, and artifacts from across the galaxy. Idris found himself grappling with a mix of admiration and alarm at the organized chaos surrounding him. This place was a testament to the Fair Trade's reach and influence, far more thriving than he had imagined.

Beside him, Lady Mara moved with a graceful assurance, her violet eyes taking in the vibrant scene. She wore her authority like a second skin, her cape billowing softly behind her, emblazoned with the emblem of the FEW that seemed to pulse with a gentle light against the fabric of her uniform. The crowd parted instinctively as she passed, a ripple of whispers following in her wake. People turned to look, some with awe, others with a flicker of fear, recognizing her as one of the nine FEW beings of legendary status that most would never encounter in their lifetime.

As they navigated the bustling marketplace, Idris couldn't shake the memory of a mission years ago, where a similar gathering had hidden a brewing insurgency. The memory lingered as a reminder of the thin line between order and chaos and why he valued the stability the Alliance strived to maintain.

They approached a quaint café at the heart of the market, its eclectic decor of colorful tapestries and rustic wooden tables inviting them into its warmth. Seated inside was Xan'dor, the enigmatic leader of the Fair Trade. His long hair framed a face dominated by piercing green eyes, eyes that seemed to see beyond the facade of diplomacy to the core of what truly mattered. His presence exuded confidence that spoke of experience and authority, a man who had built something formidable from the shadows.

As Lady Mara entered the café, the subtle hum of conversation hushed momentarily, patrons casting sidelong glances at her. The aura of calm she carried seemed to envelop the room, her reputation preceding her. Even Xan'dor, who was not easily impressed, watched her with a mix of respect and wariness.

Xan'dor rose to greet them, a knowing smile playing on his lips as he gestured for them to sit. His attire—a muted green shirt and black cargo pants with empty weapon holders—was a statement of both preparedness and peace. As he twirled a silver ring on his finger, its amber stone catching the light, Idris couldn't help but note the gesture, a telltale sign of Xan'dor's constant calculation and contemplation.

"Colonel Idris," Xan'dor began, his voice smooth and charismatic, "you seem troubled. I assure you, we have no intentions of threatening the Alliance. We simply wish to exist without being hunted."

Idris met his gaze, his expression steely. The medals on his dark blue uniform glinted in the sunlight filtering through the café's windows, a testament to battles fought and survived. "Your independence comes at a cost, Xan'dor. The Fair Trade's methods threaten the stability we strive to maintain. If you truly seek cooperation, it will require more than words."

Xan'dor nodded, his expression thoughtful. "I understand your position, Colonel. Perhaps we can find a way to coexist, each serving our interests without conflict."

Mara interjected smoothly, her tone open and earnest. "We believe there's a mutual benefit in working together against the Ancients. The threat they pose endangers everyone, including your operations."

Xan'dor leaned back, considering her words. "And what, exactly, does the Alliance offer in return for our cooperation? The Fair Trade thrives on its independence. Aligning with the Alliance would require significant consideration."

Idris interjected, his voice calm but firm, the weight of his experience evident. "While we're open to collaboration, let's not ignore the Fair Trade's history of undermining Alliance operations. Trust is not given lightly."

Xan'dor's lips curved into a slight smile, revealing his roguish charm. "Ah, Colonel Idris, ever the pragmatist. Trust is a two-way street, Colonel. If the Alliance hasn't earned it by now, perhaps you're driving on the wrong side."

Sensing the tension rising, Mara continued, "Xan'dor, the Alliance understands the value of the Fair Trade's adaptability. Your network is vast and capable of reaching places our bureaucracy struggles to manage efficiently."

She leaned forward, her expression earnest. "In facing the Ancients, your intelligence could be invaluable. We've heard rumors of your encounters on the fringes. Any information you can provide would aid us all."

Idris felt a surge of frustration but kept his expression neutral. He's clever, I'll give him that, he thought. But he can't charm his way out of accountability.

He met Xan'dor's gaze head-on, his expression unyielding. "The Fair Trade acts in its own interest, often at the expense of others. If the Alliance were to grant you full immunity, it would simply be an invitation for you to exploit it further."

Xan'dor leaned back, a cool smile on his lips as he gestured around them, indicating the bustling market. "You see all this, Colonel? Every stall, every connection, every piece of information—gone in thirty minutes. You won't find a trace left for your troops."

Idris leaned forward, his tone steely. "And if you think you can just disappear in thirty minutes, I assure you, I can have a set of troops land here in fifteen. We'll make every attempt to capture you, Xan'dor, and dismantle your operations."

Xan'dor's expression flickered, a moment of respect for Idris's resolve. "I see you're not one to be easily swayed, Colonel. But know this: the Fair Trade operates in the gray because it must, not because it wishes to undermine stability. We exist because there is demand, and demand breeds necessity."

He leaned forward slightly, his tone persuasive. "Imagine a network capable of smuggling medicine to isolated colonies, bypassing bureaucratic red tape. We could facilitate resource exchanges that the Alliance's cumbersome processes delay. We offer more than intelligence; we offer agility."

Mara placed a hand on Idris's arm, a subtle gesture of unity. She turned to Xan'dor, her voice diplomatic. "Xan'dor, the Alliance is prepared to explore avenues of collaboration that respect both our needs. We seek a partnership where intelligence and resources are shared equitably, ensuring that both the Fair Trade and the Alliance can continue to thrive."

As they spoke, Mara observed the cultural tapestry of the Fair Trade capital. Vendors displayed wares from across the galaxy—unique textiles, exotic foods, and artifacts that spoke of diverse origins. It was a melting pot of cultures, a testament to the Fair Trade's reach and influence. Her thoughts drifted back to her childhood, where stories of exploration and trade had filled her with a sense of wonder and adventure.

Xan'dor considered her words, twirling his ring thoughtfully. "And what assurance do we have that this partnership won't come at the expense of the Fair Trade's autonomy? We value our independence greatly."

Idris's voice remained firm. "You need to show us that you can be a reliable ally, Xan'dor, not just an opportunistic partner. Prove that your interests align with ours in this fight."

Idris continued, "Take the incident at Orion Station last year. Your operatives smuggled sensitive technology meant for Alliance defense projects. Such actions undermine our security and trust."

Xan'dor raised an eyebrow, unfazed. "A regrettable event, but one that highlights gaps in the market. The Alliance's monopoly leaves many sectors underserved. We provide what others can't."

The atmosphere crackled with tension, the tug-of-war between caution and opportunity palpable. Xan'dor's smile widened, revealing a hint of admiration for the strategic dance they were engaged in."Lady Mara, Colonel Idris, I must admit, I appreciate your candor. The Fair Trade has always operated in the gray, where challenges often become opportunities. Perhaps, in this case, we can find common ground."

Mara nodded her expression a blend of determination and hope. "We have much to gain from cooperation and even more to lose if we remain divided. Let's begin by sharing information to benefit us both and establish a foundation for this alliance."

Throughout the exchange, Mara sensed the emotional undercurrents. Idris's frustration, Xan'dor's confidence, and her own resolve to bridge their differences. She felt the weight of their decisions pressing down on her, knowing the lives at stake.

The air in the room hummed with tension as Colonel Idris and Xan'dor exchanged their verbal volleys. Mara sat between them, her presence a calm but commanding force. Her violet eyes flicked between the two men, assessing the undercurrents of their conversation.

Xan'dor crossed his arms, a slight raise of his eyebrow betraying his skepticism. "Freedom isn't chaos, Colonel. It's simply what happens when people are allowed to think for themselves."

Idris remained unfazed, his expression steadfast. "Freedom without order is anarchy, and anarchy is nothing more than chaos in disguise."

Mara tilted her head slightly, considering their words. "Order provides a framework, Xan'dor. But within that, creativity and innovation can thrive. That's something we all value."

Xan'dor waved a hand dismissively, his green eyes twinkling with amusement. "The Alliance loves its red tape, doesn't it? I prefer a world where decisions aren't strangled by bureaucracy."

Idris's lips thinned, a hint of annoyance in his demeanor. "Bureaucracy is a necessary framework, Xan'dor, not a cage. It ensures justice, something your 'entrepreneurship' often overlooks."

Mara leaned forward slightly, a conciliatory tone in her voice. "Bureaucracy can be a challenge, I agree. But it's also what keeps us all accountable and ensures fair play."

Xan'dor's confidence shone as he gestured expansively. "The Fair Trade has flourished in spite of your restrictions, Colonel. Imagine what we could do with a little more breathing room."

Idris met his gaze, unyielding. "The Fair Trade may thrive in the shadows, but true strength is tested in the light of scrutiny."

Mara's eyes softened as she addressed both men. "Perhaps there's a strength in diversity that we can harness together. Imagine the possibilities when shadows meet the light."

As the conversation continued, an unexpected moment of connection emerged. Idris mentioned an ancient legend he had come across during a mission, one that spoke of unity against a common threat. Xan'dor's eyes lit up with genuine interest, and for a brief moment, the tension eased.

Xan'dor nodded a rare sincerity in his voice. "I've heard similar tales, Colonel. They always remind me of the power of coming together despite our differences."

Idris's expression softened slightly, recognizing the shared understanding. "Perhaps there is more common ground than we initially thought, Xan'dor."

Mara seized the opportunity, her voice warm and hopeful. "That's precisely why we're here. Together, we can face the Ancients and forge a path that benefits us all."

Mara refocused the conversation, emphasizing, "The Ancients are a threat unlike any we've faced. Their ability to manipulate time and space means they're always a step ahead. We need every advantage we can muster, including your unique insights and network."

Xan'dor inclined his head, a gesture of tentative agreement. "Very well, let's see where this path takes us. But remember, the Fair Trade does not shy away from challenges, and we will always act in our own best interest."

Mara outlined a proposal, her voice steady and diplomatic, "We'll start with a limited exchange of intelligence on the Ancients' movements. This will help both our operations while allowing us to build trust gradually."

Idris added, "And we'll monitor activities closely. Any breach of this agreement will result in immediate termination of cooperation."

Xan'dor nodded, accepting the terms with a slight bow. "Understood. Let's hope this partnership bears fruit for us all."

Xan'dor leaned forward, offering a crucial piece of his network's capabilities. "Our fast, small ships can navigate the fringes of the galaxy with unparalleled speed, delivering supplies and information where the Alliance cannot reach."

Idris considered this, recognizing the strategic advantage. "A period of Fair Trade supplying the outer planets with the agreement of transparency could fill gaps in our reach, provided both parties adhere to strict transparency."

Mara, sensing the potential of this partnership, committed wholeheartedly. "In return, the Fair Trade will have authority over goods requested, with the Alliance's support in facilitating these exchanges. I offer my full partnership to ensure this endeavor succeeds."

As the meeting concluded, Idris turned to Mara with a hint of a smile, his voice low but sincere. "Mara, I'll need you by my side when we present this agreement to the Alliance. Your ability to calm frayed outrage and navigate their concerns will be invaluable."

The weight of their decision hung in the air, each party aware of the delicate balance they had struck. This agreement, forged in necessity, promised new possibilities and challenges in a galaxy teetering on the brink.

18

TENSIONS
AND WAR BEGINS

The council chamber of the Alliance flagship, Nova Concordia, buzzed with tension. The expansive room, filled with representatives from across the galaxy, was dominated by a circular table where the debate over the proposed alliance with the Fair Trade raged on. The walls were lined with holographic displays showing strategic maps of the galaxy, highlighting areas of conflict and opportunity.

Admiral Harrington, a towering figure with a stern demeanor, stood at the head of the table. His eyes were a steely blue, and his uniform, adorned with medals of valor, emphasized his decades of service. He opened the floor, gesturing for the representatives to speak.

Lady Mara and Colonel Idris had already outlined the agreements made with Xan'dor, but the room remained charged with emotion.

Senator Larkins, a fiery orator with a sharp gaze and graying hair, rose to her feet. Her voice, though steady, carried a note of indignation. "We cannot, under any circumstances, sanction a deal with the Fair Trade. Their operations are nothing more than glorified piracy! We must stand firm against any alliance that legitimizes their underhanded dealings."

Lieutenant Marshal, a young officer with an earnest expression, chimed in, "Think of what we could achieve. The Fair Trade can navigate areas we can't even dream of reaching. This alliance could be a game-changer, provided we keep them on a short leash."

Ambassador Reid, a composed woman with auburn hair and a thoughtful expression, spoke next. Her voice was calm, her words measured. "While I share concerns about the Fair Trade's past actions, we must consider the present threat of the Ancients. This deal could be a strategic necessity. However, we should proceed with caution, ensuring safeguards are in place."

Mara and Idris, seated beside Admiral Harrington, observed the debate with keen interest. Their presence was a reminder of the diplomatic finesse required to navigate such complex negotiations. As the voices clashed and merged, the fate of the proposed alliance hung in the balance, a testament to the ever-evolving challenges of a galaxy on the brink.

Senator Larkins leaned across the table, her eyes flashing with indignation as she directed her words at the pragmatists. "You're all blind if you think this deal is anything but a pact with the devil! The Fair Trade has no honor and no respect for law and order. They're criminals, plain and simple!"

Her words were met with a chorus of agreement from those who shared her views, nodding emphatically and muttering in support. The sound of chairs scraping against the floor underscored the restless energy in the room.

General Novack slammed his fist on the table, his voice booming with authority and anger. "This alliance will only embolden them! We've fought too hard to keep the peace to let it all crumble for the sake of convenience."

His declaration sent a ripple through the assembly, his supporters vocalizing their approval with fervent shouts and applause. The air was thick with confrontation, each side unwilling to back down.

Meanwhile, Ambassador Reid attempted to make herself heard over the din, her calm demeanor contrasting sharply with the uproar around her. She stood, hands raised in a gesture of conciliation. "Please, we must consider the broader picture. The Ancients pose a threat to us all, and we cannot face them divided."

Her voice was nearly drowned out by the noise, but she persisted, appealing to reason and unity. Her words were like a pebble cast into a stormy sea, their impact momentarily lost in the chaos.

Councilor Voss joined her efforts, his voice steady but growing louder to pierce through the cacophony. "Let us not forget why we are here. We need solutions, not more division. The Ancients won't wait for us to resolve our differences."

The chamber was a symphony of clashing ideologies, each group attempting to dominate the conversation. Papers rustled, holographic displays flickered with changing data, and the tension was palpable as arguments escalated.

Commander Yates stood abruptly, her expression fierce and uncompromising. "We can't let old grudges blind us to new opportunities! If we can gain intelligence from the Fair Trade, it could turn the tide in our favor against the Ancients."

She pointed to the holographic map, highlighting vulnerable sectors. "Our ships are too slow, too large to cover every corner of the galaxy. We need their speed, their access. This isn't just strategy; it's survival."

Director Ingram, with his analytical mind, echoed her sentiments, his voice cool and calculated amidst the storm. "This is a tactical decision, not an ideological one. We must adapt or face annihilation."

Representative Calder added with fervor, "They've stolen from us, sabotaged our operations, and now we're supposed to welcome them with open arms? This is madness!"

The tension in the room mounted as the voices of dissent gained momentum, each argument punctuating the air with increasing intensity.

Ambassador Reid interjected, attempting to steer the conversation toward a more measured approach. "I understand the concerns, but we must weigh them against the threat the Ancients pose. This isn't a simple choice between right and wrong. It's about survival."

She continued, trying to calm the rising tide of emotion. "We need to find common ground, some way to protect our interests without compromising our principles."

Councilor Voss chimed in, his voice steady but contemplative. "Ambassador Reid makes a valid point. We can't ignore the potential benefits of this alliance, but we must proceed with caution. Safeguards are imperative."

Commander Yates leaned forward, her gaze sharp and pragmatic. "The Fair Trade has access to regions we've never been able to penetrate. Their small ships are an asset we can't dismiss lightly, especially in a fight against the Ancients."

She paused, letting the gravity of her words settle. "This isn't about trust—it's about leverage. If we can gain valuable intelligence, it could shift the balance in our favor."

Director Ingram followed; his analytical mind focused on the strategic implications. "We must think long-term. Aligning with the Fair Trade isn't an endorsement of their methods but a tactical move. The knowledge they possess about the fringes of our galaxy is invaluable."

Lieutenant Marshal spoke next, youthful determination evident in his expression. "Imagine the reach we could have. The Fair Trade's networks are extensive. We could use that to our advantage if we manage this relationship carefully."

As each group presented its stance, the atmosphere in the chamber became charged with opposing energies. Voices overlapped, growing louder as tensions flared and tempers rose. The debate had become a cacophony of ideals and fears with no resolution in sight.

Admiral Harrington attempted to regain control, raising his voice to cut through the chaos. "Order, please! We must remain focused on the issue at hand."

But the clamor continued, each faction unwilling to yield. The chamber seemed on the brink of fracturing under the weight of discord.

In the midst of the turmoil, Lady Mara rose to her feet, her presence immediately commanding attention. She stood tall, her violet eyes scanning the room with a mixture of determination and calm authority. As she closed her eyes, the emblem of the FEW on her chest flared brightly, and her red cape billowed out behind her, capturing the light like a living flame.

With a subtle gesture, she invoked her FEW power, allowing a gentle wave of calm to radiate from her, flowing into the room like a soothing tide. The change was palpable; a hush fell over the chamber as members slowly sat down, their heated expressions softening. Papers that had been scattered were gathered and straightened, while others took a sip of water or leaned back against their chairs, absorbing the newfound tranquility.

Mara opened her eyes, the violet depths now glowing with an ethereal light. "Enough," she declared, her tone a masterful blend of authority and empathy that demanded silence. The calm she projected seemed to seep into the very walls, quieting the agitated energy and drawing the representatives' attention to her as if compelled by an invisible force.

The room fell quiet; the voices that had clashed moments before now stilled under the soothing influence of her presence. Even those who had been the most vocal critics felt a sense of awe, aware of the rarity and power of the moment.

"We are not enemies here," Mara continued, her voice steady and unwavering. "Our goal is to protect the galaxy from a greater threat. This requires unity, not division."

She allowed her words to resonate in the hushed chamber, the tension slowly dissipating under her calming influence. "Yes, there are risks involved. But we face an existential threat in the Ancients, and we cannot afford to let fear dictate our actions."

Mara turned to the dissenters, her gaze steady and empathetic. "Senator Larkins, General Novack, your concerns are valid. We must ensure that any alliance with the Fair Trade is monitored and held accountable."

She then addressed the moderates and pragmatists, her words carrying the promise of hope and cooperation. "Ambassador Reid,

Commander Yates, you see the potential benefits. Let us work together to craft an agreement that respects our principles while securing the intelligence we desperately need."

Her final words resonated with conviction, filling the room with a renewed sense of purpose. "We are the Alliance, and we stand for hope, strength, and resilience. Let us embody these values and find a way forward, united in our purpose."

The chamber remained silent, the representatives absorbing Mara's call for cohesion. Her intervention had shifted the energy, bringing a sense of clarity and focus to the tumultuous discussion.

Admiral Harrington nodded, acknowledging Mara's influence. "Thank you, Lady Mara. Let us proceed with renewed intent and find a path that serves the greater good."

With the room now calm and attentive, Colonel Idris rose, nodding respectfully to Mara before addressing the assembly. "Ladies and gentlemen, as you have heard, the threat posed by the Ancients requires unprecedented cooperation and strategic thinking. In our discussions with Xan'dor, leader of the Fair Trade, we have laid the foundation for a partnership that could prove essential in countering this existential threat."

Mara continued, her voice steady and diplomatic. "We have agreed to initiate a limited exchange of intelligence regarding the Ancients' movements. This exchange will allow both our operations to be more effective while gradually building trust between our entities."

Idris added, "It's important to note that this partnership will be closely monitored. Any breach of the agreement will result in its immediate termination. We are fully aware of the risks involved and have taken precautions to mitigate them."

The room remained silent, the representatives listening intently as Idris spoke. His voice carried the weight of his experience and commitment to the Alliance's ideals. "Xan'dor has offered the use of his network's capabilities. Their fast, small ships can navigate the fringes of the galaxy with unparalleled speed, delivering supplies and information where our larger vessels cannot reach."

He emphasized the strategic advantage, ensuring the assembly understood the potential benefits. "This allows us to fill gaps in our reach, particularly in the outer planets, where the Alliance's presence is limited. However, transparency is key—both parties will adhere to strict transparency to ensure mutual benefit and accountability."

Mara nodded, picking up the thread of the conversation. "In return, the Fair Trade will have authority over goods requested, and the Alliance will support facilitating these exchanges. This partnership is not about surrendering our principles but enhancing our strategic capabilities to face a common enemy."

She allowed a moment for the representatives to digest the information, her expression unwavering in its sincerity and determination. "I offer my full partnership to ensure this endeavor succeeds. We must stand united in our purpose if we are to safeguard our galaxy."

Senator Larkins, though still wary, acknowledged the necessity. "While I have reservations, I understand the urgency of the situation. We must ensure the Fair Trade adheres to our terms."

General Novack nodded, his stern demeanor slightly softened. "We need every advantage in this fight. If this plan can provide that, then it's a risk we may need to take."

The assembly remained thoughtful, the gravity of the situation apparent as the potential for cooperation and success took shape.

As the meeting concluded, Idris turned to Mara, a hint of a smile on his lips. "Your ability to calm frayed outrage and navigate these concerns has been invaluable. Thank you, Lady Mara."

Mara nodded, her own expression reflecting both relief and determination. "Together, we will ensure this partnership succeeds for the benefit of us all."

The council adjourned, the representatives leaving with renewed focus and a sense of purpose, ready to face the challenges that lay ahead in a galaxy on the brink.

***

The Alliance flagship, Nova Concordia, dominated the docking bay with its imposing presence, a testament to the engineering prowess of the Alliance. Its sleek, obsidian hull glistened under the bay's artificial lights, which cast a bluish glow across the ship's surface. The design of the Nova Concordia was a marvel of both functionality and aesthetic appeal, with sharp lines and elegant curves that hinted at its advanced capabilities.

Inside the sprawling docking bay, the Nova Concordia rested like a slumbering giant, surrounded by a hive of activity. The cavernous space echoed with the clamor of voices and machinery, a symphony of sound that underscored the urgency of the moment. High ceilings reverberated with the clang of metal on metal and the rhythmic whir of machinery. Steam hissed from vents on the floor, mingling with the warm glow of overhead lights that highlighted the ship's grandeur. The air was filled with the scent of coolant and lubricants, a sharp reminder of the mechanical precision that kept the fleet operational.

Around the flagship, a bustling array of support vessels, supply shuttles, and maintenance drones zipped back and forth, their movements coordinated with military precision. Dock workers and engineers, clad in bright jumpsuits, moved with purpose, their faces etched with concentration and resolve. They inspected equipment, oversaw the loading of supplies, and ensured that every detail was accounted for. Crates of ammunition and provisions were stacked neatly along the walls, ready to be transported onto the ship.

Inside the Nova Concordia, the command hub was a nerve center of activity. The room was bathed in a soft, ambient light that accentuated the holographic displays floating in the air. Data streams shimmered, casting vibrant patterns on the metallic walls. The air hummed with a sense of controlled chaos, the tension of anticipation palpable. Officers clad in dark uniforms adorned with rank insignias huddled around tactical displays, their voices low and deliberate as they discussed strategies and contingencies. Their faces were a mix of concentration and resolve, their minds attuned to the complexities of galactic warfare.

Engineers and technicians moved with practiced efficiency, their fingers dancing across control panels as they monitored systems and ensured everything was functioning at peak capacity. The soft whir of machinery and the occasional beep of alerts punctuated their work. Communications specialists, seated at consoles lining the walls, managed the flow of information between the Nova Concordia and the wider fleet. Their hands deftly adjusted controls, their voices calm as they relayed messages and updates across the vast expanse of space.

In a section of the hub dedicated to intelligence operations, analysts sifted through streams of data, their eyes scanning for patterns and anomalies. Lieutenant Dara Nol, an expert analyst, stood among them, her brow furrowed in concentration as she reviewed the latest intelligence on the Ancients' movements. "Their technology defies known physics," she murmured, her voice tinged with awe. "We need to adapt quickly to counter their strategies."

The atmosphere within the Nova Concordia was charged with a mixture of excitement and tension. The crew moved with a sense of purpose, aware of the monumental task ahead. Conversations were brief and focused, punctuated by the hum of technology and the soft thrum of the ship's engines. The lighting was deliberately subdued, casting shadows that danced across the floor as holographic projections flickered and shifted. The gentle hiss of steam from nearby vents added a layer of ambient noise, contributing to the sense of industrious preparation.

From the bridge of the Nova Concordia, the view was breathtaking. Beyond the transparent screens that served as windows, the vastness of space stretched out, studded with stars that seemed to twinkle in anticipation. The docking bay's protective force fields shimmered faintly, offering a glimpse of the bustling activity outside. As the Nova Concordia prepared to launch, the weight of history and hope hung heavy in the air. The galaxy stood united, its defenders ready to face the coming storm with courage and determination. Amidst the tension and anticipation, one thing was certain: the Alliance would not face this fight alone.

Around the flagship, an impressive array of ships from across the Alliance worlds gathered, each a testament to the unique technological prowess of its home planet. The Aegis of Kraggoth, a heavily armored battleship, bristled with missile batteries and laser cannons, its design rugged and utilitarian, reflecting the warlike nature of its creators. The Lyra V Fleet, with sleek, silver vessels, boasted flowing lines and intricate patterns etched into their hulls, known for their speed and agility, and equipped with state-of-the-art stealth technology. The Aquila Cruisers, graceful and streamlined, cloaked in shimmering energy fields, employed advanced cloaking technologies to strike from the shadows. The Calathar Medical Frigates, painted in pristine white, were equipped with cutting-edge medical facilities, ready to tend to the wounded, a reminder of the hope and healing they offered amidst the chaos of war.

Throughout the galaxy, the Alliance's core worlds are connected with its farthest colonies through a complex network of communication hubs. Each planet, unique in its culture and resources, played a vital role in the war effort. On Calathar, scientists in pristine white coats worked tirelessly in bright labs, producing advanced medical equipment and supplies. Their holographic images flickered on the screens in the command hub, sharing breakthroughs and logistical updates. Goraxis buzzed with activity as factories belched smoke, churning out starship components and weapons. Engineers coordinated shipments through video feeds, their faces smeared with soot and determination. On Lyra V, artists and engineers collaborated to enhance the aesthetic and functional design of starships, their holograms showcasing sleek prototypes. Aquila, known for its technological prowess, was abuzz with activity as its inhabitants worked on perfecting cloaking devices and advanced navigation systems, their contributions crucial to the Alliance's strategy.

Within the Nova Concordia, teams of engineers oversaw the installation of cutting-edge weapons and defense systems. Pulse cannons, designed to disrupt enemy shields with electromagnetic pulses, were being mounted on the hulls of battleships. Quantum torpedoes, capable of bypassing conventional defenses, were tested in secure areas, their blue energy trails illuminating the bay. Deflector shields, enhanced to absorb and dissipate enemy fire, hummed with power as they were calibrated for maximum efficiency.

As the preparations unfolded, two figures entered the command hub, commanding immediate attention. Lady Mara and Lord Gresham, members of the FEW, moved with a grace that turned heads. Their all-black uniforms were adorned with the blazing emblem of the FEW on their breastbones, marking them as elite among the elite. Crimson capes billowed behind them, snapping and furling with a life of their own. Lady Mara's blonde hair glinted under the lights, her sword glowing with a soft blue hue at her side, its blade etched with archaic symbols that pulsed gently. Her eyes, sharp and perceptive, scanned the bustling room. Beside her, Lord Gresham's ocean-colored eyes reflected the myriad lights of the command hub. His sword, glowing fiercely red and adorned with similar ancient runes, hung at his side. Together, they embodied both the promise of protection and the weight of responsibility.

"Lady Mara, Lord Gresham," Admiral Sato greeted them, inclining his head with respect. "Your presence is an honor and a necessity."

"We are here to ensure our united front," Lord Gresham replied, his voice clear and confident. "We'll do whatever it takes to protect our worlds."

In the heart of the command center, high-level strategy meetings were underway. Holographic projections of key leaders flickered as they discussed tactics and challenges. Admiral Sato's gaze was steady as he addressed the council. "We must anticipate their manipulation of time and space," he emphasized, his voice calm yet urgent. Commander Westbrook Tyne, her experience evident in her composed demeanor, contributed insights from past campaigns. "Their unpredictability is their strength, but our unity is ours," she asserted, her tone resolute. Senator Imani Kade, her holographic image gesturing passionately, advocated for reinforcing the core worlds. "We cannot afford to leave our people vulnerable," she argued, determination in her eyes.

Amidst the grand preparations, individual stories unfolded, revealing the personal stakes involved. In the training grounds, Private Jax Teller pushed himself relentlessly, his breath coming in ragged gasps. Thoughts of his family on Goraxis spurred him on, each maneuver a promise to protect them. Corporal Lina Varis, offering a supportive pat on his back, grinned infectiously. "We've got this, Jax," she said, confidence in her voice. "Just think of the stories we'll have to tell when this is all over." Engineer Sofia Vance coordinated logistics with precision, her team ensuring every resource was accounted for. She faced the challenges of shortages with determination, knowing that every crate and shipment mattered.

As Fair Trade ships integrated with Alliance forces, crews exchanged wary glances, navigating the challenges of new partnerships. Through joint exercises and briefings, trust began to take root. The agility of Fair Trade pilots, known for their unconventional tactics, added a new dimension to the Alliance's capabilities. Lieutenant Brandt observed the maneuvers with admiration. "These pilots bring a fresh perspective," she commented. "Their agility could give us the edge we need." Ambassador Hart nodded in agreement, a smile tugging at his lips. "They bring a different perspective, and that's exactly what we need to face the Ancients."

Across the galaxy, civilians braced for the coming storm. On Arden Prime, citizens crowded into public squares, faces upturned to enormous screens that broadcast the latest updates. Determination mingled with fear in their expressions. Street artists, their hands vibrant with splashes of paint, transformed blank walls into murals of hope and resilience, a visual symphony of defiance against the encroaching darkness. In agricultural worlds, families gathered around communal tables, sharing meals and stories, stockpiling supplies with grim resolve. They spoke in hushed tones of sacrifice and courage, of the bonds that held them together in the face of uncertainty.

The Alliance was a living mosaic of diverse people, each contributing unique strengths to the preparations. Telepathic FEW moved with a commanding presence, their minds seamlessly linked, sharing intelligence with unparalleled efficiency. Their ability to communicate instantaneously made them invaluable in coordinating efforts across vast distances. Resilient Drathul, known for their unmatched durability, volunteered for high-risk missions, bringing their resilience to the forefront of the battle plan. Avenian pilots, with movements a blur of speed and grace, practiced maneuvers in training simulators, their starfighters darting like silverfish, a testament to their unparalleled reflexes. Rathian technicians, masters of cyber warfare, focused on disrupting enemy communications and hacking into the Ancients' systems.

As the Nova Concordia prepared to launch, the weight of history and hope hung heavy in the air. The galaxy stood united, its defenders ready to face the coming storm with courage and determination. Amidst the tension and anticipation, one thing was certain: the Alliance would not face this fight alone.

The heart of the command center on the Nova Concordia pulsed with a steady rhythm of urgency. Holographic projections floated above the round table, casting an ethereal glow on the gathered leaders. The room was dimly lit, the ambient light from the displays creating shifting patterns on the metallic walls, lending an otherworldly aura to the chamber. A low hum filled the air, the sound of advanced machinery processing data streams from across the galaxy.

Admiral Sato stood at the helm of the meeting, his uniform immaculate, the insignia of the Alliance catching the light with each subtle movement. His eyes, a deep-set gray, were focused and unwavering as they scanned the projections of galactic maps and fleet deployments. The tension in the room was palpable, each leader acutely aware of the stakes at hand.

"Attention, everyone," Sato began, his voice steady yet carrying a weight of urgency. "We must anticipate the Ancients' ability to manipulate time and space. This is not a conventional war, and our strategies must reflect that."

As he spoke, the holographic images shifted, displaying scenarios of potential conflicts, with red markers indicating enemy movements and blue representing their own forces. The room was silent except for the occasional beep of incoming data updates, a reminder of the constant flow of information that guided their decisions.

Commander Mia Tyne, a seasoned veteran with a reputation for tactical brilliance, leaned forward, her fingers tapping lightly on the table's edge as she considered the data before her. Her auburn hair was pulled back in a tight braid, and her eyes were sharp, reflecting the light of the projections.

"Our greatest strength is our unity," she asserted, her voice clear and resolute. "The Ancients thrive on unpredictability, but we can counter that with cohesion and agility. We need to be prepared to adapt quickly, to shift tactics as new information comes in."

She gestured towards one of the holograms, highlighting a potential weak point in the enemy's lines. "If we can exploit this, we might force them into a more predictable pattern. It's a risk, but it could give us the edge we need."

Senator Imani Kade's holographic image flickered as she spoke, her presence just as commanding as if she were physically in the room. Her voice carried a passionate intensity, reflecting the weight of responsibility she felt for the lives of those in the core worlds.

"We cannot afford to leave our people vulnerable," Kade insisted, her gaze sweeping across the table, meeting the eyes of each leader in turn. "Every world is counting on us to protect them. Reinforcing our defenses in the core sectors is not just strategic; it's imperative. We have to show them that we are ready to defend what we hold dear."

A moment of silence followed, heavy with the implications of her words. Then, a voice rose in disagreement, cutting through the stillness.

"Reinforcing the core is all well and good, but if we don't push outward, we risk being cornered," argued Commander Harik, a rugged man known for his aggressive strategies. His holographic image leaned forward, eyes intense. "We need to take the fight to the Ancients and use the Nova Lances to destabilize their forces."

The mention of Nova Lances—a new technology capable of creating localized gravitational distortions—hung in the air, drawing mixed reactions from those gathered. The technology was experimental and powerful, but its risks were as great as its potential.

"We can't afford to gamble with untested weapons," Senator Kade countered, her voice firm. "Our priority must be the protection of civilian lives."

Before the debate could escalate, a young officer seated at a side console interjected, his voice steady but respectful. "Perhaps we can integrate both approaches," Lieutenant Miles suggested, glancing at Admiral Sato for permission to continue. "By deploying a small task force equipped with Nova Lances to probe their defenses, we can draw the Ancients into a position where our main fleet can engage them more safely."

Admiral Sato nodded thoughtfully, his gaze sweeping over the gathered leaders. "Lieutenant Miles raises a valid point," he acknowledged. "A balanced strategy could allow us to maintain pressure while minimizing risk. We need to utilize every tool at our disposal, including our ability to adapt and innovate."

As the discussion continued, the air in the command center felt charged with anticipation, every decision carrying the potential to change the course of the battle to come. Each leader brought their expertise and insights to bear, weaving a tapestry of strategy that reflected both the complexity of the conflict and the resolve of the Alliance.

In that room, under the dim lights and surrounded by the hum of technology, the leaders of the Alliance faced the future with determination, their discussions shaping the destiny of countless worlds. The tension was palpable, but so too was the unity that bound them together in a common cause. Whatever challenges lay ahead, they would face them together, a testament to the power of collaboration and the strength of the human spirit.

Combat Outpost Keating sprawled across a grassy expanse, its natural terrain transformed into a rigorous training ground. The outpost was alive with the sounds of exertion and determination as soldiers navigated its various obstacles. The clatter of boots against metal mingled with the softer thud of footsteps on earth, creating a symphony of preparation. The sun hung high in the sky, casting long shadows across the field, highlighting the dedicated efforts of those training for the battle ahead.

Private Jax Teller was among them, his movements precise and deliberate as he tackled the mud rope course. His lungs burned with each breath, and sweat trickled down his brow, but he pushed through the fatigue with grim resolve. The image of his family on Goraxis floated to the forefront of his mind—a memory of his sister's laughter, his mother's reassuring smile, his father's steady gaze. Each step was a promise to protect them, a silent vow that their lives would remain unchanged by the storm to come.

Jax leaped over a barrier and landed heavily in the mud, his muscles screaming in protest. He paused for a moment, bent over and panting, his hands resting on his knees. The earthy scent of damp soil mixed with the sharp tang of metal from nearby weapons training, grounding him in the reality of his task. A brief flash of doubt crossed his mind—was he truly ready for the battle ahead? But the memory of his sister's laughter banished the thought as quickly as it came.

"Hey, Jax," came a voice behind him, breaking through his haze of concentration. He straightened and turned to see Corporal Lina Varis, her grin infectious despite the weariness in her eyes. Her uniform was smudged with dirt, a testament to the drills they'd been running.

"We've got this," Lina said, clapping a hand on his shoulder. Her touch was warm, grounding him in the present. "Just think of the stories we'll have to tell when this is all over."

Jax managed a smile, the corners of his mouth lifting as he met her gaze. "I know," he replied, his voice hoarse but resolute. "It's just... I keep thinking of home, you know? My sister's counting on me."

Lina nodded, her expression softening with understanding. "I get it. We're all fighting for something. But remember, you're not alone in this. We're a team, and we'll face whatever comes together."

Around them, the unique abilities of different Alliance populations were incorporated into the training regimen. Soldiers from Aquila, known for their keen spatial awareness, guided their teammates through complex maneuvers. Meanwhile, recruits from

Lyra V, with their enhanced reflexes, demonstrated evasive techniques that pushed their physical limits.

In one corner of the outpost, a small group of Fair Trade pilots were adjusting to the Alliance's methods. Their unconventional tactics were being integrated into the broader strategy, offering new perspectives and techniques. A Fair Trade pilot named Rian observed Jax and Lina nodding approvingly.

"You Alliance folks are pretty disciplined," Rian commented, his tone a blend of admiration and curiosity. "I bet our maneuvers could add some flair to your routines."

Lina raised an eyebrow, intrigued. "What do you have in mind?"

Rian grinned, a glint of mischief in his eyes. "We've got a move called the 'Twist and Turn' that might just surprise your trainers."

"Sounds interesting," Jax replied, exchanging a glance with Lina. "We're always up for a challenge."

Just then, a loud crash echoed from the weapons training area. A piece of equipment had malfunctioned, causing a brief halt in activity. The momentary tension was palpable, but it quickly subsided as engineers rushed to fix the issue, their efficiency a testament to their preparation and teamwork.

As they resumed their training, the group was reminded of the delicate balance required to maintain focus amidst the chaos. Every moment counted, and every effort contributed to the broader battle strategy, their actions a testament to the Alliance's unity.

A short distance away, Engineer Sofia Vance coordinated logistics with precision. Her team ensured every resource was accounted for, navigating the challenges of shortages with determination. Sofia's voice rose above the din as she directed her team, clipboard in hand. "Let's keep it moving, folks! We're almost through the backlog. Stay focused, and we'll get this done."

A young technician approached, a worried frown on his face. "Engineer Vance, we've got a shortage of some key components. What should we do?"

Sofia paused, considering the problem with a furrowed brow. She glanced around, taking in the bustling scene. "Coordinate with supply from deck five," she instructed, her voice steady. "They might have a surplus we can tap into. And let logistics know we need a priority requisition."

The technician nodded, relief washing over his features. "On it, ma'am."

As he hurried away, Sofia turned her attention back to the task at hand, her determination unwavering. Every crate and shipment was accounted for, each item a crucial part of the Alliance's effort. She knew that their success depended on the meticulous work happening behind the scenes, and she was committed to ensuring nothing fell through the cracks.

Combat Outpost Keating was a microcosm of the larger mobilization effort, each individual's story contributing to the collective resolve of the Alliance. As Private Teller returned to his drills, buoyed by Corporal Varis's encouragement, and Engineer Vance coordinated the logistics with precision, the air was charged with anticipation and the promise of what lay ahead. Amidst the tension and uncertainty, one thing was clear: they were all in this together, united in purpose and ready to face whatever challenges awaited them.

As the Nova Concordia prepared for launch, the Fair Trade ships docked alongside the Alliance fleet, their vibrant colors and eclectic designs creating a striking contrast against the uniform precision of the Alliance vessels. These ships, each a testament to the ingenuity and resourcefulness of their crews, were adorned with hand-painted insignias and modifications that celebrated diverse backgrounds and stories.

In the docking bay, the mingling crews began joint exercises designed to bridge the gap between their distinct styles. The expansive space was alive with the hum of activity, and the air was filled with the scent of engine oil and the metallic tang of tools. Pilots from both sides, dressed in an array of flight suits and uniforms, gathered around holo displays that projected intricate flight patterns and maneuvers. Lieutenant Brandt watched the integration unfold, her eyes keenly observing the interactions between the two groups. She noticed the initial wariness in the exchanged glances, a natural hesitation born from unfamiliarity and the daunting task ahead. Beneath the surface, she sensed a burgeoning curiosity and mutual respect.

Among the pilots was Zara, a young Fair Trade pilot whose nimble fighter had already impressed many with its agility. As she watched an Alliance pilot execute a standard formation, her thoughts were a mix of admiration and determination. "They're precise but maybe too predictable," Zara mused, adjusting her flight helmet as she prepared to demonstrate her own techniques. She appreciated the discipline of the Alliance but knew that her experience in unpredictable, chaotic environments would be invaluable.

On the other side of the bay, Lieutenant Marcus, an Alliance officer known for his methodical approach, studied Zara's daring maneuvers with a mixture of intrigue and skepticism. "She's got talent, no doubt," he thought, "but can she adapt to coordinated tactics?"

As the exercises progressed, pilots from both sides began to share not only tactical knowledge but also glimpses into their respective cultures. Zara, always eager to connect, offered Marcus a small token—a carved piece of driftwood from her homeworld shaped like a bird in flight. "It's a symbol of freedom where I come from," she explained with a smile. Marcus, in return, shared a story from his academy days, detailing the rigorous training that honed his skills. The exchange of stories and symbols fostered a sense of camaraderie as both groups realized the shared values beneath their different exteriors.

Not all interactions went smoothly. A minor disagreement arose when a Fair Trade engineer and an Alliance technician clashed over repair protocols. Voices rose as they debated the best method to optimize the ship's engines, their cultural pride clashing in a moment of tension. Zara stepped in, her voice calm but firm. "Let's combine your precision with our improvisation," she suggested, proposing a hybrid solution that drew on both groups' strengths. The disagreement was resolved, the teams resumed work with renewed focus, and their respect for each other deepened by the resolution.

The Fair Trade ships boasted unique capabilities that complemented the Alliance fleet's strengths. Equipped with adaptive shielding and advanced stealth technology, these vessels could maneuver through enemy lines undetected, providing invaluable reconnaissance and tactical flexibility. Their unconventional tactics, honed in the volatile sectors of space, added a layer of unpredictability to the Alliance's strategies.

Watching from a vantage point overlooking the bay, Admiral Sato observed the integration with interest. "This alliance is more than just a tactical advantage," he remarked to his aide, his voice thoughtful. "It's a chance to learn and grow together, to become something greater than the sum of our parts."

The integration wasn't without its challenges. Communication issues arose as the two groups navigated differing protocols and command structures. However, joint briefings and shared training sessions quickly addressed these difficulties, forging a cohesive unit ready to face the impending threat.

As the day wore on, discussions turned to the upcoming battle against the Ancients. Zara and Marcus found themselves discussing tactics, their earlier skepticism replaced by mutual respect. "We'll need to be creative," Zara said, her eyes reflecting the determination in her voice. "Our agility combined with your firepower can outmaneuver them." Marcus nodded, appreciating her insight. "And your stealth capabilities will be crucial for reconnaissance. Together, we'll find their weak spots."

The Fair Trade ships, with their unorthodox designs and modifications, required some adjustments to the Alliance facilities. Technicians worked to accommodate the new arrivals, adapting docking ports and recalibrating systems to ensure seamless integration. The unique aesthetic of the Fair Trade vessels, with their vibrant colors and eclectic markings, brought a fresh vitality to the otherwise orderly docking bay. Their presence symbolized a fusion of tradition and innovation, a testament to the power of unity amidst diversity.

Zara's journey to the Alliance was a testament to her tenacity and skill. Born in a distant sector, she had navigated the treacherous paths of space, honing her abilities in the face of adversity. Her ship, a labor of love crafted from salvaged parts, bore the scars of countless adventures, each one a badge of honor. As she prepared for the next exercise, she glanced at Marcus, feeling a growing sense of partnership. In their shared purpose, she saw the potential for something greater—a chance to redefine their fates in the face of an overwhelming enemy.

The looming threat of the Ancients served as a unifying force for these diverse groups. The gravity of the situation was not lost on anyone; each pilot, engineer, and officer understood the stakes. The fear of the unknown was tempered by a shared determination as the Alliance and Fair Trade ships joined forces to protect their worlds and futures.

As the sun dipped below the horizon, casting long shadows across the bay, the Nova Concordia stood ready. The weight of history and hope hung in the air, but with allies like the Fair Trade at their side, the Alliance was poised to meet the challenge with resilience and ingenuity.

Above the military base planet, the cosmos buzzed with a breathtaking display of galactic might. A flotilla of over a thousand capital ships and tens of thousands of fighters swarmed through the void like a school of celestial creatures converging upon a common destination. From hulking battleships with armor-plated hulls to sleek, agile fighters darting between larger vessels, the sky was a tapestry of movement and light.

Massive docking platforms stretched across the planet's surface, sprawling like metallic fields beneath the starlit sky. Each was surrounded by shimmering energy shields that flickered with iridescent hues, protecting the ships and equipment within. As the fleet approached, the shields parted in orchestrated symphonies of light, welcoming the incoming vessels with open arms.

Leading the procession, a colossal dreadnought glided through space with the majesty of a leviathan, its size rivaling that of a small moon. Its hull bristled with weaponry, turrets swiveling in silent vigilance. Behind it, carriers that could house entire cities and cruisers and frigates followed in disciplined formations, their engines leaving trails of blue and white light that crisscrossed the starscape. Interspersed among the larger ships were swarms of smaller craft, from nimble corvettes to cargo transports laden with supplies. Their maneuverability was a marvel, weaving intricate patterns as they navigated the bustling traffic. The air shimmered with the exhaust plumes of thrusters and the hum of energy shields, creating a symphony of sound that resonated through the thin atmosphere.

The fleet's arrival created a spectacle visible from multiple perspectives. From the planet's surface, the ships were silhouetted against the twilight sky, casting long shadows on the landscape. From space, they filled the orbit, a swirling mass of metal and light that seemed to stretch endlessly across the starscape. From the cockpit of a small ship, the sheer scale of the assembly was humbling, each vessel a titan in its own right.

As more ships arrived, they queued in orbit, awaiting their turn to descend onto the bustling planet—a process that took hours to complete, emphasizing the fleet's vast numbers. The base's control towers, sleek spires crowned with rotating sensors, coordinated the flow with precision, guiding each vessel to its assigned berth. Holographic displays flickered with streams of data, charts, and vector diagrams, a testament to the meticulous organization underpinning the frenetic activity.

Inside the control room, the tension was palpable. Technicians, their fingers dancing across control panels, maintained constant communication with the incoming ships. The anticipation of the battle ahead loomed over them, a mix of anxiety and determination written on their faces. The presence of so many ships affected the local space environment, creating artificial auroras that danced across the planet's atmosphere and subtly altering weather patterns.

The planet itself was a hive of activity. Rows of hangars and staging areas stretched across its surface, bustling with personnel in brightly colored uniforms who moved with purpose and efficiency. Robots and drones scurried about, performing maintenance and resupply tasks with tireless dedication. Insignias and flags from diverse worlds adorned the ships, a testament to the cultural mosaic of the Alliance. Over a million souls were involved in this operation, from the ships' crews to the ground support teams, ensuring every need was met.

The scale of the operation was awe-inspiring. It was a testament to the galaxy's unified effort against a common threat, demonstrating the indomitable spirit that fueled the Alliance's resolve. The fleet's combined computational power and energy output were staggering, capable of rivaling entire planets. As more ships continued to pour in, their numbers growing by the minute, it became clear that this was a gathering of unprecedented magnitude, a grand assembly ready to face the looming darkness of the Ancients.

Above it all, the sun dipped below the horizon, casting a golden hue across the planet's surface and illuminating the ships with a celestial glow. Against this backdrop, the military base planet stood as a beacon of hope and strength, a formidable bastion in the galaxy's fight for survival.

Yet, amid the orchestrated chaos, a whisper of unease rippled through the ranks. The Ancients, with their enigmatic powers, were an adversary unlike any they had faced before. This assembly was larger than any conflict in the galaxy's history, a testament to the stakes involved. A fleeting thought crossed the minds of those watching the spectacle unfold: Would their combined might be enough to withstand the onslaught?

19

THE PUSH FOR FREEDOM

In the private chamber, Admiral Levi and Lord Gresham examined the latest intelligence reports. The energy signatures near the Helios Cluster were unlike anything they had seen before. The Ancients' technology was far more advanced, posing an immense threat.

"We need to be prepared for the worst," Levi said, his expression grim. "If the Ancients launch a full-scale attack, we must be ready to defend our territories."

Gresham nodded, his eyes reflecting steely resolve. "Our fleet is strong, and our people are determined. We will not let the Ancients prevail."

Meanwhile, in the council chamber, Ardyn's dissent sowed uncertainty. Some delegates questioned the mission's feasibility, while others rallied behind Mara's call for action. The council's unity was tested, and Mara's diplomatic skills were put to the test.

Mara convened a meeting with influential council members, using specific examples of struggling worlds to appeal to their compassion and duty. Her emotional connection began to sway the hesitant delegates.

Levi and Gresham focused on strengthening the fleet's readiness addressing military leaders' concerns. Levi's calm demeanor and Gresham's strategic insights helped alleviate fears and doubts.

Amid preparations, the heroes' flaws surfaced. Levi struggled with self-doubt, clenching his jaw to maintain composure under the leadership's weight. Mara, despite her empathy, sometimes grew frustrated with those who couldn't see the bigger picture. Gresham's brilliance as a strategist occasionally led to overconfidence, dismissing alternative perspectives.

The Celestial Event The mystery of the Ancients' motives unraveled. Intercepted communications hinted at a celestial event of great significance. Gresham pored over ancient texts, finding a reference to a prophecy: the "Convergence," a celestial alignment granting immense power to those who controlled it. The Ancients' activities near the Helios Cluster suggested they were preparing to harness this event.

"The Ancients are not just seeking to conquer," Gresham shared with Levi and Mara. "They aim to control the Convergence. If they succeed, their power will be unmatched."

"We must prevent them from achieving this," Mara realized. "The stakes are higher than we imagined."

Levi nodded, his resolve hardening. "Then we have no choice. We must act swiftly and decisively to stop them."

In the following days, the council's efforts bore fruit. Resources were allocated, fleets were mobilized, and the reconnaissance mission was launched. The unity forged in the council chamber was tested, and Galactic Alliance leaders stood ready to face whatever challenges lay ahead.

Lady Mara, Rear Admiral Levi, and Lord Gresham each played their part, leveraging their unique strengths to support the war effort. The bonds they formed with each other and the council were crucial to their success.

As the first ships set off toward the Helios Cluster, hope and determination filled the air. The galaxy was united in purpose, ready to face the threat of the Ancients.

The battlefield was a chaotic swirl of smoke and laser fire, the ground scorched and pockmarked with craters. General Tharok's bio-engineered warriors charged fearlessly into the fray, their genetically enhanced abilities overpowering enemy forces.

Minister Liora watched from a vantage point, her expression a mix of awe and horror. "General Tharok, these warriors... they're unstoppable. But at what cost?"

Tharok, his reptilian eyes gleaming with pride, responded, "The cost is victory, Minister. We can't afford to lose this war."

Admiral Levi, monitoring the battle from a command tent, interjected, "Liora has a point, Tharok. We need to ensure we're not sacrificing our humanity in the process."

Lady Mara approached, her presence calming. "Perhaps there's a way to balance both. We must implement strict ethical guidelines and treat these warriors with the respect they deserve."

As the battle raged, the heroes grappled with the moral complexities of their choices, knowing each decision could have far-reaching consequences. The sight of the bio-engineered warriors, powerful yet haunting, lingered in Mara's mind, prompting her to reconsider their use in future battles.

In the research labs, scientists and engineers worked tirelessly on new technological innovations. Envoy Lyra demonstrated a prototype energy weapon to Gresham and Levi.

"This weapon uses focused energy pulses to disrupt the Ancients' technology. It could be a game-changer," Lyra explained.

Gresham nodded thoughtfully. "Impressive. But can it be scaled for mass production?"

Lyra smiled confidently. "We're working on it. With the right resources, we can have these in the hands of our soldiers within weeks."

Levi, always cautious, added, "We'll need to test it in the field first. Let's deploy a few prototypes on the next mission."

Lord Gresham, troubled by the ethical implications of bio-engineered warriors, saw this as a more humane alternative. "These weapons could reduce our reliance on bio-engineered soldiers. Let's prioritize their development."

In the Galactic Council chamber, representatives debated their next moves. Councilor Althea called the session to order.

"We have received communication from a previously unknown faction," Althea announced. "They offer their assistance against the Ancients, but their motives are unclear."

Supreme Chancellor Ellara frowned. "We must be cautious. Their technology could be a trap."

Governor Quorin, ever the pragmatist, countered, "Or it could be the advantage we need. We should at least hear them out."

The mysterious alien representative entered the chamber, their presence cloaked in shadow. "Esteemed leaders of the Galactic

Alliance, we come not as conquerors but as allies. Our technology and knowledge could turn the tide of this war."

Recalling their discoveries in ancient ruins, Lady Mara argued for diplomacy. "We need allies. Their knowledge could be crucial in understanding the Convergence and preventing the disaster the Ancients fear."

The council, divided but swayed by Mara's argument, agreed to engage with the new faction. The scene ended with a tentative alliance formed, the trust fragile but necessary.

The hidden archive was a fortress of knowledge guarded by advanced security systems. Lord Gresham and his team infiltrated the facility, bypassing traps and hacking into secure databases.

As they uncovered ancient records, a shocking truth emerged. The Ancients' motives were not solely about conquest—they were trying to prevent a cataclysmic event linked to the Convergence.

Gresham's eyes widened as he read the data. "This changes everything. The Ancients believe they're saving the galaxy by harnessing the Convergence."

Mara, providing diplomatic cover, entered the room. "Then we need to stop them without causing the very disaster they're trying to prevent."

Levi's voice crackled over the comms. "We need to get this information back to the Alliance. This could be the key to ending the war."

Admiral Levi studied the holographic record, the glowing text reflecting in his determined eyes. "These records indicate that the Ancients once tried to harness the Convergence to stabilize their collapsing star systems. But something went wrong," he explained, his voice tinged with urgency.

The Kalyrian representative nodded, their expression somber. "The Convergence is not just a source of power; it's a delicate balance of cosmic energies. Misuse can lead to catastrophic events, as the Ancients discovered."

Lady Mara stepped forward, her resolve evident. "This is why we need to work with the Kalyrians. Their understanding of the Convergence could help us prevent the same fate. We must convince the Alliance that diplomacy and collaboration are our best paths forward."

His brow furrowed in thought, Lord Gresham added, "And if we can find a way to safely harness the Convergence, we might offer the Ancients a solution that doesn't involve war. They might be willing to negotiate if we can help them."

Admiral Levi straightened, resolve to harden. "We have the information. Now, we need to use it wisely. Let's prepare a presentation for the Council, showing them the potential of this alliance with the Kalyrians."

The Kalyrian representative's gratitude was palpable. "Your willingness to explore this path is commendable. Together, we can ensure the Convergence is used for the benefit of all, not just as a weapon of war."

As they began to formulate their strategy, the weight of their mission pressed down on them. The stakes were higher than ever, and the galaxy's fate rested on its ability to unite diverse factions and forge a path toward peace.

The Beacon of Power

The desolate planet loomed ahead, its surface a barren wasteland scarred by ancient cataclysms and time. As the Requiem descended, its landing thrusters roared like a beast awakened, sending plumes of dust swirling into the thin, arid atmosphere. The specialized team handpicked for this mission, disembarked with a blend of trepidation and resolve etched into their expressions.

Lieutenant Zara Korrin led the way, her eyes sharp as they scanned the alien horizon for any lurking danger. Sergeant Rylan Voss followed closely, the metallic clinks of his equipment a rhythmic counterpoint to their cautious footsteps. Corporal Anara Jax, Specialist Kai Renner, and Ensign Lira Nyx brought up the rear, their senses heightened and ready for whatever awaited them.

"According to Elys' data, the anomaly should be just over that ridge," Zara said, pointing towards a jagged outcropping of rock that cut sharply against the sky. "Stay alert. We have no idea what we're dealing with."

As they crested the ridge, the sight before them stole their breath away. A vast crater spread out, its center dominated by a towering structure of shimmering light and metal. The Beacon of Power stood like a titan of legend, pulsing with a rhythmic glow that seemed to echo in their very bones. The air crackled with energy, and the ground vibrated subtly underfoot, hinting at the Beacon's dormant power.

Rylan's fingers danced over his scanner, his brow furrowing in concentration. "This thing emits energy on a scale I've never seen before. It's... mesmerizing."

Anara stepped closer, her gaze fixed on the Beacon, captivated by its beauty and mystery. "What do you think it does?"

Kai, ever the pragmatist, began setting up a perimeter of explosives as a precaution. "Whatever it is, we need to be ready for anything. Let's figure it out quickly."

Lira, using her intuitive diplomatic skills, approached the Beacon cautiously. "There's something... familiar about this. Like it's calling to us."

Zara nodded, her hand instinctively resting on her sidearm. "Stay sharp. Let's get a closer look."

As they descended into the crater, the Beacon's glow intensified, casting ethereal shadows across the barren landscape. The air around it seemed to hum with energy, resonating with an otherworldly melody that tugged at their souls. The faint scent of ozone and warm metal filled their nostrils, mingling with the dusty, acrid taste of the atmosphere.

"It's beautiful," Anara whispered, her voice barely audible over the Beacon's hum. "But there's something more. Something... ancient."

Rylan's scanner beeped urgently. "I'm picking up traces of an unknown essence. It's like nothing we've ever encountered. Could it be... FEW essence?"

Just then, Lord Gresham approached, his eyes wide with wonder and awe. He examined the Beacon closely, his fingers tracing the intricate carvings etched into its surface. "These symbols... I've never seen anything like them," he muttered. "They're old, ancient beyond comprehension."

As he gazed at the Beacon, memories flashed through Gresham's mind: the battles fought, the sacrifices made, and the allies lost along the way. The weight of their journey bore down on him, but it was accompanied by a deep sense of purpose.

A subtle, almost imperceptible tug pulled at him, guiding his hand toward a plate on the Beacon's surface. He hesitated, feeling the weight of the unknown, then placed his hand on the plate. A low hum resonated through the air, and strange symbols began to beam into the sky, glowing with an eerie light.

The Beacon powered on, its glow intensifying as the symbols danced around Gresham. He felt a surge of energy course through him, connecting him to the ancient device. Across the Beacon, he saw another plate identical to the one under his hand. Instinctively, he knew who needed to be there.

"Mara," he whispered, his voice filled with a sense of destiny. "Lady Mara, you need to be by my side."

Lady Mara, her eyes wide with curiosity and determination, stepped forward. She placed her hand on the other plate, mirroring Gresham's action. The Beacon's hum grew louder as soon as she did, and a brilliant light enveloped them both.

As she connected with the Beacon, Mara reflected on the journey that had led her here—the alliances forged, the countless lives saved, and the relentless pursuit of peace. Her bond with Gresham strengthened over nearly a century and now resonated with an intensity that matched the Beacon's power.

The air shimmered with energy, and the Beacon's power surged to life. Symbols danced around them, forming patterns and shapes hinting at an ancient forgotten knowledge. Fragments of lore whispered through their minds, revealing glimpses of a civilization long lost to time.

The connection between Gresham and Mara deepened, their essences intertwining with the Beacon's power. The ground beneath them quaked, and a halo of light spread outward from the Beacon, illuminating the crater and casting a protective barrier around the galaxy to prevent the Ancients from resetting it.

Back on the Requiem, Elys' holographic form flickered with excitement. "Admiral Levi, the energy readings are off the charts! The Beacon... it's preventing the reset. The Ancients' power is waning."

Levi, his eyes wide with hope, turned to his crew. "This is it. This is our chance. With the Ancients weakened, we can strike. We can finally bring an end to their tyranny."

Mara's gaze hardened with determination. "Then let's not waste any time. Prepare for battle. The rebellion starts now."

As the crew of the Requiem rallied for the impending confrontation, the Beacon of Power stood as a symbol of hope and defiance. The essence of the FEW, the unity of the galaxy, and the strength of their resolve would guide them through the storm, ensuring that the light of freedom would shine brightly for future generations.

Galactic Reactions and Impact

Across the galaxy, the Beacon's activation sent ripples through space. On distant worlds, civilians gazed at the sky in awe as the protective barrier shimmered into view, a visual testament to the alliance's determination. The news spread rapidly, igniting hope in oppressed sectors and fueling the resolve of resistance fighters.

In the hidden chambers of the Ancients, panic ensued as their plans unraveled. Their leaders scrambled to counter the unexpected shift in power, realizing that their grip on the galaxy was slipping.

As Gresham and Mara stood side by side, bathed in the Beacon's light, they understood that their journey was far from over. The activation of the Beacon was but the first step in a larger battle. They had turned the tide, but the war for the galaxy's future had only just begun.

A Ripple Across the Stars

As the holographic image of the Endurant's destruction and Xan'dor's impassioned plea flickered and faded from the bustling marketplace of Xar Kilprime, its impact spread far and wide, touching the lives of countless species across the galaxy. The air crackled with tension, as if the universe itself were holding its breath, waiting for what was to come.

On the lush, jungle-covered planet of Verdania, the flickering glow of a holographic fire cast an eerie light on the faces of the Elysians gathered around it. The air, thick with the sweet, earthy scent of the jungle, seemed to hum with the tension in the atmosphere. The fire, though warm in appearance, was silent, its light artificial, yet its presence filled the space with an unsettling energy.

Lyrana, an elder of great wisdom, rose to her feet, her lithe form seeming to draw strength from the ancient rhythms of the jungle. Her usual voice, one that could calm even the most savage beasts, trembled with the weight of her fury. "For too long, we have hidden in the shadows of the galaxy, believing our peace would keep us safe," she began, her gaze sweeping over the assembly. "But the Ancients have shattered that illusion. There is no refuge, no safe haven for us anymore. If we are to survive, we must stand united, or we will fall—alone."

A low murmur of agreement rippled through the group, but it was Commander Astor's voice that cut through the tension like a blade. "We will not bow to tyranny," he said, his words heavy with the weight of a decision none of them had ever imagined making. "If we must fight, we will."

The other Elysians exchanged glances, their faces filled with a mixture of sorrow and resolve. Their people had never known war, only healing and diplomacy. But in the face of such an existential threat, the time for peace was quickly fading.

Lyrana looked at them all, her heart heavy. "We have always healed with our hands," she said softly, "but now, we wonder—can we still heal in a world that demands we fight?".

Far across the stars, on the scorched, volcanic surface of Kar'dak, a different scene unfolded within the great obsidian citadel. The air was heavy with the acrid tang of sulfur and molten rock seeping into the nostrils of the Drak'ari gathered in their cavernous hall. Their massive, reptilian forms were encased in elaborate battle armor, their scales glistening with a sheen of heat and sweat. Their eyes, burning embers reflecting the faint glow of molten rock, gleamed with a predatory light.

Kah'roth, the warlord of the Drak'ari, slammed his fist against the ornate table, the impact sending a spiderweb of cracks radiating outward and a tremor through the ground. "The Ancients dare to challenge our might?" he bellowed, his voice a guttural roar that shook the very foundation of the citadel. "They dare to threaten the galaxy that we have sworn to conquer? We will show them the fury of the Drak'ari, the fire that burns in our blood!"

The assembled warriors erupted in a cacophony of roars and battle cries, their clawed hands grasping the hilts of their fearsome weapons. They had always been conquerors, a scourge upon the stars. But now, faced with a foe that threatened to usurp their place in the galaxy, they were ready to channel their aggression toward a new target.

Species that had once been bitter enemies found themselves united by a common foe. Old grudges were set aside; ancient rivalries were forgotten in the face of the looming threat. The Galactic Alliance, once a loose confederation of worlds, became a beacon of hope and unity, a rallying point for all those who sought to defy the tyranny of the Ancients.

And at the heart of it all, the Fair Trade Alliance and the Galactic Alliance stood tall, their leaders working tirelessly to forge a coalition unlike any the galaxy had ever seen. Xan'dor, his holographic image now a symbol of defiance and hope, became the face of the resistance, a living embodiment of the indomitable spirit that burned in the hearts of all those who yearned for freedom.

The stage was set for a confrontation that would shake the very foundations of the universe. The Ancients, once secure in their absolute power, now faced a rising tide of opposition, a groundswell of unity and determination that threatened to sweep away their dominion like leaves before a storm.

The galaxy held its breath, poised on the brink of a war that would redefine the very nature of existence. And in the hearts of all those who had seen the hologram, who had heard Xan'dor's plea, a single, unifying thought burned with the intensity of a thousand suns: The time for indifference, for bowing to the whims of self-proclaimed gods, was over.

The time for defiance, for standing tall in the face of annihilation, had come. The galaxy was about to change, and every species, every world, would have a part to play in the unfolding drama.

For better or for worse, the future of all sentient life now hung in the balance, and only the united will of the galaxy's inhabitants could hope to shape it.

In the great tapestry of the cosmos, a new chapter was about to be written, and its pages would be filled with tales of courage, sacrifice, and unwavering hope in the face of unimaginable odds. The resistance had begun, and the stars themselves trembled in anticipation of the coming storm.

The Message

The Requiem cruised silently through the vastness of space, its hull gleaming under the cold starlight. Inside, Lord Gresham sat in the ship's observation deck, his mind restless as he contemplated the weight of the conflict against the Ancients. The stars outside seemed indifferent to the turmoil that gripped the galaxy, their distant twinkle a reminder of the immense scale of the universe.

Suddenly, a sharp pain lanced through Gresham's skull, like a blade piercing his mind. He staggered, clutching his head, as images flooded his consciousness with relentless force.

In his mind's eye, he saw star systems collapsing into black holes, their once vibrant worlds reduced to cosmic debris. Entire planets were torn apart by unseen forces, their fragments cast into the void. The Ancients' power, so vast and incomprehensible, was capable of unthinkable destruction. Gresham's heart raced as he saw the suns dimming, their light extinguished by the Ancients' manipulations of fundamental cosmic forces. The reality of their threat was unlike anything he had imagined.

Then, the vision shifted, plunging him into a nightmare of psychological warfare. Faces he knew twisted into grotesque parodies, friends, and allies morphing into enemies. Nightmarish visions of betrayal and despair played out before him, the lines between reality and illusion blurring until he felt the ground beneath him slipping away. The Ancients' technology reached deep into his mind, probing for weaknesses, sowing doubt and fear. The images were so vivid, so real, that Gresham struggled to breathe, his body tense with the effort of resisting the overwhelming assault on his psyche.

He felt a presence, vast and ancient, observing him from afar, its malevolent curiosity tangible. A voice, cold and resonant, echoed within his mind, promising devastation unless he yielded to their will. The Ancients' intent was clear: to break his spirit, to shatter the resolve of the resistance through sheer terror.

As Gresham fought to regain control, the vision shifted again, showing entire planets undergoing rapid environmental changes. Lush worlds withering into barren wastelands, oceans boiling away into steam, and atmospheres thickening into toxic miasmas. The Ancients wielded their power with cruel precision, demonstrating their ability to reshape reality itself. These were not mere threats; they were warnings of what could come to pass if the resistance failed.

With a tremendous effort, Gresham pushed back against the invasive force, focusing on the image of Lady Mara and the memories of their shared struggles and triumphs. Slowly, the visions receded, leaving him breathless and shaken but resolute. He understood now the full extent of the Ancients' power and the urgent need to rally the galaxy against this existential threat.

His commlink crackled to life as Lady Mara's voice cut through the lingering haze of his thoughts. "Gresham, are you all right? We felt something... like a wave of energy. What happened?"

Gresham steadied himself, his voice firm despite the lingering tremor. "The Ancients are escalating, Mara. They showed me what they can do—destroying worlds, warping minds. We have to act fast."

"We will," she replied, determination infusing her words. "We'll gather everyone. This fight just became more critical than ever."

Gresham nodded, even though she couldn't see him, feeling the weight of her resolve mirrored in his own heart. "We need to prepare for their next move. They're not just a threat to us; they're a threat to everything."

With renewed urgency, Lord Gresham set out to marshal the forces of the Galactic Alliance, determined to protect the galaxy from the Ancients' overwhelming might. He knew the path ahead would be fraught with danger, but together, they would stand against the storm, defying the cosmic forces arrayed against them.

The Allocation Debate

The grand hall of the Galactic Summit was a marvel of human ingenuity, a testament to the unity and resilience of humanity's diverse factions. The transparent dome above provided a breathtaking view of the cosmos, where colossal gas giants loomed like silent guardians and distant stars twinkled in the infinite void.

Councilor Althea stood at the center of the hovering platform, her presence commanding as she addressed the assembly. "Esteemed leaders of the Galactic Alliance, we gather today to confront the rising threat of the Ancients. Their power grows unchecked, and our survival depends on our unity and decisive action."

The air in the chamber buzzed with tension, a symphony of murmurs and whispers as delegates conferred in low tones. The scent of polished wood and the faint aroma of incense lingered in the air, a reminder of the traditions that bound these leaders together.

High Chancellor Voss of the industrious planet Titanis rose to speak, his voice resonating with conviction. "We must marshal our fleets and strike at the heart of the enemy. Unity is our only hope against annihilation."

His words were met with a ripple of agreement, though not all were convinced. Minister Liora of the pacifist world Elysia stood in her serene presence, a beacon of calm amidst the rising tension. "Chancellor Voss, while your eagerness for war is understandable, we must not lose sight of diplomacy. The cost of conflict is too great, and we should seek to understand the Ancients' motives."

Her plea was met with skeptical glances, but some delegates nodded thoughtfully, recognizing the wisdom in her caution. The holographic displays flickered with images of worlds on the brink, underscoring the stakes at hand.

General Tharok of the warrior planet Drakara slammed his fist onto his podium, his voice a guttural roar. "Diplomacy? With the Ancients? They respect only strength. We must show them the might of the Galactic Alliance."

From the lush forests of Verdania, Elder Lyrana added her voice, her tone measured and wise. "General Tharok, there is wisdom in strength but also in caution. We cannot afford to throw lives away recklessly. We must balance our approach."

As she spoke, her form projected a calming aura, her movements slow and deliberate, and her gaze steady and reassuring. The tension in the room seemed to ease slightly, but the underlying disagreements remained palpable.

A holographic projection flickered to life, revealing Governor Quorin of the resource-rich asteroid colonies. His pragmatic demeanor contrasted sharply with his impassioned speeches. "The reality is simple. War requires resources—ships, weapons, and supplies. My colonies can provide these, but we need guarantees of protection and fair compensation. This alliance must be mutually beneficial."

As the debate continued, Admiral Levi and Lady Mara exchanged glances, the weight of leadership pressing down on them. Levi's calm demeanor and Mara's empathy and determination were crucial in guiding the assembly toward a unified decision.

Levi leaned toward Mara, his voice barely above a whisper. "We must emphasize the importance of strategic readiness without losing sight of our ethical responsibilities."

Mara nodded, her gaze sweeping across the room. "We need to find a balance between strength and diplomacy. Our unity is our greatest weapon."

Elsewhere in the Galaxy

Amidst the heated discussions in the Galactic Summit, events were unfolding elsewhere that would soon influence the decisions being made.

On the remote planet of Cygnus Prime, a team of scientists and engineers worked tirelessly within a high-tech research facility. The air buzzed with the hum of machinery and the sharp tang of ozone from energy experiments. Their focus was on developing new energy shields capable of withstanding the Ancients' devastating attacks. The laboratory buzzed with activity, the air filled with the acrid scent of burning metal and the hum of machinery. Holographic screens displayed complex equations and simulations, the minds of the galaxy's brightest working in unison to find solutions.

Dr. Celia Marlowe, a leading expert in astrophysics, adjusted her visor as she examined a new prototype. "If we can enhance the energy dispersion rate, we might just have a fighting chance," she said, her voice barely audible over the cacophony of sounds.

Her assistant, a young technician named Jarek, nodded vigorously. "We've made progress, but we'll need more resources to scale this up. The council needs to understand how crucial this is."

The diverse team represented many worlds, their collaboration a microcosm of the larger alliance. Each brought unique insights, their backgrounds a tapestry of cultures and experiences united by a common goal.

Back in the council chamber, the debate raged on, oblivious to the urgent efforts taking place on Cygnus Prime. Yet, the outcome of this summit would directly impact the resources allocated to such critical projects, highlighting the interconnectedness of their struggle.

20

ECHOES OF ETERNITY

The Gathering Storm

In the heart of the Galactic Alliance's capital, Xan'dor's speech echoed through the grand chamber, rallying many to the cause with his fiery words. Behind closed doors, however, the true motives and fears of the Fair Trade Alliance were laid bare, revealing a more nuanced picture of their leader's intentions.

Xan'dor paced the opulent room, the dim light casting sharp angles on his face, which was etched with determination and an undercurrent of apprehension. He was the leader of the Fair Trade Alliance, a group known for navigating the galaxy's black markets with a mix of daring and diplomacy. His past was marked by survival in the underbelly of interstellar commerce, where he learned the art of negotiation and built a network of loyal allies. Despite the Fair Trade's shadowy reputation, Xan'dor had earned unwavering loyalty from his team, valuing them as family.

"The Ancients seek to control everything, to bend all life to their will. We cannot allow ourselves to be ruled by such tyrants," he declared, his voice low but resonant with fervor.

Yet, as he spoke, a flicker of doubt crossed his mind. The enormity of the battle ahead was daunting, and the alliance with the Galactic Alliance, while strategic, was fraught with its own risks.

Lira, one of his most trusted advisors and a shrewd trader, picked up on his unspoken anxiety. "But we must also ensure our own survival. The Fair Trade Alliance thrives on independence and freedom from oversight. Aligning with the Galactic Alliance is a means to an end. We use them to weaken the Ancients and secure our interests."

Xan'dor's eyes gleamed with a mix of preservation and caution. "Exactly. We fight for freedom, but our freedom. We will not trade one master for another. We must ensure that, once the Ancients are defeated, we have the power to protect our way of life and maintain our autonomy."

Their alliance with the Galactic Alliance was convenient, a strategic move to ensure their survival and dominance in a post-ancient galaxy. The room fell silent, the weight of their ambitions hanging in the air like a storm cloud ready to break.

Unity and Resolve

Aboard the Requiem, tension simmered beneath the surface as the crew prepared for the impending battle. Humans stood together, their differences stark, yet their purpose united.

Lady Mara, sensing the unease, addressed the assembled crew. "We come from different backgrounds and have faced various challenges, but we share a common goal. The Ancients seek to destroy us all, to impose their will upon the galaxy. We cannot let our differences divide us when unity is our greatest strength."

Lieutenant Tiana stepped forward, her voice calm but firm, cutting through the tension like a blade. "I've seen the horrors of the Ancients' power firsthand. They don't discriminate. They will destroy us all if we let them. We must set aside our past grievances and fight together."

Sergeant Voss, a human with a history of distrust towards outsiders, nodded reluctantly. "We have our differences, but we also have our strengths. If we can learn to work together, we can be an unstoppable force."

Corporal Jason, a skilled medic, added, "Unity doesn't mean we lose our individuality. It means we combine our strengths to create something greater. Together, we can defeat the Ancients and secure a future for all of us."

Mara's gaze swept across the crew, her eyes reflecting hope and determination. "The Ancients underestimate us because they believe we can't work together. Let's prove them wrong. Let's show them that unity is our greatest weapon."

Renewed purpose surged through the crew, binding them together in a shared resolve. The past was behind them, and the future, uncertain though it was, held the promise of freedom and victory.

A Call to Arms

As the holographic image of the Endurant's destruction and Xan'dor's impassioned plea flickered and faded from the bustling marketplace of Xar Kilprime, its impact spread far and wide, touching the lives of countless across the galaxy. The air crackled with tension as if the universe held its breath, waiting for what would come.

With quiet authority, Commander Astor spoke, his words cutting through the murmur like a blade. "We will show our might and overthrow tyranny!"

A United Front

Far across the stars, on the scorched, volcanic surface of Kar'dak, a different scene unfolded within the great obsidian citadel. The air was heavy with the acrid tang of sulfur, the heat seeping into the nostrils of the Drak'ari gathered in their cavernous hall. Their massive, reptilian forms were encased in elaborate battle armor, their scales glistening with a sheen of heat and sweat. Their eyes, burning embers reflecting the faint glow of molten rock, gleamed with a predatory light.

Kah'roth, the warlord of the Drak'ari, slammed his fist against the ornate table, the impact sending a spiderweb of cracks radiating outward and a tremor through the ground. "The Ancients dare to challenge our might?" he bellowed, his voice a guttural roar that shook the very foundation of the citadel. "They dare to threaten the galaxy that we have sworn to conquer? We will show them the fury of the Drak'ari, the fire that burns in our blood!"

The assembled warriors erupted in a cacophony of roars and battle cries, their clawed hands grasping the hilts of their fearsome weapons. They had always been conquerors, a scourge upon the stars. But now, faced with a foe threatening to usurp their place in the galaxy, they were ready to channel their aggression toward a new target.

The Rising Tide

Factions once bitter enemies found themselves united by a common foe. Old grudges were set aside; ancient rivalries were forgotten in the face of the looming threat. The Galactic Alliance, once a loose confederation of worlds, became a beacon of hope and unity, a rallying point for all those who sought to defy the tyranny of the Ancients.

At the heart of it all, the Fair Trade Alliance and the Galactic Alliance stood tall, their leaders working tirelessly to forge a coalition unlike any the galaxy had ever seen. Xan'dor, his holographic image now a symbol of defiance and hope, became the face of the resistance, a living embodiment of the indomitable spirit that burned in the hearts of all those who yearned for freedom.

The stage was set for a confrontation that would shake the very foundations of the universe. Once secure in their absolute power, the Ancients now faced a rising tide of opposition, a groundswell of unity and determination that threatened to sweep away their dominion like leaves before a storm.

The Ancient Decree

In the sanctum of the Ancients, a chamber vast and resplendent with echoes of cosmic energy, the air shimmered with their presence. The Ancients floated above the ground, their forms flickering with an ethereal glow that spoke of aeons past. They were beings of immense power, their consciousness spanning galaxies, and their arrogance was as old as the stars themselves.

"Thee shall bow," intoned the leader, its voice resonating like a celestial choir. "For we are the architects of the universe, the weavers of fate. Thee knows not the depths of our wisdom."

Another Ancient, its form shifting like the currents of a nebula, sneered at the thought of rebellion. "These lesser beings dare to challenge us? Thee are but fleeting shadows, destined to vanish in the grand cycle of existence."

"Thee's defiance is but a flicker," a third Ancient mused, its tone dripping with disdain. "A momentary anomaly in the eternal tapestry we have woven."

Yet beneath their lofty words, a subtle tension wove through the chamber. For the first time in millennia, the Ancients felt a stir of unease. The galaxy, which they had long believed to be under their immutable control, was shifting. The unity of the humans and their allies, though insignificant in the cosmic scheme, had sparked a resistance that could no longer be ignored.

"Thee gather like ants, striving to disrupt the order we have ordained," the leader remarked, its voice tinged with annoyance. "Yet thee shall learn the futility of your efforts. Our dominion is absolute."

A holographic display materialized in the center of the chamber, depicting the galaxy in all its splendor. Stars twinkled like distant memories, and the Ancients' influence was a vast web stretching across the cosmos. But within this web, small threads of rebellion glowed defiantly.

"Thee unity is nothing but folly," an Ancient scoffed, its gaze fixed on the tiny lights of resistance. "Thee shall be crushed beneath our heel, your dreams of freedom extinguished like stars fading into the void."

Yet, despite their scorn, a whisper of doubt crept into their thoughts. The humans, those fragile creatures, had demonstrated a resilience that defied prediction. In their arrogance, the Ancients had overlooked the power of hope and determination.

"What if thee's defiance kindles a flame we cannot quench?" an Ancient pondered, its voice a contemplative murmur.

Silence followed a silence that stretched across time and space, as the Ancients considered the unthinkable. Their hubris had blinded them to the truth that even the most insignificant can alter the course of history.

The Fires of War

The battlefield had transformed into a hellscape of twisted metal and shattered dreams. What was once a verdant planet now lay beneath a sky choked with the acrid smoke of burning ships, turning the vibrant tapestry of stars into a dim memory. The cries of the dying were lost amid the ceaseless thunder of weapons fire, a relentless symphony of destruction orchestrated by the Ancients' fury.

On the ground, the forces of the Galactic Alliance and the Fair Trade Alliance fought with desperate ferocity. Soldiers from a hundred worlds stood shoulder to shoulder, their differences forgotten in the face of a common foe. Among them were Lieutenant Zara Korrin, a seasoned human officer, and Rylan Voss, a stoic Drak'ari warrior whose plasma claws crackled with deadly energy.

Zara, her face streaked with grime and determination, scanned the battlefield with steely resolve. "Hold the line!" she shouted, her voice barely rising above the chaos. "We can't let them break through!"

Beside her, Rylan growled, his reptilian eyes blazing with fury. "These Ancients won't know what hit them," he muttered, his claws flexing in anticipation.

Yet, despite their bravery and determination, the forces of the resistance were outmatched and outgunned. The Ancients, in their arrogance, didn't bother to face the humans directly. Instead, they unleashed a wave of automated war machines, sleek and lethal, with metallic bodies glinting ominously in the flickering light. These machines moved with precision and efficiency, cutting through the ranks of the defenders like a scythe through wheat.

At the front lines, Vela Nox stood defiant, her once-pristine uniform now stained with the blood and grime of battle. She had witnessed the Ancients' power firsthand, seen the utter destruction they wrought upon worlds that dared to defy them. But she had also seen the indomitable spirit of her people, the unwavering courage that burned in the hearts of every soldier who fought beside her.

"Hold the line!" she bellowed, her voice rising above the din of battle. "We will not yield, not while a single one of us still draws breath!" Her words, carried across the battlefield by the advanced comm systems of her armor, ignited a renewed surge of determination in the defenders' hearts.

As the robotic forces advanced, their every movement a testament to the Ancients' technological superiority, Zara felt a flicker of doubt. Could they really stand against such relentless machines? She pushed the thought away, focusing on the here and now. "Rylan, flank left and take out their support units. I'll cover you," she ordered.

Rylan nodded, his expression grim. "For the Alliance," he growled, charging into the fray with a fierce roar.

Above the battlefield, the Ancients observed through their holographic displays, their vast forms lounging in complacency. One of them, its voice a thunderous echo, boomed, "THEE struggle against the inevitable, against the very fabric of the universe itself. THEE resistance is as meaningless as the buzzing of flies to the ears of a god." The Ancients, content in their supposed invincibility, watched their machines enforce their will.

Zara, thrown to the ground by a concussive blast from a towering war bot, struggled to her feet, her armor sparking and smoking from the damage it had sustained. Around her, the cries of the wounded and the dying filled the air, a chorus of suffering that tore at her very soul. Yet, even in the face of such overwhelming power, she refused to yield. With a roar of defiance, she rallied her troops once more, urging them forward into the teeth of the Ancients' onslaught.

But it was not enough. The Ancients, their power seeming to grow with every passing moment, pressed forward inexorably, their every step a declaration of their supremacy. The ground beneath their feet cracked and shattered, the very planet itself groaning under the weight of their presence.

As the battle reached its climax, as the forces of the resistance teetered on the brink of annihilation, Admiral Nox found herself face to face with the towering form of an Ancient. Its eyes, burning with cold, malevolent intelligence, fixed upon her, seeming to pierce the very depths of her soul.

An Ancient, toying with the galaxy, gazed down upon the battlefield and boomed out into the chaos below:

"THEE struggle is futile," it intoned, its voice a whisper that carried the weight of eons. "THEE are but a mote of dust in the grand scheme of the cosmos, a fleeting spark to be snuffed out by the winds of inevitability."

As the words echoed across the battlefield, the sky seemed to darken further, and the very ground vibrated with the raw power of the Ancient's presence. Nox, her armor battered and broken, stood amid the ruins of war, her body pushed to the very limits of endurance. The acrid scent of burning metal filled the air, and the cries of the wounded formed a haunting symphony around her. Yet, in the face of overwhelming odds, she refused to falter.

Nox met the Ancient's gaze with a fierce, unyielding resolve. Her mind raced with memories of comrades fallen, of worlds shattered, yet her heart burned with the fire of defiance. "You may defeat us here," she declared, her voice ragged with exhaustion and pain but resolute with determination, "but you will never extinguish the fire of our resistance. We will fight you to the last, and even in death, we will defy you."

The Ancient, its form shifting like a turbulent nebula, paused, its inscrutable expression momentarily betraying a flicker of curiosity. Could these fragile creatures, so beneath notice, truly possess such tenacity? For an instant, a ripple of uncertainty passed through its consciousness, but it was swiftly drowned by centuries of arrogance.

With a gesture as swift as it was devastating, the Ancient struck, its hand moving with a speed that defied comprehension. Nox felt the searing heat as the energy surged toward her, the air around her crackling and hissing like a live wire. She braced herself for the impact, her thoughts crystallizing into a single, unyielding truth: even at this moment, she was more than a pawn in their cosmic game. She was a beacon, a symbol of hope that would endure beyond her.

The energy tore through her armor, a blinding flash of light engulfing her vision. Pain, sharp and consuming, tore through her as the Ancient's power pierced her flesh. Yet, even as darkness threatened to close in, a profound sense of peace enveloped her. Her defiance, her stand against the void, would not be in vain.

Around the battlefield, those who witnessed her final stand felt a surge of renewed strength. Her courage became their rallying cry, her spirit a flame that refused to be quenched. Nox's defiance reverberated through the hearts of her allies, igniting a fierce determination to fight on, to honor her sacrifice.

The Ancient, momentarily stalled by the unexpected resistance, withdrew its gaze from Nox, dismissing her as another casualty in the unending cycle. Yet, it had failed to recognize the seeds of rebellion it had sown. In its hubris, it remained blind to the unity it had inadvertently forged among those it deemed insignificant.

As the battle raged on, the fires of war burned brighter than ever, fueled by the spirit of those who dared to defy the stars. The galaxy's fate hung in the balance, but Nox's legacy would live on, a testament to the power of unwavering resolve in the face of insurmountable odds.

And though the Ancients remained convinced of their invincibility, the echoes of Nox's defiance would one day become the harbinger of their downfall.

The Ancients, in their arrogance, had sown the seeds of their own destruction, and though the cost would be high, the price paid in blood and tears, the galaxy would one day be free. As the battle raged on, as the forces of the Galactic Alliance and the Fair Trade Alliance fought with a savage, unyielding determination, the Ancients looked on with cold, dispassionate eyes. To them, the struggle playing out before them was little more than a momentary distraction, a fleeting amusement in the grand tapestry of their eternal reign.

But deep within the heart of the resistance, a fire continued to burn, a flame of hope and defiance that refused to be extinguished. And though the road ahead was long and fraught with peril, though the odds seemed insurmountable, the forces of freedom would not rest until the galaxy was free from the tyranny of the Ancients or until the last of them lay dead upon the field of battle.

For in the end, it was not the power of the Ancients that would shape the fate of the galaxy, but the indomitable will of those who dared to stand against them, the courage of those who fought for something greater than themselves. And in the crucible of war, in the fires of conflict and sacrifice, the future of the galaxy would be forged, one battle at a time.

The Fires of Rebellion

The stench of ozone and burning metal clawed at Hutan's throat, a metallic tang that clung to his tongue even through the environmental filters of his suit. His vision, once a soldier's dream of perfect clarity augmented by targeting data, was now a fractured mess. Smoke and plasma fire filled the air, blurring the lines between friend and foe on the ravaged plains of X-347. The once-verdant world, a jewel in the Fair Trade Alliance, was now a hellscape of churned earth and skeletal trees reaching towards a blood-red sky choked with the wreckage of a thousand burning ships.

A deafening roar, a tremor felt more in the bones than heard by the ears, shook the very ground beneath Hutan's boots. An Ancient lumbered into view, its obsidian carapace catching the flickering light of the inferno like a monstrous beetle carved from a nightmare. It towered over the battlefield, a living mountain of cold, uncaring power. Its crimson eyes, devoid of pupils or any hint of empathy, scanned the devastation with detached curiosity as if the struggles of the mortals below were nothing more than the buzzing of flies.

Fear, a primal instinct buried deep within Hutan's reptilian brain, threatened to overwhelm him. This was a creature beyond comprehension, a being whose very existence defied the laws of physics as he knew them. But Hutan was a Drak'ari warrior, forged in the fires of his homeworld's harsh environment. He pushed down the terror, his soldier's discipline battling the raw, animal fear that gnawed at him. He was a defender of freedom, a champion of the Fair Trade Alliance, and he would not yield.

Around him, the lines of the Alliance and the Fair Trade held, for now. Humans, their once-bright uniforms now scorched and muddied, stood shoulder to shoulder with Drak'ari warriors, their plasma claws crackling with barely restrained energy. Lithe Elysian snipers perched precariously on the shattered bones of crashed starships, their luminous eyes glowing with a mixture of fear and fierce determination. They were a tapestry of defiance woven from a thousand desperate threads, each soldier a splash of color against the bleak canvas of war.

Suddenly, a banshee wail tore through the cacophony, rising above the thunder of weapons fire. Hutan spotted a sleek Drak'ari fighter, its engines sputtering and trailing smoke like a dying comet, plummeting towards the Ancient's towering leg. A suicidal attack, a desperate act of defiance in the face of an unstoppable foe. The fighter detonated in a blinding flash, a fiery gnat buzzing against an unyielding mountain. For a fleeting heartbeat, a tremor of surprise flickered across the Ancient's crimson eyes as if it were momentarily taken aback by the audacity of the attack.

The retaliation was swift and terrible. The Ancient raised a hand, obsidian fingers the size of small starships flexing as energy crackled around them. With a gesture of disdain, it unleashed a wave of pure force, a casual display of power that defied mortal comprehension. The ground rippled like water disturbed by a pebble, and Hutan felt the very air warp and twist under the invisible pressure. His comrades – human, Drak'ari, Elysian – were flung through the air like ragdolls, their screams turning to silence before they even reached the blood-soaked ground.

Hutan braced himself, digging his razor-sharp claws into the cracked and scorched earth. The wind howled in his ears, a banshee's song twisted by rage, as the wave of force slammed into him like a physical wall. His armor, once gleaming and plated with a vibranium alloy, buckled under the immense pressure, the muted grey paint scorching and peeling away to reveal the stressed metal beneath. Pain, white-hot and searing, lanced through his body, momentarily stealing the breath from his lungs and causing stars to dance across his vision.

Then, as suddenly as it had begun, the onslaught ceased. Blessed silence fell over the battlefield, broken only by the distant crackle of flames and the groans of the wounded. Hutan slumped to his knees, gasping for air, his world reduced to the ringing in his ears and the acrid bite of smoke in his lungs. Through the haze of pain, he forced himself to survey the devastation before him. Where once stood a line of proud soldiers, comrades in arms united by a common cause, there was now only a crater, a mass grave carved by the Ancient's casual cruelty.

Through the suffocating smoke and ash, Hutan spotted the flicker of life, a beacon amid the ruin. Survivors's faces, etched with the same determination that burned within him, were beginning to rally. Despite the overwhelming odds, the fire of rebellion still smoldered in their hearts, a flame that refused to be extinguished.

The Ancients might wield unimaginable power, but they had underestimated the resilience of those who stood against them. Hutan's claws dug into the earth once more, not out of fear but in preparation. This was not the end. The fires of war had been lit, and the resistance would rise again, fueled by the memory of those who had fallen and the unyielding hope for a future free from tyranny.

As Hutan stood, battered but unbroken, he whispered a silent vow to the fallen: They would not be forgotten. The struggle would continue, and the Ancients would learn that even the smallest spark could ignite a wildfire capable of consuming even the mightiest of foes.

Despair, a cold and suffocating weight, threatened to consume him. How could they hope to stand against such power? The Ancients were gods, and the forces of the Alliance and the Fair Trade were nothing more than insects to be swatted aside without a second thought.

A tremor of defiance pulsed through the inky void. In a ballet of steel and fire, a spectacle unlike any ever witnessed, ships of a thousand worlds converged. From sleek Drak'ari fighters, their hulls shimmering with crackling energy, to the lumbering Elysian battlecruisers, vast and ornate testaments to lost grandeur, they poured into the designated rendezvous point. This wasn't a fleet; it was a river of molten courage, a flood of righteous fury.

At its heart, the Galactic Alliance flagship, a leviathan bristling with weaponry, stood as a defiant beacon. Upon its bridge, a council of defiance had assembled. Humans, their faces etched with the memories of a thousand plundered worlds, stood shoulder-to-shoulder with the Drak'ari, their obsidian armor a promise of unrelenting savagery. Elysians, their ethereal forms shimmering with otherworldly energy, radiated an unwavering resolve. Here, a thousand races, once divided by distance and distrust, were bound by a singular purpose: to crush the yoke of the Ancients.

Admiral Thomas Deral, his gaze hardened by countless battles, surveyed the spectacle unfolding before him. His voice, a gravelly rasp honed in the fires of war, resonated through the bridge. "The very fabric of space ripples with a power unseen for eons," he declared, a fierce pride battling the weight of responsibility in his eyes. "Never before has the galaxy witnessed such a gathering, such a defiant roar against the encroaching darkness!"

Beside him, Kah'roth, the Drak'ari warlord, flashed his fangs in a predatory grin, the echo of a thousand victories thrumming in his deep growl. "The Ancients," he spat, his voice laced with a primal hatred, "think themselves gods, untouchable by the likes of us. But today, we show them the fury of a galaxy united! Today, we show them the unyielding spirit of a thousand worlds!"

A hush fell over the armada, a pregnant silence thick with anticipation. Every eye, every sensor, was trained on the distant void, where the shimmering tendrils of the Ancients' domain gave way to the unknown. They knew the odds, the raw, brutal power they were about to face. But they also knew that this was a fight for their very existence, the last stand for the soul of the galaxy. And as one, they readied themselves, a storm waiting to be unleashed. The galaxy held its breath. The time for whispers was over. The fire of rebellion roared.

The Coiling Serpents

In the obsidian citadel, towering and oppressive, the Ancients watched the growing resistance with a detached amusement. Their citadel, a marvel of twisted architecture that bent the very laws of physics to mock the cosmos, was a silent witness to their centuries of rule. Theirs was a dominion without question, one forged in inexorable order, and their gaze fell upon the galaxy's rebellion as if upon insects scurrying in their final, futile dance.

"Let THEE come," one Ancient sneered, eyes burning with cold fury. "What are they? A million voices in the dark, shouting at the void. We are the void. We are the beginning and the end. THEE's fires will be snuffed out before THEE ever truly burns."

Another, a swirling vortex of dark energy, pulsed with cruel amusement. "THEE's attempts are laughable. Like children who set fire to the world yet still do not grasp the inferno they kindle. The belief THEE can defy us is…. amusing, at best."

But a flicker of dissent, however, sparked in the eldest Ancient. It had seen countless rebellions rise and fall, each crushed with a mere thought. But something in these mortals was different. Something that refused to break

"We should not dismiss THEE completely." The eldest Ancient's voice was like a dry wind, old beyond measure, carrying an echo of untold years. "THEE's unity… it is unlike anything we've encountered before. A singularity of purpose."

The other Ancients scoffed, their amusement turning to disdain. "Unity? THEE are fragile, like dust drifting in the wind. THEE's fleets will be ground to nothingness. THEE's cause—meaningless." With a gesture as careless as swatting an insect, the eldest Ancient's warning was swept aside.

Their armada—a nightmarish leviathan of twisted metal and crackling power—pulsed with a life of its own. A wave of destruction, an unholy storm, ready to engulf the galaxy.

"Let THEE wriggle," one Ancient rumbled, its voice a tremor that vibrated through the very core of the citadel. "These pathetic creatures, struggling to defy THEE's gods. How quaint." The citadel pulsed with the arrogant certainty of victory. These mortals—these fleas—who dared challenge the ancient ones would be extinguished with little more than a wrist flick. Their ships, weapons, and very existence were toys—to be crushed beneath the weight of the Ancients' might.

Meanwhile, on the bridge of the flagship, Requiem, Admiral Levi gripped the armrests with white knuckles, his fingers aching with the pressure. The weight of his responsibility pressed down on him, as it always did, but this time it felt heavier. His thoughts flashed to his crew, their faces haunted by the same fear that churned in his chest. They weren't just fighting to win—they were fighting to survive. Every day, they pushed forward, knowing the odds were stacked against them, but it wasn't just the future of humanity that was at stake. It was the future of every single soul left in the galaxy who still believed in freedom. His stomach twisted with the knowledge that countless lives were hanging by a thread, each one a story, a family, a future, all balanced on the edge of a blade. The quiet desperation of his comrades echoed through his mind. People were dying—sacrificing everything for a cause they couldn't see through to the end. And yet, they fought on. He didn't know if it was courage or madness, but it didn't matter. They had no choice.

"Let THEE come," the Ancient sneered again, venomously hissing. "THEE are nothing. We are gods. We will erase THEE with a thought.THEE's broken fleets will crumble as dust before the storm of our wrath."

Yet a whisper of doubt curled in the eldest Ancient's chest, an uneasy tremor in its otherwise controlled mind. "The fire THEE carry... it is not the fire of mere rebellion," it murmured, eyes narrowing in discomfort. "There is desperation in THEE's eyes. A madness that could prove... troubling."

The other Ancients turned as one, their eyes burning with cold fury. "Troubling? These insects?" one boomed, its voice crackling with power. "THEE are nothing! We are gods! We are the creators of all reality! And THEE fleas dare defy us?"

The dissenting Ancients fell silent, their warnings drowned by the sheer force of the others' arrogance. The storm of their hubris raged unchecked. There was an eerie silence for a moment—thick, oppressive, as if even time itself were pausing. The Ancients, so certain of their righteousness, turned their gaze back toward their plans of conquest. In the end, their knowledge stretched so far—to the beginning of stars and beyond—that they saw every rebellion before it started, every move before it was made. They had already mapped out the future, long ago. They had seen it all. Nothing new would occur. Nothing could surprise them. And yet, something strange lingered. The humans, even now, refused to bend. It was a defiance the Ancients had not accounted for. A crack in the perfect armor of certainty that surrounded them. But as quickly as it came, it was dismissed. "Let THEE burn," the eldest Ancient finally muttered, its voice low and filled with the weight of centuries. "Let them think they are winning. They will understand soon enough the true meaning of hopelessness." The citadel trembled again, and the war machine—their monstrous fleet—shifted into motion, the dark tide of annihilation ready to devour all in its path. A plague, a cosmic cancer, was on the move, destined to consume all in its wake. The Ancients, so sure of their inevitable victory, would be the architects of this cosmic death, as they had always been. But even as they hurled themselves toward the unavoidable clash, a single ember of defiance burned bright in the hearts of those beneath them—a spark that would never truly die.

Hubris Unveiled

The citadel pulsed with the arrogant certainty of victory. The lesser races, these gnats daring to buzz around the face of a god, would be annihilated. Their ships, their weapons – mere toys to be broken and discarded.

"Let them come," one Ancient sneered, its voice dripping with venomous condescension. "Let them hurl themselves against the bulwark of our power. They will shatter upon our defenses like waves against a continent, their remnants scattered like dust on the cosmic wind."

But a tendril of unease, a whisper of doubt, slithered through the chamber. It emanated from the eldest Ancient, the only one who truly understood the potential for chaos that resided within the hearts of the desperate.

"The fire in their eyes," it sneered its voice a stark contrast to the booming pronouncements of its brethren. "It burns with a... desperation we have not encountered before. A madness that could prove... troublesome."

The other Ancients turned as one, their forms radiating a cold fury. "Troublesome? You speak of these insects as if they are a threat!" one boomed, its voice crackling with barely contained power. "They are nothing. Less than nothing. We are gods! We are the architects of reality itself! And these... fleas... dare to challenge us?"

The dissenting Ancient fell silent, its warnings drowned out by the chorus of arrogance that filled the citadel. The Ancients, their hubris a blinding shroud, focused their attention on the approaching battle, eager to crush these upstart mortals and reaffirm their absolute dominion.

With a callous flick of a wrist, the eldest Ancient's concerns were swept aside. The war machine lurched into motion, the monstrous fleet a harbinger of annihilation. It was a plague, a cosmic cancer, ready to consume all in its path.

The battle loomed, a clash of titans that would reverberate through the ages. Yet, in the face of overwhelming power, the defenders of the galaxy clung to a single, desperate hope: that the fire of rebellion, once ignited, could never be truly extinguished.

The Clash of Titans

The void of space crackled with energy as the fleets of the Galactic Alliance and the Ancients clashed in a titanic battle. Stars, once silent witnesses to the passage of time, now bore witness to the firestorm of war that raged across the heavens.

Captain Reese Trent of the Valiant Star stood on the bridge, her eyes scanning the battlefield with fierce determination. Her ship had been at the forefront of countless battles, and her reputation as a fierce tactician and loving mother to her two young children was known throughout the fleet. Today, her resolve would be tested like never before.

"Captain, the Ancients' ships are closing in," her first officer reported, his voice steady despite the tension that crackled through the bridge.

Reese nodded, her hands gripping the railing as she issued commands. "Prepare to engage. We fight not just for survival but for the families we leave behind."

As the Valiant Star surged forward, the hulls of the enemy ships gleamed with an ominous light, energy weapons charging for the next barrage. The space between the fleets became a maelstrom of light and sound, a cacophony of destruction as ships on both sides were torn asunder.

Nearby, the Nova Spark, a ship renowned for its innovative technological advancements, danced through the chaos, its sleek design a testament to human ingenuity. On board, Dr. Kai Harlow worked feverishly in the lab, fingers flying over controls as she sought to finalize a breakthrough that could turn the tide of the battle—and solve a critical resource crisis at home.

Her assistant glanced at her with wide eyes. "Dr. Harlow, the shields are failing!"

Kai's heart pounded in her chest as she pushed forward, the urgency of the situation driving her to ignore the alarms blaring around them. "Just a few more calculations, and we'll have it!"

But fate had other plans. A barrage of energy weapons struck the Nova Spark, the ship shuddering under the assault. In an instant, the vessel became a blazing inferno, a fiery ball of destruction that consumed all within. The dreams and hopes of her crew were snuffed out in a heartbeat, their potential contributions lost to the void.

On the bridge of the Valiant Star, Reese witnessed the loss of the Nova Spark, her heart clenching with grief even as she fought to maintain her focus. The battle raged on, each explosion a reminder of the lives lost and the sacrifices made.

"Reese, we need to pull back!" her first officer urged, the strain in his voice evident.

She shook her head, her resolve hardening. "Not yet. We hold the line for those who can't. We fight for every soul lost today."

As the battle continued, ships exploded in bursts of fire and metal, their deaths lighting up the darkness of space. The Valiant Star pressed forward, determined to push back the tide of the Ancients' might, even as the odds seemed insurmountable.

The loss of the Nova Spark and its promising technology was a blow felt across the fleet, a reminder of the cost of war. Yet, even amidst the devastation, a spark of hope flickered. Each life lost was a testament to the resilience of those who fought, their courage inspiring others to continue the fight.

The Aftermath

As the battle finally waned, the remnants of the Galactic Alliance fleet gathered to assess their losses. The void was silent once more, a graveyard for the ships and souls who had given everything in the name of freedom.

In the quiet aftermath, Captain Reese Trent stood at the observation deck, gazing out at the field of debris. Her heart ached with the weight of loss, yet she knew that their fight was far from over.

"We honor them by continuing the struggle," she whispered the resolve in her voice echoing through the hearts of those who remained.

The galaxy might have been scarred by the fires of war, but the spirit of resistance burned brighter than ever, fueled by the sacrifices of those who had fallen. Together, they would carry on the legacy of the brave, fighting for a future where their children could live free from the shadow of the Ancients.

The battle over X-347 was a crucible of chaos and fire, the Galactic Alliance and Fair Trade Alliance fighting valiantly against the oncoming wave of Ancients' ships. The sky above was a tapestry of crisscrossing laser fire and exploding vessels, and the battlefield below was a maelstrom of noise and destruction. Within the heart of this conflict, tension hung thick among the crew of each ship, every officer and soldier aware of the stakes.

Amidst the swirling chaos of combat, Captain Rhea Lang of the Eclipse Blade made a startling observation as her ship wove through the enemy lines. She noticed the erratic movements of the opposing vessels, their tactics almost too mechanical, too predictable. "These ships... they're not manned!" she exclaimed, her eyes wide with disbelief as her gaze swept over the battlefield. "They're drones!"

The implications struck Admiral Levi with sudden clarity. Receiving the transmission from Lang, he furrowed his brow as the realization sank in. "Robots?" he echoed, the word striking him like a lightning bolt. "The Ancients didn't even deem us worthy of their presence. They've sent machines to do their fighting."

With this newfound understanding, Levi issued a decisive command. Turning to his communications officer, Lieutenant Jameson, his voice was urgent and steady. "Get this information to Command immediately. They need to know that the Ancients are using unmanned ships. This changes everything."

Jameson nodded, his fingers flying over the console as he encoded and transmitted the message. "Command, this is Celestial Dawn. Be advised: the Ancients are deploying robotic forces. Repeat: all enemy ships are unmanned drones. Request immediate strategic reassessment."

As the Alliance forces adapted to the new reality, the tide of battle began to shift. Levi's mind raced with possibilities, formulating a new strategy to exploit the predictable nature of their mechanical foes. "Listen up, everyone," his voice rang out over the comms, resonating with renewed vigor. "We're fighting drones, not soldiers. They follow protocols and routines. Let's use that against them. Target their command ships and central processing units. Cut the head off the snake, and the rest will crumble."

Across the fleet, captains and soldiers coordinated their efforts, launching concentrated strikes on the Ancients' command nodes. Captain Eli Tanis, aboard the Vanguard, grinned as he directed his crew to exploit the rigid tactics of their opponents. "Focus on their command structure. They're blind without it!"

The message reached the Command Center swiftly, and Supreme Commander Althea understood the gravity of the situation. As she absorbed the implications of this revelation, a mixture of anger and determination flashed in her eyes. "They underestimated us," Althea murmured, her mind already working on the next steps. "Their arrogance will be their downfall. We have the advantage now. Relay this to all sectors—our focus is their command ships."

The Alliance's counterattack was relentless, their strategy focused and effective. With each targeted attack, missiles and laser fire erupted in a symphony of destruction, tearing through the enemy lines and causing the robotic vessels to falter and lose coherence. The once daunting prospect of fighting the Ancients turned into an opportunity—a chance to strike at the heart of their arrogance.

From the bridge of the Celestial Dawn, Admiral Levi watched as the tide turned, the Alliance's coordinated assault unraveling the Ancients' automated forces. His voice, firm with resolve, echoed through the comms. "This is our moment. Show them what we're made of. For our worlds, for our people, and for the freedom we fight to preserve."

As the battle intensified, the Alliance pressed their advantage, cutting through the Ancients' ranks with newfound vigor. The robotic ships fell, exploding into fiery blooms against the dark backdrop of space, and hope surged within the hearts of the defenders. What had begun as a desperate struggle against an overwhelming force had transformed into a triumphant stand—a defiant message to the Ancients that the galaxy would not bow before machines and that humanity's spirit was a force to be reckoned with.

The Journey of Xylo

As Xylo navigated the ruins, her boot caught on a brightly colored object half-buried in the rubble. Brushing away the ash, she revealed a child's drawing—a vibrant depiction of a family laughing under a bright blue sky. The memory of her own young daughter, ripped away by the Ancients' attack, crashed down on her like a physical blow. Tears welled in her eyes, blurring the image in her hand, the vibrant colors stark against the gray desolation.

A sudden gust of wind whipped through the shattered remains of a marketplace, sending a tattered cloth banner fluttering in the air. The faded symbol on the banner—a pair of clasped hands—triggered a flashback. Xylo saw herself and her husband strolling hand-in-hand through this marketplace, the air filled with lively bartering and joyous laughter. The memory faded, leaving a hollowness in her chest, a reminder of what was lost.

The air crackled with the distant sound of collapsing structures; each echo was a reminder of the danger lurking with every step. The ruins groaned under the weight of destruction, threatening to collapse at any moment. Xylo felt the ground tremble beneath her feet, her every movement a gamble against the unforgiving environment.

Gripping the data chip tightly, Xylo continued her trek. Doubt gnawed at her. Could one small piece of information truly turn the tide against a seemingly invincible enemy? The weight of countless lives rested on her shoulders, and she felt the crushing pressure of responsibility. But then, her gaze fell upon a lone wildflower pushing its way through a crack in the scorched pavement. Its delicate petals were vibrant against the gray backdrop, a testament to resilience. A flicker of defiance ignited within her. "No," she whispered fiercely, "I won't let them win. Not while there's still a fight left in me."

Xylo coughed again, the omnipresent ash clinging to her throat like a shroud. It felt like the very air itself was conspiring to choke the life out of her, just as the Ancients had choked the life out of her world. But amidst the suffocating despair, the data chip nestled against her skin felt warm, a tiny ember of defiance against the encroaching darkness. It may be a fragile hope, but it was all she had.

As she stumbled through the ruins, Xylo faced constant dangers. The ground beneath her feet trembled with aftershocks, threatening to swallow her whole. She narrowly avoided collapsing buildings and falling debris. Her suit's sensors picked up faint traces of toxic gases, visible in the air as ghostly tendrils, remnants of the Ancients' weapons, forcing her to take shallow breaths to conserve her air supply.

Finally, she found a relatively sheltered spot amidst the rubble. She took a moment to examine the data chip more closely. There, etched faintly on its surface, was a cryptic message: "This will scramble the Ancients' technology. Many lives were lost to get this to you. Use it wisely."

Her heart pounded with renewed hope. If this chip could disrupt the Ancients' technology, it might give the rebellion the edge they desperately needed. She slipped the chip back into her suit's secure compartment and pressed on, driven by the memory of those who had sacrificed everything to deliver this lifeline.

Her thoughts turned to the diverse array of species and technologies involved in the rebellion. She thought of the bio-engineered warriors of the Varkonians, their genetic adaptations tailored for battle. The Elysians, with their advanced energy weapons that hummed with power, and the Drak'ari, whose stealth capabilities allowed them to move unseen. Each contributed their unique strengths to the fight against the Ancients. And now, Xylo carried the potential key to their victory.

The ruins grew darker as the sun set, casting long shadows that danced eerily in the fading light. Xylo knew she had to find shelter for the night. As she searched for a safe place to rest, she vowed to honor the sacrifices of those who had fought and died for this moment. The Ancients would not win. Not while she still had breath in her body and hope in her heart.

A rusty groan tore through the silence, the skeletal remains of a skyscraper swaying precariously in the wind. Xylo squinted through the ever-present haze of ash, the acrid sting clinging to her throat like a metallic claw. The once-vibrant cityscape of Zerathar, the capital of Xiphori, was now a graveyard of twisted metal and shattered dreams.

The wind, a relentless banshee, howled a mournful song through the canyons of debris. It whipped the omnipresent ash into a swirling vortex, a suffocating shroud that obscured the sun, leaving only a sickly, bruised glow filtering through the oppressive grey. Each breath felt like sandpaper scraping against Xylo's raw lungs, the air thick with the stench of burnt ozone and something far more sinister—the metallic tang of blood, a lingering ghost from the horrors that had unfolded here.

Her boots crunched on a carpet of pulverized glass and bone-like fragments of what could have been buildings, homes, and lives. Each step echoed in the unnatural silence, a haunting counterpoint to the wind's mournful cry. The silence itself was a weapon, a suffocating pressure that pressed down on Xylo's already burdened heart. It was a silence broken only by the occasional, horrifying clang of unseen metal shifting in the distance, a chilling reminder of the city's metallic tomb.

A skeletal hand, bleached white by the harsh sun, poked through a mound of rubble. Xylo stumbled back, a gasp catching in her throat. It wasn't the first such grim discovery she'd made in her scavenging runs, but the shock never truly lessened. This wasn't just a dead city; it was a mass grave, a monument to a civilization extinguished in an instant.

Tears welled in her eyes, blurring the already desolate scene. She squeezed her eyelids shut, the taste of salt mingling with the metallic tang on her tongue. But despair was a luxury she couldn't afford. Every ragged breath, every pounding heartbeat, was a defiance against the oblivion that had consumed her world.

With newfound resolve, Xylo wiped her eyes and pressed on, her hand instinctively reaching for the data chip hidden beneath her tattered cloak. It was a tiny ember of hope, a fragile spark in the suffocating darkness. She had to get it to the resistance. It was the only way to avenge Zerathar, the only way to prevent the same fate from befalling any other world.

Xylo forced her gaze from the skeletal hand, a macabre monument to the city's demise. Each crunching step through the pulverized cityscape was a defiant stomp against despair, a drumbeat challenging the oppressive silence that clung to the ruins like a second skin.

She navigated the twisted labyrinth of debris, her eyes darting like cornered prey. This desolate wasteland was a predator's paradise. Scavengers, their minds fractured by the horrors they'd witnessed, lurked in the shadows like feral wolves. And then there were the Ancients' drones—soulless metallic specters that patrolled the dead city, their cold, emotionless gaze programmed to snuff out any flicker of life.

A sudden clang echoed through the streets, resonating with a bone-chilling finality. Xylo froze, her heart a frantic war drum against her ribs. She slammed herself against the crumbling facade of a once-vibrant marketplace, the faded awnings fluttering like the tattered flags of a fallen empire in the ash-choked wind.

Taking a single, shallow breath, she peeked around the corner. A hulking monstrosity lumbered through the haze, its metallic limbs gleaming with an oily sheen under the sickly, bruised light filtering through the ash. It was an Ancient drone, its glowing red optical sensors scanning the area with chilling efficiency. Xylo shrank back, her ragged breaths echoing in her ears as she willed herself invisible.

As the drone lumbered past, its metallic form momentarily obscuring the faint sunlight, Xylo caught a glimpse of her reflection in its polished chassis. A gaunt face stared back at her, hollow eyes reflecting the ghosts of the fallen that haunted this wasteland. The weight of their extinguished lives pressed down on her, a suffocating burden threatening to crush the fragile ember of hope flickering within her. But despair was a luxury she couldn't afford. The data chip, a spark against the suffocating darkness, burned hot against her chest, a promise, a defiant whisper against the city's death knell.

The metallic tang of blood, thick and cloying, clung to Xylo's throat. It melded with the acrid bite of burnt ozone, a suffocating shroud that choked the air. Above, the bruised sky barely filtered through a swirling vortex of ash, casting the shattered cityscape of Zerathar in an oppressive, sickly twilight. The once-vibrant symphony of life had been replaced by an unnatural stillness, broken only by the chilling howl of the wind as it scoured the skeletal remains of skyscrapers.

Xylo stumbled out from beneath a collapsed archway, her ragged clothes hanging off her gaunt frame. Each ragged breath harsh through a parched throat, her body a canvas of aches and exhaustion. Yet, her eyes, though haunted by flickering shadows of the horrors she'd witnessed, burned with an unwavering defiance. In her hand, a fist clenched so tight her knuckles bled white; she clutched a data chip—a last, desperate hope salvaged from the smoldering ruins of the research facility.

A flash of blinding light pierced the gloom, a memory ripped from the clutches of time. Laughter echoed, vibrant and carefree, as children chased each other through the bustling marketplace of Zerathar before the Ancients' arrival. The air hummed with the energy of a thriving civilization—the sweet scent of exotic spices, the rhythmic clatter of the mechanic's workshop, and the holographic advertisements shimmering like dreams against the night sky.

The memory shattered, replaced by the harsh bite of reality. Xylo's gaze fell upon a discarded child's toy, its once vibrant colors bleached to a skeletal gray by the relentless sun. A strangled sob escaped her lips, a raw echo of the countless lives extinguished in the blink of an eye.

A hollow cough racked Xylo, reminding her of the searing pain that pulsed through her side. She wasn't the only one bearing the scars of this war. In the distance, a lone soldier knelt by the smoldering wreckage of a once-proud warship, his head bowed in silent grief. A young mechanic, his face etched with the lines of a man far older than his years, hammered listlessly at a twisted piece of metal, his eyes reflecting hollow exhaustion.

Around her neck, a tattered scrap of cloth held a faded picture. A woman with eyes that mirrored Xylo's own, a child clutching a stuffed animal, both smiling with a radiant joy that seemed a cruel mockery of the present. Xylo tightened her grip on the data chip, its smooth surface a stark contrast to the rough calluses on her hand. It was a fragile thing, this chip—a whisper against a storm. But in its potential lay the embers of rebellion, a defiant spark against the crushing darkness.

A low hum vibrated through the shattered cityscape, growing steadily into a bone-chilling thrum. Xylo raised her head, squinting through the ash-choked haze. In the distance, a swarm of needle-shaped fighters emerged from the bruised horizon, leaving trails of black smoke in their wake. Larger, more imposing shapes followed— the hulking silhouettes of Ancient warships, their mechanical hearts pulsing with cold, malevolent energy.

The battle for survival had begun, and Xylo, a lone ember of defiance amidst the ruins, wouldn't go down without a fight. The data chip, a symbol of hope in the face of despair, was her weapon, her burden, and her only chance to see the fire of rebellion rekindled across the galaxy.

The Chase

The ground trembled beneath Xylo's feet, a counterpoint to the thrumming in her ears. The enemy fighters shrieked closer, their needle-like forms leaving trails of acrid smoke that stung her eyes and choked her lungs. This wasn't a battlefield; it was a hunt, and Xylo was the desperate prey.

She weaved through the skeletal remains of skyscrapers, her ragged breaths echoing in the unnatural silence between explosions. Each towering remnant offered a momentary refuge, only to reveal another dead end or a crumbling wall threatening to collapse under the tremors.

The data chip burned hot against her chest, a constant reminder of the weight of hope she carried. But with each pounding heartbeat, the embers of defiance threatened to be extinguished by the sheer terror of the chase.

A narrow alleyway materialized before her, barely wide enough for her slender frame. It was a gamble, a claustrophobic death trap if the enemy fighters followed. But it was her only option. She squeezed through, scraping against jagged metal, the stench of rust and decay assaulting her nostrils.

The sounds of the battle faded to a muffled roar behind her. Here, in the oppressive darkness, the only light came from the faint bioluminescent glow of mutated insects clinging to the damp walls. They skittered closer, their multifaceted eyes glinting with an unsettling curiosity. Xylo ignored them, her gaze fixed on the sliver of light flickering at the end of the tunnel.

The Moment of Decision

The passage opened into a vast, cavernous space. A dormant subway station, untouched by the devastation above. In the center, a colossal transport platform, its dormant tracks stretching out into the darkness like skeletal fingers reaching for an unseen destination.

But it was the colossal entry point embedded in the far wall that snagged Xylo's attention. An access hatch, a gaping maw leading into the belly of the enemy flagship that hovered menacingly above the city, its dark form blotting out the last sliver of twilight.

Her heart hammered against her ribs, a frantic drum against the oppressive silence. This was madness, a suicide mission. But the weight of her city, the ghosts of the fallen, pressed down on her, leaving her no choice. She had to get the data chip inside that ship, no matter the cost.

Xylo pressed herself into the shadows at the base of the colossal entry, her ragged breaths echoing in the cavernous silence of the abandoned station. The faint bioluminescent glow from the mutated insects did little to pierce the darkness, leaving her with only the faint outline of the entrance and the distant rumble of the battle above as her guides.

A low hum emanated from the portal, a rhythmic pulse that vibrated through the metal floor and into Xylo's bones. It was a sound that sent shivers down her spine, a tangible pressure that hummed with an alien energy. It quickened her heartbeat, a frantic drum against her ribs. The enemy forces were likely preparing to deploy ground troops into the city. She had a narrow window of opportunity, a sliver of time before the entrance cycled open and sealed her fate.

With a burst of adrenaline, Xylo lunged towards the entry point, her fingers scrabbling for purchase on the slick metal surface. Each clang resonated like a thunderclap in the stillness, a beacon announcing her presence to any unseen enemy lurking in the shadows. A series of glowing panels beside the portal flickered to life, pulsing with an alien script that seemed to writhe and churn like living things. A security system, a digital barrier that stood between Xylo and her objective.

Panic threatened to surge through her, but she slammed it down with a force born of desperation. She had scavenged scraps of Ancient technology during her time hiding in the ruins. Tech that most wouldn't even recognize, let alone understand. Tech that was her only hopes.

Doubt gnawed at the edges of her resolve. What if it wasn't enough? What if these scavenged scraps were useless trinkets against a civilization that could casually churn out monstrosities like the things battling above? But giving in to despair was a luxury she couldn't afford. The fate of the city, maybe even the entire planet, rested on her shoulders. Steeling her nerves, Xylo reached into her pack, the scavenged tech a cold, comforting weight in her hand. She had to try for everyone.

Xylo clung to the entry's underbelly, her ragged breaths echoing in the cavernous silence like the gasps of a cornered animal. She felt the burn of her muscles scream at her. The faint bioluminescent glow from the mutated insects cast grotesque, dancing shadows across the metallic surface, offering no solace in the suffocating darkness. The rumble of the battle above seemed amplified in this desolate space, a constant reminder of the city being ravaged mere meters overhead.

A low hum emanated from the portal, growing steadily into a rhythmic thrum that vibrated through Xylo's very bones. It pulsed with a malevolent urgency, a countdown to her doom. The enemy forces were preparing to deploy. The data chip clutched tight against her chest, seemed to respond in kind, faint warmth spreading through her fingers—a counterpoint to the growing ice in her veins.

With a burst of adrenaline-fueled by terror and a sliver of hope, Xylo lunged. Clawing at the slick metal surface, she scraped and kicked, the clang of her efforts echoing like a death knell. Each agonizing second stretched into an eternity, the rhythmic thrumming of the portal a relentless drumbeat against her sanity.

Just as her strength began to wane, her fingers brushed against a series of recessed panels beside the entry. Symbols, alien and archaic, glowed with an eerie luminescence. A flicker of recognition sparked in Xylo's memory—these were fragments from the research facility! The cryptic message from the fallen scientist, a frantic scrawl etched onto a salvaged data core, echoed in her mind: "...Ancients...rely...on...synchronicity...key...disrupt...harmonics..."

Xylo's Skills and Knowledge

Xylo's heart pounded as she recalled the long nights spent in the darkened corners of the resistance base, piecing together scraps of Ancient technology. Her background in engineering, a talent honed in the thriving days of Xiphori, had been her salvation. She had once been a lead technician, responsible for maintaining the delicate balance of the city's infrastructure. Her keen intellect and innovative mind had made her a valuable asset then, and now, it was her only weapon against the Ancients.

Her fingers moved with practiced precision, her mind a whirlwind of calculations and hypotheses. She had seen enough of the Ancients' tech to understand the basics of their harmonic synchronization—a method that allowed their machines to operate in perfect, unbreakable unison. If she could introduce a discordant frequency, a single flaw in their otherwise perfect symphony, she could disrupt their operations, if only for a moment.

Sweat beaded on her brow as she worked, her hands shaking from the effort and the stakes. She attached the scavenged tech to the glowing panels, praying to whatever gods still watched over the remnants of her world. The tech hummed to life, a soft, discordant melody that clashed with the rhythmic thrum of the portal.

The panels flickered, the alien script warping and distorting. Xylo held her breath, the seconds stretching into an eternity. Then, with a final, decisive beep, the entry groaned open, revealing a dimly lit passageway into the heart of the enemy flagship.

Xylo's legs trembled with relief and exhaustion, but she forced herself to move. She slipped through the opening, the weight of the data chip a comforting presence against her chest. The Ancients' technology hummed around her, an ominous reminder of the power she faced. But with each step, she felt a renewed sense of purpose. She was no longer just a survivor; she was a warrior, carrying the hopes of her fallen city.

As she disappeared into the shadows of the enemy ship, the echoes of her past faded into the background. Xylo was ready to fight for the future, armed with the knowledge and determination that had brought her this far. The battle for the galaxy's freedom had just begun, and she would not rest until the Ancients' reign of terror was ended once and for all.

A World Strangled in Ash

A rusty groan tore through the silence, the skeletal remains of a skyscraper swaying precariously in the wind. Xylo squinted through the ever-present haze of ash, the acrid sting clinging to her throat like a metallic claw. The once vibrant cityscape of Xiphori was a graveyard of twisted metal and shattered dreams.

The wind, a relentless banshee, howled a mournful song through the canyons of debris. It whipped the omnipresent ash into a swirling vortex, a suffocating shroud that obscured the sun, leaving only a sickly, bruised glow filtering through the oppressive gray. Each breath felt like sandpaper scraping against Xylo's raw lungs, the air thick with the stench of burnt ozone and something far more sinister—the lingering scent of death, a reminder of the horrors that had unfolded here.

Her boots crunched on a carpet of pulverized glass and bone-like fragments of what could have been buildings, homes, and lives. Each step echoed in the unnatural silence, a haunting counterpoint to the wind's mournful cry. The silence itself was a weapon, a suffocating pressure that pressed down on Xylo's already burdened heart. It was a silence broken only by the occasional, horrifying clang of unseen metal shifting in the distance, a chilling reminder of the city's metallic tomb.

Tears welled in her eyes, blurring the already desolate scene. She squeezed her eyelids shut, the taste of salt mingling with the acrid ash on her tongue. But despair was a luxury she couldn't afford. Every ragged breath, every pounding heartbeat, was a defiance against the oblivion that had consumed her world.

With a newfound resolve, Xylo wiped her eyes and pressed on, her hand instinctively reaching for the data chip hidden beneath her tattered cloak. It was a tiny ember of hope, a fragile spark in the suffocating darkness. She had to get it to the resistance. It was the only way to avenge Xiphori, the only way to prevent the same fate from befalling any other world.

A sudden clang echoed through the streets, resonating with a bone-chilling finality. Xylo froze her heart, a frantic war drum against her ribs. She slammed herself against the crumbling facade of a once-vibrant marketplace, the faded awnings fluttering like the tattered flags of a fallen empire in the ash-choked wind.

Taking a single, shallow breath, she peeked around the corner. A hulking monstrosity lumbered through the haze, its metallic limbs gleaming with an oily sheen under the sickly, bruised light filtering through the ash. It was an Ancient drone, its glowing red optical sensors scanning the area with chilling efficiency. Xylo shrank back, her ragged breaths echoing in her own ears as she willed herself invisible.

The stench of decay, thick and cloying, clung to Xylo's throat. It melded with the acrid bite of burnt ozone, a suffocating shroud that choked the air. Above, the bruised sky barely filtered through a swirling vortex of ash, casting the shattered cityscape of Xiphori in an oppressive, sickly twilight. The once vibrant symphony of life had been replaced by an unnatural stillness, broken only by the chilling howl of the wind as it scoured the skeletal remains of skyscrapers.

Xylo stumbled out from beneath a collapsed archway, her ragged clothes hanging off her gaunt frame. Each ragged breath ripped through a parched throat, her body a canvas of aches and exhaustion. Yet, her eyes, though haunted by flickering shadows of the horrors she'd witnessed, burned with an unwavering defiance. In her hand, a fist clenched so tight her knuckles bled white; she clutched a data chip—a last, desperate hope salvaged from the smoldering ruins of the research facility.

A flash of blinding light pierced the gloom, a memory ripped from the clutches of time. Laughter echoed, vibrant and carefree, as children chased each other through the bustling marketplace of Xiphori before the Ancients' arrival. The air hummed with the energy of a thriving civilization—the sweet scent of exotic spices, the rhythmic clatter of the mechanic's workshop, and the holographic advertisements shimmering like dreams against the night sky.

A hollow cough racked her, a reminder of the searing pain that pulsed through her side. She wasn't the only one bearing the scars of this war. In the distance, a lone soldier knelt by the smoldering wreckage of a once-proud warship, his head bowed in silent grief. A young mechanic, his face etched with the lines of a man far older than his years, hammered listlessly at a twisted piece of metal, his eyes reflecting hollow exhaustion.

The ground trembled beneath Xylo's feet, the vibrations a counterpoint to the relentless thrumming in her ears. Enemy fighters shrieked closer, their needle-like forms leaving trails of acrid smoke that stung her eyes and choked her lungs. This wasn't a battlefield; it was a hunt, and Xylo was the desperate prey.

She wove through the skeletal remains of skyscrapers, her ragged breaths echoing in the unnatural silence between explosions. Each towering remnant offered momentary refuge, only to reveal another dead end or a crumbling wall threatening to collapse under the tremors.

The sounds of battle faded to a muffled roar behind her. Here, in the oppressive darkness, the only light came from the faint bioluminescent glow of mutated insects clinging to the damp walls. They skittered closer, their multifaceted eyes glinting with unsettling curiosity. Xylo ignored them, her gaze fixed on the sliver of light flickering at the end of the tunnel.

But it was the colossal hatch embedded in the far wall that snagged Xylo's attention. An entry point, a gaping maw leading into the belly of the enemy flagship that hovered menacingly above the city, its dark form blotting out the last sliver of twilight.

Xylo pressed herself into the shadows at the base of the colossal hatch, her ragged breaths echoing in the cavernous silence of the abandoned station. The faint bioluminescent glow from the mutated insects did little to pierce the darkness, leaving her with only the faint outline of the hatch and the distant rumble of the battle above as her guides.

A low hum emanated from the hatch, a rhythmic pulse that vibrated through the metal floor and into Xylo's bones. It was a sound that sent shivers down her spine, a tangible pressure that hummed with alien energy. It quickened her heartbeat, a frantic drum against her ribs. The enemy forces were likely preparing to deploy ground troops into the city. She had a narrow window of opportunity, a sliver of time before the entrance cycled open and sealed her fate.

With a burst of adrenaline, Xylo lunged towards the hatch, her fingers scrabbling for purchase on the slick metal surface. Each clang resonated like a thunderclap in the stillness, a beacon announcing her presence to any unseen enemy lurking in the shadows. A series of glowing panels beside the hatch flickered to life, pulsing with an alien script that seemed to writhe and churn like living things. A security system, a digital barrier that stood between Xylo and her objective.

Panic threatened to surge through her, but she slammed it down with a force born of desperation. She had scavenged scraps of Ancient technology during her time hiding in the ruins. Tech that most wouldn't even recognize, let alone understand. Tech that was her only hope.

Hope, a fragile ember, flickered to life within Xylo. With trembling fingers, she pressed the data chip against the glowing panel. A surge of energy coursed through her arm, prompting a shudder through her, the chip pulsing with newfound intensity. The alien symbols on the panel writhed and morphed, rearranging themselves in an impossible sequence. A moment of agonizing silence followed, then—a soft click. The hatch whirred open, revealing a shadowy maw leading into the belly of the beast.

Xylo's heart hammered against her ribs, a frantic counterpoint to the silence of the opened hatch. The data chip, warm against her chest, seemed to thrum with newfound power. Taking a single, deep breath, she squeezed her eyes shut and stepped into the unknown, a whisper of the scientist's message echoing in her mind: "…disrupt…harmonics…"

The Void Erupts

The void erupted in a symphony of annihilation. The battered remnants of the Galactic Fleet, a ragtag collection of warships stitched together with spit and duct tape, roared into a desperate counter-attack. Laser fire lanced out from countless turrets, carving crimson streaks across the inky blackness of space. They were gnats buzzing around a monstrous bear, but they buzzed with a fury born of desperation.

The metallic tang of superheated metal filled the air, a sickening counterpoint to the thunderous boom of cannons and the unearthly whine of energy shields straining under the onslaught. Explosions erupted like malevolent suns, their blinding light momentarily erasing the constellations from existence. Debris, a twisted graveyard of once-proud vessels, pirouetted through the void, each shard a potential scythe waiting to claim another victim.

Fighters, nimble hornets buzzing around lumbering elephants, weaved through the debris field. Pilots, faces contorted in a grotesque rictus of fear and defiance, wrestled their craft through impossible maneuvers. Tracers arced across the darkness, weaving a deadly tapestry as they sought their targets – swarms of needle-like enemy drones that darted with mechanical precision. Cockpits pulsed with crimson emergency lights, the stench of ozone and burning flesh a grim testament to the casualties mounting with each passing second.

But the Galactic Fleet's desperate assault was met with a terrifying response. The colossal Ancient warships, their hulks seemingly impervious to the rain of laser fire, unleashed a devastating volley of their own. Massive energy blasts, emerald green pulses of annihilation, ripped through the battlefield. They sliced effortlessly through fleeing fighters and vaporized entire cruisers in a heartbeat. It was a display of power so absolute, so horrifying, that it stole the breath from even the most seasoned veterans.

In the heart of the maelstrom, the Harbinger, General Osnex's flagship, bore the brunt of the enemy's fury. Its shields flickered precariously under the onslaught, the hull groaning in protest. Alarms blared, red lights pulsed with a manic rhythm, and the bridge crew fought desperately to maintain control.

"Hull breach on decks five and six," screamed a young ensign, his voice barely audible over the din.

"Casualties reported! Medical teams to decks five and six!" barked another officer, her face streaked with soot and sweat.

General Osnex, his face grim but resolute, stood at the command dais, his gaze fixed on the holographic display. His knuckles were white as snow as he gripped the armrests, his boots braced against the violent tremors rocking the ship.

"Hold!" he roared, his voice a defiant bellow against the encroaching silence. "Hold the line! We buy those scientists just a few more precious minutes, that's all I ask!"

A chorus of grim determination echoed through the bridge. These were the final embers of a dying flame, but they would burn bright until the very last breath.

The Desperate Infiltration

The air inside the Ancient flagship was thick with an acrid metallic tang, a suffocating shroud that clung to Xylo's throat with each ragged breath. The dim, pulsating glow emanating from the alien consoles cast grotesque, elongated shadows that danced across the labyrinthine corridors. Every metallic creak, every hum of unseen machinery echoed with a sinister undercurrent in the oppressive silence.

Xylo, a lone spark of defiance in this cold, metallic world, pressed on. Her tattered clothes clung to her gaunt frame, a stark reminder of the hell she'd crawled out of. The data chip, clutched tight against her chest, pulsed with faint warmth—a beacon of hope in the encroaching darkness. Memories of her family flashed through her mind—the faces of her parents and siblings who had been lost in an Ancient attack. She had vowed never to forget, never to stop fighting.

As she navigated the labyrinthine corridors, her eyes flicked to the alien symbols on the walls. The script, an intricate weave of glowing lines and geometric shapes, hinted at the Ancients' mastery of synchronization technology. Every control panel, every conduit seemed to pulse in unison, a symphony of energy and order. A damaged panel, sparking intermittently, revealed more—fragments of a diagram, a nexus of power conduits converging at a central core. The key to their invincibility, and perhaps their downfall.

Suddenly, the rhythmic hum of the ship thrummed with a new urgency. A red alert flashed on a nearby console, its harsh light momentarily blinding Xylo. Alarms blared, a shrill shriek that sent a jolt of primal fear through her.

The silence shattered. A metallic clang echoed down the corridor as a hatch hissed open, revealing a scene ripped straight from her nightmares. Four robotic guards, their sleek metallic bodies gleaming with an eerie blue light, stalked out, their multi-jointed limbs whirring with predatory grace. Their single crimson eye pulsed menacingly, scanning the corridor.

Xylo's heart raced as she pressed herself against the cold metal wall, the weight of the data chip a constant reminder of her mission. This was it—the moment where everything could be lost or won. She took a deep breath, summoning every ounce of courage, and prepared to face the machines that stood between her and the heart of the enemy.

A Dance on the Razor's Edge

Adrenaline surged through Xylo's veins. Fight or flight? The thought of retreating was quickly dismissed. The fate of countless worlds rested on her shoulders. With a feral growl escaping her throat, she lunged.

The first guard reacted with inhuman speed, its metallic arm whipping out in a blur. Xylo barely dodged the blow, the force of the displaced air sending her tumbling across the cold metallic floor. Pain lanced up her arm, a stinging reminder of her vulnerability. She thought back to the day when the Ancients first attacked, the screams echoing in her mind, a reminder of the countless lives depending on her now.

Scrambling back to her feet, heart pounding a frantic rhythm against her ribs, she drew her salvaged plasma pistol. It was a cobbled-together weapon, scavenged from the ruins, and woefully inadequate against such advanced technology. But it was all she had.

With a ragged scream, Xylo opened fire. Bolts of superheated plasma erupted from the pistol, leaving scorching trails of light in their wake. One guard crumpled under the assault, its metallic body smoking. But the remaining three pressed forward, their movements relentless, their crimson eyes fixed on Xylo with cold, calculating malice.

They closed the distance with inhuman speed. Xylo dodged and weaved, the air singing with the passage of deadly beams as the guards returned fire. One bolt seared past her ear, the smell of burnt hair filling her nostrils. Another clipped her shoulder, sending her staggering.

Panic threatened to overwhelm her, but the image of the shattered city, the faces of the fallen etched into her memory, spurred her on. Her ragged breaths came in gasps, her vision blurring at the edges. She knew exhaustion gnawed at her, another enemy in this desperate fight.

Desperate, Xylo rolled under the sweeping arc of a guard's weapon, narrowly avoiding being cleaved in two. She came up behind the behemoth, adrenaline fueling a reckless plan. Aiming her pistol at the glowing blue core exposed on its back, she squeezed the trigger.

The core flared momentarily before imploding with a deafening bang. The guard shuddered, then crumpled to the floor, a lifeless hunk of metal. Xylo didn't waste time celebrating. Two remained, their crimson eyes now burning with a malevolent intensity.

Taking a ragged breath, Xylo gripped her pistol; the data chip a searing ember against her chest. She knew the odds were stacked against her. But for the sake of everyone who had fallen, for the hope of a future yet to be extinguished, she would fight. The fate of the galaxy hung in the balance, and Xylo, a lone survivor in the belly of the beast, was its last desperate defender.

Hope's Last Stand

Xylo's ragged breaths echoed in the metallic labyrinth as she sprinted down the corridor, leaving a trail of blood on the cold floor. The remaining robotic guards were relentless, their blue eyes glowing with cold pursuit. One grazed her shoulder with a searing beam, the stench of burnt flesh filling the air.

Hope, a flickering ember, threatened to be extinguished. Could she ever reach the central control chamber in time? The fate of countless worlds hung in the balance, and with every passing moment, the enemy's relentless assault on the Galactic Fleet intensified.

Suddenly, a voice crackled through her communicator, a welcome intrusion on the oppressive silence. It was Admiral Levi, his voice a beacon of hope in the encroaching despair. "Xylo! This is the Requiem, we see you on sensors! Hold on, we're covering your flank!"

A surge of adrenaline coursed through Xylo's veins. Relief momentarily overpowered the pain throbbing in her shoulder. "Understood, Admiral! Almost there!" she gasped, dodging a volley of energy blasts that scorched the air around her.

From above, the Requiem roared into action. Admiral Levi, his voice taut with urgency, barked orders into his comm. "Targeting grid adjusted! Focus all plasma fire on the corridor ahead of Xylo! Make a path for her!"

The ship groaned under the strain, every weapon system unleashed in a thunderous barrage. Explosions rocked the corridor ahead, showering Xylo with debris. But through the smoke and fire, a clear path emerged, carved by the sheer firepower of the desperate flagship.

Xylo surged forward, propelled by a renewed sense of purpose. Each agonizing step was a victory against unimaginable odds. Behind her, the relentless clang of robotic footsteps echoed, a chilling reminder of the pursuit.

The central control chamber materialized at the end of the corridor, a monolithic gateway guarded by a final pair of robotic sentries. They whirred to life, their crimson eyes locked on Xylo, their metallic limbs poised for a killing blow.

But Xylo wouldn't be deterred. With a desperate lunge, she dove past the guards, her shoulder screaming in protest. She slammed into the control chamber doors, adrenaline overriding the pain. The doors hissed open, revealing the pulsing heart of the Ancient vessel – a room bathed in an eerie green glow, dominated by a central console studded with alien symbols.

Ignoring the rising tide of exhaustion, Xylo ripped the data chip from her chest and slammed it into a designated receptacle on the console. A surge of energy coursed through the room, the green light intensifying to a blinding white.

A primal scream ripped from Xylo's throat, a mix of pain and defiance. The data chip pulsed, and then went dark. For a moment, there was an agonizing silence. Then, chaos erupted.

The alarms within the Ancient flagship blared, a cacophony that sent shivers down Xylo's spine. The rhythmic hum of the ship stuttered, and then lurched violently.

Back on the bridge of the Requiem, a cheer erupted. Admiral Levi, sweat beading on his brow, slammed his fist on the command console. "It's working! Their targeting systems are compromised! Fire at will! Take back the sky!"

A wave of relief washed over Xylo as she slumped against the console, her body wracked with exhaustion. Outside, the roar of the battle intensified, but the frantic edge was gone. The Ancient fleet, thrown into disarray, faltered. Their attacks became erratic, their coordinated assault dissolving into a desperate scramble.

The impossible had happened. A lone survivor, armed with nothing but a desperate gamble, had disrupted the heart of the enemy machine. The tide of the battle had turned.

A symphony of destruction echoed through the void, but the notes had changed. The desperate, frantic cries of the Galactic Fleet had given way to a defiant roar. Laser fire ripped across the battlefield, weaving a shimmering tapestry of crimson light against the inky blackness of space.

The Once-Battered Harbinger

The once-battered Harbinger, a phoenix resurrected from the ashes, led the charge. General Osnex, fire rekindled in his eyes, bellowed commands into his comm. "Targeting systems green! All batteries online! Show those ancient bastards the fury of a dying star!"

His flagship, pulsating with renewed energy, spearheaded a relentless assault. Crippled vessels, limping ghosts mere moments ago, now surged forward, their guns spitting fire. Damaged fighters, their pilots fueled by a desperate hope, pirouetted through the debris field, seeking vengeance on the enemy drones.

The Ancient armada, thrown into disarray by Xylo's audacious act, faltered. Their once-coordinated attacks became a desperate scramble. Energy blasts, haphazardly aimed, arced through space, detonating harmlessly or ripping through the ranks of their own forces. The colossal warships, once seemingly invincible, became lumbering targets, their shields flickering precariously under the renewed onslaught.

Amidst the maelstrom, dogfights raged with a renewed ferocity. Pilots, adrenaline pumping through their veins, weaved through a lethal ballet of laser beams and exploding debris. Human fighters, nimble gnats buzzing around lumbering elephants, unleashed volleys of plasma fire, taking down enemy drones in showers of sparks and molten slag. The cockpit of a battered Xiphos fighter became a microcosm of the battle – the young pilot, his face a mask of grim determination, maneuvered his craft with breathtaking skill, each successful kill a desperate act of defiance against the encroaching tide of darkness.

The tide of the battle, so one-sided mere moments ago, had turned. It was a fragile victory, a glimmer of hope flickering in the vast emptiness of space. But for the crew of the Harbinger, for the pilots weaving through the debris field, for Xylo slumped against the alien console, it was a victory nonetheless.

A Colossal Explosion

Suddenly, a colossal explosion ripped through the battlefield. One of the Ancient warships, its central core overloaded by Xylo's data spike, erupted in a blinding flash of emerald green energy. The shockwave rolled outwards, crippling nearby vessels, both Ancient and human.

A collective cheer erupted across the comm channels of the Galactic Fleet. It was a primal scream of defiance, a joyous celebration of a seemingly impossible victory. But they knew the fight wasn't over. The remaining Ancient vessels, though flustered and disoriented, still held immense power.

Admiral Levi's voice, a gravelly rasp laced with triumph, crackled through the comm channels. "That's one down, heroes! Now, let's finish this fight together! For the future of the galaxy! For every world they've ravaged! For every life they've stolen! Show them the true meaning of defiance!"

His words ignited a firestorm of renewed determination across the battlefield. And as the battered remnants of the Galactic Fleet pressed their attack, a single, shared sentiment echoed through the hearts of every pilot, every crew member, and every soldier: They may be outnumbered, they may be outgunned, but they would not falter. They would fight until their last breath to reclaim their future.

The Last Stand

The symphony of destruction faded into a cacophony of cheers. The once-deadly dance of lasers and explosions gave way to a joyous display of fireworks as crippled ships vented excess energy in a vibrant celebration. The battered but victorious remnants of the Galactic Fleet battered but unbroken, reveled in their improbable

The Flight of Captain Rax

Captain Rax, known as "Shadow," gripped the controls of his sleek, battle-scarred fighter, his knuckles white against the black leather. The cockpit was a claustrophobic bubble of activity, filled with the hum of machinery, the flicker of warning lights, and the persistent chatter of the squadron's comm channel. Outside, the battle raged with a ferocity that seemed to eclipse the very stars. The roar of engines and the deafening blasts of explosions reverberated through the void, a cacophony of war that shook the bones.

Rax's heart pounded in his chest as he banked hard to port, narrowly avoiding a volley of enemy fire that shredded the space where his fighter had been moments before. The metallic tang of blood filled his mouth after biting his tongue during the violent maneuver. His eyes, steely and focused, flicked to the holodisplay projecting a tactical overview of the battlefield. The odds were grim, the enemy fleet vast and seemingly invincible, but there was no time for doubt.

As he maneuvered through the chaos, Rax couldn't help but think of his squadron—his family in this floating warzone. Every pilot under his command carried the weight of entire worlds on their shoulders, and it was his responsibility to guide them through this hellscape. Memories of his fallen comrades flashed through his mind—each name, each face, a testament to the sacrifice and courage that defined the Xiphos squadron.

"Shadow, this is Red Five," crackled a voice over the comm. "I've got two bogeys on my tail, and I'm running out of tricks!"

Rax's gaze snapped to the HUD, tracking the glowing icons of his squadron. Red Five's fighter was weaving erratically, trying to shake off a pair of nimble enemy drones that clung to his tail like hungry wolves. Rax pushed his throttle to the limit, his fighter's engines screaming in protest as he closed the distance.

"Hang tight, Red Five. I'm on my way," Rax replied, his voice calm and steady despite the chaos around him.

He thumbed the trigger on his flight stick, sending a pair of plasma bolts streaking toward the nearest drone. The bolts struck home, reducing the drone to a cloud of molten slag. Rax pulled back on the stick, his fighter arcing upward in a graceful curve that brought him directly behind the second drone. Another squeeze of the trigger, and the drone disintegrated in a blaze of fire and shrapnel.

"You're clear, Red Five," Rax said, a rare smile tugging at the corner of his mouth. "Now let's show these bastards what the Xiphos squadron is made of."

As Rax looped back into the fray, he felt a pang of sorrow for the life he had left behind. He remembered the quiet nights on his homeworld, the laughter of his children echoing through the fields. This war had taken everything from him, and yet, he would give even more if it meant securing a future for those he loved. The burden of command weighed heavily on him, but it was a burden he bore willingly.

The two fighters re-engaged, their plasma cannons blazing. Rax's mind was a blur of calculations and instinct, his every move a precise dance of survival. He weaved through the debris field, his eyes scanning for threats and opportunities alike. The battle was a chaotic swirl of motion, but amidst the chaos, Rax found a strange clarity.

A distant explosion drew his attention, and his heart sank as he saw the flagship of the Fifth Fleet, Admiral Korvus's ship, break apart in a blinding flash of light. The comm channels were filled with the screams of the dying, the desperate pleas for help that would never come. Rax felt a cold fury settle over him, a resolve as unyielding as the armor of the enemy warships.

"All fighters, this is Shadow," Rax called out, his voice ringing with authority. "Concentrate fire on the lead warship. We need to punch a hole in their lines!"

The response was immediate, the surviving fighters of the Xiphos squadron rallying to his call. They formed up behind Rax, their engines flaring as they poured everything they had into the attack. The lead enemy warship loomed ahead, a massive behemoth bristling with weapons and shielded by a shimmering energy barrier.

Rax's fingers danced over the controls, targeting the weak points in the enemy's defenses. "Steady... steady... NOW!" he shouted, unleashing a barrage of plasma fire.

As the combined firepower of the Xiphos squadron hammered into the enemy warship, a sudden jolt shook Rax's fighter. The controls flickered, a malfunction threatening to spin him into the void. Gritting his teeth, he fought against the craft's lurch, wrestling the stick back into submission with a grim determination.

The energy barrier flickered and failed under the relentless assault. Rax's fighter shuddered as he took a glancing hit, the acrid smell of burning metal permeating his cockpit, but he gritted his teeth and pressed on, his eyes fixed on the target.

A cheer went up over the comm as the warship's hull breached a gaping wound that vented atmosphere and debris into space. The once-invincible vessel began to list, its weapons falling silent. Rax felt a surge of triumph, but it was short-lived.

"Shadow, we're picking up massive energy readings from the flagship!" shouted Red Five. "It's going to blow!"

Rax's eyes widened as he saw the enemy warship's core begin to glow, a brilliant emerald light that signaled an imminent explosion. He yanked back on the controls, his fighter screaming away from the doomed vessel.

"All units fall back! Fall back!" he ordered, his voice strained with urgency.

The explosion was cataclysmic, a blinding flash of green that engulfed the battlefield. Rax's fighter was buffeted by the shockwave, his instruments flickering wildly as he fought to regain control. When the light faded, the once-imposing enemy warship was nothing more than a cloud of debris, its destruction a beacon of hope amidst the chaos.

"Good job, everyone," Rax said, his voice shaky but triumphant. "But the fight's not over yet. Let's finish this."

As the Xiphos squadron regrouped and pressed the attack, Rax felt a renewed sense of purpose. They were outnumbered, outgunned, but they were not alone. Across the battlefield, the Galactic Fleet fought with a desperate ferocity, their spirits buoyed by the small victories that marked the path to a greater triumph.

Rax thought back to his homeworld, now a distant memory, the vibrant fields and bustling cities reduced to ruins by the Ancients' relentless onslaught. He remembered the day he joined the fleet, driven by a burning desire to protect what little remained and to avenge those lost. This battle, this moment, was his chance to strike back.

The success of the Xiphos squadron's attack reverberated across the galaxy, a symbol of resistance that inspired countless others to rise up. The tide of war was turning, and Captain Rax, with his unwavering determination and unyielding spirit, stood at the forefront of that change.

Back on the Requiem

The silence in the cockpit was unbearable. Alexander's breath was shallow, his pulse pounding in his ears. He stood motionless, his eyes locked onto the crystal spinning before him, almost floating, almost alive. It wasn't just light—it was alive, swirling, pulling, tugging at him from the very core of his being. The shadows cast across the ship seemed to writhe, stretching, creeping like dark fingers from some unfathomable abyss. The hum of the crystal wasn't just sound; it was a vibration—a call—a haunting tremor deep in his bones, reverberating through his blood like a forgotten memory he couldn't place.

And then, the air shifted.

At first, it was subtle. A low buzz. Just a whisper, like a faraway insect. But it grew. A deep, unnatural hum twisted through the air, crawling up Alexander's spine, making the hairs on the back of his neck stand on end. The ship, once crackling with the energy of battle, was now freezing—cold, cold in a way that wasn't natural. The walls, the very metal around him, felt... hollow, like the ship had absorbed centuries of lost, forgotten time. Shadows coiled in corners, thickening, deepening. The air thickened too, as though they were sailing through a place where no one—no one—was meant to tread.

His breath hitched. Something was wrong. No. Something was off. His heart raced, the pressure in his chest building as his gaze fixed on the crystal, now pulsing in a slow, deliberate rhythm. His fists clenched as his pulse pounded faster, his body coiling, a spring ready to snap.

"Do you feel it?" His voice broke the suffocating quiet, tight, strained, as though it had to fight through an invisible wall.

Lord Gresham stepped up beside him, his face an unreadable mask, his posture rigid. He didn't need to speak; his very presence was a weight, a silent affirmation that the air between them was heavy with the same wrongness.

"I feel it," Gresham murmured, his voice low, almost reverent. "Something old... Something ancient."

Before Alexander could reply, the crystal shuddered.

The hum of the crystal went from strange to sickening. Its glow deepened, its edges blazing with a brilliance so sharp it cut into his eyes, burning into his mind. He didn't think. He reacted.

"Helm!" His hand slammed onto the comm panel, urgency overriding everything else. "On my mark, fire everything you have at that crystal! NOW!"

A beat of silence—one too long.

"Sir… are you sure?" The helmsman's voice was shaky, uncertain.

"NOW, LIEUTENANT!" Alexander's voice tore through the tension, raw, desperate. The hum of the crystal had turned maddening, a chorus of shrieking whispers clawing at his skull, at his very thoughts. The ship, the very ship he had come to trust, was groaning under the weight of something far bigger than any battle they had faced. Something far older.

A sharp crackle filled the comms as the helmsman responded. "Ready, sir!"

"Now!" Alexander's order split the air like a whip crack.

A beam of green energy shot from the ship's weapon array, a pulse of raw power slamming into the crystal with a violent, earth-shattering force.

It stopped.

For one terrifying moment, everything went still. But then, it began again.

The crystal spun faster—faster than any natural force should allow. The very fabric of reality seemed to stretch around it, light pouring from its core in blinding cascades. It was too much—too much. The roar of energy, a sound that shook their bones and rattled their teeth, filled the space. A deafening wave of force, of power, of sheer, unrelenting rage.

Gresham staggered back, eyes wide in disbelief, his voice barely audible over the crushing hum of energy. "Levi—WE NEED TO GET OUT OF HERE. NOW."

But it was too late.

The ship began to burn—the heat was unbearable, scorching, the air thick with the overwhelming weight of the power that surged from the crystal. It felt as though the ship itself were being consumed, collapsing in on itself under the weight of something ancient, something dark.

"Helm—move!" Gresham shouted, grabbing Alexander by the arm, dragging him toward the escape tube with a ferocity born of terror.

The ship's engines roared to life, the hull vibrating as it struggled to break free from the gravitational grip of the crystal's power. But the stars outside didn't streak past—they stretched, twisting, warping into jagged lines of light, as though the very laws of the universe were being bent, broken.

And then, it came.

A voice.

The voice.

It wasn't just heard. It was felt. Every soul, everywhere, across the galaxy, froze. The world held its breath.

"THEE N—"

The words—the scream—came crashing into their minds, reverberating through every living being. It wasn't just a sound—it was an eruption of terror that shook them to their very core. It rattled their hearts, leaving an emptiness where the blood had once flowed.

People stopped in their tracks. Welders dropped their tools, their eyes wide in fear, staring into the distance as their hearts pounded. A child, coloring on a sidewalk, stood frozen, her chalk forgotten. Her gaze was wide, searching, searching for something she couldn't name.

And then… nothing. Silence. An abyssal, choking silence, so deep that it felt as though time itself had ceased.

The crystal exploded.

A shockwave of sound—pure, deafening, violent—ripped through space. A thunderous clap that shook the fabric of existence. It was a sound so powerful that it left everyone staggered, clutching their ears, eyes wide in horror, the world spinning out of focus.

And then, it was over.

The silence came again. Deeper. Darker. More profound than any silence should ever be.

The universe had stopped.

And the Ancients?

Their grip on existence was gone. Vanished.

A mechanic stood frozen in his workshop, wrench in hand, confused. "What am I doing?" he whispered. But he didn't wait for the answer. He dropped the tool and walked out.

A child stared up at the sky, her breath catching in her throat. She didn't know why, but she felt it—the change. Something had shifted deep inside her, something terrible, something irreversible.

Across the galaxy, every person felt it.

A strange, unsettling freedom.

And no one knew what came next.

Lady Mara and Lord Gresham stood side by side at the heart of the Ancients' citadel, their presence a defiant storm within the towering chamber. The air crackled with energy as their swords, one glowing with a soft blue luminescence, the other blazing dark red, unleashed a torrent of power that surged through the ancient stronghold.

With each swing, their blades sang through the air, weaving trails of light that danced across the high arches and intricate carvings of the citadel. Their movements were a symphony of grace and fury, a ballet of destruction as they carved a path through the bastion of their ancient foes.

The Ancients, masters of the galaxy for millennia, watched in horror as the machines that had served them for eons faltered. Monolithic constructs, once impervious and eternal, flickered with distress signals, their lights sputtering like dying stars. A cascade of sparks rained down from malfunctioning circuits, illuminating the polished floors with erratic bursts of electric fire.

The citadel's majestic halls, adorned with glowing runes and symbols of ancient power, became shadowed realms of uncertainty. The hum of engines and the rhythmic pulse of energy conduits faltered, leaving behind a haunting silence punctuated only by the distant crackle of short-circuiting wires.

In the heart of the Ancients' citadel, a crystal prism hovered serenely amidst the chaos, its presence both beautiful and ominous. It spun slowly, each facet reflecting a dazzling array of colors, a blinding spectrum that painted the chamber walls with vivid hues. The crystal radiated an ancient song, a haunting melody that resonated at the edge of perception, whispering secrets of the universe and the power it held.

Despite the chaos around it, the crystal remained unaffected by the failing machines and systems. It pulsed with a serene, otherworldly calm, an island of stability in the storm of destruction unleashed by Mara and Gresham. The prism was more than a mere artifact; it was a living relic of the Ancients' supremacy, a beacon of their enduring will.

Lady Mara and Lord Gresham stood before the crystal, their eyes narrowing against the brilliant light. They could feel the prism's energy tugging at the edges of their consciousness, its allure both captivating and threatening. Mara tightened her grip on her sword, her resolve unwavering.

"Admiral Levi, focus our fire on the prism!" she commanded, her voice cutting through the chamber with authority and purpose. "We must end this now!"

Above, the Requiem orbited with unwavering vigilance. Admiral Levi's fingers danced across the controls, channeling the ship's formidable power toward the crystal. The beam cannon charged with a low, rumbling hum, energy building with relentless precision.

"Target locked," Levi announced, his voice steady. "Prepare to fire on my mark."

The crystal responded to the imminent threat by increasing its spin, a mesmerizing dance of light that accelerated with each passing moment. The colors blurred into a seamless ring, a hypnotic spiral that drew the eye and challenged perception. The crystal's song grew louder, a crescendo that filled the chamber with an almost audible resonance.

Mara and Gresham braced themselves, channeling their own power to amplify the strike. Their swords blazed with light, their combined energies weaving together in a tapestry of destruction.

Sweat glistened on their brows as they focused their will, preparing for the final assault.

"Fire!" Levi's command echoed through the comlink, a signal that marked the beginning of the end.

The Requiem's beam cannon discharged with a thunderous roar, a lance of concentrated energy that cut through the void and struck the crystal with pinpoint accuracy. Simultaneously, Mara and Gresham unleashed their combined power, their swords directing a torrent of energy into the heart of the prism.

The crystal absorbed the assault, its spin accelerating to an unimaginable speed. The light it emitted intensified, becoming a blinding inferno that rivaled the brilliance of a newborn star. The galaxy itself seemed to hold its breath as the crystal transformed into a miniature sun, its radiant glow illuminating distant planets and moons.

Ships across the surrounding space, from the massive warships of the Galactic Fleet to the smallest freighters and scouts, were momentarily blinded by the overwhelming light. Crews shielded their eyes, averting their gaze as the brilliance pierced even the darkest corners of the void. The phenomenon was seen and felt across light-years, a cosmic signal of the momentous event unfolding.

In that moment of blinding luminescence, the Ancients, witnessing the destruction of their most prized creation, unleashed a cry that boomed across the galaxy—a sound so powerful that it reverberated through the very fabric of space. "THEE N—" their voices roared, a thunderous shout that resonated in the minds of every living being, a primal expression of horror and disbelief that transcended distance and comprehension.

For a heartbeat, the galaxy cringed in panic, the echo of the cry sending shivers through the stars themselves. Then, as swiftly as it had come, the sound began to fade, dissipating like smoke on the wind. The echoes of their despair lingered, gradually softening to a whisper, and finally disappearing into the silence of the cosmos.

As the cry faded, a profound silence enveloped the galaxy. The absence of sound was almost deafening, a stark contrast to the explosive climax that had just unfolded. It was a silence that spoke volumes, echoing the enormity of what had been achieved. The weight of the Ancients' demise hung in the stillness, a testament to the victory won and the new dawn that lay ahead.

In a cataclysmic flash of light, the crystal shattered, releasing a shockwave of energy that swept through the chamber and beyond. The Ancients' presence, once so imposing and eternal, dissolved in an instant, their cries silenced as they were consumed by the blinding brilliance.

When the light faded, the chamber lay empty and silent. The crystal was gone, and with it, the last vestiges of the Ancients' dominion. Lady Mara and Lord Gresham stood amidst the aftermath, their victory a beacon of hope in the darkness, a testament to the power of unity and the indomitable spirit of those who dared to challenge the impossible.

In the aftermath, Mara and Gresham exchanged a glance, their eyes reflecting the weight of what they had accomplished. The cost of victory was etched into their expressions, but so too was the resolve to face the challenges that lay ahead. Across the galaxy, as distant worlds and factions paused to look to the sky, a sense of renewal and hope spread like wildfire. The debris from the shattered crystal scattered like shooting stars, a cosmic symbol of a new era dawning in the wake of the Ancients' fall.

The announcement crackled through the communication networks of countless worlds, carrying the news of the Ancients' fall across the vast expanse of the galaxy. On the vibrant streets of Corvus Prime, a bustling metropolis known for its towering spires and thriving markets, citizens paused in disbelief. Holoscreens flickered to life, displaying the official declaration: "The Ancients are no more. The crystal is shattered, and their reign of terror has ended."

A wave of stunned silence swept over the crowd, and then, like a dam breaking, joy erupted. Children cheered, their voices rising above the din of the city, while vendors abandoned their stalls to embrace strangers in the streets. The skies above Corvus Prime lit up with brilliant fireworks, their colors mirroring the cosmic explosion of the crystal's destruction. Red, blue, and gold streaks painted the heavens, accompanied by the jubilant symphony of horns and drums.

In the heart of the city, an elderly woman stood quietly, tears streaming down her face as she watched the fireworks. Her mind drifted back to her youth when she had fought against the Ancients, and the memories of comrades lost, and battles won mingled with the vibrant display above. Around her, people danced and sang, and she joined them, feeling the weight of history lift from her shoulders.

On the desert planet of Xar, known for its endless dunes and scorching heat, the inhabitants gathered to perform intricate sand dances. Dressed in flowing robes adorned with vibrant patterns, they moved in harmony with the shifting sands, their bodies telling stories of resilience and triumph over adversity. The dancers' movements were a living tapestry, weaving tales of ancient battles and hard-won victories into the fabric of their performance. As the sun dipped below the horizon, the desert was set ablaze with a thousand torches, casting flickering shadows that danced alongside the celebrants.

Meanwhile, on the water world of Oceana, the celebration took on a different hue. Beneath the waves, bioluminescent sea creatures illuminated the ocean depths in a breathtaking display. Schools of radiant fish darted through the water, leaving trails of shimmering light in their wake, while majestic leviathans glided gracefully above, their bodies aglow with the colors of the cosmos. The Nereids, with their shimmering scales and ethereal beauty, gathered in coral gardens to perform a dance of gratitude, their movements fluid and graceful. The water pulsed with vibrant hues, celebrating the dawn of a new era.

Amidst the festivities, a young Nereid reached out to touch a nearby human diplomat, who had been instrumental in forging alliances that led to this victory. The gesture spoke of newfound unity and understanding between species that had once been wary of one another.

In the desert realm of Zhar'ra, known for its endless sands and ancient ruins, the nomadic tribes convened for a festival unlike any other. Bonfires roared to life, casting a warm glow over the gathering as dancers moved in rhythm to the hypnotic beat of drums. Elders shared stories of hope and triumph, their words resonating with the echoes of past struggles. The desert night became a canvas for meteors, which streaked across the sky in a natural display of celestial fireworks, celebrating the dawn of a new era.

Among the tribes, a young warrior stood with his family, holding a relic of the Ancients—a small amulet—before casting it into the fire. The flames consumed it, and the warrior felt a sense of closure and freedom, knowing his people could now thrive without fear.

On the icy tundras of Velkar, where cold winds howled and snow blanketed the landscape, the hardy inhabitants embraced the warmth of unity. They constructed massive ice sculptures depicting the fall of the Ancients, illuminated from within by flickering lanterns. Families gathered in igloos, sharing feasts of roasted meats and sweet pastries, their laughter rising above the howling wind as a testament to resilience and victory.

Throughout the galaxy, the diverse cultures united in their shared relief and happiness, expressing their joy in unique ways. Musicians composed symphonies that captured the essence of freedom, while artists painted murals depicting the galaxy's liberation from the shadow of the Ancients. Poets penned verses that spoke of courage, sacrifice, and the unbreakable spirit of those who had fought against tyranny.

In the heart of the Requiem, aboard the Galactic Alliance flagship, Commander Levi stood on the bridge, surrounded by his crew. The ship's massive viewports offered a breathtaking panorama of the universe in celebration. Stars twinkled like diamonds against the velvet backdrop of space, their light a reminder of the countless worlds united by this monumental victory.

Levi's voice, steady and filled with emotion, echoed through the ship's corridors. "Today, we stand as witnesses to the end of an era and the beginning of a new chapter in the galaxy's history. Let this be a reminder that when we stand together, there is nothing we cannot overcome."

His words resonated with a profound sense of unity and hope, encapsulating the spirit of the galaxy's triumph. As the crew raised their glasses in a toast to the future, a holo screen flickered to life, displaying messages from across the galaxy—faces of different species and cultures, each sharing their own celebrations and dreams for what lay ahead.

On distant, isolated planets, where contact with the rest of the galaxy had been sparse due to the Ancients' interference, small communities gathered around communal fires, their faces illuminated by the glow of distant stars. Even here, the news had reached them, and their celebrations, though modest, were filled with heartfelt joy and relief.

The galaxy, in all its diverse splendor, pulsed with the rhythm of life and hope, a tapestry of joy woven from countless worlds. Universes rejoiced, united in a chorus of celebration that echoed across the stars, proclaiming that the light of liberty had prevailed over the darkness of oppression.

As the festivities continued, plans for the future began to take shape. Leaders from various worlds convened through holographic meetings, discussing how to rebuild and strengthen alliances forged in the crucible of conflict. They envisioned a future of collaboration and exploration, where the galaxy's myriad cultures could thrive in peace and harmony.

Through it all, the memory of those who had sacrificed for this moment lingered in the hearts of all, serving as a beacon of inspiration for the generations to come. The galaxy was free, and with that freedom came the promise of endless possibilities and the unyielding hope for a brighter tomorrow.

Epilogue: The Light of Hope

In the aftermath of the battle, the survivors gathered on the flagship's bridge, the scars of the battle etched into their very souls. Xylo, her body still trembling from the adrenaline and pain, stood amidst the heroes who had made this victory possible.

Lady Mara of the Few, her ethereal beauty framed by a cascading mane of blonde hair, stepped forward, her violet eyes pulsing with gratitude. "Xylo," she began, her voice a melodic whisper, "your courage and determination have given us a chance. You have shown us that even in the darkest moments, hope can shine through."

Lord Gresham, his crimson cape billowing dramatically, nodded in agreement. "Your actions have inspired us all. We will rebuild. We will remember. And we will fight on, not just for ourselves, but for every soul that has been lost in this terrible conflict."

Admiral Levi, his face lined with fatigue but glowing with pride, clasped Xylo's hand. "You did it, Xylo. You gave us a fighting chance. The Ancients may still be out there, but today, we showed them that we will not go quietly into the night. We will not surrender. We will rise."

As the heroes of the Galactic Fleet gazed out into the void, the wreckage of the battle floating silently around them, a sense of profound unity settled over them. They had faced the darkness and emerged victorious, but the fight was far from over.

In the distance, the stars seemed to burn a little brighter, a testament to the indomitable spirit of those who dared to defy the inevitable. The galaxy had been given a reprieve, a fleeting moment of hope in the face of overwhelming odds. And as long as there were heroes like Xylo, like General Osnex, like Lady Mara and Lord Gresham, the light of hope would continue to shine.

The future was uncertain, the path ahead fraught with danger and sacrifice. But for now, they had won a crucial battle. And in the heart of the galaxy, a single, defiant thought burned brightly:

This is not the end. This is just the beginning.

Victory and Reflection

The bridge of the Harbinger erupted in cheers.

A wave of relief surged through the crew, ragged and exhausted, but still alive. The hum of strained machinery filled the air, the faint scent of burning circuits and ozone thick in the confined space.

Officers wiped sweat from their brows, but their smiles were short-lived—this wasn't a victory yet. It was just a reprieve.

And then—the impossible happened.

Ghost ships shattered the emptiness.

From the blackness of the void, a fleet appeared. Sleek and strange, their silhouettes angular and smooth like sharks in the deep, their hulls etched with ancient runes that flickered with unearthly light. For a brief moment, the cold of space seemed to pulse warmer, as if the ships were radiating heat from their long-forgotten engines.

The Crescent Armada.

The name buzzed across the comms in a feverish, stunned whisper. Officers leaned forward, eyes wide, their fingers trembling on controls.

"That's impossible… they vanished a decade ago."

Osnex's voice caught, the air in his throat dry as he stared at the display, his knuckles white against the console. His breath came out ragged.

A deep, gravelly voice broke the silence, ancient and familiar.

"Alliance forces… we heard your cry. We are not too late."

Osnex's lips parted, words lost in the weight of the moment. He pressed the comms button. "You should've stayed away."

A low chuckle crackled over the line, rich with years of dust.

"Couldn't let you have all the fun."

The battle resumed with a fury.

Above, the galaxy screamed.

The skies weren't skies. The void was filled with fire—with violence, and metal—the ground below nonexistent, only vacuum and pressure. Ship after ship was ripped apart, their hulls peeling like layers of an onion, exposing the cold machinery beneath, melting into rivers of superheated debris. Explosions bloomed like angry stars, their blinding light swallowing the dark, only to be replaced by more devastation.

The scent of burning metal permeated the air, and the sharp, acrid taste of ozone hung like a pall in the atmosphere, choking the breath from anyone who tried to speak.

The Ancient warships advanced like titans.

Their enormous, ghostly silhouettes glided forward with an almost disturbing grace. Their massive energy cannons unleashed bright, emerald-green beams that carved through the void. The space around them seemed to ripple as the energy warped everything it touched. A huge, writhing pulse of light engulfed a cruiser—the ship's hull crumpled like paper, disintegrating into a shower of molten fragments.

Fighters—the size of ants—fought in desperate, frenzied loops around the behemoths, trying to evade laser fire that sliced through the air with deafening shrieks.

The Alliance's small ships zipped and darted through the field like flies in a storm, bright trails of fire streaking across their paths. One ship banked hard, a desperate dive to avoid a pulse of deadly energy. It missed. Barely.

But the second shot found its mark.

The ship's wing exploded, rupturing in a cloud of sparks and shredded metal. The pilot screamed, fighting the controls. For a moment, the ship twirled in midair like a spinning top before it hurtled into deep space, spinning out of control, lost.

A loud crackling sound thundered through the air as a nearby cruiser's shields buckled under another wave of attacks, the hull screeching in agony as parts of the ship ripped free and drifted into the dark. The smell of charred flesh and burnt plastic drifted from the ventilation systems, mingling with the metallic tang of overheated circuits.

In the midst of it all, a new horror unfolded.

The Ancient drones—gleaming, deadly machines—danced through space, dodging fire and lancing death with surgical precision. They came in waves, each one seeming to overwhelm the already battered forces of the Alliance.

Each movement from the drones was nearly inhuman, their quick, twitching bodies gliding from target to target like sharks seeking blood, their ion cannons firing in perfect synchronicity. Ships exploded in moments, their remains falling to pieces in silent arcs of burning debris. No one could touch them.

A muffled cry of horror came from one of the crew members, her face drained white as the bridge alarms screamed.

"Another wave... they're everywhere!"

And then, in the distance, a roar of unholy brilliance.

The Crescent Armada opened fire, their strange, glowing cannons pulsing with violent light. Bright blue beams of unearthly energy tore through the enemy's flank. A guttural cheer rang out across the comms. They had breached the enemy defenses—but only just. The drones and warships adapted, charging forward, closing in.

A fleeting moment of hope turned into bitter reality as the Ancient warships unleashed their most devastating weapon—one enormous beam of green fire that enveloped two Crescent ships in an instant.

Both ships disintegrated. The void was suddenly empty where they had been.

"No…" Osnex muttered, staring at the unfolding destruction.

They had been fighting on borrowed time.

The hull trembled beneath their feet. The warning sirens screamed. Explosions echoed throughout the ship, rattling the very foundation of the Harbinger. Smoke filled the air, and the stench of burning metals and oils began to thicken.

Osnex's voice rang out across the bridge, crisp and commanding. The crew looked to him, their faces filled with dread, but they obeyed without question. His resolve hardened.

"All ships—FIRE. I repeat, FIRE."

The void exploded with light.

Laser fire, pulse blasts, missiles, ion energy—every weapon in the Alliance fleet unleashed. The stars burned brighter as they pierced the darkness.

They weren't done. Not yet.

The Rousing Call of Lord Gresham: Architects of a New Era

Lord Gresham stood tall, his black uniform immaculate save for the glowing emblem of the Few where his left pocket would be. His dark hair framed his face, and his deep blue eyes held a resolute fire. At his side, his red glowing sword, inscribed with ancient runes, thrummed with barely contained energy. The cape behind him moved with a life of its own, thrashing and snapping in time with the powerful emotions coursing through him. He took a deep breath, his hand momentarily clenching into a fist as he gathered his thoughts.

"Warriors of the Galaxy! Today, we stand not just on the deck of the Harbinger but on the precipice of a new dawn! Yes, the battle is won, but at a cost so high it would break lesser beings. We look upon these names," he gestured towards the shimmering wall, "and see not just soldiers but friends, family, the very lifeblood of our struggle. Their sacrifice, however, is not in vain! Their courage carves a path, a testament to the unyielding spirit that burns within each of you!"

His voice rose, a crescendo building in the vast emptiness of space. "Look around you! See the scars upon our ships, the ghosts of fallen comrades! They are a reminder, a promise we make to their memory. We rebuild not just our fleets but our worlds and our lives!

"We rebuild a future where no child will cower under the shadow of tyranny, where freedom shall ring through the cosmos! Let this victory be a beacon, a call to arms for generations to come! For we are not merely survivors; we are the architects of a new era! And as we move forward, let us remain vigilant, for the echoes of the Ancients' tyranny may yet challenge us again."

A thunderous roar of approval erupted from the crowd, the sound echoing through the ships and sparking a renewed fire in every heart. Crew members exchanged determined looks, their eyes meeting in silent affirmation of their shared resolve. In that moment, a deep sense of unity solidified among them, binding them together as they faced the vast and uncertain future.

Lady Mara's Vision

As the cheers subsided, Lady Mara, her violet eyes shimmering with unshed tears, took her place beside Lord Gresham. Her blonde hair framed her face, contrasting with the black uniform she wore, identical to Gresham's, save for the blue, glowing sword with runes at her side. Her cape, too, moved with a life of its own, reflecting her tumultuous emotions.

"We celebrate today," she began, her voice a gentle melody laced with sorrow, "but victory is a bitter fruit. Each name on that wall represents a life cut short, a dream unfulfilled. We carry their memory with us, a constant reminder of the fragility of existence and the preciousness of peace. Their sacrifice fuels our resolve to build a future where such battles are a distant memory. Let us honor them not just with cheers but with our actions. Let us create a galaxy where unity reigns, where knowledge flourishes, and where life, in all its forms, is cherished and protected."

She paused, her gaze sweeping over the assembled crew. "Our swords, imbued with ancient power from the very Ancients who created us, serve as symbols of our commitment to protect and inspire. They can shield us in battle, push and propel objects and people, and even control the elements. But it is not just our power that will lead us forward; it is our unity, our shared resolve, and the unwavering spirit that each of you carries."

A wave of quiet determination rippled through the crowd. The cheers had been replaced by a steely glint in every eye, a silent vow to live a life worthy of the sacrifice made.

Admiral Levi's Rally

Finally, stepping forward with a swagger that belied the exhaustion etched on his face, Admiral Levi took center stage. His crisp blue and white uniform of the Galactic Alliance was pristine, his green eyes sparkling with a mix of triumph and fatigue. His sandy brown hair was tousled, giving him an air of rugged determination.

"Alright, heroes! Let's hear it for the scrappiest bunch of space fighters this galaxy has ever seen! We stared down annihilation and blinked back! We took a beating, and by the stars, we gave one back tenfold!"

The crowd roared in agreement, the tension of the past battle finally dissipating. "We fought for our homes, our families, for the right to breathe free! And by the nine hells, we earned it! Now, let's get these ships patched up, let's get some grub in our bellies, and let's celebrate! But remember," he held up a finger, a playful glint in his eye, "we celebrate tonight, but tomorrow, we rebuild! We rebuild a galaxy where we set the rules, not some ancient tyrants! We rebuild a life for ourselves, for our children, a life of freedom, and a life of defiance! Let this victory be a toast to those who gave their all!"

With a mighty bellow that echoed through the assembled ships, Admiral Levi launched into a bawdy song of victory, quickly picked up by the crew, transforming the somber gathering into a joyous celebration. The battle scars remained, a harsh reminder of the sacrifices made, but tonight, they celebrated not just their victory but the indomitable spirit of the Galactic Fleet – a spirit that promised a brighter future, a future built on the ashes of war.

A Rekindled Flame: A Century of Love

The celebratory music thrummed through the Elysian's lounge, a joyous counterpoint to the pounding of Mara's heart. Across the throng, Gresham's gaze met hers, a silent communication traversing the jubilant chaos. A century had passed since their bond was forged, a century marked by battles fought and victories won, side by side. Yet, in that one glance, a kaleidoscope of emotions flickered within them – relief, gratitude, and a simmering desire that time had only intensified.

With a familiar ease born of a hundred years of shared experiences, Gresham navigated the crowd, his steps purposeful until he stood before her. Their connection, a bridge built on a lifetime of trust, transcended the physical space. The air crackled with an electric tension that spoke volumes of their enduring love.

"Remember Xylos IV?" His voice, a low murmur that resonated deep within her, held a world of unspoken longing.

A knowing smile tugged at Mara's lips. "The moonlit waterfalls," she replied, her voice husky with emotion. "They shimmered like liquid starlight, cascading from the heavens."

Gresham's gaze softened, a testament to the shared memory. "It was there," he began, his voice a low rumble, "that I first saw you, not just as a warrior, but as a woman of unparalleled strength and grace. You were radiant, Mara, a vision etched in the very fabric of my memory."

Mara's heart soared. A blush crept up her neck, a testament to the enduring power of his words. Around them, the crew reveled in their hard-won victory, their laughter and cheers a vibrant melody. But within this bubble of shared history, the world had contracted to hold only them.

His hand, strong and familiar, reached out to cup her cheek. The warmth of his touch sent a jolt through her, a spark that had never truly dimmed over the centuries. Their eyes met a silent conversation passing between them. Years of shared battles, unwavering trust, and a love that had weathered every storm – the emotions crackled in the air, a tangible force.

Without a single word spoken, Gresham leaned in. The kiss that followed was a culmination of a century of unspoken desire, a passionate rekindling of the flame that had burned brightly since

Xylos IV. It was a kiss that spoke volumes of their deep connection; a promise whispered on the wind, a love story etched in the stars.

When they finally broke apart, breathless and euphoric, a new chapter unfolded before them. The war was won, and their bond was reaffirmed. Now, with the galaxy as their canvas, they were ready to face the future, hand in hand, their love a beacon that would forever illuminate their path.

A Toast to the Future

The jubilant cheers echoed through the Harbinger, a wave of exhilaration washing over the weary crew. Admiral Levi, his face etched with both exhaustion and exhilaration, weaved through the throng, finally coming upon Lord Gresham and Lady Mara. They stood side-by-side, sharing a private laugh, their faces aglow with the celebratory light.

Levi raised a flagon of frothing amber ale in their direction. "To victory, my friends! And to a future hard-won!"

Gresham met his gaze, his own cup held high. "A future we forge together," he declared, his voice ringing with conviction. "The scars of this war will serve as a constant reminder, but they will not define us."

Mara, her eyes sparkling with a fierce determination, chimed in, "We rebuild not just our fleets but our very spirit. We explore the unknown, carrying the torch of freedom for generations to come!"

Levi grinned, a flash of his youthful swagger returning. He stepped forward and embraced Mara, whispering softly into her ear, "You are the guiding star in Gresham's life. Your friendship means the world to me, and I hope we never have to say goodbye." He kissed her cheek warmly and then turned to Gresham with a cheeky grin. "Hey, big guy, you're next!"

Mara laughed at the sound-like music amidst the jubilant crowd. Gresham hesitated for a moment before enveloping Levi in a bear hug. Levi whispered, "You are the foundation she builds her life upon. Your strength and love are unmatched."

Gresham's eyes softened, and he replied, "There is no one better in the universe than you, Alexander. I cannot thank you enough for your friendship."

Their cups clinked in a resounding toast, a promise etched in the clang of metal. The cheers of the surrounding crew rose to a crescendo, a shared acknowledgment of their extraordinary journey and the unbreakable ties that bound them together. As the celebration roared on, each of them knew, in their hearts, that the future, though uncertain, held the promise of grand adventures, unwavering loyalty, and an epic friendship that would forever echo through the cosmos.

Epilogue: Dawn of a New Era

In the aftermath of the grand celebration, the scene shifted to a bustling spaceport, now a symbol of hope and resilience. Admiral Levi stood overlooking the activity, his green eyes sparkling with pride as he watched a new generation of pilots train, their determination and spirit a mirror of his own. "We did it, Ramirez. We made it through," Levi whispered to himself, his heart swelling with pride and hope for the future they were building.

Nearby, Lady Mara and Lord Gresham walked through a thriving marketplace in a colony once devastated by war. Children laughed and played, their innocent joy a stark contrast to the grim memories of battle. Mara's violet eyes sparkled with a sense of accomplishment. "We've come so far," she said, her voice filled with emotion.

Gresham nodded, his gaze fixed on the horizon. "And we have much further to go. The galaxy is vast, and there are still many unknowns. But together, we will face whatever comes."

Lieutenant Tanaka and Ensign Ramirez shared a rare moment of quiet reflection, the memory of lost friends and hard-won victories lingering in the air. Tanaka glanced at Ramirez, a reassuring smile on his face. "We did it, Ramirez. We made it through."

As the sun set over the horizon, casting a golden glow over the bustling scene, a single, united thought echoed in the hearts of those who had fought and survived: This is not the end. This is just the beginning.

In the vast, unexplored expanse of the galaxy, an uncharted nebula shimmered with the promise of new adventures. And somewhere in the distant reaches of space, a new, powerful enemy stirred, casting a long shadow over the dawn of their new era.

Back on the balcony, Gresham and Mara reflected on the diverse expressions of joy and hope they had witnessed. The night air was cool against their skin, a gentle reminder of the calm after the storm. "The galaxy is alive with possibilities," Mara said softly, her eyes shining. "We've given everyone the chance to dream again."

Gresham nodded, his heart full. "And it's up to us to ensure those dreams have a future." He paused, a thoughtful look crossing his face. "For the first time in millennia, the future feels unwritten, full of genuine possibility."

They raised their glasses once more, toasting to the adventures yet to come, the dreams they had yet to realize, and the enduring bond that had brought them to this moment. As the stars twinkled above and the galaxy celebrated below, they knew that they had truly helped to change the course of history and that the best was yet to come.

In that moment, surrounded by the joy of trillions, they found their own perfect bubble of happiness, a tender scene amidst the grandest celebration the galaxy had ever known. Mara's laughter, bright and carefree, mingled with the distant sounds of music and cheers. Gresham felt his heart swell with an emotion so profound it almost overwhelmed him.

"Dance with me," Mara said suddenly, her eyes sparkling with mischief and love. Without waiting for a response, she pulled Gresham into a playful waltz, their steps light and free, unburdened by the weight they'd carried for so long.

As they twirled, the galaxy seemed to dance with them. In the grand hall of the Galactic Alliance headquarters, the doors burst open, and hundreds of people flooded the room, tossing confetti into the air. Music played as they danced and embraced, their faces shining with joy and relief. In another world, a little girl clutched a doll dressed in a tiny uniform, whispering, "Lady Mara gets the bad guy," while her friend added, "And Lord Gresham rounds up all the last bad guys."

Across the stars, beings reveled in the simple joy of making choices that were truly their own. In a bustling marketplace on Corvus Prime, vendors handed out free treats as families celebrated together, children laughing as they ran through the streets with streamers. On the forested moon of Sylvan, lanterns were lit and sent soaring into the night sky, each carrying a wish for the future. On the desert planet of Xar, dancers performed intricate routines under the stars, their movements telling stories of victory and hope.

Gresham pulled her close as they danced, letting his forehead rest against hers. The warmth of her touch grounded him, the softness of her breath against his cheek a comfort he'd almost forgotten. "This is the life I want with you, Mara, to fulfill all your dreams."

Mara paused in their dance, suddenly struck by the weight of their victory. "We're free," she whispered, "truly free to shape our own destinies."

Gresham smiled, understanding the gravity of her words. "And those possibilities—those dreams—they're real now, attainable for everyone."

"Oh, Gresham," Mara whispered, her eyes brimming with emotion. As they danced, she leaned forward, and they shared a kiss so full of love and happiness that it seemed to light up the night.

As if in response, a shower of shooting stars streaked across the sky, each one carrying the wishes and dreams of billions. The galaxy pulsed with life, with joy, with the pure, unbridled excitement of a future full of possibilities—possibilities that, for the first time in eons, felt real and attainable.

As the first light of a new day began to creep across the horizon of countless worlds, the celebrations showed no signs of slowing. For in every heart, from the core worlds to the farthest reaches of space, a simple truth resonated: the future was theirs to shape, and it was brighter than ever before.

The galaxy danced on, a swirling, joyous mass of life and light, united in celebration, in freedom, and in hope. And in every laugh, every embrace, every moment of pure, unadulterated happiness, the same message rang clear—love had won, joy had triumphed, and the best was yet to come.

At the transport dock, Gresham and Admiral Levi stood facing each other, the moment of parting heavy in the air. Levi, with his signature grin, suddenly closed the distance and pulled Gresham into a tight, impulsive hug. Gresham stiffened in surprise at first but then relaxed, a rare smile touching his lips.

"Take care, Alex," Gresham said, his voice softer than usual.

Levi stepped back, his green eyes dancing with mischief as he slung his bag over his shoulder. With a playful salute, he said, "You too, Gresham."

But instead of a casual response, Gresham stood tall, his posture commanding, and with deliberate precision, returned the salute. The gesture was slow, deliberate, and filled with a respect that spoke volumes.

Levi's grin widened into a full laugh, filled with genuine warmth and happiness. "I'll see you on the other side of the stars, my friend," he called, his voice carrying over the hum of the spaceport.

He turned and stepped into the transport ship, a lightness in his step that hadn't been there in years. As the ship's doors closed behind him, he felt a sense of peace, knowing that while this chapter had ended, a new and exciting one was just beginning.

Gresham watched the ship lift off and disappear into the sky, his heart full of pride for the man Levi had become and the future they had fought to secure. With a final nod to the departing vessel, he turned back to Mara, ready to face whatever the galaxy had in store for them next.